The Oil Vendor and the Courtesan

Also by Ted Wang and Chen Chen

Chen Chen: *Come Watch the Sun Go Home* (Marlowe, 1998)
Ted Wang and Chen Chen: *The Abbot and the Widow* (Eastbridge, 2004)

The Oil Vendor and the Courtesan

TALES FROM THE MING DYNASTY

Feng Menglong

Translated by Ted Wang and Chen Chen

Introduction by Teresa Chi-ching Sun

WELCOME RAIN PUBLISHERS
NEW YORK

Welcome Rain Publishers
532 LaGuardia Place #473
New York, NY 10012 USA

PAPERBACK EDITION
ISBN-13: 978-1-56649-139-6
ISBN-10: 1-56649-139-8

HARDCOVER EDITION
ISBN-13: 978-1-56649-140-2
ISBN-10: 1-56649-140-1

The cover design reproduces a section of the twelfth-century scroll, *Springtime on the Bian River*, by Song Dynasty artist Zhang Zeduan. The original scroll is over 17 feet long (208.5" x 10.06") and hangs in the Palace Museum in Beijing.

Woodcut illustrations retouched by Cheng Z. Lu
Chinese calligraphy by Shaoyong Wang

Library of Congress catalog information is available from the publisher.

To Dr. E-tu Zen Sun

Professor Emerita of Chinese History, Pennsylvania State University,
a cousin, a friend,
whose immense knowledge and informative involvement
gave us the confidence to present these translations to the world.

CONTENTS

Preface

Chen Chen

It is with pleasure that we present this volume of short stories—the second of a projected series—selected and translated from among a total of two hundred such tales written almost four hundred years ago during China's Ming dynasty by two writers, Feng Menglong and Ling Mengchu.

Feng Menglong (1574–1646) wrote 120 tales evenly divided among three books—*Instructive Tales to Enlighten the World*, *Popular Tales to Admonish the World,* and *Lasting Tales to Waken the World*—that have been commonly referred to as the "San yan," or "Three Tales."

Ling Mengchu (1580–1644), inspired by Feng's volumes, also wrote two books of forty tales each, naming them *Slapping the Desk in Astonishment: Book One* and *Slapping the Desk in Astonishment: Book Two.* They were popularly known as the "Er pai," or "Two Slaps."

While the ten tales in our first volume of translations have all been selected from the "Two Slaps" by Ling, the second volume comprises eight tales from Feng's "Three Tales."

Neither of the two translators, Ted Wang or myself, have graduated from Chinese or English departments; nor have either of us, during our professional careers, been associated with Chinese studies—Sinology, if you will—be it in history, politics, anthropology, or culture. We are also blissfully ignorant of the "Who's Who" of Chinese studies, either in China or the West. With no restraints from peers or from arcane academic conventions, we embarked on this adventurous endeavor with absolute freedom. Should we offend any scholarly sensibilities with this publication, the offense is unintentional.

Our intention, as lovers of Chinese and English books from the time we each emerged from infancy, is to treat an interested English-reading public to a delectable selection of toothsome stories. We believe that students of Asian studies will be able to informatively spice up their reading lists with these tales. More importantly, the tales may be of interest to readers who are related in some way to Asia, be they multi-generational Chinese Americans—whose forebears came to the Americas in the nineteenth and twentieth centuries—or people related to China by marriage, adoption, vocation, or history, such as old China hands, the progeny of ministry families and others. There may also be not a few people among the general readership who simply would like to read some really good stories, the durability of which is shown by the fact that the tales have survived some four hundred years in a country with a redoubtable literary legacy.

My acquaintance with the Ming tales began in China before I entered my teens with editions censored, of course, for sexual content. I read and re-read them because of their brevity and varied elements, especially in later years after I obtained the complete and unabridged volumes of these tales. However, it was not until I settled down in the United States and finished writing my memoir *Come Watch the Sun Go Home* that I conceived the idea of translating a selection from these tales wider in range than the sporadic and individual renditions I was told were currently available.

This ambition could not have taken off without the main force behind these volumes: my longtime collaborator Ted Wang, a veteran translator known for his eloquent and elegant style and whom the renowned late film director King Hu called a *qi cai* (wonder talent) of Chinese to English translation.

Ted Wang was familiar with the English and French classics but had never come in contact with these nonclassic Chinese tales. From the moment he read his first tale, he was captivated by the richly detailed descriptions of an erstwhile everyday life unknown to most contemporary Chinese, the characterization of the protagonists, and the authors' narrative skills. We agreed it would be a great waste if these delightful, vivacious, folksy, and even ribald tales were not made available to a wider English-reading audience.

We worked up some six or seven tales randomly selected from all five books and showed the translations to a few interested parties. It so happened that Ted met our then future-publisher-to-be, Doug Merwin, and told him about our project. Doug kept it in mind and, when the time came, launched the first volume, *The Abbot and the Widow*.

Thereafter, Ted and I embarked on a fairly intensive period of translation—on top of the work we each do for a living. First, I re-read all two hundred tales several times to gauge their respective merit and value for current and future selections. What naturally came to mind were the English and Italian classics *Canterbury Tales* and *The Decameron*. When these works were presented to their respective audiences in fourteenth- and fifteenth-century Europe, China's popular literature had already emerged from the era of the "The Legends of Tang (618–907) and Song (960–1279)," which were originally told in teahouses and evolved into the rudimentary dramatizations known as the "Miscellaneous Plays of Yuan (1271–1368) and Ming (1368–1644)." The earliest of these per-formances date from some three hundred years before Shakespeare and, in their later years, overlapped with his emergence in England. The Yuan and Ming plays were also performed at teahouses and fairgrounds, like their predecessors, the storytellers' tales.

This development of drama in turn enhanced and improved the nar-rative content and techniques of storytelling honed by centuries of prac-tice. Since most of the storytellers were semiliterate, they passed on their stories primarily by word of mouth and with the help of prompt books. These stories gradually emerged in written form, and some were even presented before emperors for their entertainment, and then recycled back to the populace through the palaces' back doors.

Thanks to the efforts of writers like Feng Menglong and Ling Mengchu, we can now share with our readers these fascinating tales about merchants, scholars, housewives, magistrates, craftsmen, courtesans, abbots, nuns, and even children, spanning a broad spectrum of Chinese urban and rural life, including seafaring travel of some four hundred and more years ago. While a few of the tales deal with supernatural powers, the majority are about everyday people in everyday situations, about their lives and loves and triumphs and tragedies, and about their strengths and weakness-es, virtues and vices.

Throughout the translation process, I could not help but marvel at the techniques employed by these long-ago writers, at the precision of their narrations, at the structuring of the plots and subplots, and at their skillful use of suspense, flashbacks, and flashforwards—in many ways as smooth and seamless as any of their twentieth-century counterparts. In some tales, the characters are so well crafted that each has a distinctive speech pattern.

While no good literary translations should be verbatim, we have kept as close to the original texts as feasible for informative and entertaining reading, but stayed away from untranslatable plays on words, flowery poetic flourishes, and extraneous narrative elements. For exact research, scholars in Chinese literature should go to the original Chinese texts.

Both translators wish to thank my cousin, Dr. E-tu Zen Sun, Professor Emerita of Chinese History, Pennsylvania State University, for the unstinting and invaluable support she has given us since we first started on the translations several years ago. We laypersons have had to ask her an array of questions about things ranging from China's imperial and academic systems all the way down to details like dwellings and tools. She patiently read all the manuscripts we sent her and, to our embarrassment, even corrected our typos. E-tu's informative and instructive involvement bolstered our confidence in this endeavor.

We also wish to thank Dr. Hong Cheng, Chinese Studies Librarian at UCLA Library, for his scholarly and erudite assistance throughout the translation of our stories.

Along the way, we engaged the assistance, as "readers," of some of our friends who, by gender, ethnicity, age, profession, and general interest, represent to some extent the diversity of the readership we envision. They furnished us with candid feedback after going through the draft manuscripts, and their positive reactions gave us great encouragement. Those we wish to thank are: Alice Chi, Russell Good, Sue C. Hoy, Janice Lance, Sally Morgan, John Wang, and Robert Zivnuska.

We were also fortunate to secure enthusiastic support from Dr. Teresa Chi-ching Sun who wrote, at very short notice, the enlightening introduction to this volume. Her essay greatly increases the instructive aspect of this series of books and lends academic clarification and dignity to the "fun" that this project is meant to provide.

I consider ourselves extremely fortunate to have obtained another platform for this current volume soon after the appearance of *The Abbot and the Widow*. The person who was essential in the publication of my memoir, Dr. Charles Defanti, came again into the picture. Again through him, we are reunited in working with our former publisher and editor, John Weber and Mara Lurie. We, as translators, are confident that the Welcome Rain team will bring to our readers an excellently crafted volume of tales from some four hundred years ago.

Introduction

Teresa Chi-ching Sun, Ed. D.

Popular fiction in Chinese literary history has had a long and delayed development. Traditionally, the Chinese had ignored this particular genre ever since their civilization came into being. Fiction and drama writing were regarded as a sort of trivial craftsmanship that had no place in the "grand hall of literature," and the stigma of this tradition is to be seen to this day in the name by which novels are still referred—*xiao shuo* (little talk). It was not until the coming of Western literature to China that the Chinese, amazed by the value other cultures placed on the art of fiction writing, began to perceive their own precious literary legacy. Thereafter, fiction assumed a prominent position in Chinese literature.

There is little doubt that one factor in the development of literature in China was the interdependent nature of literary talent and public affairs within the Chinese political, cultural, and historical context. Up to the turn of the twentieth century, the influence of Confucianism as the intellectual and moral source of Chinese civilization overwhelmingly dominated social mobility. The goal of life for almost every intellectual during China's imperial ages was to cultivate oneself morally according to the Confucian teachings and thus be able to serve the imperial house by governing the populace according to these teachings. The educated elite won respect from their families and fellow scholars by rising in public officialdom through a system of imperial civil service examinations, during which they displayed their knowledge of the Confucian classics by producing essays in a literary writing style, and thereby acquired a position on the social and political ladder. Acquisition of knowledge of the classics as well as of the written medium in which these classics were couched demanded long-term devotion from the literati. In this process, they zealously perpetuated this literary style within their elitist circle in the writing of poetry, prose, essays, tribunes of opinions, and official documents.

This jealously preserved literary writing style differed considerably from the colloquial language spoken by the common people, a language which was deemed unworthy of the efforts of scholars. Such discrimination left little room for any acceptance of fiction and drama as literary genres.

During the Ming period, however, parallel with the formal writing style, a trend toward writing in the colloquial language arose. This fresh literary activity was due mainly to economic prosperity and ubiquitous commercial development, which prompted creative story writing among individual authors for the entertainment of the middle class in urban centers. The vigorous development of such story writing attracted the interest of intellectuals, many of whom applied their literary talent to—and executed with the colloquial writing style—numerous works of fiction, drama, and short stories. Their formal writing training considerably enriched and articulated the colloquial writing style, and their education helped them perceive with deeper insight the life of the common people around them and touch upon their sorrows, joys, separations, and reunions. Most of these authors were disappointed scholars who had failed the civil service examinations or were unable to climb higher within the bureaucratic system, and they wrote novels to amuse themselves or, in many cases, to keep food on the table. Thus, with the diversion of a group of creative and talented writers away from the formal writing style and the Confucian tradition, a new literary genre took shape. The tales they wrote were interesting and popular among the common people, yet the genuine artistic value of the genre only began to grab the attention of literary critics toward the end of the Qing Dynasty. It is unfortunate that the splendor of their achievements had to wait until centuries later to be recognized and perceived by their fellow Chinese. Among their more outstanding productions are such masterful works as *Journey to the West* (Xi you ji), *Tales of the Marshes* (Shui hu zhuan), *Romance of the Three Kingdoms* (San guo yan yi), *A Dream of Red Mansions* (Hong lou meng), and *The Golden Lotus* (Jin ping mei), all of which have been translated into other languages and widely read by people around the world.

A great many short stories were also written along with the full-length novels listed above. In the closing years of the Ming period, two large sets of such stories appeared in South China along the lower reaches of the Yangtze River. Known popularly today as the "Three Tales" (San yan) and "Two Slaps" (Er pai) and based in large part on the tales told by storytellers in teahouses and other places of popular entertainment, these two sets of stories acquired a unique position in the repertoire of Chinese fiction. Their writers did much to develop the creative aspect of short stories. They showed considerable maturity in terms of narrative enrichment, plot arrangement, and the articulation of narrative language, and delighted and fascinated generations of readers with short and medium-length narratives of many different aspects of society in Ming and earlier times.

The "Three Tales" consist of three volumes each containing forty stories and entitled respectively *Instructive Tales to Enlighten the World* (Yu shi ming yan), *Popular Tales to Admonish the World* (Jing shi tong yan), and *Lasting Tales to Waken the World* (Xing shi heng yan). These titles clearly reveal the elitist background of the writer Feng Menglong (1574-1646), as they declare his intention to educate the general public with sincere moral messages—a typical response to worldly affairs on the part of Confucian scholars. Most of these realistic stories end happily with victory for the virtuous and punishment for the wicked and regale readers with the triumphs of folk justice. Feng based many of his stories either on the manuscripts used by storytellers of Song and early Ming times, or on fragments of folktales, or hearsay, or unconfirmed historical occurrences. A few were tales of his own invention. Whatever their origin, his stories displayed considerable maturity of form as he combined oral storytelling skills with literary techniques. He was an innovator, not just an imitator.

The "Two Slaps," or *Slapping the Desk in Astonishment: Book One* and *Slapping the Desk in Astonishment: Book Two,* consist of a total of eighty stories in two volumes. At a time when the Three Tales mentioned above were creating quite a stir in the popular book trade, another writer, Ling Mengchu (1580-1644), was stimulated by the short-story writing trend to write his own tales. Also a poor scholar and frustrated official, Ling wished to create tales in his own manner. This he did by shaking off influences from Feng Menglong's writing style, deviating further from the Confucian norm than Feng, and writing stories centered around a different theme—wonder and amazement, without giving especial consideration to moral messages. With his literary pen he elaborated realistic oral accounts of the marvels and unusual events he encountered or heard about while wandering on the streets of cities during the turbulent years of the late Ming period. These ranged from romances between successful scholars and ladies from upper-class families and the adventures of merchants and travelers, to murders, unjust trials, and the seamier doings of beggars, thieves, prostitutes, and lascivious monks and widows. His aim was always to excite the readers' emotions and elicit exclamations of "how astonishing!"

At the time of this writing, apart from a rendition entitled *Stories from a Ming Collection*, done almost five decades ago by Cyril Birch and containing seven tales from one book among the *Three Tales*, there have been few concerted efforts to translate these popular Ming Dynasty tales into English. Aficionados will be glad to know that the translators of the current *The Oil Vendor and the Courtesan*, Ted Wang and Chen Chen, have published another collection, *The Abbot and the Widow* (2004). These two collections are a long overdue contribution to the treasury of translated Chinese literature.

The Oil Vendor and the Courtesan

賣油郎獨占花魁

In the last years of the Song Dynasty, Emperor Huizong placed his trust in a covey of corrupt ministers. Neglecting affairs of state, he emptied the empire's coffers to build parks and gardens for himself and frittered away his time in revelry. As the entire populace complained bitterly, the Jin barbarians in the north availed themselves of the dynasty's corruptness to rise up and lay waste to vast regions of this splendorous land. It was only after the Song emperor fled south of the Yangtze River and the country was split asunder that people found some respite. However, for scores of years, the ordinary folk suffered most grievously.

This is the story of one family in the village of Anle in the outskirts of the capital Bianliang. The father's name was Xin Shan, and his wife was from the Ruan family. They owned a small grain store in which they sold not only rice and other cereals but also wheat flour, beans, tea, liquor, oil and salt, and that afforded them a fairly comfortable living. By the time they were in their forties, they had only one daughter, whom they named Yaoqin. An exquisite child, Yaoqin was endowed with great intelligence, and when she was sent to school at the age of seven she could commit to memory a thousand words in a single day. By the time she was ten years old she was already reciting and composing poetry. And at the age of twelve she had learned to perform on the lute, play chess, and paint. Nor was she lacking in women's skills; needle and thread virtually flew under her fingers. All these accomplishments were to be attributed more to her natural talents than to instruction and training.

Xin Shan had no son, so he wished to bring a son-in-law into the household to provide for his wife and himself in their old age. Because of their daughter's multifarious talents, however, it was difficult to find a match for her. Not that there was any lack of suitors. There were many, but none of them met Xin Shan's expectations.

Just at this time, the Jins went on a rampage and besieged the capital Bianliang. Though there were many forces loyal to the emperor in the surrounding regions, the prime minister decided to enter into negotiations with the Jins and refused to do battle. As a consequence, the Jins became all the more arrogant and overbearing. Storming the capital, they abducted the two young crown princes. Residents outside the capital were terror stricken. All people, young and old, left their homes and fled for their lives, among them Xin Shan and his wife and twelve-year-old daughter. With bundles slung over their shoulders, they joined the flood of refugees.

They met no barbarians on their way, but soon came upon a band of soldiers who had been defeated in battle. When the latter caught sight of these fugitives laden with bundles, they raised a false alarm, yelling, "The barbarians are coming!" and set fire to the grass by the roadside. Darkness was falling and, as the terrified civilians took to their heels, many families were separated. The soldiers availed themselves of the refugees' panic to plunder their belongings, cutting down those who refused to surrender their bundles. It was a scene of utter chaos, and of utter misery. Xin Yaoqin tripped and fell while running from the soldiers, and by the time she had picked herself up, her parents were nowhere in sight. She dared not call out for them, so she spent the night hidden among some old grave mounds by the roadside.

At daybreak, she came out of hiding, and all that met her eyes was a windswept, dusty road littered with dead bodies. The refugees who had been with her the night before were nowhere to be seen. Yaoqin wept tears of longing for her parents. She wished to go in search of them but knew not which direction to take. The girl finally headed southward and trudged along, sobbing every step of the way. She walked two *li*'s distance, miserable and hungry, and came upon a mud hut. Assuming it to be inhabited, she thought of begging the occupants for a bowl of broth. But when she came closer to the house, she saw it was empty and in a state of decrepitude. All the residents had fled. She sat down against a wall and cried bitterly.

As the saying goes, "There are no tales without coincidences." A person happened to walk by the wall. His name was Bu Qiao, and he had been a close neighbor of the Xins. This man was an ill-behaved good-for-nothing, a freeloader who was in the habit of cadging food and money from others. People called him Bu the Big One. He, too, had been separated from his fellow refugees by the marauding soldiery and was now traveling alone. On hearing the sound of weeping, he had come to investigate. Yaoqin, who had known him since she was born, and was now bereft of kinsfolk in this time of adversity, felt as though she had found a close relative. Quickly drying her tears, she rose to her feet, asking, "Uncle Bu, have you seen my parents?"

Bu Qiao thought to himself, "Yesterday the soldiers robbed me of my belongings and I have no more money for the road. Now that Heaven has sent me this windfall, I must take as good care of her as I would of precious piece of merchandise." So he lied, saying, "Your parents are looking for you and are greatly distressed. They have pressed forward, but before leaving they said to me, 'Should you see our daughter, be sure to bring her along and return her to us.' They even promised me a generous reward." Yaoqin was not an unintelligent girl, but dazed as she was in her hapless plight she suspected nothing and went along with Bu Qiao.

Bu Qiao gave Yaoqin some food he had brought along, and then admonished her, "Your parents left the night before and we may not be able to catch up with them. In that case, we shall have to cross the river and look for them at Jiankang Prefecture. As we travel, I shall say you are my daughter, and you shall address me as 'Father.' There would be much inconvenience if it were said that I had picked up a lost girl." Yaoqin agreed. So they addressed each other as "father" and "daughter" as they walked along and crossed the river by ferry boat.

When they reached Jiankang Prefecture, however, they learned that the Fourth Prince of the Jin barbarians was about to cross the river with his troops and the prefecture was no longer safe. Then they heard that Prince Kang had ascended the throne and made Hangzhou his capital city, renaming it Lin'an. So Yaoqin and Bu Qiao sailed to Runzhou, crossed the Suzhou, Changzhou, Jiaxing, and Huzhou regions, and ended up in Lin'an where they took up temporary lodgings in an inn. It was to Bu Qiao's credit that he had been able to bring Yaoqin all the three thousand *li* from Bianliang to Lin'an. The little silver remaining in his possession was exhausted, and he even had to remove his outer garments as payment to the innkeeper. All that was left to him was Yaoqin, and now he was ready to dispose of this "precious merchandise."

Before long, Bu Qiao heard that a woman called Ninth Mother Wang, owner of a brothel in the environs of West Lake, wished to purchase a girl. He brought Ninth Mother Wang to the inn, showed her his merchandise, and haggled with her over the price. Ninth Mother Wang, pleased with Yaoqin's comely appearance, agreed to pay a price of fifty taels of silver. So when Bu Qiao was paid in full, he took Yaoqin to the brothel owner's house. "Yaoqin is my own flesh and blood," said the wily

Bu Qiao to Ninth Mother Wang, "and it is a pity that she must end up in a brothel. Treat her kindly, and she will eventually come around. Be patient with her." To Yaoqin, he said, "Ninth Mother is a close relative of mine. Stay with her for the time being. I will come back for you when I shall have discovered the whereabouts of your parents." Yaoqin was satisfied with this arrangement and agreed to stay.

Ninth Mother Wang presented the newcomer with a set of new garments and installed her in a room at the back of the cluster of courtyards. She plied Yaoqin with good food and fine tea to hasten her return to health and lavished kind words and attention on the girl to warm her heart. Yaoqin was content with her lot. But as the days passed and Bu Qiao did not come back, she began to miss her parents. With tears welling in her eyes, she asked Ninth Mother, "Why does Uncle Bu not come back?" Puzzled, Ninth Mother inquired, "What Uncle Bu?" Yaoqin replied, "The Uncle Bu who brought me here." Ninth Mother said, "But he told me he is your father." Yaoqin protested, "His family name is Bu, mine is Xin!" She then recounted her family's flight from Bianliang, how she became separated from her parents, how she met Bu by happenstance and was taken to Lin'an, and how Bu Qiao had coaxed her into coming here, whereupon Ninth Mother remarked, "So that's how it is! You are a waif, a crab without legs!" She then continued, "Let me tell you in all frankness. That Bu sold you to this house for fifty taels of silver. This is a brothel and we make our living by providing men with carnal services. I shelter three or four girls here, but none of them is outstanding. Your fairness has caught my fancy and I regard you as my own daughter. I promise you that as you grow older, you will have the best food and clothing and will not lack for anything for the rest of your life."

Yaoqin realized now that Bu Qiao had deceived her. She began to wail disconsolately, and it took Ninth Mother a long while to talk her around.

Ninth Mother changed Yaoqin's name to Wang the Lovely, and the entire household came to address her as Miss Lovely. She was taught to play on the flute and the lute, and learned to sing and dance to perfection. And by the time she was fourteen, she was already a ravishing beauty. All the rich young men in Lin'an were allured by her charms and came with lavish gifts in the hope of meeting her. Others who admired her talent and her literary skills haunted the gate of the brothel, asking for poems and samples of her calligraphy. As her fame grew, people began calling her "Mistress Queen of Flowers." A young man in the West Lake region even composed a song extolling her virtues, the lyrics of which were as follows,

> Quite rare is the girl who can stand with this flower;
> For none can match her skills with the brush or the lute,
> Her beauty is greater than that of any other,
> So many are those who would die for her love.

However, Ninth Mother worried lest her business would be hurt by Yaoqin's continued inaccessibility, so she tried to persuade the girl to start taking in clients. However Yaoqin demurred and announced, "I will agree to do so only after I see my parents." Ninth Mother was very much displeased but still doted on the girl and did not insist. More time passed until, one day, Second Master Jin, a man from a very rich family, offered to pay three hundred taels of silver for deflowering Miss Lovely. Ninth Mother could not resist such a huge fee. She had an idea. Discussing the matter with Second Master, she explained to him what should be done if he wished to have his way, and Second Master Jin agreed. Thus, on the fifteenth day of the eighth moon, he invited Miss Lovely to join him in watching the full moon over the lake waters. They embarked on a boat with three or four other persons who were privy to the scheme. There was much singing and playing of drinking games, until Miss Lovely fell in a faint from imbibing too much wine. She was then borne, unconscious, back to Ninth Mother's house and put to bed. Unclothing her took little time, as she was lightly clad for the warm summer weather. Ninth Mother herself undertook to restrain Miss Lovely in case she attempted to struggle. But the girl's arms and legs were limp and unresisting, and the man took her without effort.

When Miss Lovely awoke before daybreak, she realized that she had been tricked into ceding her virginity. She felt violated and was overcome by feelings of self-pity. After relieving herself, she put on her clothing and lay down on a rattan couch, turned toward the wall, and wept quietly. Second Master Jin came over and attempted to force his attentions upon her, but she showered him with blows, leaving bloody scratches on his face.

Sorely put out, Second Master Jin announced to Ninth Mother, "I am leaving," and stormed out of the gate before the madam could detain him.

It has always been the custom for clients who have deflowered a novice courtesan to be congratulated the next morning by the madam. All other courtesans in the brothel also offer their compliments, and banquets are held for the next two or three days. Some of these clients may even stay on for two or three months, or at least fifteen to twenty days. Second Master's precipitous departure, so early the next morning, was quite without precedent. With exclamations of surprise and consternation, Ninth Mother threw on some clothes and hastened upstairs. She realized what had happened when she saw Miss Lovely lying on the rattan couch, crying her heart out. Ninth Mother tried to cajole the girl and offered profuse apologies, but Miss Lovely said not a word. There was nothing Ninth Mother could do but go downstairs again. Miss Lovely cried the whole day, taking neither food nor drink. From that day on she feigned illness and would not go downstairs. She even refused to come out and greet clients.

Ninth Mother was greatly concerned. If she treated Miss Lovely abusively, she feared the headstrong girl, instead of coming to heel, would harden her heart for good. Yet the madam's purpose in adopting Yaoqin was to make money, and if the girl refused to accept clients, what good use would she serve even if she stayed on until she was a hundred years old? Ninth Mother mulled on this for several days without coming up with any ideas. Suddenly, she thought of Fourth Mother Liu, a sworn sister of hers with whom she had frequent contact. Fourth Mother had a ready tongue and, besides, was on good terms with Miss Lovely. Why not have her talk to the girl? There was much to be gained if Fourth Mother could prevail upon the girl to change her mind. Ninth Mother instructed a servant to invite Fourth Mother Liu to the brothel. And once the two women were seated in the front hall, Ninth Mother poured out her grievances.

Fourth Mother Liu heard her out, then declared, "As you know, I, your older sister, have a persuasive tongue—one that is capable of talking a clay Buddha into a love affair and making the Moon Fairy yearn for a mate. Just leave this matter to me." Ninth Mother said, "If you can talk her into it, I shall get on my knees and kowtow to you. So have some more tea, lest your mouth becomes parched from too much talking." To which

Fourth Mother Liu replied, "My mouth is like the sea. I could talk the night through and not feel thirsty."

Fourth Mother finished her cup of tea, and then proceeded to the rear of the building. Finding the door tightly shut, she tapped on it lightly and called out, "Open up, my niece!" Miss Lovely, recognizing her voice, came to unbolt the door, and the two greeted each other. Fourth Mother seated herself next to the table, facing the room, while Miss Lovely took a seat to one side. On the table was a square of fine silk with an as yet uncolored portrait of a beautiful girl traced on it. Fourth Mother exclaimed, "Wonderful! What skillful fingers you have! Ninth Mother is indeed fortunate to have acquired a daughter like you. Why, one could spend several thousand taels of gold and not find a girl of your beauty and your accomplishments!" Miss Lovely protested, "Do not make fun of me! But what wind has blown you here today, Auntie?" To which Fourth Mother Liu replied, "I have always wished to visit you, but there is so much to do at home I could never find time. I heard you have been happily deflowered, so I stole away to congratulate Ninth Sister." At the mention of the word "deflowered," Miss Lovely blushed and bowed her head. Observing that the girl was embarrassed, Fourth Mother drew her chair forward and took Miss Lovely's hands in her own. "My child," she said, "girls in our trade cannot afford to behave like soft-shelled eggs, so do not be so tender and thin-skinned. How will you earn big money if you are so sensitive?" Miss Lovely retorted, "Why should I want to earn big money?"

Fourth Mother Liu explained, "You may not want to earn big money, my child. But your mother who brought you up will wish to gain something from her investment. As the saying goes, 'Those who live next to mountains make their living by the mountains, and those who live next to the sea make their living by the sea.' Ninth Mother has several girls, but none that can hold a candle to you. Of all the vines in the melon patch, you are the only one that will bear luscious fruit. Ninth Mother treats you better than the others. You are a clever girl and should know what is expected of you. I hear you have refused to entertain clients after you were deflowered. What do you think you are doing? If we were a family of silkworms, who would feed you mulberry leaves if you were to behave in this manner? Since your Mother favors you so much, you should try to bring credit to her and not do anything to incur censure from the other girls."

Miss Lovely retorted, "Let them censure me! Little do I care!" "Silly girl," replied Fourth Mother Liu. "Criticism is but a small matter. Do you not know the rules of the game at brothels?" Curious, Miss Lovely asked, "And what might those be?"

Fourth Mother Liu explained, "People in our trade depend on our daughters for food, clothing, and our livelihood. For us, finding a pretty girl is like a windfall, just as acquiring a piece of good farmland or property is a windfall for those affluent households. If the girl is still too young, we only hope that clement winds and rains will cause her to grow up more quickly. The day she comes of age is harvest time—the time when we look forward to reaping our benefits, to welcoming new clients at the front door, and sending off old ones at the back door, to seeing Master Zhang bring us rice and Master Li come with firewood. A courtesan becomes famous only when clients beat a well-trodden path to her door!"

"How humiliating!" protested Miss Lovely. "I would never let such things happen!" Fourth Mother Liu chuckled, covering her mouth with her hand. "Never let such things happen? That is not for you to decide. The Mother makes all decisions in the household, and when a girl disobeys her, she may whip the girl until she' is barely alive. Then the girl does what she says, have no fear! Ninth Mother has never pressed or importuned you, for she treasures your wit and beauty and realizes you have had a coddled childhood. She respects your virtue and wishes to save you your dignity. However, she has spoken at length to me just now. She said you do not know what is good for you, that you fail to understand the difference between a feather and a millstone. She is highly displeased and has asked me to reason with you. Should you continue to disobey her, and should she lose her temper and scold and beat you, where can you go to for refuge? To Heaven? Do not start out on the wrong foot. You may be beaten morning and night, and when you can no longer endure such treatment, you will still have to entertain clients. But by then your value will have greatly diminished, and you will have become the butt of other girls' jokes. Let me tell you, a bucket that has fallen in the well is difficult to fish out again. Why do you not seek happiness, make everyone happy, and throw yourself into Ninth Mother's arms? You yourself would find life much more pleasant."

"I was born in a good family," said Miss Lovely, "and it only by mischance that I have landed in this house of prostitution. Nothing would make me happier than your helping me find a husband and becoming a decent woman. I would die rather than have to stand at the doorway to welcome and send off patrons with a simpering smile on my lips." Fourth Mother Liu replied, "Becoming a decent woman, or 'going straight' as we call it, is indeed the right thing to do. That, I do not gainsay. However, going straight comes in different ways and takes different forms." Miss Lovely asked, "What do you mean by that?" Fourth Mother explained: "Well, there is true going straight and false going straight. There is bitter going straight and felicitous going straight. Or going straight may take place when times are still good, or may be done in desperation. Going straight may be final, but it may also be unfulfilled. Bear with me, my child, as I explain these choices to you.

"What is true going straight? The best match is, of course, between a handsome scholar and a beautiful woman. Such a good thing occurs quite infrequently and is indeed rare. But once two such persons are fortunate enough to meet, it is love at first sight, with the man willing to take the woman, and the woman willing to give herself. With them, it is like the mating of moths that cling together until they die. This is true going straight.

"So what is false going straight? A patron may fall in love with a girl, but she does not love him. She has no real wish to marry him but uses the word 'marriage' to titillate his passions and have him splurge his money on her. Should a deal be concluded, however, she is likely to seek excuses to go back on it. There are also some single-minded fellows who insist on marrying the girl, even though he knows full well that she has no liking for him. He pays the madam of the house a big sum of money to overcome the girl's objections. She marries him reluctantly, and then purposely flouts the rules of the household in all possible ways, everything from creating scenes and throwing tantrums to openly carrying on with other men. This she does until the family can no longer countenance her, and in a year or even a few months' time they drive her out of the house and she goes back to prostitution. Going straight is, in her case, a means to make money, and is false.

"What is bitter going straight? A patron may like a girl who dislikes him but is cowed by his power. The Mother, too, is afraid there will be trouble and agrees to the match. Thereafter, the girl has no more control over her own destiny. She marries with tears in her eyes, and entering the doors of that powerful family is like plunging into a bottomless ocean. The rules of the household are so strict she cannot lift her head. Her position is one of half-servant and half-concubine, up to the day she dies. That is bitter going straight.

"So what is felicitous going straight? That is when a girl, who is seeking someone to marry, comes across a man with a mild temper and considerable means. He also has an agreeable first wife who has no children of her own and counts on the girl to give birth to a son after marrying into the family. If the girl does produce an heir, her position will be that of principal mother. Thus, by marrying the man, she can count on a comfortable life today and a good status in future. That is felicitous going straight.

"What, then, is going straight when times are still good? When the girl is still enjoying a life of moonlight and flowers, when she is still at the height of her popularity, she entrusts me with finding a satisfactory husband, having made up her mind to turn her life about before she falls out of favor. This is going straight when times are still good.

"What is going straight in desperation? That is when the girl has no desire yet to marry but is compelled to do so because of some lawsuit, or because she is suffering abuse at the hands of rich and powerful clients, or because she owes so much money she will never be able to discharge her debts. So she swallows her pride and marries whoever will take her, simply to find refuge and obtain some peace.

"What is final going straight? That is when the girl, who is approaching middle age but is still going strong, meets an honest patron with whom she shares much in common. Both furl their sails, and they spend the rest of their years together. That is called final going straight.

"What, on the other hand, is unfulfilled going straight? It happens when both the man and the girl apparently desire each other with a fiery passion and she goes to live with him. But their love turns out to be merely a passing fancy, devoid of permanent objectives, and friction arises. Or it may be that the man's parents will not countenance her, or his wife is consumed by jealousy. At any rate, after a number of set-tos, the family sends the girl back to the brothel and demands a refund of the price paid for her. Or, the family may fall on bad times and can no longer provide for her. Unable to bear poverty, she goes back to her old ways and, like a third-class whore, resorts to soliciting patrons at restaurants and teahouses. That is called unfulfilled going straight."

Miss Lovely asked, "I wish to go straight properly, so how should I do that?"

Fourth Mother Liu replied, "A girl who steps through the door of matrimony is expected to be pure and unsullied. However, your body has already been defiled. Even if you were to marry this very night, you would not be a virgin. Your biggest misstep was coming to this place. But such is your fate. Your Mother has spent a great deal of time and money on you, and she will not let you out of these doors if you do not help her in her business and make a few thousand taels of silver for her. Moreover, if you intend to go straight, you will first have to choose a good man. Surely, you would not wish to go off with one of those clients who have foul-smelling mouths and filthy faces! But if you refuse to entertain any clients today, how will you know which is the right man to marry? If you stubbornly reject all clients, your Mother will have no recourse other than to sell you to the first man who is willing to pay the price, and you will end up as his concubine. That, too, might be called going straight. However, the man may well be decrepit, or unsightly, or he may be an illiterate dolt, and that would make you an object of scorn and derision. Better that you fell into a river and drowned, for then people might hear the splash and feel some pity for you! It is my opinion that you would do well to bend to your Mother's will and receive clients. Your talent and beauty will deter run-of-the-mill clients from seeking your favors. Your patrons will be princes and royalty, men from noble and powerful households. Such men will not demean your existence. You should enjoy the good life while you are still young. You should also help your Mother build up her fortunes. And, last but not least, you should set aside some money of your own so that you will not be beholden to other people in future. After five or ten years, you may come across a man after your own heart, a man with whom you can converse and share your feelings. Then I, as your match-maker, will marry you off in state, and your mother will have no objections to letting you go. Is that not the best for both of you?"

Miss Lovely smiled, but said nothing. Fourth Mother Liu knew she had had a change of heart, so she said, "All I have said is for your own good. Follow my advice, and in the future you will be grateful to me." So saying, she rose to her feet.

As Miss Lovely saw out her visitor, she bumped right into Ninth Mother who had been eavesdropping by the door. Miss Lovely, covered with confusion, hurriedly withdrew into her chambers while Fourth Mother went with Ninth Mother to the front room. Sitting down, Fourth Mother stated, "My niece is quite headstrong. However, I have used my powers of persuasion and the iron has now become malleable. Find her a second patron as quickly as possible, one who will be acceptable to her. When that has happened, I will come to offer my congratulations."

Ninth Mother Wang thanked Fourth Mother profusely. She prepared a dinner, and the two, after drinking all the wine they could hold, took leave of each other.

In the meantime, Miss Lovely had thought over Fourth Mother's words and found that they made sense. Thereafter, she willingly received clients who sought her, and after her second patron they came in a steady stream. In fact, so many applied for her favors she had hardly a moment's respite and her fame grew. Clients vied for her, even at the price of ten taels of silver for a night's enjoyment. And while Ninth Mother rejoiced over the money that rolled in, Miss Lovely kept an eye out for someone with whom she could share her heart. But such a man is not to be found in haste, for,

> More easy is it to find a precious stone,
> Than it is to discover a caring mate.

Now, to the other side of this story. There lived outside Qingbo Gate of Lin'an city an oil merchant who went by the name of Tenth Elder Zhu. Three years earlier, he had adopted a young boy named Qin Zhong who was also a refugee from Bianliang. Qin Zhong's mother had passed away while he was still a child, and when he was thirteen his father had sold him and gone off to Upper Tianzhu Monastery to serve as a tender of censers. Tenth Elder Zhu was getting old and had no offspring of his own. Moreover his wife had died quite recently. So he treated Qin Zhong like he would his own kith and kin, changing his name to Zhu Zhong and teaching him the oil trade. Things went well while there were only the two of them. However, Tenth Elder began to suffer from excruciating back pains that had him sitting up nine nights out of ten. No longer able to do any work, he hired a clerk by the name of Jing Quan to help out at the store.

Time flew by, and four years passed almost unnoticed. By this time, Zhu Zhong had turned seventeen and was now a handsome young man. Yet he had not married though he had come of age. In the Zhu household lived a maidservant, a girl in her twenties named Lan Hua. She had her eye on the Young Master and tried several times to seduce him. However, Zhu Zhong was a well-behaved person and, moreover, shunned the girl since he found her to be slovenly and unattractive. Seeing that Young Master resisted her wiles, Lan Hua turned her attention elsewhere and set her sights on Jing Quan. The clerk, being almost forty and still unmarried, fell for her at once. Thereafter, the two fornicated in secret on more than one occasion. But, for some perverse reason, they felt that the Young Master was a hindrance to them, so they conceived the idea of driving him out of the house. Together they planned a concerted attack on Zhu Zhong. Lan Hua, putting on a show of aggrieved virtue, went to Tenth Elder Zhu and complained, "The Young Master is constantly taking liberties with me. He is quite ill-behaved!" Hearing this piqued Tenth Elder Zhu, since he himself had been making advances to Lan Hua. Then Jing Quan hid away some of the silver earned by the store and told Tenth Elder Zhu, "Young Master Zhu goes out to gamble and is a man of little gumption. Silver has been missing from the till because he steals from it."

At first, Tenth Elder refused to believe this. But after hearing several such accusations, and because he was in his dotage and knew no better, he summoned Zhu Zhong and gave him a dressing down. Being no fool, Zhu Zhong knew that Jing Quan and Lan Hua were conspiring against him. He thought of defending himself, then realized that doing so would only lead to disputes in which he would end up as the loser if Tenth Elder refused to listen to him. On a sudden inspiration, he said to Tenth Elder Zhu, "Business at the store has been slack and does not merit two clerks. Jing Quan could tend to the store, while I sell oil by carrying casks around on a tote pole. Since I would bring back the daily receipts, that would double our business, would it not?"

Just as Tenth Elder Zhu was on the verge of agreeing to this proposal, however, Jing Quan remarked, "He is not the sort that would go out peddling goods with a shoulder pole. He has pilfered enough silver for his own cache these last years. Besides, he harbors a grudge against you for not finding him a woman and does not wish to work here any longer. He is merely seeking a pretext to go out, acquire a wife, and set up his own house." Tenth Elder Zhu sighed, saying, "So that is how he repays me for treating him like a son! Heaven is not kind to me. But so be it! Since he is not of my own flesh and blood, there is no natural bond between us. Let him go." He gave Zhu Zhong three taels of silver and showed him the door. As a mark of consideration, he allowed the boy to take along a set of summer and winter clothing as well as his bedding. Knowing he could not expect to be kept any longer, Zhu Zhong kowtowed four times and tearfully took his leave.

Zhu Zhong's father, Qin Liang, had never told his son that he gone to Upper Tianzhu Monastery. Thus, after leaving Tenth Elder Zhu's house, Zhu Zhong rented a tiny room at the foot of Zhong'an Bridge, deposited his belongings, bought a large lock with which to secure the door, and then roamed the streets and lanes in search of his father. This he did for several days without, however, obtaining any news. Unwillingly, but seeing no alternative, he deferred his quest for the time being.

In the four years that he had worked at Tenth Elder Zhu's house, he had been scrupulously loyal to his benefactor and had not laid aside any savings of his own. All he possessed now were the three taels of silver with which he had been sent packing, and that did not give him sufficient capital for any sort of business. The more he thought about the matter, the more he felt the only business he was familiar enough with was the oil trade. The owners of most of the city's oil presses knew him, and vending oil as a street peddler could provide him with a stable living. With these thoughts in mind, he proceeded to purchase a tote pole and the necessary appurtenances, then used the remaining silver to buy oil from the oil presses. The owners of the oil presses all knew Zhu to be an honest, upright fellow. Moreover, they had learned that this lad, previously a store clerk, now had to peddle oil in the streets on account of the machinations of his colleague Jing. Aware that he had suffered an injustice and wishing to help, they let him have their clearest oil and were most liberal with their dippers. Given these advantages, Zhu Zhong was also generous to his own customers. So he was able to sell more than other peddlers. Thrifty by nature, he spent the profits he made for purchasing only daily necessities and clothing. The rest of it he saved.

Only one matter now weighed on his mind—his father. He reflected, "People call me Zhu Zhong, and no one knows that my true name is Qin. Were my father to look for me, he would have nothing to go by." He therefore changed his family name back to Qin.

Now, when a man of superior position or power changes his name, he submits a petition to the imperial court or to one of the yamens in charge of rites, imperial studies, or national academics in order to have the records amended and his new name announced to the public. But who makes it known when an oil vendor assumes another name? Qin Zhong had an idea. On one side of his casks of oil he inscribed the word "Qin," and on the other side, the word "Bianliang." These markings, which everyone could see, served him as his hallmark, and from then on he became known in the marketplaces of Lin'an as Oil Vendor Qin.

During the second moon, when the weather was neither too cold nor too warm, Qin Zhong learned that the monks of Zhaoqing Monastery were to perform nine days and nights of meritorious rites. Surmising that they would have need of goodly quantities of oil, he carried his oil casks to the monastery and began to hawk his wares. The monks knew the name Oil Vendor Qin and had heard that his oil was better and cheaper than that of other vendors, so they brought all their business to him. Thus for a full nine days, Qin Zhong frequented the Zhaoqing Monastery.

On the ninth and last day, Qin Zhong, having sold all his oil, toted his casks out of the monastery. It was a clear, sunny day and visitors swarmed about like so many ants. Qin Zhong trotted along a river and saw in the distance the Lake of Ten Scenes, with its peach-red flowers, green willows, and colorfully painted boats floating on the lake to the music of flutes and hand drums. Tourists strolled here and there, enjoying the scenery and having a good time. After walking a while, Qin Zhong felt tired and turned his steps toward a clearing to the right side of the monastery. Here, he set down his load and sat down on a rock to take a rest. Close by, there happened to be a house that overlooked the lake. Within its gold-painted latticed gate and scarlet fence stood a grove of delicate bamboos. One could not see inside the house, but the entrance hall looked clean and well kept. Three or four men wearing the kind of headdresses affected by scholars or officials came out, accompanied by a young woman. When they reached the gate, the woman folded her hands, bade the men farewell, and went back toward the house. Qin Zhong stared at her. He had never seen anyone with such an exquisite complexion and graceful figure. He stood there transfixed, unable to speak or move. Being a well-behaved young man, he was ignorant about the trade of prostitution, and he wondered what sort of family resided in that house.

As he puzzled over the matter, a middle-aged woman and a young maidservant stepped out of the house. The older woman saw the oil casks and remarked, "We are running short of cooking oil and here is a peddler. Why not purchase some from him?" The maidservant and the older woman came out of the gate and approached Qin Zhong, calling, "Oil vendor!" Realizing that they were addressing him, Qin Zhong replied, "I am sold out, but if Mother wishes to have some oil, I can deliver it tomorrow." The maidservant, who could read a few characters, saw the inscription on the casks and told the older woman, "Mother, this vendor's name is Qin." The older woman had heard it said there was an oil vendor named Qin who was honest and reliable in his dealings, so she said to Qin Zhong, "We use oil in my family every day. If you are willing to deliver the oil, I will give you the business." "I thank you for your patronage. You may rely upon me," Qin Zhong replied. The older woman and the maidservant then went back into the house. Qin Zhong thought to himself, "I wonder what the relationship is between the woman and that beautiful girl. If I can sell oil here every day, as well as making a handsome profit I will have the good fortune of feasting my eyes on her beauty!"

As he was about the pick up his tote pole and leave, two bearers carrying a sedan chair with a black silk canopy sped up to the house and stopped in front of the gate. Two young lackeys alighted and went into the house. Qin Zhong thought to himself, "How odd! Whom can they be coming for?" A few moments later, two maidservants came out of the house, one bearing a bundle wrapped in a red blanket and the other, an intricately carved bamboo box. These they handed to the carriers, who stowed the articles under the seat of the sedan chair. Then the beautiful girl emerged, followed by the two lackeys. One was carrying a lute case, the other clutched a number of manuscripts and had a jade flute hanging from one of his wrists. When the beautiful girl had mounted the sedan, the bearers shouldered their poles and returned the way they had come, with the maidservants and young lackeys following on foot. Qin Zhong had caught another glimpse of the beautiful girl, but his puzzlement only increased. Picking up his tote pole, he departed.

Having walked a short distance, he came to a tavern by the river. Qin Zhong seldom drank liquor, but after seeing the beautiful girl on the sedan he felt both elated and depressed. Setting down his casks, he stepped into the tavern and seated himself at a small table. The waiter asked, "Are you entertaining guests, or will you be drinking alone?" Qin Zhong replied, "I am alone. Bring me three cups of your best wine and two or three dishes of fruit and nuts. No meat courses." As the waiter poured out his wine, Qin Zhong inquired, "What sort of people live inside the golden lattice gate?" The waiter informed him, "That garden belongs to a nobleman named Qi, but is now being used by Ninth Mother Wang." Qin Zhong then asked, "A young woman left the garden by sedan chair just a while ago. Who is she?" The waiter replied, "That is the famous courtesan Miss Lovely, who is known to all the local people as the Queen of Flowers. A refugee from Bianliang, she was stranded here some time ago. She plays music, sings, dances, writes, and paints to perfection. Her clients are all men of consequence, and those who wish to spend the night with her must put up ten taels of silver. That should apprise you she is beyond the reach of ordinary men. They used to live outside Flood-of-Gold Gate, but the premises were too small. And, as they are on good terms with Commander Qi, he has lent the garden to them for their use."

The information that Miss Lovely was also from Bianliang filled Qin Zhong with feelings of nostalgia and gave him fresh food for thought. He had a few more drinks, paid his bill, picked up his casks, and left. As he jogged along, he thought, "What a pity such a beautiful woman should end up in a brothel!" Then with a wry smile, he reflected, "But if she were not in a brothel, I, an oil vendor, would never have had the opportunity to see her." His cogitations wandered on, "Grass survives a single season, and a man lives but one life. I would die happy if I could hold this beauty in my arms and sleep with her for just one night." Then he rebuked himself, "I make my living by toting around casks of oil and earn no more than a few coins a day. It is not for me to think such thoughts! I am like a warty toad in a sewer that dreams of dining on swan's flesh. She deals only with princes and nobility, and I am but an oil vendor. Even if I had the money she would not accept me." But a moment later he contradicted himself, "Yet I hear that pimps and madams look only at your purse. They would accept even a beggar if he had money. And that is to say nothing of the fact that I am a merchant and a respectable person. Yes, she would receive me if I had the money! But where will I find such money?" Thus he indulged in such thoughts, muttering and mumbling to himself as he walked along.

Tell me, has such a simpleton ever existed in the world of men? A paltry ped-dler, whose entire capital amounts to no more than three taels of silver, obsessed with the idea of taking to bed a famous courtesan whose price for a single night is ten taels of silver? Talk about spring dreams!

Yet as the saying goes, where there is a will, there is a way. By dint of cudgeling his brains, Qin Zhong devised a plan. He told himself, "Starting from tomorrow, I will deduct my costs from my daily earnings and save up all the rest. By laying aside one *fen* of silver each day, I will have amassed three taels and six *qian* in a year, and in three years I will have achieved my purpose. If, on the other hand, I save two *fen* each day, I will need only a year and a half. And should I succeed in saving even more, then one year will probably suffice." With this plan in mind, he arrived at his home. Unlocking the door, he went in. Thanks to the day's flights of fantasy, he felt no pleasure as he looked at his dreary pallet. He went to bed without supper and spent the night tossing and turning sleeplessly and thinking about Miss Lovely.

When morning finally arrived, he clambered out of bed, filled his oil casks, and prepared himself some breakfast. Then he hastened straight to Mother Wang's house and entered the gate. He dared not go in any fur-ther, however, and merely leaned his head against the door and tried to look in. Mother Wang had just risen from her bed and, with hair still uncombed, was giving the servant girl instructions about the day's shop-ping. Qin Zhong recognized her voice and called out, "Mother Wang!" Ninth Mother Wang looked out and, seeing Oil Vendor Qin, smiled, say-ing, "Good fellow! You are as good as your word." She asked him to come in with his casks, had him fill a jar with about five catties of oil, and offered him a fair price, which Qin Zhong accepted without argument. Evidently quite pleased, Ninth Mother Wang said, "This bit of oil will last my household only two days. If you deliver some every other day, I will not take my business elsewhere." Qin Zhong promised to do so and left. He felt disappointed that he had not caught sight of Miss Lovely, but he consoled himself with the thought, "I should be glad to get this client, for even if I have not seen the girl this time, there will be a second opportunity, and a third one after that. The only problem is that coming so far out for just one customer is not the best way to do business. Zhaoqing Monastery is close by, and although they do not perform meritorious rites every day, surely they still need cooking oil. It would do no harm to find out. If I should succeed in making customers of all the priors, I could make Qiantang one of my routes and sell an entire load of oil here."

Thus Qin Zhong went to the monastery. As it turned out, the moment was quite opportune, as all the priors had been thinking about him. All bought oil from him, some more, some less. Qin Zhong came to an understanding with the priors that he would bring oil every other day. That particular day happened to be an even day by the calendar. So starting from then, Qin Zhong plied other routes on odd days and came to Qiantang on even days. Once out of Qiantang Gate, he would make straight for Ninth Mother's house to deliver oil, using this as a pretext to see the Queen of Flowers. On some days he would come across her, on other days he did not. He would pine for her on days he missed seeing her, and pine for her even more when he did see her.

Time flew, and by the next year Qin Zhong had entered the door of Ninth Mother Wang's house so frequently that everyone in the household, old and young, knew him. His business had been good on some days, less so on others. But he had managed to set aside two or three *wen* of the purest silver on ordinary days, and at least one *wen* even on days when sales were slow. Whenever he had a few *qian* of silver to spare he would wrap these in a small package. And now, after weeks and months of careful hoarding, he possessed a big bagful of silver, although he had no idea exactly how much there was since it had accumulated bit by bit.

One day—an odd day—it was raining heavily, so Qin Zhong decided not to go out on his rounds. He felt most happy with his bag of silver. "Since I am taking this day off," he thought, "I might as well weigh it out and see how much I have." With an oilpaper umbrella as protection from the rain, he went to the silver store across the street to use a balance. The silversmith surveyed him disdainfully, thinking, "How much silver does an oil vendor have, that he must use a balance? If I let him use a five-tael counterweight, his silver will not even make the first notch." Qin Zhong opened his package to display all his loose silver. As we all know, silver looks more voluminous in loose pieces than when it is presented in the form of ingots. The silversmith, a petty man with a small soul, goggled at the sight of the pile of silver, thinking to himself, "The sea cannot be measured with a bushel, nor can a man be judged by his appearance!" He hastened to set up a balance and to bring out a collection of counterbalances, large and small. Qin Zhong weighed the silver in his package. There were exactly sixteen taels—or one catty if ordinary scales were used. Qin Zhong determined, "This is more than enough for a night's enjoyment of flowers and willows, even if I subtract my original capital." Then he thought, "How could I pay with such bits and pieces of silver? People would certainly look down at me. However, I can avail myself of this silversmith to combine the pieces into a bigger ingot that will be much more imposing in appearance." Thus he measured out a full ten taels to be melted down and cast as one large ingot. Then he had a smaller ingot made, weighing a tael and eight *qian*. Of the four taels and two *qian* that remained to him, he gave a small piece to the silversmith as payment for the smelting, then bought himself a pair of shoes with piping, some clean socks and a pleated coif. At home, he washed and starched a set of garments and, with some fragrant incense, scented these over and over again.

On the next sunny day, he rose early and began to dress himself up. When he was satisfied with his appearance, he secreted the ingots in his sleeve pocket, locked his door and set out for Ninth Mother Wang's house. He was in high spirits at first, but by the time he arrived at the gate of the house feelings of uneasiness set in. He thought, "I have always come to this brothel to sell oil. But now that I am visiting it as a paying client, what should I say?" As he stood undecided, the door suddenly squeaked open and Ninth Mother stepped out. At the sight of Qin Zhong, she exclaimed, "Why, Young Master Qin! I see you are all dressed up. Are you not doing business today? What important matter brings you here?" Taken unawares, Qin Zhong quickly covered his embarrassment by bowing with folded hands. Ninth Mother had to return the courtesy. Then Qin Zhong said, "This humble person has come for no other purpose than to bring you my regards." However, the worldly-wise procuress had noted his demeanor and attire as well as his assurances that he had come for a visit. She surmised, "I'll wager he has an eye on one of my girls and wishes either to spend the night with her or take her to a room for a quick turn. Although he is no big Buddha, his silver is as good as anyone else's. Even if I get no more than a *qian* or two out of him, I can always use that to buy groceries." Thus, wreathing her face in a smile, she said aloud, "Young Master Qin, you will not regret this visit." Qin Zhong said, "There is something that I hesitate to say, that I know not how to put into words." Ninth Mother Wang replied, "There can be no harm in speaking it out. Let us go inside and sit down, and you can tell me what you have to say."

Qin Zhong had delivered oil at this house on hundreds of occasions, yet his posterior had never once made acquaintance with the chairs in the parlor. Now they would meet for the first time. Ninth Mother showed Qin Zhong to the parlor, seated him in a visitor's chair, and called for tea to be served. The servant girl who brought in tea on a tray recognized Qin Zhong as the oil vendor and wondered why he was being treated like a patron. Lowering her head, she giggled. Ninth Mother snapped, "What is so funny? Do you not know how to behave toward guests?" The girl stopped giggling and went out with the tray. Ninth Mother Wang asked, "So what is it that Young Master Qin wishes to tell me?" Qin Zhong replied, "It is just that I wish to share a cup of wine with one of the sisters in your house." Ninth Mother inquired, "Is that all you want? To share a cup of wine? Surely, you would also wish to lie with her. But you are a well-behaved fellow. When did you conceive the idea of enjoying such pleasures?" Qin Zhong replied, "The desire has grown in me over many years, and not just overnight." Ninth Mother continued, "Well, you know all the girls in my house. Which one has caught your fancy?" Qin Zhong replied, "I wish for nothing more than to spend a night with the Queen of Flowers."

Ninth Mother thought Qin Zhong was trifling with her. Frowning, she said, "Watch your tongue! Are you trying to mock me?" Qin Zhong replied, "I am a simple man. Why would I say anything that is not true?" Ninth Mother said caustically, "Even a night pot has two ears! Have you not heard of the price commanded by my house's most beautiful girl? You could not pay for half a night with her even if you pawned all of your oil-vending chattels. You had better make do with another girl." Qin Zhong shrugged his shoulders and stuck out his tongue, "That is tall talk, Ninth Mother. Dare I ask how many thousands of taels of silver it costs to spend a night with the Queen of Flowers?"

Ninth Mother surmised that Qin Zhong was jesting. Her anger receded and she said with a smile, "Oh, not that much! But one would need ten taels of the best silver. That does not include the cost of hosting and other sundry expenses." Qin Zhong said casually, "In that case, there is no problem." Reaching into his sleeve, he drew out a big, shining ingot of silver and handed it to the madam with the words, "This is ten taels, of full measure and the best quality. Please accept it." He then extracted a smaller ingot and continued, "Here is another ingot, a full two taels. Please prepare a dinner for two. Mother, do me the favor of helping me fulfill this humble person's wish. I will not forget this favor as long as I live, and will make it up to you some day." Ninth Mother was loath to let go of so much silver, but she worried that Qin Zhong was acting on impulse and might eventually regret the loss of his seed money. So she attempted one last time to dissuade him. "It is no light matter for a merchant like you to save ten taels of silver," she said. "You should really give the matter more thought." Qin Zhong, however, replied, "I have made up my mind, so do not trouble yourself on my account."

Ninth Mother thereupon secreted the two ingots in her sleeve, saying, "Well, that's that. But there may be other difficulties." Qin Zhong inquired, "What other difficulties might there be, Mother? After all, you are the head of the household." Ninth Mother replied, "My beautiful girl consorts with princes, aristocrats, and the rich and powerful. As one might say, 'She converses and jests with the learned and has no truck with dolts.' She knows you as Vendor Qin and there is little likelihood that she will accept you." Qin Zhong pleaded, "Mother, I place my reliance on your skills of persuasion. If you make this thing happen, I shall forever be indebted to you." Seeing how determined Qin Zhong was, Ninth Mother knit her brows. Suddenly, an idea occurred to her. "I think I have a device that will succeed. If it does, do not exult. If it fails, do not reproach me. Yesterday, Mistress Beautiful went to drink with the guests at a banquet given by Li the Academician and has not come home. Today she has an appointment with the scion of Magistrate Huang to go boating on the lake. Tomorrow, she is going to a poetry society at the invitation of Man-of-the-Mountains Zhang and his companions. And on the day after tomorrow, a banquet will be held here, hosted by the son of Minister Han. So come and try your luck on the day after the day after tomorrow. However, a word of advice! For the sake of decorum, do not come here to sell oil the next few days. Also, the cotton garments you wear do not give you the appearance of a high-class client. Next time, come dressed in silks and satins, so that even the maidservants will not recognize you. That will make it easier for me to concoct a story about you." Qin Zhong said, "This humble person understands." Bidding farewell, he left. The next three days, he stopped doing business altogether and bought a ready-made second-hand silk robe at a pawnshop, then sauntered around the neighborhood, rehearsing the gait and mien of a cultured person.

On the fourth day, Qin Zhong rose at the crack of dawn and went to Mother Wang's house. He was much too early, however, and the gate was still shut when he arrived. He decided to walk around some and return later. However, he dared not go to Zhaoqing Monastery for fear that the monks there might make fun of his unwonted attire, so he went for a long stroll by the Lake of Ten Scenes. When he returned to Mother Wang's house, the gate was open, but a sedan chair and several horses stood by the door and many servants and attendants were sitting around. Qin Zhong was not a devious person, but neither was he lacking in artifice. He beckoned surreptitiously to a hostler and asked, "To whom do the sedan chair and horses belong?" The hostler replied, "To the Han Residence. They are here to pick up their young master." Thus Qin Zhong was apprised that Young Master Han had slept over and had yet to leave. So he went away again and found a small restaurant nearby where he ordered some food and sat for a while. Returning to the Wang house, he found that the sedan and horses were gone. However, Ninth Mother Wang met him at the door with the words, "It is all this older person's fault. Your chance will not come today. Young Master Han insisted on taking her to see the first plum blossoms at his East Homestead. I could not argue with him, as he is a longtime patron. I learned they will be going from there to Lingyin Temple to play a game of *go* with the temple's chess master. Furthermore, the scion of Commander Qi has been here two or three times to seek an appointment. I cannot refuse him either, as he is my landlord. And whenever he comes he stays between three to five days, so I am unable to set a date for you. Young Master Qin, if you are set on sleeping with the girl, you will have to be patient for few more days. Otherwise I can pay you back the full amount you gave me the other day." Qin Zhong hastened to reply, "My only fear is that Mother will not go through with this matter. I lose nothing by waiting some more time." Ninth Mother said, "Since you put it that way, making an arrangement will be easier for me." Qin Zhong bade her farewell and was about to leave, when Ninth Mother stopped him, saying, "Young Master Qin, this older person has another suggestion. Do not come so early the next time. Wait until midday. By then I will be able to say for certain whether there is another patron. Take my word for it, the later you come the better, and, pray, do not misunderstand my intentions." Qin Zhong hastened to assure her, "Of course not, of course not."

That day, Qin Zhong did not do any business, but the next morning he readied his tote pole and oil casks and went out on his rounds, dropping, however, the Qiantang Gate route. After coming back from work each day, he dressed up and went to Ninth Mother Wang's house to make inquiries, but no opportunities presented themselves. This went on for another month or so.

Heavy snow fell on the fifteenth day of the twelfth moon and, after it stopped, a westerly wind rose, hardening the snowdrifts into ice. It was bitterly cold, but the ground was dry, so Qin Zhong was able to go out for half a day's business. In the afternoon, dressed up as usual, he went to try his luck. Ninth Mother Wang was all smiles as she came forth to greet him. "This is your lucky day. The odds are nine points to one in your favor." Qin Zhong asked, "And what is the missing point?" Ninth Mother laughed, "That one point? The principal player has yet to come back." Anxiously, Qin Zhong inquired, "Will she be coming back?" Ninth Mother reassured him, "Today's appointment was to enjoy the snow scenes at the residence of Prefectural Chief Yu. The banquet is being held in a boat on the lake, but Prefectural Chief Yu is in his seventies and the days of wind-and-moon trysts are past for him. The agreement was to send her home before nightfall. Go to her room and have a cup of warm wine, and wait for her at your leisure." Qin Zhong said, "Then I must trouble you to lead the way."

Ninth Mother Wang took Qin Zhong through a series of winding corridors, not, however, to the two-story building but to a three-room suite with high ceilings. The maidservant's room on the left was currently unoccupied but equipped with bed, couch, table, and chairs and was used on occasion for entertaining clients. The room on the right was the Queen of Flower's bedchamber; the door to it was locked. Both these chambers had small side rooms. The room in the center, which served as a parlor, was decorated with a famous artist's landscape painting. An ancient bronze vessel with burning incense stood on a table, and sideboards on both sides held various curios and antiques. The walls were hung with poems and calligraphic writings, but Qin Zhong, painfully aware that he was no literary man, did not subject these to close inspection. He thought to himself, "If the outer room is so well appointed, the inner room must certainly be quite magnificent. And all of it is mine for this one night. Ten taels of silver is not too high a price."

Ninth Mother asked Qin Zhong to take the guest's seat while she herself sat down at the hostess's place. A few moments later, maidservants brought in lamps plus a table for eight, upon which they placed bowls of fresh fruit and nuts and a number of dishes containing viands so fragrant they tickled the palate even before one tasted them. Ninth Mother filled a cup with wine, saying, "All the girls have clients this evening, so this old one will dine with you. Relax, and enjoy a few cups of wine." However, Qin Zhong, never a big drinker and presently somewhat preoccupied, only drank half a cup, and after a while declined any further libations. Ninth Mother said, "Young Master Qin, you must be hungry. Have some food first and drink later." A maidservant set a bowl of rice before Qin Zhong and kept refilling it as he ate, then brought him tureen of soup consisting of a variety of ingredients. The madam, a good drinker, ate nothing but drank while keeping her guest company. When Qin Zhong laid down his bowl and chopsticks, Ninth Mother insisted, "The night will be long, you must eat more." So Qin Zhong accepted another half bowl of rice. Then a maidservant came with a lantern and said, "The water has been heated, please take your bath." Qin Zhong had already bathed but could not refuse, so he went to the bathhouse and washed himself with soap and scented water. When he had dressed himself and returned to the table, Ninth Mother had the food dishes removed and a warming pot brought in for heating wine. By then, the last light of dusk had waned, and even the Zhaoqing Monastery's bell had tolled.

As the saying goes, "Those who anticipate are the most impatient." Qin Zhong had waited so long for the courtesan he was becoming irritated. The madam, meanwhile, chattered about this and that, cracked salacious jokes, and kept urging him to drink. And thus another two hours passed.

Then a commotion was heard outside. The Queen of Flowers had come home. As a maidservant announced her arrival, Ninth Mother got up to meet the girl. Qin Zhong also rose from his seat. Miss Lovely was drunk and the maidservants had to help her into the house. As she walked through the door and saw, with drink-dazed eyes, the brilliantly lit room and the table strewn with leftovers, she came to a halt and asked, "Who is drinking here?" Ninth Mother replied, "My child, it is the Young Master Qin I mentioned to you, the one who admires you and frequently sends you gifts. He has been waiting for more than a month now, since you have not had time for him. But you are free this evening, so I asked him to keep you company for the night." Miss Lovely retorted, "I have never heard of any Young Master Qin in Lin'an County! I will not receive him." She turned around to leave, but Ninth Mother spread out both arms to bar the way. "He is an honest-to-goodness person," said Ninth Mother. "I would not try to deceive you."

Miss Lovely had no choice but to turn back. As she stepped into the parlor, she looked up at the patron and thought he looked familiar but, being too inebriated, was unable to place him. She said, "Mother, I know this man. He is not a person of renown, and if I receive him I will be laughed at." To which Ninth Mother replied, "My child, he is Young Master Qin who owns a silk store inside Yongjin Gate. You may have met him when we lived there. That is why he looks familiar. But do not get him wrong. He has asked for you in all earnestness. I agreed and cannot go back on my word now. For my sake, just put up with him for this one night. I know I am at fault and will make things up to you tomorrow." As she spoke she prodded Miss Lovely's shoulder. Miss Lovely could not prevail against Ninth Mother and went in to meet her customer.

Qin Zhong had overheard every word of the exchange but he feigned ignorance. Miss Lovely greeted him and sat down to one side of the table. The more she looked at Qin Zhong, the more suspicious and displeased she became, and she refused to speak. She told the maidservant to bring wine and fill a large cup. The madam thought the wine was for the client, but Miss Lovely downed it at one gulp. Ninth Mother protested, "You have had too much already, my child. Do not drink any more!" But Miss Lovely would not listen. "I am not drunk," she said, and emptied another ten or more cups of wine.

All that wine, after previously having imbibed so much, made her all the more drunk. She herself realized now that she could no longer stand on her own, so she ordered the maidservant to unlock the door to her bedroom and light the silver lamp. Without removing her hair ornaments or her garments and only kicking off her shoes, she collapsed onto the bed. Much embarrassed by the girl's behavior, the madam said, "My daughter has always been pampered and is quite willful. For some reason she is not herself today. Do not take offense." Qin Zhong replied, "I assure you none is taken!" The madam attempted again to persuade him to drink some more wine, but he repeatedly declined, so she took him to the bedroom and whispered in his ear, "She has had too much to drink. Be gentle with her." Raising her voice, she said aloud, "Child! Get undressed and go to bed properly!" However, Miss Lovely was already asleep and made no reply. Seeing there was nothing else she could do, the madam left. Meanwhile, the maidservant cleared away the cups and dishes and took her leave with the words, "Sleep well, Young Master." Qin Zhong said, "Bring me a pot of hot tea if you have any." The maidservant made a pot of hot, strong tea and brought it into the bedroom, then shut the door and retired to a side room.

Qin Zhong gazed at Miss Lovely. She was fast asleep, facing the wall and lying atop her silken coverlet. People who have had too much to drink must be sensitive to the cold, he thought. However, he was afraid of waking her up. Looking around, he saw a bright red silk coverlet draped over the railing of the bed, took it down, and carefully covered Miss Lovely with it. He then trimmed down the wick of the lamp, removed his shoes, took the pot of hot tea to the bed and lay down beside the girl, clasping the pot of tea to his chest with his left hand and placing his right hand on Miss Lovely. He lay still, not even blinking his eyes.

Miss Lovely slept until midnight. When she woke up, she felt the wine she had drunk churning up irresistibly in her gorge. She struggled to a sitting position in the folds of her coverlet and retched. Qin Zhong quickly sat up and put down the teapot, aware that she was about to throw up. He stroked her back. Soon, Miss Lovely could hold out no longer and suddenly opened her mouth to vomit. Concerned lest the coverlet be soiled, Qin Zhong spread out a sleeve of his robe and covered Miss Lovely's face with it. Oblivious of all else, Miss Lovely heaved with all her might. Afterwards, still with her eyes shut, she asked for water with which to rinse out her mouth. Qin Zhong got out of bed, carefully divested himself of the robe and laid it on the ground, then poured out a big cup of strong, fragrant tea and handed it to Miss Lovely. She drank two cups in succession and felt much better. Still feeling drowsy, however, she lay down facing the wall again and fell asleep. Qin Zhong rolled up his robe, wrapping the dirtied sleeve within its folds, and placed the bundle beside the bed. Then he lay down once more and held Miss Lovely as before.

Miss Lovely woke up at dawn. Turning around, she saw a man lying at her side and asked, "Who are you?" Qin Zhong replied, "This humble person's name is Qin." The name brought back memories of the previous night, but the details were hazy and Miss Lovely asked, "I was quite drunk last night, was I not?" Qin Zhong assured her, "It was not too bad," and when Miss Lovely inquired, "Did I throw up?" he replied, "No." Relieved, Miss Lovely said, "That's good." Then, after a moment's reflection, she said, "I do recall throwing up, and also asking you for tea. Was that just a dream?" Only then did Qin Zhong own up. "You did throw up. This humble person observed that you had had a drink too many, so I kept the teapot warm with my body. You asked for tea after you threw up, so I poured some out for you. You graciously accepted two cupfuls." Miss Lovely was appalled. She declared, "How disgusting! Where did I throw up?" Qin Zhong replied, "On the sleeve of my robe. I was afraid you would dirty the coverlet." Miss Lovely asked, "And where is the robe now?" Qin Zhong said, "Rolled up and hidden over there." Miss Lovely said contritely, "I am sorry to have ruined it." Qin Zhong replied, "I am glad that robe of mine could be of service to you." Hearing these words, Miss Lovely thought, "What an obliging person!" Actually, she was already beginning to like him.

By now it was broad daylight. As Miss Lovely got up to relieve herself, she took a good look at Qin Zhong and recognized him as Oil Vendor Qin. "You had best tell me the truth," she said. "Who are you? And why were you here last night?" Qin Zhong replied, "Since the Queen of Flowers asks, this humble person dares not lie. I am, in fact, Qin Zhong, the person who has been delivering oil to this residence." He then launched into an account of how he had for the first time seen her sending clients off, then how she had mounted a sedan chair, and how much he admired her and saved up money to sleep with her. "I have now had the chance to be with you one night. Such good fortune is sufficient to last me three lifetimes, and I am fully satisfied."

Miss Lovely was filled with compassion. She said, "I was too drunk last night to tend to you. Do you not regret wasting so much silver?" Qin Zhong replied, "You are a goddess from Heaven. I already feel most fortunate that I have done nothing to merit reproach from you. I dare not hope for things I do not deserve." Miss Lovely commented, "You are a merchant, and should use the money you saved to support your family. This house is no place for the likes of you." Qin Zhong told her, "I am a single person with no wife or children." Miss Lovely was silent for a moment, and then asked, "Will you be coming again after you leave today?" Qin Zhong replied, "The memory of being close to you for one night will comfort me all my life. I cherish no more illusions." Miss Lovely mused to herself, "This is a rare person, a sincere and kindly man who lives by his principles. He is one in a thousand. It is a pity he comes from common stock. Were he a man of consequence, I would gladly commit myself to him."

While Miss Lovely thought these thoughts, the maidservant came in with a basin of water and two bowls of ginger brew. Qin Zhong washed his face, but did not have to comb his hair as he had not removed his headwear the night before. Taking a few gulps of ginger brew, he began to bid farewell. Miss Lovely attempted to detain him. "Stay a little longer," she said. "I would like to talk to you." But Qin Zhong demurred, "This humble person greatly admires the Queen of Flowers and would gladly stand by her for a while, but I know my position. It was already foolhardy enough of me to stay the night here, and I fear your illustrious name will be tarnished if someone else finds out. I had best leave as quickly as possible." Miss Lovely nodded, then sent the maidservant out of the room and hastened over to her personal casket. She extracted twenty taels of silver and offered them to Qin Zhong with the words, "I apologize for last night. Use this silver for your business, and do not tell anyone."

Qin Zhong naturally refused to take the silver, but Miss Lovely insisted, saying, "I come by it easily enough. This is to repay you for the consideration you showed me last night, and I shall continue to help you in future. Let the maidservant cleanse the robe I dirtied. It shall be returned to you later." But Qin Zhong declined. "My rough clothing does not warrant your attention. I can wash it myself. Besides, accepting such a favor from you would not be right." Miss Lovely chided him, saying, "Why make such a fuss!" She tucked the silver into Qin Zhong's sleeve and spun him around. Realizing that any further protest would be futile, Qin Zhong made a deep obeisance, picked up his bundled robe, and walked out. As he passed the madam's door, the housekeeper saw him and called out, "Mother! Young Master Qin is leaving!" Ninth Mother Wang was sitting on a commode, relieving herself. She shouted, "Young Master Qin, why are you leaving so early?" Qin Zhong replied, "I have some small matters to attend to. I will come back to thank you some other day." He then departed.

As for Miss Lovely, although she had shared no intimacies whatsoever with Qin Zhong, she knew him now for an honest and sincere man and regretted her behavior toward him. She suffered from a hangover, so she declined invitations from clients and stayed at home that day to take a rest. Despite being acquainted with a great many rich and powerful men, she thought of no one else the whole day but Qin Zhong.

Let us now go back to events at Tenth Elder Zhu's home.

Taking advantage of the fact that Tenth Elder Zhu was now ill and bedridden, Jing Quan and Lan Hua had, without the least compunction, carried on a torrid love affair. And when the old man had several more attacks of back pains, they cooked up a scheme. Sequestering all valuables and money in the store, they disappeared without a trace in the middle of the night. Tenth Elder only found out the following morning that they had absconded. He asked neighbors to help him make a list of lost articles and then instituted a search, but with no result. He now bitterly regretted that he had allowed himself to be deluded by Jing Quan into driving Qin Zhong away. Truly, he thought, time tells good men from the bad. Having been informed that Qin Zhong had rented a room at the foot of Zhong'an Bridge and was peddling oil from door to door for a living, Tenth Elder Zhu decided the best thing to do would be to bring Qin Zhong back. He would thus have someone to support him in the final years of his life. Yet he feared that Qin Zhong might be nursing a grievance against him, so he asked neighbors to persuade Qin Zhong to come home and let bygones be bygones.

When Qin Zhong heard this message, he gathered together his belongings and moved forthwith back to Tenth Elder's house. Both shed tears as they were reunited. Tenth Elder turned over to Qin Zhong all that remained of his property. Qin Zhong, who now had more than twenty taels of silver to serve him as capital, had the storefront repaired and repainted and sat at the counter to sell oil. And since he had returned to the Zhu household, he changed his surname back to Zhu.

About a month later, Tenth Elder's condition turned for the worse and, when all treatment proved ineffective, he died. Zhu Zhong wept and pounded his breast just as though he had lost his own father. He had funerary garments made for the deceased and performed charitable deeds on the seventh day of the seventh week after Zhu's death. He then buried Tenth Elder in the Zhu family's cemetery outside Qingbo Gate and personally conducted the funeral ceremony. All the rituals were observed, and all the neighbors praised him for doing things the right way.

When all these matters had been disposed of, Zhu Zhong reopened the store. The Zhu Oil Store was an old establishment that had always enjoyed good business, but much of its clientele had been driven away by Jing Quan's mean and unscrupulous practices. Now that Young Master Zhu was back at the shop, everyone wished to help out, and soon business was better than it had ever been before. Finding it more and more difficult to manage the store alone, Zhu Zhong urgently sought an experienced helper.

One day, Master Jin, a well-known go-between, brought a man in his fifties to the store. This man was Xin Shan from Anle village outside Bianliang city, the man who had come with his wife to the South to find refuge from the warfare of past years and had been separated from his daughter, Yaoqin, by rampaging soldiery. The couple, miserable and frightened, had wandered here and there during all these years, scraping together an existence as best they could. They had heard that Lin'an was now a prosperous city and that many refugees from the North had settled down here, and they thought their daughter might also be in the city. So they had come in search of the girl but had found no trace of her. They were in desperate straits, having spent all their money, and they owed money for food and were constantly being pestered by the keeper of the inn where they were staying. It was by mere chance that they heard Go-between Jin mention that the Zhu Oil Store was looking for a helper. Xin Shan, who had once operated a grain store and was familiar with the oil business, also learned that Young Master Zhu had come from Bianliang and was a fellow townsman. He therefore entreated Master Jin to take him to the oil store.

As between fellow townsmen, Zhu Zhong asked Xin Shan in detail about his circumstances and was deeply touched. "Since you have no place to go, both of you may stay at my house and will we treat one another as village kin. Take your time looking for your daughter. When you find her, we shall make further dispositions." He gave Xin Shan two strings of cash to repay the money owed to the innkeeper for food and lodgings. He then asked to meet Xin's wife, Mistress Ruan, and furbished a vacant room for the elderly couple. Thereafter, Xin Shan and his wife did all they could to help deal with affairs both in and outside the shop, much to Zhu Zhong's gratification.

Time flew, and another year passed. Many people who had watched Young Master Zhu grow up saw his business flourish and knew him as an honest and sincere man. Aware that he was still single, they were more than willing to give him their daughters without seeking anything in return. However, Zhu Zhong had seen the Queen of Flower's beauty and was not interested in the ordinary run of girls. He was determined to find someone exceptional before making up his mind to tie the marriage knot. And so, day after day, the matter dragged on unresolved.

Now let us return to Miss Lovely at Ninth Mother Wang's house.

Fame brought her, night and day, all the pleasures she could desire. Indeed, it was surprising that she had not yet tired of all the rich foods she ate and all the silken and embroidered garments she wore. Yet she thought about Young Master Qin and his goodness whenever something went against her wishes, or when a patron mistreated her or abandoned her for another prostitute, or when she was sick or drunk and woke up in the middle of the night with no one to dote on her, and she regretted that there was no chance of meeting him again. However, her days of wine and peach blossoms were soon to end, and her destiny was to take another turn. A year later, an incident took place.

There lived in Lin'an County a man called Eighth Scion Wu, whose father, Wu Yue, was governor of Fuzhou. After his father took office, Eighth Scion Wu had rolled in gold and silver. His favorite pastimes were gambling and drinking and frequenting houses of pleasure. He had heard the name "Queen of Flowers" but had never had the opportunity to meet the courtesan in person, and so had sent people to make him appointments for securing her sexual favors. However, Miss Lovely had learned about his discreditable ways and, unwilling to meet him, each time made excuses to decline his proposals. Eighth Scion Wu had also come together with some ne'er-do-well cronies to Ninth Mother Wang's house but had not found Miss Lovely.

There was one day, however, when Miss Lovely stayed at home. This was during the Qingming Festival when families visited their ancestors' graves and took trips to the countryside. Miss Lovely was exhausted after several days of spring excursions, and besides, owed many of her acquaintances paintings and calligraphic inscriptions, so she told the household, "If any client comes for me, tell him I am not available today." Shutting herself in her room, she lit a censer of the best incense, laid out her writing and painting implements, and had just picked up a brush when she heard a commotion outside.

Eighth Scion Wu had come with ten or more ruffianly retainers to take Miss Lovely out for a tour on the lake. Knowing that the madam had pretended in the past that Miss Lovely was not in, he created a scene in the central parlor and searched the premises, smashing furniture and other objects, until he found the girl's quarters. The door was locked from the outside. This is an old device used in whorehouses to get rid of undesirable clients. The girl is concealed in the room, the door locked from outside, and the client told she is not at home. Gullible clients are in general duped by this subterfuge. Eighth Scion Wu, however, was an old hand at such matters and tricks like that could not fool him. He had his retainers break the lock, and then kicked the door open. Miss Lovely tried to conceal herself but was not fast enough. Eighth Scion caught sight of her and ordered two of his servants to seize her, one on each side. Yelling and cursing, they dragged her out of the room. Ninth Mother stepped forward with a mind to making them desist and apologize, but she realized that matters had gotten out of hand and quickly made herself scarce. By now, not a shadow was to be seen of other members of the household, either young or old. The ruffianly retainers rushed out of the door with Miss Lovely in tow and, heedless of her tiny slippers and lily feet, sped down the road with Eighth Scion Wu triumphantly bringing up the rear.

When the group reached the bank of the West Lake, the girl was flung into a boat. Miss Lovely, who had had been coddled and cosseted since the day she came to Ninth Mother Wang's house at the age of twelve, had never suffered such indignities. Turning toward the bow of the boat, she covered her face with her hands and broke into loud sobs. Eighth Scion Wu pulled a long face. Flanked by his retainers, he angrily seated himself on a chair facing the water and ordered the boat to set forth, all the while cursing and railing at Miss Lovely. He cried, "You, trash! You whore! Do you not know when someone is doing you a favor? Stop that sniveling, or I shall have you thrashed!" Miss Lovely was not intimidated and kept on crying. When the boat reached Mid-Lake Island, Eighth Scion Wu ordered his retainers to place hampers of food in the pavilion on the island. He then disembarked and said to his retainers, "Tell that trash to come and drink together with me." Miss Lovely refused to budge. She wrapped her arms around the rail of the boat and started to weep and wail. Disgusted, Eighth Scion Wu tossed down a few cups of wine all by himself, then had the food put away. He then returned to the boat and seized Miss Lovely by the arm. The girl kicked and struggled and wailed all the more loudly. Flying into fury, Eighth Scion Wu commanded his retainers to rip the hairpins and clasps from Miss Lovely's hairdo. Her hair rumpled and askew, Miss Lovely ran to the bow of the boat to cast herself into the water but was restrained by the retainers. Eighth Scion Wu sneered, "Do you think throwing such a tantrum frightens me? Even if you die, your death will only cost my family a few taels of silver. A small matter! On second thought, however, letting you die would be a sin. So if you stop crying, I will cease pestering you and let you go."

Miss Lovely did indeed stop crying when she heard he would let her go. Eighth Scion had the boat moved to a secluded spot outside Qingbo Gate. He then removed Miss Lovely's embroidered slippers and foot bindings and bared her jade-like lily feet. Ordering his retainers to help her onto the shore of the lake, he yelled, "You little hussy! Since you are so clever, you can try to walk back. No one here will take you home." So saying, he had the boat poled from the bank toward the middle of the lake.

It was impossible for Miss Lovely to walk with bare feet. In despair, she thought to herself, "Talented and beautiful as I am, I have been abused like this because I am a prostitute. And of all those rich and powerful clients I have come to know, not one will help me when I am bullied and need them most. Even if I go back, how shall I live this matter down? Better that I were dead! Yet I shall have gained all my fame and reputation in vain if I die like this, for no good reason. As I stand now, even a peasant woman is much better off than I am. This is all the fault of Fourth Mother Liu and her glib tongue. I would not have ended up like this had she not persuaded me to leap into the pit of prostitution. Alas, misfortune has always bedeviled beautiful women, yet I doubt that any have been as unfortunate as I am!" The more she thought about it, the more miserable she felt, and she broke into loud sobs.

Purely by coincidence, Zhu Zhong had come this day to visit the grave of Tenth Elder Zhu outside Qingbo Gate. After burning sacrificial offerings and sweeping the grave, he had sent the sacrificial implements back by boat and decided to go home by himself on foot. As he walked along, he heard someone weeping and looked around to see who it was. Although Miss Lovely's hair was flying loose and tears stained her face, her beauty was still beyond compare, and Zhu Zhong recognized her at once. Shocked by her appearance, he asked, "Queen of Flowers, how can you have ended up in such a state?" Hearing a familiar voice amid her misery, Miss Lovely stopped crying, only to see the caring and sympathetic countenance of Young Master Qin. In her present plight it was like being reunited with a close family member, and Miss Lovely poured out her tale of woe.

Zhu Zhong was so distressed that he, too, shed tears. He happened to have a white silken scarf, five feet in length, in one of his sleeves. Tearing the scarf lengthwise in strips, he gave these to Miss Lovely to wrap around her feet. He also brushed the tears from her face with his fingers, helped coil up her hair, and all the while comforted her with soothing words. When she had stopped crying, he went to hire a sedan chair. He then seated Miss Lovely on the conveyance and walked beside her all the way to Ninth Mother Wang's house.

Ninth Mother Wang had been making anxious inquiries right and left after Miss Lovely had been taken away and was overjoyed when Young Master Qin brought her back. It was like being given back a precious jewel. Moreover, she had not seen Young Qin delivering oil to her house any longer, and had heard many people say that he had inherited the Zhu oil business, that he had more money to spend, and that his status had much improved. That, of course, made the madam see him in a different light. And, having asked why Miss Lovely was in such a sorry state, she learned how the girl had suffered and how Young Master Qin had rescued her. Ninth Mother Wang made a deep obeisance and forthwith ordered that wine be brought to thank him.

The hour was getting late, however, and after drinking a few cups of wine, Qin Zhong stood up to take his leave. Miss Lovely of course would not let him go. She said, "I have always had you on my mind and hoped to see you again. I will not let you go just like that." The madam, too, insisted that he stay for the night. Qin Zhong was delighted beyond words.

That night, Miss Lovely played the flute and the lute and sang and danced, displaying all her skills for Qin Zhong's benefit. For Qin Zhong it was like being in the dreamland of the gods, and he waved his hands and stamped his feet in transports of joy. When the night was deep and both had had their fill of wine, the two put their arms around one another and repaired to the bedchamber. . . .

After a while, Miss Lovely said, "I wish to ask you something from the bottom of my heart, and you must not refuse me." Qin Zhong replied, "If there were anything I could do for you, I would do so even if it means going through fire and boiling water. I would not refuse you." Miss Lovely then said, "I want you to marry me." Qin Zhong laughed and said, "Miss Lovely could marry ten thousand times before my turn would come! Do not make fun of me, as that might break my run of fool's luck."

Miss Lovely assured him, "I have spoken in full sincerity. I have wanted to go straight from the day I was made drunk and turned into a prostitute by Ninth Mother. The only reason I have not yet done so is that

I have not found the right man, or have not been able to tell good men from the bad, and was afraid a wrong choice would hurt the most important thing in my life. I have been with many men, but all of them are rich drunkards and debauchees who count on their money to obtain sensual and carnal pleasures. They do not know the meaning of true love. I have looked high and low, and the only good and honest man I have found is you. I also hear you are still single. If you do not despise me as a lowly woman of mists and flowers, I would gladly kneel before you and serve you until my hair turns white. If, however, you reject me, I will take three feet of white silk and hang myself before you to prove my sincerity. That, in any case, would be better than dying at the hands of that villain Eighth Scion Wu, dying for no good reason and mocked by all." Having said all this, she began to cry.

Qin Zhong said, "Do not grieve, young mistress. Your love, albeit misplaced, is a rare, Heaven-sent gift I have always desired, and I shall never reject it. However, you are worth ten thousand taels of gold while I am but a poor man with puny resources. What can I do? I do not have the wherewithal to fulfill such a desire." Miss Lovely replied, "That is not a problem. To tell you the truth, I have laid many things aside and placed them in safekeeping elsewhere for the day I would go straight. You need not worry about buying my freedom."

Doubtfully, Qin Zhong asked, "Assuming you buy your own freedom, how could you live in my humble home, accustomed as you are to luxurious mansions and silken garments and rich viands?" Miss Lovely assured him, "Should I have to wear cotton cloth and eat coarse fare for the rest of my life, I would die content." Qin Zhong asked one last question, "That may be your intention, but will your mother be agreeable?" Miss Lovely replied, "I have my ways. We shall do this and that and thus and thus." The two of them talked until dawn.

Miss Lovely had left chests and bundles in safekeeping at the homes of people she knew well, among them Academician Huang's scion, Minister Han's son, and Commander Qi's wife. She now told them she needed these things and would have them placed in a secret location. Having done that, she asked Qin Zhong to come and see her and instructed him to take the objects to his home. She then took a sedan chair to Fourth Mother Liu's house and told her she was going straight.

Fourth Mother Liu commented, "I talked to you once about such matters. However, you are still young. Who are you marrying?" Miss Lovely replied, "Never you mind who the man is, Auntie. But I will tell you that I am taking your advice. Mine will be a genuine marriage, a felicitous marriage, and a final marriage. It will not be one of those false, desperate, or unfulfilled ventures. If Auntie is willing to help, I am certain my mother will listen to you. The only way I, as your niece, am able to show my filial gratitude is by presenting you with ten taels of gold, for you to make into whatever kind of jewelry you like. So be sure to put in a word for me with my mother. This gold is besides the matchmaker's gift you will get after the matter is concluded."

At the sight of the gold ingots, Fourth Mother Liu grinned so broadly her eyes were reduced to mere slits. She protested, "Since you are like my own child and I will be doing a truly good thing for you, I can hardly accept this gift! Let us just say I am taking this gold to place in safekeeping for you. You can leave this matter to me. However, your mother sees you as the goose that lays the golden eggs, and is not likely to let you go so easily. I am afraid she will ask for a thousand or more taels of silver. Is your man willing to pay that much? This older person must meet him and have a talk with him." Miss Lovely countered, "That, Auntie, is none of your business. Let us just say that I, your niece, will herself be buying her freedom." Fourth Mother Liu then asked, "Does your mother know that you have come here?" Miss Lovely replied, "No, she does not." Fourth Mother Liu said, "Then stay here for a simple meal while I go to your home and talk to your mother. I will come back and tell you if she agrees or not."

Fourth Mother Liu hired a sedan chair and set out for Ninth Mother Wang's house. Ninth Mother met her at the door and ushered her in. Fourth Mother Liu began by asking about the affair with Eighth Scion Wu. After Ninth Mother Wang told her what had happened, she said, "For us in the brothel business it is best to have girls not too good and not too inferior and who make money for us in a safe and secure manner. They are willing to take any kind of client and work every day without a pause. Our niece has become too famous. She is like a fragrant morsel of fish that drops on the floor—every ant wants to taste of her. That brings in a good deal of business, yet one feels ill at ease. The price she charges for a night is high, but real income is less than it would seem, for the princes and scions she receives are likely to be accompanied by several hangers-on who stay all night and require too much attention. They also bring many servants who demand good service, and when these are dissatisfied they curse you roundly and even smash up your property. But you cannot complain to their masters, you have to keep your anger to yourself. On top of all this, there are those poets and literati and those members of poetry societies and chess societies, not to mention the summons to appear at official functions several times a month. All these rich and high-placed people vie and compete for her favors. Oblige the one, and you offend the other. Make one party happy, and you risk incurring the ire of the other party. The incident with Eighth Scion Wu is most frightening. Any misstep could cost you everything you possess. And you cannot sue an official's family. You can only bear such things in silence. Fortunately for you, the matter ended quickly and nothing came of it. If a showdown had taken place, you would forever rue the day. I have heard it said that Eighth Scion Wu, that malevolent monster, might come here again to raise a ruckus. As we both know, my niece has quite a temper and refuses to oblige others. This is most unfortunate, as it is a source of trouble."

Ninth Mother said, "That is precisely what worries me all the time. This Eight Scion Wu comes from a famous family and is no small fry. But the girl adamantly refuses to receive him, and that is what led to all the trouble. She used to listen to me when she was younger. Now that she has become famous, all the praise and pampering she gets from those rich aristocrats have turned her head and she is more than likely to make her own decisions. She entertains a client if she is so inclined. If not, nine oxen cannot drag her into changing her mind." Fourth Mother Wang commiserated, "All girls are like that, once they acquire a bit of status."

Changing the subject, Ninth Mother Wang said, "There is something I have wanted to discuss with you. I feel it would be best to sell the girl, if someone is willing to pay the price, and get the matter off my mind. That would be better than being perpetually haunted by all those terrible thoughts." Fourth Mother Liu quickly agreed. "That is an excellent idea! By selling one girl, you could purchase five or six others, or even ten or more if you should happen upon the right buyer. I would go for such a good deal if I were you." Ninth Mother Wang continued, "I have it all fig-ured out. Rich and powerful men are usually unwilling to pay a good price, as they prefer to get things cheaply. As for those who are willing to disburse a few taels of silver, my daughter may find them lacking, get on her high horse, and refuse to consider them. Should you find a suitable candidate, arrange a match for the girl. And please talk to the girl if she is unwilling. That girl does not listen to me. You are the only person who has her confidence and can make her change her mind."

Fourth Mother Liu chuckled and said, "I have come today precisely for the purpose of making a match for my niece. How much money do you want for letting her go?" Ninth Mother Wang said, "Sister, you are familiar with such things. In our trade, we buy cheap but never sell cheap. Besides, Miss Lovely has for years been famous throughout Lin'an, and everyone knows her as the Queen of Flowers. I would certainly not let her out of my door for a mere three or four hundred taels. The least I am willing to accept is a thousand." Fourth Mother Liu stood up, saying, "Let me go and ask someone. If the man agrees to pay that amount, I will return and discuss the matter further with you. If the price does not meet his conditions, I shall not come back."

As she was about to leave, she deliberately asked, "Where is my niece today?" Ninth Mother Wang replied, "Do not talk about that. After the maltreatment she received at the hands of Eighth Scion Wu, she is afraid he will come back and make more mischief. She goes out on her sedan chair and stays all day at this or that house. The day before yesterday she was at Commander Qi's place, yesterday she went to Academician Huang's mansion, and who knows where she has gone today."

Fourth Mother Liu had one last admonition, "Now that you have come to a decision, you must stand firm on it and not let my niece reject the match. In case she does, I shall get her to come around. And don't you make excuses and change your mind after I have found a buyer." Ninth Mother assured her, "I have said I agree and will not tell you otherwise." She saw her visitor all the way to the gate, whereupon Fourth Mother Liu excused herself and mounted her sedan chair.

As soon as Fourth Mother Liu got home, she said to Miss Lovely, "I have told your mother this, that, and the other, and she has agreed. The matter will be concluded as soon as she sees the silver." Miss Lovely said, "The silver is ready. Auntie, make sure to come to my home tomorrow to see that everything goes well. If for any reason the deal goes sour, renegotiating it will call for a lot more talk." Four Mother Liu assured her, "I will of course be there. That is the agreement." Miss Lovely took leave of Fourth Mother Liu. At home, she said not a word about the matter.

At the noon hour of the following day, Fourth Mother arrived as promised. Ninth Mother Wang asked her, "How is the matter we talked about progressing?" Fourth Mother Liu replied, "It's virtually a done deal. However, I have yet to tell my niece about it." So saying, she went to Miss Lovely's chambers. The two greeted each other and exchanged some small talk before Fourth Mother came to the point. She asked, "Has your man come yet? Where are the things we need?" Pointing toward the foot of her bed, Miss Lovely replied, "Everything is in those chests." She opened up five or six chests. They contained valuables and a number of packages, each weighing approximately fifty taels. She then took out thirteen or fourteen of the packages and chose some gold ornaments, pearls, rubies, and jade articles, estimating their value until she had a full one thousand taels' worth in silver.

Fourth Mother Liu was so astounded her eyes bulged and saliva drooled from her lips. She thought, "So young, and yet so shrewd! How did she manage to put away so much? Those trollops at my house take in clients in the same way as she does, but none of them comes anywhere near to her in this respect. They have no idea how to make or save money. If they do have a few coins in their purses, they spend them on watermelon seeds and sweets and other such snacks. Why, they even ask me to buy cloth for foot bindings when theirs are worn out and need to be replaced! Ninth Mother is indeed fortunate. As well as being a good buy and making a good deal money for Ninth Mother over the years, my niece has saved all this wealth for the time she leaves this house. And since the money she uses to buy herself comes from within the house, Ninth Mother will be saved the trouble of going out to collect payment."

These, however, were her own thoughts, and she did not say them aloud. Miss Lovely observed Fourth Mother's pensive look and feared the madam was concocting some difficulty or other in order to collect a bigger reward. So she hastily took from her chests four bolts of the finest silk, two jewel-studded bracelets, and a brace of phoenix-headed jade hairpins, placed them on the table, and said, "Auntie, take these as a mark of my appreciation to you for serving as my matchmaker."

Fourth Mother Liu was elated. To Ninth Mother Wang she said, "My niece is willing to buy herself at the price you ask and not one cent less. That is better than a patron buying her, for you would then have to ask an outsider to act as middleman. You would squander good wine and food and, on top of that, you would have to pay him a commission to thank him." But when Ninth Mother Wang learned that her daughter's chests contained so much silver and so many valuables, her face darkened.

Do you know why? Madams the world over are greedy people. A madam is only happy when her girls place all the money they manage to make into her own hands. Should one of the girls secrete a private hoard in her boxes and chests and the madam gets wind of this, she waits until the girl goes out of the house and then pries open locks and ransacks boxes and chests and takes all she can find. Ninth Mother Wang had not dared to transgress upon Miss Lovely without good cause, partly because of the big money she made from the girl's clients, all of them rich and powerful, and partly because of Miss Lovely's unpredictable temperament. Thus she had never set foot in Miss Lovely's bedroom and did not know she was so rich.

Fourth Mother Liu guessed what Ninth Mother was thinking from the somber expression on her face. She quickly said, "Ninth Mother, don't you have second thoughts. My niece saved these things for herself, and you have no claim to this money. It would not be there had she decided to spend it. You would not even know the money existed had she heedlessly used it to support some ne'er-do-well who took her fancy. Actually, it is a good thing she is such a frugal person. Would you have chased her out of the door without a stitch on her back if she had no money of her own? You would have had to dress her from head to toe, and dress her well, so that she would be presentable when she married into another family. Now that she is able to produce this money, I'll wager she will not trouble you for a single stitch or thread. You can tuck all the money you save into your own pocket. Besides, she will still be your daughter after she buys her freedom and, as filial duty demands, will bring you gifts on holidays and other occasions if her husband makes good money. And since she has no parents of her own, you will be the grandmother of her children and receive all the treatment a grandmother deserves."

Feeling much better after hearing these words, Ninth Mother Wang consented to the deal. Fourth Mother Liu brought out the silver and ver-ified the packages one by one before handing them to Ninth Mother Wang. She then pointed out to Ninth Mother the value of each and every item of jewelry, stating, "I am intentionally giving you low estimates. You stand to gain several dozen taels of silver if you should pass these on to other people." Although a madam, Ninth Mother Wang was, after all, an uncomplicated person and took Fourth Mother Liu at her word.

After Ninth Mother Wang accepted the payment, Fourth Mother Liu asked a procurer to write out the marriage agreement. When this was done, she gave the agreement to Miss Lovely, who then said, "I wish to bid a formal farewell to my parents while Auntie is still here. And Auntie, are you willing to let me stay at your house for a few days and to help me choose an auspicious day for going straight?" Fourth Mother Liu was more than anxious to get Miss Lovely out of the house and bring the matter to a conclusion, since she had accepted a great number of gifts from Miss Lovely and feared that Ninth Mother Wang might change her mind. So she agreed with alacrity, saying, "That is precisely what should be done."

Miss Lovely went to her chambers and assembled her makeup acces-sories, notion caskets, chests, and bedding without, however, touching anything that belonged in Ninth Mother Wang's house. When everything was packed, she proceeded with Fourth Mother Liu to the front parlor, kowtowed a farewell to a pretended father and mother and took leave of all her sisters in the brothel. Then she hired porters for her luggage, mounted a sedan, and followed Fourth Mother to the latter's house. Fourth Mother Liu vacated a nice, quiet room for her and deposited her belongings in it. And soon, all the girls in the house came to offer their congratulations. Meanwhile, Zhu Zhong had sent Xin Shan to make inquiries at Fourth Mother Liu's house and was apprised that Miss Lovely had already purchased her freedom. An auspicious date was selected and an orchestra consisting of pipes, flutes, and drums was engaged for the wedding. Fourth Mother Liu, as the primary matchmaker, gave away the bride at the ceremony. That night, Zhu Zhong and the Queen of Flowers lit ceremonial candles in the nuptial chamber, and happiness reigned.

The next day, Xin Shan and his wife asked to meet the bride. The old couple and the girl immediately recognized one another and, after inquiring about their respective travails, the three blood kin fell into one another's arms and wept. Zhu led his newly found father- and mother-in-law to the seats of honor, after which the young couple kowtowed to them. The news of this reunion created quite a stir among friends and neighbors. That same day, a banquet was held to celebrate this twofold happiness, and it only concluded when all the guests had quaffed and caroused to their hearts content.

Three days later, Mistress Lovely asked her husband to prepare several generous gifts. These were presented to the families of her acquaintances who had kept chests and bundles in safekeeping for her, and also to inform them that she had already gone straight. Mistress Lovely was not one to leave loose ends untied. Gifts were also delivered to Ninth Mother Wang and Fourth Mother Liu, and both were very grateful.

When they had been married for a full month, Mistress Lovely opened her chests. They were full of gold and silver objects and the best silks and satins. Numbering in the hundreds, these articles were worth no less than three thousand taels of silver. Mistress Lovely handed the keys to the chests to her husband and told him to purchase, at his leisure, houses and fields, and to refurbish their house. The oil business was now under Xin Shan's management. Within a year, their assets had grown impressively, they had retainers and maidservants, and their affairs were in splendid condition.

Zhu Zhong, in his gratitude for the blessings conferred upon him by heaven and earth and the gods, presented incense and candles to every major monastery and temple and provided them with three months' supply of oil for their altar lamps. He fasted and bathed and went in person to light sticks of incense and chant prayers, commencing with Zhaoqing Monastery and then proceeding to Lingyin, Faxiang, Jingci, and Tianzhu monasteries in that order.

We shall only mention Tianzhu Monastery where joss sticks are burned to the goddess Guanyin. It consists of Upper Tianzhu, Middle Tianzhu, and Lower Tianzhu, all of which are accessible by mountain paths but cannot be reached by boat. Zhu Zhong had his retainers carry one load of incense and candles and three loads of the clearest oil, while he himself rode on a sedan chair. The first place they came to was Upper Tianzhu. Monks took them to the upper hall where Qin Gong, the elderly tender of censers, was in charge of lighting candles and replenishing the burners with sticks of incense. By this time, Qin Zhong's changed lifestyle had altered his bearing and filled out his physique. Stalwart and well built, he looked quite different from the stripling of former years, and it was not surprising that Qin Gong failed to recognize his son.

Qin Gong was, however, intrigued by the characters "Qin" and "Bianliang" respectively painted in big characters on two of the oil casks. It was purely by coincidence that the two casks were being used on the trip to Upper Tianzhu. After Zhu Zhong had lit an offering of incense sticks, Qin Gong brought a tea tray and the head monk poured tea for Zhu Zhong. Qin Gong then asked, "May I venture to inquire of this benefactor why those three characters are written on the oil casks?"

Zhu Zhong recognized his Bianliang accent and inquired in return, "Why do you ask, old fellow townsman? Can it be that you are also from Bianliang?" Qin Gong replied, "That is so." Zhu Zhong pursued, "What is your name? Why have you come to this monastery? And for how many years?" Qin Gong told him his name and the names of the county and township he hailed from, and then added, "It was in those years of warfare that I took refuge here. Since I could not make a living, I left my thirteen-year-old son, Qin Zhong, with the Zhu family. That was eight years ago. As I am old and in poor health, however, I have not been able to leave this mountain to inquire about him."

Zhu Zhong threw his arms around Qin Gong and broke into tears, saying, "I am Qin Zhong. All these years I have been in the Zhu family's business of peddling oil. I wrote those three characters on the caskets as a sort of mark, hoping these would help me discover your whereabouts, but I never thought we would meet again in this place! This is indeed the will of Heaven!" Learning that father and son had been separated for eight years and had now been reunited, all the monks in the monastery declared that a miracle had taken place.

Zhu Zhong stayed at Upper Tianzhu that night. He shared a room with his father, the better for them to exchange reminiscences about the events of the last few years. The next morning, Zhu Zhong rewrote the laudatory inscriptions he would burn on the altars at Middle and Lower Tianzhu, changing his name from Zhu Zhong back to Qin Zhong.

After visiting these two monasteries, he returned to Upper Tianzhu

and asked his father to come home with him to live a blissful and boun-
teous life. Qin Gong, accustomed as he was to frugal fare and a monastic
existence, did not wish to go to his son's house, but Qin Zhong argued,
"Father, you and I have been separated for eight years, and I have been
remiss in serving you as behooves a son. Besides, I have married recently,
and my wife should meet her father-in-law."

Qin Gong could only comply. Qin Zhong placed his father on the
sedan chair, while he himself walked all the way home. There, Qin
Zhong produced a set of new clothes for his father to put on, seated him
the main parlor and, together with his wife, kowtowed before Qin Gong.
Then Xin Shan and his spouse also came to meet their new in-law. The
same day, a big banquet was held, at which Qin Gong refused to eat meat
and partook only of vegetarian food and wine. The next day, friends and
neighbors pooled money to hold several banquets. The first was for the
newlyweds, the second, to celebrate the reunion of the bride's family,
the third, to celebrate the reunion of father and son, and the fourth, to
mark Young Master Qin's resumption of his own name. All these were
events of great rejoicing, and the banquets lasted several days.

Despite all the comforts he enjoyed, Qin Gong did not wish to live
at his son's home. He missed the serene solitude of life at Tianzhu. Qin
Zhong dared not go against his father's will, so he had a special abode
constructed at Tianzhu at the cost of two hundred taels of silver and prevailed on his father to live in it. He also had his father's daily necessities
delivered to the house every month. He himself visited his father every
ten days, and went with his wife to see him every three months. Qin
Gong lived until he was well over eighty years old and passed away seated
in meditation. He was then interred on the mountain in accordance with
his last instructions. But that is another story.

Qin Zhong and his wife lived as man and wife to a ripe old age. They
had two sons, both of whom achieved fame for their literary accomplishments. To this day, Qin Zhong is talked about in the streets and lanes of
Lin'an, and anyone who helps others in times of need is dubbed "young
master Qin," or simply "oil vendor."

Governor Teng Craftily Resolves a Family Dispute

滕
大
尹
鬼
斷
家
私

During the Yong Le reign of the Ming Dynasty, there lived in Xianghe County of Shuntian Prefecture near Beijing a prefect whose name was Ni Shouqian, and who had accumulated much wealth as well as many fertile lands and good houses. His wife, Mistress Chen, bore him a single child whom they named Shanji, and when the boy had grown up and married, Mistress Chen passed away. Lord Ni subsequently retired from office and lived as a widower. Although advancing in years, he remained in excellent health and spirits, and kept all matters pertaining to the collection of rents and issuance of loans under his personal purview.

When he attained the age of seventy-nine, however, his son Ni Shanji commented, "It is generally acknowledged that seventy is a rare old age, but you will have attained eighty next year. Why do you not leave the family affairs in my care and spend your days in more leisurely pursuits?" But the old man shook his head and replied, "For each day that I live, I shall remain in charge and shall devote my mind and efforts to earning our keep. Only when my toes point upward will these matters be of no further concern to me."

In the tenth moon of each year, Lord Ni would personally go through the villages to collect rents, staying away from home for as long as a month at a time. The villagers would bring out their mellowest wines and plumpest pullets for his delectation.

That year, he went out again for a few days, and one afternoon, having nothing better to do, strolled around the village to enjoy the scenery. All at once he caught sight of a young maiden, who, together with a white-haired old woman, was scrubbing clothes on some rocks by a rivulet. Though the maiden was clad in rough peasant garb, she was most comely in appearance, with raven-black hair, large, liquid eyes, and a willowy body that would have done justice to the richest silks and satins.

The former prefect stood entranced by the maiden's appearance, which awoke in him long forgotten desires. And when the maiden was done with her washing and had left with the older woman, he took careful note of the way they went. He observed them pass several cottages and enter a small, white-painted trellis gate. Lord Ni then promptly returned and summoned the village head, instructing the latter to investigate the maiden's circumstances and whether or not she was betrothed. He added, "If not, I would have her as a consort, should she be willing."

Being eager to ingratiate himself with Lord Ni, the village head made haste to comply. The maiden's family name apparently was Mei and her father had been a minor scholar. Both the father and mother having passed away when she was a child, however, the girl was now residing with her maternal grandmother. She was seventeen years of age and unbetrothed.

Girded with this information, the village head approached the grandmother, saying, "The Old Lord has been taken by your granddaughter's comeliness, and proposes to engage her as his consort. Though she will be a lesser consort, the Old Mistress passed away several years ago and the girl will be at the behest of no one. And once she is married, not only will she enjoy a life of comfort and ease, but even you will be provided with clothing, tea, and rice, and when you die you will be given a decent funeral. What better could you desire?"

Having heard these glowing promises, the grandmother forthwith gave her consent. The village head then made his report to Lord Ni, who was mightily pleased. Agreement was reached on the amount of presents for the bride's family and—after consulting an almanac—on a propitious date for the wedding, which Lord Ni decided would be held in the village for fear that his son might raise objections. And after the wedding ceremony, the newlyweds, one old and one young, spent the night in embraces no less ardent than those enjoyed by the groom when he was still a youth.

Three mornings later, a sedan chair was called to take the bride to her new home where she was presented to the son and daughter-in-law. All members of the household kowtowed to her and called her "Little Mistress," and Lord Ni distributed gifts of cloth and silk so that all were highly pleased. The only person who was less than happy was Ni Shanji.

He said nothing to his father's face, but he and his wife had many comments to make behind the father's back. "The old man's behavior is most unbecoming," they complained. "At his age, when a breath could blow his taper out, he should consider the consequences of his actions. He must know that he only has a few more years to live, so why does he enter into such a messy affair? Marrying that little frump and keeping her satisfied will wear him out. He cannot, after all, ignore her and maintain her as a wife in name only. There is no lack of old men who acquire a young wife and then are unable to keep pace with her, whereupon in desperation she takes a lover and brings about a scandal that besmirches the family name. Moreover, these young women marry older men as an escape from want, and once the time is ripe they abscond. They pilfer things left and right and accumulate a private hoard, which they salt away here and there. Or they coax and wheedle clothes and jewelry from their husband, and when the old tree falls they fly away with their booty to another nest. These women are like termites in the wood and weevils in the rice, and any family that is afflicted with one of them will surely be sapped of its vitality."

They also said, "That girl minces and simpers like a whore and lacks the graces of a woman of good upbringing. She is best, no doubt, at sashaying around and seducing men. While she is with Father, she should be regarded only as a part-concubine and part-servant and be addressed as Aunty or Sister, which would leave us some leeway after he is gone. But, befuddled as he is, he insists she be called Little Mistress. Does he expect us to address her as Mother as well? We cannot allow her to become so pampered that she forgets what she is and attempts to lord it over us!"

The couple's interminable mutterings soon reached the ears of Lord Ni, but he refrained from comment despite his displeasure. Fortunately, Mistress Mei was of a mild and gentle disposition, and her comportment toward people of all positions, high or lowly, was such that peace reigned in the household.

Mistress Mei became pregnant two months later but kept the news from everyone except Lord Ni. So when she gave birth to a son after ten months, the entire household was stunned. The infant was given the pet name Nine-nine, since he was born on the ninth day of the ninth moon. The eleventh day of the same moon happened to be Lord Ni's birthday— his eightieth—and well-wishers flocked through the gate. Lord Ni gave a grand banquet to entertain them. The festivities were to mark both his birthday and the third day of the birth of his child, an event commonly celebrated with a "soup-and-unleavened-bread" dinner. Among the many speakers, one said, "That you have acquired a new son at your venerable age is a sign of your undiminished virility and continuing longevity."

Lord Ni was highly gratified by these words, but Ni Shanji observed in private, "A man's seed dries up by the time he is sixty. Yet he is eighty. Who has ever seen a withered tree put forth blossoms? That infant is someone's bastard and does not carry our father's blood line, and I certainly will not acknowledge him as my brother!" This, too, reached the ears of Lord Ni but still he made no comment.

Time sped by, and another year passed almost unnoticed. On Ninenine's first birthday, the family prepared to observe the custom called "choosing from the tray," whereby the infant was allowed to grasp one of several objects on a tray to determine his natural bent. Kinsmen and friends came again to join the festivities.

But Shanji would not meet them and left the house. His father, aware of what was passing through his mind, did not send servants after him. Instead, the old man himself entertained the guests and drank with them all day long.

Although Lord Ni said nothing about the incident, he could not but feel discouraged. As the saying goes, "A filial son sets his father's mind at ease." But it was obvious that Shanji, being mean and grasping by nature, refused to acknowledge his younger brother for fear of having to share the family's wealth with the child once the latter grew up, and his malicious utterances were designed to put mother and son at his mercy at some future date. Lord Ni, a learned man and an official, clearly discerned these machinations. But he was also painfully aware of his age and of the fact that he would not live to see Nine-nine grow up. The child would be dependent upon his elder brother for a living, so it would not do to aggravate Shanji's hostility at this time. The only thing he could do was to exercise forbearance. Lord Ni cared deeply for the small child and pitied the young mother. He found himself by turns pensive, melancholy, angry, and regretful.

Four years later, when the boy turned five, the old lord decided that the bright, mischievous youngster should take lessons at home with a private tutor. Nine-nine was given a formal name Shanshu, in line with his elder brother's name Shanji. An auspicious day was chosen and the boy was taken to meet his tutor with gifts of wine and fruit. This tutor had been engaged to teach the old man's grandson, Shanji's son, and for the sake of convenience the nephew and the young uncle would study in the same classroom.

Shanji, however, was not of the same mind as his father. He had already felt displeased when the boy had been named Shanshu, thus placing him and the boy hierarchically on the same generational level; and now, rather than let his own son sit in the same classroom and address Shanshu as "uncle"—which, if this became habitual, would place his son at a disadvantage in later life—he preferred to take him out and engage another tutor. This he did on the very same day, offering the excuse that his son was indisposed.

Lord Ni assumed that his grandson was indeed not feeling well, until several days later when the tutor remarked, "I fail to see why your eldest son should engage another tutor and set up a second classroom." Now that the truth was out, Lord Ni, in his fury, was about to summon his eldest son and have him explain himself, when he reflected, "He was born ill-disposed, so there is no sense in arguing with him. Let him have his way."

Still simmering with rage, however, he returned to his chambers and accidentally stumbled on the doorsill. Mistress Mei hurriedly raised him to his feet and had him sit down on a recliner, where he soon lapsed into a swoon. A hastily summoned physician said the old lord had suffered a stroke. A brew of ginger root was quickly administered to bring him back to his senses, and he was carried to his bed. His mind was lucid, but his limbs were numb and unable to move. Mistress Mei sat by his bed, brewing medicaments, which she fed to him. The old man showed no sign of improvement, however, and the physician's diagnosis was as follows: "It is only a matter of time. There is no hope of recovery."

Shanji visited his father once or twice and, learning that the old man was not expected to rise again, promptly assumed the role of master of the household, shouting, issuing orders, beating the young houseboys and scolding the servants. The sound of his voice merely added to the old man's vexations. Mistress Mei could do little else but weep, and even the child stopped attending classes to stay at his father's bedside.

When the old man sensed that the end was near, he called his eldest son to his bedside. Placing in Shanji's hands a register in which was recorded the family's land, houses, and other property as well as the names of debtors and the amounts owed, he said: "Shanshu is but five years of age and even needs someone to clothe him, whereas Mistress

Mei is too young to take charge of the household. Since it is senseless to give them a portion of the family property, I am leaving all of it with you. And when Shanshu has become a man, do me the service of obtaining him a wife and giving him a small house with fifty or sixty *mu* of good farmland so that he will not suffer from cold and hunger. All this has been written down in the register and will serve you as a testimonial when dividing the family property. Mistress Mei may remarry if she wishes, but do not force her to do so if she desires to stay with her son. Should you carry out all these instructions after I die, you may count yourself as a filial son, and I shall rest in peace by the Nine Fountains of the nether world."

Shanji opened the register and saw that all was clearly recorded as his father had stated. Wreathing his face in smiles, he babbled, "Do not worry, I shall do exactly as instructed." Then he departed, exultantly clasping the register to his breast.

Once he was out of earshot, Mistress Mei tearfully pointed to the child and said to Lord Ni, "He is your own flesh and blood, too, is he not? How will he and I keep body and soul together, now that you have given everything to your elder son?" Lord Ni replied, "There are circumstances of which you have no conception. Shanji, in my estimation, is not a good fellow and, had I divided the property equally, even the child's life would be endangered. It is best to give Shanji everything, for he will thus be gratified and no longer feel jealous."

Mistress Mei wept, saying, "That may be true, but as the saying goes, 'All sons are equal regardless of their provenance.' You will be laughed at for being so inequitable." Lord Ni sighed and said, "I am beyond caring about such things now. But while I am still alive I shall entrust the child to Shanji's care. You are still young. After I die, wait at most a year, or at least half a year, and then choose a good man with whom to spend the rest of your life. Do not stay here to be tyrannized by the others."

Mistress Mei protested, "How can you say such things? I, too, come from a scholar's family and know that a woman should remain faithful to one man till she dies. Besides, there is the child. I cannot abandon him. I must stay with him through thick and thin." Lord Ni asked, "Do you really intend to remain faithful for the rest of your life? You may, in time, regret that decision." As Mistress Mei proceeded to utter solemn vows, the old man interrupted her, saying, "If that is indeed your firm resolve, then rest assured that you and the child will be provided for."

He fumbled beside his pillow and extracted an object, which he proffered to Mistress Mei. At first, she assumed it to be another property register, but it turned out to be a small scroll about a foot wide and three feet long. She inquired, "Of what use is this?" Lord Ni replied, "This portrait of myself contains a clue. Keep it hidden from other eyes until the child is a grown man. Even if Shanji refuses to care for the boy, keep your own counsel and wait till you find a wise and able official. Entrust your case to him together with this scroll, and tell him it is my deathbed wish that he carefully scrutinize it. Dispositions will ensue that will amply provide for you and your son's needs."

Mistress Mei accepted the scroll. Lord Ni lingered a few more days, and one night suffered a congestion from which he never regained consciousness. He died at the age of eighty-four.

Meanwhile, having obtained the property register as well as the keys to all the storerooms and warehouses, Ni Shanji busied himself every day counting and verifying the family's wealth and had found no time to visit his ailing father. It was not until the old man died and Mistress Mei had sent a maidservant with the evil tidings that Shanji and his wife came and wailed "Father!" a few times. Less than an hour later they departed, leaving Mistress Mei to keep the wake.

Fortunately, the coffin and burial garments had been prepared in advance and did not require the attentions of Shanji. When the old man was in his coffin and lay in state in the family's memorial hall, Mistress Mei and the child remained at his side, weeping from morning till night. Shanji did little more than come out to greet mourning relatives and friends, and that without manifesting the least sign of grief.

Seven days later the coffin was buried. On the night of "soul's return day," Shanji and his wife had Mistress Mei's chambers ransacked lest the father had secreted some money there. The quick-witted Mistress Mei, fearing that they would discover and seize the portrait, opened her two dowry coffers without being asked, to show that they contained little else than some worn clothing. Disarmed by Mistress Mei's apparent openness, Shanji did not examine the coffers closely. After having rummaged around a bit more, he and his wife departed. Mistress Mei was so mortified that she wept, whereupon the child, seeing his mother in such despair, cried heartbrokenly.

The next morning, Shanji had a carpenter inspect the chambers, announcing that they would be refurbished to serve his own son as living quarters. Mother and child were relegated to three small storerooms in a rear courtyard and given one small bed and a few crude tables and stools, but not a single article of decent furniture. Shanji also called away the elder of the two maidservants who had attended upon Mistress Mei, leaving only an eleven-year-old girl whose duties consisted solely of fetching some rice from the common kitchen; whether or not there were any other dishes to go with the rice was of no one's concern. Finding this most inconvenient, Mistress Mei asked to be given some uncooked rice, which she prepared herself on a makeshift stove built with clay. She did needlework from morning till night, and with the earnings purchased a few vegetables to eke out their fare. She also paid tutoring fees for the child who now attended classes at a neighbor's house.

Shanji more than once asked his wife to persuade Mistress Mei to remarry, and desisted only after the latter had adamantly refused. Thereafter he paid scant attention to the mother and her child, for Mistress Mei bore all his spite and cruelty in silence.

The years passed, and few people remarked the fact that Shanshu had already turned fourteen. Mistress Mei, being of a most discreet nature, had never once told her son about past events, for fear that a slip of the tongue on his part might worsen their plight. But now that the boy was fourteen and had become more acute in his perceptions, it was no longer possible to keep the truth from him.

One day, he asked his mother for a new silken gown, and when she told him she could not afford to purchase one, he remarked, "My father was once a prefect and had only two sons. How is it that my elder brother is so wealthy while I cannot have even a new gown? Since you do not have any money, I shall ask my brother for some."

He turned to leave, but Mistress Mei restrained him, saying, "My son, why is a gown of such great importance that you should go begging for one? There is a saying, 'Wear cotton when young and silk when old.' Those who wear silk as children may not have even cotton to wear when they grow up. When you advance to higher studies in two years' time, I shall indenture myself as a servant for money to make clothes for you. But do not importune your brother, for he is a hard man to deal with."

Shanshu replied, "You are right, Mother." But privately he disagreed with her and thought, "My father possessed much wealth which should have been shared between my brother and myself. Besides, I am not an adopted child brought over from a previous marriage, so why does my brother slight me so? I find it incomprehensible that my mother should indenture herself to clothe me, as though I had no right to even one bolt of silk! And why should I fear my brother? He is not a man-eating tiger!" And so, without telling his mother, he made his way to the main courtyard.

When he had found his brother, he greeted him with the words, "My obeisance." Shanji, surprised, inquired why he was here. Shanshu replied, "I am the son of an official, but my garments are so shabby that people mock me. I have come to ask you for a length of silk to make a gown for myself." Shanji retorted, "Go ask your mother if you want a new gown." Shanshu then said, "Our father's property is in your hands, not my mother's."

Shanji's face became suffused with anger at the mention of the word "property," for this was no trivial matter. He parried, "Who put these words into your mouth? Have you come today to beg for a gown, or to contend over family property?" To which Shanshu replied, "There will no doubt be a reckoning over property some day, but today I have come for a gown to keep up appearances." Shanji snapped, "What does a bastard want with appearances! True, my father amassed considerable wealth, but that was for his own flesh and blood and had naught to do with wayside spawn like yourself! And who has been inciting you to pick crumbs from my table? Do not nettle me, lest you and your mother be left with no place to stay!" Shanshu replied, "Why should I be a bastard, when both of us were begotten by the same father? And what will you do if I nettle you? Murder my mother and me so that you may have the family property all to yourself?"

Infuriated, Shanji roared, "How dare you talk back to me, you little brute!" He caught Shanshu by the sleeve and belabored the boy's head with his fist until it was black and blue. Shanshu broke free and ran, sobbing, to his mother. When he had recounted everything, she scolded him, saying, "I told you not to make trouble, but you would not listen. It serves you right!" But even as she uttered these words, she patted his bruises with the hem of her black cotton gown and wept in spite of herself.

Having pondered the matter, Mistress Mei, fearing that Shanji would nurse his anger, dispatched the maidservant to him to say that the boy was young and ignorant and was sorry now that he had offended his elder brother. Shanji, however, was not assuaged. Early the next morning, he invited a number of clansmen to his house and showed them his father's handwritten testament concerning the division of the family property. Then he asked Mistress Mei and her son to be present for a public reading of the testament.

At the reading, Shanji said, "Honored clansmen, do not imagine that I am unwilling to care for the mother and child and wish to drive them out. The fact is, however, that Shanshu argued with me yesterday over the family property and uttered many unfounded accusations. I honestly fear he will level more accusations at me as he grows older, so I intend to divide the property today and have them live apart from the family. They will receive a house in East Village as well as fifty-eight *mu* of farmland. This is in accordance with my late father's behests, which I dare not misrepresent, and to the veracity of which I now beg you, my clansmen, to attest."

The clansmen were all aware that Shanji was not a man to be trifled with and, since the will had been written by the old prefect in person, none saw any call to incur Shanji's enmity by making unwelcome observations.

So all said things he desired to hear. Those who wished to flatter him declared, "A thousand pieces of gold cannot change a dead man's written word. I have nothing to say about the division." Even those who pitied the mother and son merely philosophized, "There is a saying that 'Men should not eat up their inheritance and women should not wear their dowry.' Many are those who begin life with empty hands. With this house and the farmland, Mistress Mei and her son are not without some support upon which to base their future endeavors. Nor should they complain about the gruel being too thin, for each man has a different fate."

Mistress Mei had known she would not be allowed to stay forever in the back courtyard, so she agreed, albeit reluctantly, to the division. She thanked the clansmen, made her last obeisance at the ancestral shrine, and bade farewell to Shanji and his wife. Then she engaged porters for her several articles of old furniture and the two coffers containing her dowry, hired a beast of burden, and rode away to East Village.

The house was hardly fit for habitation. Weeds choked the grounds, and the loosely laid roof tiles had not been repaired for many years, so that the floor was damp with leaking rain. After cleaning up two rooms as best she could, she installed the beds and furniture. Then she summoned the tenant farmers and inquired about the fields. These were of the most inferior quality, she was told. In the best of years they yielded only half the normal harvest, and in bad years even seed grain could not be recovered. Mistress Mei was close to desperation.

It was her sharp-witted son who brought up the question: "Why was the division of property so unfair, since both of us were born of the same father? There must be some reason. Perhaps the testament was not written by my father. In any case, it is an ancient axiom! 'Apportionment of property has naught to do with the age of the beneficiaries.' Why do you not appeal to the authorities for adjudication? Then there would be no complaints, regardless of the ruling they pass down."

Now that her son had broached the subject, Mistress Mei confided to him the secret she had kept hidden in her heart for ten or more years. She said, "Do not question the testament, for it was indeed written by your father. He said you were still young and he feared your elder brother would take your life, so he willed all the property to Shanji in order to gratify him. Just before he passed away, however, he left me a scroll and repeatedly enjoined me that it contained a clue, and that I should wait till I found a wise and able official to whom I should appeal our case. He promised that you and I would be provided for and that we would not live in poverty." Shanshu exclaimed, "Why, then, did you not say anything about this earlier? Where is the scroll? Let me see it!"

Mistress Mei opened one of her coffers and took out a cloth bundle. This she undid to reveal the scroll, wrapped in oilpaper. Mistress Mei hung the scroll over the back of a chair and, as both she and her son kowtowed before it, said, "Forgive us for not having any incense or candles in this rustic abode." Having kowtowed, Shanshu approached the scroll to examine it more closely.

It was an exceedingly life-like portrait of Lord Ni wearing a black official cap on his gray hair and sitting on a chair with a child in his arms. He was pointing at the ground with one hand. Mother and son studied the portrait for a long time, but, failing to discover any clue in it, put it away again. Both felt very much depressed in spirit.

A few days later Shanshu went to South Village to seek a teacher who could explain some literary passages. As he was passing by the Temple of Lord Guan, Mentor of Upright Officials, he noticed a group of villagers bearing pigs and sheep to be sacrificed to Lord Guan. As Shanshu stopped to watch, an old man with a bamboo staff, who was also observing the proceedings, asked one of the villagers, "What is the occasion for this sacrifice?" The villager replied, "Some time ago we were wronged in a court case. Happily the case was put to rights by a wise and able official. So now we are making good a promise we made to the gods."

The villager recounted how a local tailor had been murdered by his wife and her lover, who then made it appear that the murderer was this villager who had previously had a drunken altercation with the victim. The villager had been sentenced to death by the authorities, and all families in his *jia*—the neighborhood group responsible for the conduct of its members—were punished for not reporting his crime. By chance, the case had come to the attention of Governor Teng, who thereupon reinvestigated the circumstances and found discrepancies in the accounts presented by the lover and the wife of the victim.

The villager said, "Because Governor Teng succeeded in discovering the truth, the two were brought to justice and I was set free. Now my relatives and neighbors have raised money to purchase these offerings of thanks to the gods. Old man, can you imagine the injustice I have suffered?" Whereupon the old man observed, "Rare indeed are such wise and able officials. The inhabitants of this county are fortunate in having such a Governor."

Shanshu went home and related to his mother what he had seen and heard. He said, "Since there is such a good official here, we should go to him with the scroll and our appeal. I see no reason to wait any longer." Having agreed upon this course, mother and son informed themselves of the date of the next tribunal hearings. And on that day, Mistress Mei rose before dawn and, with her fourteen-year-old son and the scroll, went to the county yamen.

Governor Teng was very much surprised that they submitted nothing more than a scroll. He questioned Mistress Mei about this matter, and was told about Shanji's behavior and his father's last behests. The governor then took the scroll and instructed Mistress Mei to return after he had examined it.

Governor Teng withdrew to his residence when the hearings had ended and opened up the scroll. Having scrutinized it, he mused, "It goes without saying that the child is Ni Shanshu, but what does the hand pointing to the ground signify? Did he wish this official to remember him as he lay buried under the ground and to render him assistance?" But then he reflected, "I can do nothing to help him, since he wrote the testament with his own hand. Yet he said the scroll contains a secret, so there is undoubtedly another aspect to the matter. If I do not succeed in finding it, I shall have in vain regarded myself as a man of intelligence."

And so, whenever he returned from the yamen he would open the scroll and mull over it. Several days passed, however, without a solution presenting itself.

It was a chance occurrence that provided him with the clue. One day after lunch, as Governor Teng was poring over the scroll, a maidservant brought him a cup of tea. He extended his hand to take the cup but fumbled, spilling some of the tea onto the scroll. The governor set the cup down and went to the terrace with the scroll, holding it up to the sun to dry the damp spots.

As the sunlight shone through the scroll, he remarked the outlines of some writing within it. Curious, he separated the painting from the mounting and found a sheet of paper inserted between the two. The writing on the sheet of paper was Lord Ni's:

> I, an official meriting a chariot of five horses, have lived four score years and more, and as I approach death I have no regrets. However, my young son Shanshu is but a year old and his helplessness occasions me anxiety. I fear he may suffer harm at the hands of my son from my first wife, namely Shanji, who is lacking in filial qualities. Therefore, Shanji shall inherit the two large

houses I have recently purchased and all the farmland. Shanshu shall be given the older house. Though it is smaller, under the wall on the left side is buried five thousand taels of silver in five jars. Under the wall on the right side is buried six jars containing five thousand taels of silver plus a thousand taels of gold, which will suffice to purchase farmland. After some wise and able official shall have ruled on this case accordingly, Shanshu shall present him with three hundred taels of gold.

Written by the hand of Ni Shouqian in his eighty-first year

The portrait had been executed before the old man celebrated his second child's first birthday. Truly, "No one knows his sons better than their father," as the old saying goes.

Governor Teng was a man of inconstant character, and the mention of so much gold and silver aroused his cupidity. It took him but a moment's reflection to concoct a plan. He then dispatched an attendant to summon Ni Shanji to the courthouse, saying he wished to see him about some matter.

Meanwhile, Ni Shanji, much pleased that he had secured sole possession of the property, had been spending his days at home in revelry. The abrupt appearance of the messenger bearing a summons that brooked no procrastination left him with no alternative but to go forthwith to the county yamen.

Governor Teng was presiding at a court trial when the messenger announced, "Ni Shanji is here." The governor called Shanji over to bench and inquired, "Are you the elder son of Lord Ni?" Shanji replied, "I am he." Governor Teng continued, "Your stepmother Mistress Mei has lodged a complaint against you, claiming that you have evicted her and her son and have appropriated to yourself all the houses and land. Is this true?"

Ni Shanji protested, "Since childhood my stepbrother has been under my care, and it is only recently that he and his mother asked to live apart from the family. I did not evict them. As concerns the property, it was divided in conformity with a testament written by my late father which I followed to the letter." Governor Teng asked, "Where is this testament?" To which Shanji replied, "It is at my house. Permit me to fetch it for your perusal." The governor observed, "Mistress Mei claims in her complaint that the family property comprises tens of thousands of taels of silver. That is no small amount. Nor is it clear whether the testament was truly written by your father. Since you are the son of a prominent official, however, I shall not press you too hard. I shall summon Mistress Mei tomorrow and go personally to your house to inspect the property. If it has indeed been inequitably divided, the matter will be dealt with according to law, for this is more than just a private matter."

He then ordered bailiffs to escort Shanji to his home and to summon Mistress Mei and her son to attend the next day's hearing. For a small consideration from Shanji, however, the bailiffs permitted the latter to go home on his own and departed for East Village to serve the summons on Mistress Mei.

Shanji was greatly alarmed by the harsh tone employed by the official. The division of the family property had, after all, been conducted not by his father in person, but on the strength of a testament, to the authenticity of which he would now need the testimony of his clansmen. The very same night, he took gifts of silver to all the three branches of his relatives—paternal, maternal and marital, entreating them to be present at his house the next day and to give him their full support should the governor inquire about the testament.

Ever since the old man's death, however, none of these relatives had seen a single dish or box from Shanji, nor had he invited them to share so much as a cup of wine on festive occasions. The large ingots of silver he now brought them were as the offerings of a man who "burns no incense when all is quiet, but grovels at Buddha's feet in times of peril." Snickering and sneering, they accepted the silver to purchase delicacies for their own tables, but resolved to see which way the wind blew when the official arrived on the morrow, before committing themselves one way or the other.

The summons apprised Mistress Mei that the governor had taken up her case, and early the next morning she and her son went first to the county seat to see Governor Teng.

The governor said, "Out of compassion for you, an orphan and a widow, I feel I should render you assistance. But I hear that Shanji is in possession of a testament written by the deceased, and I am at loss as to what to do." Mistress Mei replied, "There is indeed such a testament, but it was made to protect the child and does not convey my late husband's real intentions. Your Excellency will understand the reason once you see the register of the family's property." Whereupon the governor cautioned, "It is difficult for even the best of judges to rule fairly in family disputes. I shall see to it that you and your son are adequately nourished and clothed for the rest of your days, but do not entertain excessively high expectations."

Mistress Mei thanked him, saying, "We would be content with being spared from hunger and cold. We do not hope to become as wealthy as Shanji." Governor Teng instructed mother and son to precede him to Shanji's house and wait there upon his arrival.

Ni Shanji had already had the main hall tidied up, an armchair spread with a tiger skin placed in it, and fine incense lit in the burner. He had also urged relatives and clansmen to come early and to be in attendance before the governor appeared.

Mistress Mei and Shanshu arrived to see a large assemblage of relatives and clansmen. Mother and son greeted the guests one by one and took the opportunity to say a few words soliciting their indulgence. Shanji was furious, but since he could not vent his ire here, he, like everyone else, concentrated on what to say to the governor.

Before long, the shouts of way-clearers in the distance heralded the approach of Governor Teng. Shanji straightened his apparel to meet the official. Seniors and the more sophisticated among the relatives stepped forward, while the young and timid peered from behind the wall which screened the gateway to catch a glimpse of the proceedings.

What they saw were attendants marching in pairs before a black silk canopy appropriate for an official of Governor Teng's rank. When the company came to the Ni family's gate, the attendants knelt and uttered a loud shout. Mistress Mei and all members of the Ni household dropped to their knees, remaining thus until the governor's personal assistant called "Rise!" The bearers then set down the sedan chair and Governor Teng unhurriedly emerged from it.

As he was about to enter the gate, however, he suddenly clasped his hands together and bowed again and again at thin air, mouthing salutations as though the master of the house had come out to greet him. Everyone looked at the governor in bewilderment. They watched him as he entered the main hall, bowing all the way and making small talk. In the hall, he clasped his hands toward the armchair with the tiger skin, seemingly in response to an invitation to be seated. Then he made haste to draw up another chair, which he placed in front of the armchair, and sat upon it after addressing at empty space many modest refusals to take the seat of honor. All those present stared in stupefaction as he communed apparently with some spirit or ghost, and none dared approach him.

Having bowed once more toward the seat of honor, Governor Teng broached the subject of his visit, saying, "Your wife submitted a complaint to this later-born person about the sharing of the family property. What are the dispositions made in this regard?" Then he appeared to listen attentively. After a long interval, he shook his head, clicked his tongue and commented, "Your elder son is unkind." He listened a while longer, then spoke again, asking, "How, then, will your younger son survive?" A moment later he inquired, "What is there in the small courtyard on the right side?" Then he exclaimed repeatedly, "Quite so, quite so!"

After a while, he said, "So this is also to be given to your younger son? I shall proceed as instructed." After another pause he clasped his hands together and demurred, "I dare not accept such a weighty consideration." Then, after many more refusals and protestations, he conceded, "The earnestness of your request leaves me no choice but to accede. I shall have an acknowledgment of receipt written out for your younger son." So saying, he stood up and bowed deeply several times with the words, "This later-born person will attend to the matter." The assemblage watched as though transfixed.

Then, as Governor Teng straightened up, he looked around and enquired, "Where is Lord Ni?" His assistant hastened to report, "I have not seen any Lord Ni." To which Governor Teng replied, "That is strange!" Calling Shanji to his side, he said, "Your honored father greeted me at the gate and conversed with me all this while. Surely, you must have overheard everything." Shanji replied, "I heard nothing!"

Governor Teng proceeded to explain, "There was a tall man with a thin face, high cheekbones, narrow eyes, bushy eyebrows and large ears. His whiskers fall in three long, silvery-white strands. And he is wearing an official's cap, black boots, a scarlet gown, and a golden sash. Surely that is Lord Ni!"

All who heard this description broke into a cold sweat and exclaimed, "That is precisely what he looked like before he passed away!" Governor Teng asked, "Why did he suddenly depart? He said there are two principal courtyards and a smaller, older one to the east of them. Is that the case?" Not daring to conceal anything from the governor, Shanji admitted this was so. Governor Teng then commanded, "Let us go to the eastern courtyard. I shall have something to say there."

Everyone present was convinced that the old Lord had indeed manifested himself, and they stood with jutting tongues and fluttering hearts. How could they know that Governor Teng was duping them, that his description of Lord Ni had been culled from the scroll, and that not a word he spoke was the truth?

With Ni Shanji showing the way and the rest of the people following behind, Governor Teng walked to the eastern courtyard. This had been Lord Ni's residence before his appointment to prefectureship, but after the newer courtyards were built, it had been converted into storerooms for miscellaneous cereals and housed only a family of domestics.

Governor Teng walked around the courtyard, then seated himself in its main hall and said, "Your father, with whose spirit I was doubtless conversing, gave me a clear account of your family property and asked me to rule that this old courtyard be given to Shanshu. What do you think?" Shanji kowtowed, saying, "Let it be as Your Excellency decides."

Governor Teng then asked for the family property register. As he perused it, he more than once remarked, "A large property indeed!" And when he came to the testament of the deceased regarding the division of the property, he laughed, saying, "The old gentleman did indeed write this, but just a while ago he had much to say about Shanji's misdeeds. He is quite unpredictable, the old gentleman!" He called Shanji before him, saying, "However, since he has willed it so, these lands and properties should go to you, and Shanshu may not presume to gainsay this decision."

Overcome with distress, Mistress Mei was about to plead with the governor. But before she could do so, he announced, "This old courtyard and all that is in it shall be Shanshu's, nor may Shanji presume to dispute this decision." Shanji reflected, "The old furniture in this courtyard is worth little, whereas most of the grain stored here was sold last month and hardly any is left. I shall be getting off very cheaply." So he vouchsafed his agreement, saying, "Your Excellency's decision is most sagacious."

Governor Teng continued, "The two parties have both consented to this decision, and neither may recant. To this, all here who are their clansmen shall bear witness. Now, old Lord Ni told me earlier today that five thousand taels of silver, divided among five jars, are buried under the left-hand wall of this house, and that this should be given to his younger son." Shanji did not believe him, so he declared, "If indeed there is something hidden there, it belongs to my brother, even though it were ten thousand pieces of gold. I will not contest that." Governor Teng snapped, "Nor would I permit you to do so!" He ordered his men to bring picks and shovels.

When that had been done, Mistress Mei and her son led a crew of laborers to the east wall where a trench was excavated under its foundations, bringing to light five large jars. These were opened and found to be filled with gleaming ingots of silver. One of the jars was weighed and proven to contain exactly one thousand taels of silver. All present were flabbergasted. Shanji was fully convinced now that his father's spirit had appeared and told the governor about the hidden treasure, for how could the latter have known about it when even he himself had ignored its existence?

Governor Teng ordered that the jars be lined up before him, and then informed Mistress Mei, "Five more jars with the same amount of silver are buried under the right-hand wall. In addition, there is one jar filled with gold, which by Lord Ni's instructions should be given to me as recompense for my services. I attempted to decline the gift, but Lord Ni was so insistent that I felt constrained to accept it." Whereupon Mistress Mei and Shanshu kowtowed and said, "The five thousand under the east wall have already exceeded our expectations. Should there be more under the right-hand wall, it goes without saying that we will obey the instructions of the deceased."

Governor Teng declared, "I know about the treasure because of what the old gentleman told me, and I believe his words to be true." He ordered the laborers to dig under the west wall and, sure enough, they uncovered six big jars, five with silver and one containing gold.

At the sight of all this yellow and white metal, Shanji's eyes smoldered with greed and he was sorely tempted to snatch up one or two of the ingots. But having already given his word, he dared not utter a single word in protest. Governor Teng wrote out a receipt, which he gave to Shanshu, then ruled that the family of domestics be assigned to Mistress Mei and her son. Delighted beyond measure, the mother and son kowtowed their gratitude to the governor. Shanji, utterly chagrined, also kowtowed a few times and grudgingly muttered, "I thank Your Honor for passing this judgment." Governor Teng wrote his name on several slips of paper, which were used to seal the jar containing the gold. The jar was then placed on his sedan chair to be transported to his residence.

Everyone present took it for granted that the gold had truly been given him by Lord Ni, and consequently no one presumed to raise objections. It was as the saying goes: "The fisherman profits when the snipe and the clam grapple." Had Shanji been an honest and kindly man on good terms with his younger brother and willing to share the family property in an equitable manner, the thousand taels of gold would have been divided between the two brothers instead of falling into the hands of Governor Teng. As it turned out, all of Shanji's machinations had but the result of playing into another man's hands, of putting himself in a vile mood, and of gaining himself the reputation of an unfilial son and unworthy brother. He had, in effect, hoisted himself with his own petard.

But let us return to our story. Mistress Mei and her son went to the county seat the next day to thank Governor Teng, whereupon he gave the scroll back to them, but only after removing the hidden sheet of paper and remounting the portrait. Only then did mother and son realize that the hand pointing to the ground indicated the presence of buried treasure.

With the ten jars of silver they now possessed, they purchased farmland and homesteads and, in time, became one of the wealthiest households in the county. Shanshu took a wife and had three sons who eventually achieved fame as scholars. In fact, theirs was the only branch of the Ni clan that prospered, for Shanji's two sons turned out to be wastrels who dissipated their family property. After Shanji died, his sons sold the family's two large courtyards to their uncle Shanshu. And all who knew about the Ni family's fortunes declared that these occurrences were no more than the consequences of Heaven's requital.

The Faithful Old Servant

徐老僕義憤成家

This is the story of a servant who single-handedly helped his widowed mistress set up a prosperous family business, married out her three daughters, and obtained wives for the two young masters, but had not an iota of wealth to his name when he died. To this day, his name remains inscribed in the annals of history.

The events in this story took place during the reign of Emperor Jiajing of the current Ming Dynasty, in the village of Jinsha, a few *li* from Chun'an County Town in Zhejiang's Yanzhou Prefecture. In this village there lived a family of three brothers surnamed Xu. The eldest brother, Xu Yan, and the second brother, Xu Zhao, each had one son. However, the third brother, named Xu Zhe, had two sons and three daughters.

In compliance with the last will and testament of their deceased father, the three brothers ate from one communal pot and tilled their fields together, and had together purchased an ox and a horse. They also possessed an old servant, named Ah Ji, who was married and more than fifty years of age and had sired a son less than ten years earlier.

Ah Ji had grown up in this village. He had sold himself to the Xu family after his own parents had passed away, since he had lacked the money to give them a proper funeral. Faithful and circumspect, he rose early and turned in late and worked hard on the land. The brothers' father had profited greatly from his toil, and had consequently treated him well in every respect. But his sons viewed the old servant with displeasure after they had taken over the family's affairs, for they felt he was growing too old. Ah Ji, moreover, was quite outspoken and attempted strenuously to dissuade the brothers when their actions seemed inappropriate. Xu Zhe would now and then hearken to his well-meant persuasions, but his brothers, both of whom were presumptuous and opinionated, accused him of nagging and meddling, and would loudly rebuke him and even mete him a few peevish blows.

Ah Ji's wife advised him, "You are getting along in years and should take a less active part in things. The brothers belong to the new generation, to a world where things have changed and keep changing. So why must you voice your opinions and invite their abuse?" Ah Ji replied, "The old master was my benefactor. I cannot refrain from saying what I must."

But the woman argued, "It is no fault of yours if they do not listen to your repeated admonitions!"

So Ah Ji accepted his wife's advice. He stilled his tongue and minded his own business, and this spared him a good deal of humiliation. As the ancients said, "Shut your mouth and tuck away your tongue, and you will enjoy safety and security."

One day, the youngest brother Xu Zhe was stricken with an ague and died seven days later. His wife and children wept heartbrokenly as they put the deceased in his coffin and buried him, and performed the requisite rituals.

Two months later, Xu Yan sought Xu Zhao and spoke to him thus: "We both have but one son, whereas our younger brother produced two sons and three daughters. Their share from the family's earnings is more than ours combined. That was unfair even when there were three of us to work the land; it is even less fair now that our brother has died. We must now toil day and night to feed a gaggle of useless mouths. But there is worse yet to come. When the children grow up and we have found wives for our own sons, we shall have to marry off his children as well. We shall thus be providing them with four more shares of property than either of us will get. I propose that we divide up the property now into three shares and rid ourselves of this deadweight. It will then be no longer any concern of ours how they exist. The only difficulty is that the old man has stated in his will that the family property should not be divided up. Others will talk about us if we disobey his instructions. So what should we do?"

Xu Zhao, the younger brother, might have attempted to dissuade Xu Yan had he been a man of good conscience, but the truth is that he himself had long entertained the same thoughts. He replied, "The old man's will and testament are but the words of a dead man, not an imperial edict that must be obeyed implicitly. Moreover, these are purely family affairs, and I would like to see the outsider who has the temerity to interfere!"

Xu Yan agreed, and the brothers proceeded in secret to apportion the family property, leaving only the least desirable objects to their nephews. Xu Yan asked, "What shall we do with the livestock?" Xu Zhao pondered a while, and then replied, "That poses no difficulty. Ah Ji and his wife are getting old and cannot work very much longer. They and their son are three useless mouths to feed while they live, and will cost us two coffins after they die. Count them as a share of livestock and assign them to our brother's family. In that way we shall also rid ourselves of a burden."

Once all matters had been settled between them, they prepared some wine and food, and on the next day invited a number of friends and neighbors to their house. Then they summoned Xu Zhe's widow Mistress Yen and their two young nephews, who were still addressed by the pet names. The older boy, Fu-er, or Son of Fortune, was only seven years old; the younger one, Shou-er, or Son of Longevity, was five. They came into the front hall with their mother, who knew not why they had been called.

Xu Yan rose to his feet. "I wish to make a statement before our respected relatives," he said. "Our father left us no great inheritance, and it was we brothers who accumulated the small property we now possess, in the hope that we could hold it together until our old age and let our sons and nephews share it after we died. Sadly, a big change has occurred in our youngest brother's household, and our sister-in-law, being a simple housewife, knows nothing about the state of our property. A family's fortunes may wax, or they may wane. It would indeed be good if we henceforth made more money and could share some of it with our nephews. But should our fortunes wane, people would accuse us of dishonesty and of taking advantage of orphans and widows. That would hurt the relationships between kith and kin. Hence, my brother and I have agreed that it would be most advisable to divide the property into three shares while it is still in a good state, and let each household take a share for its own use. That will forestall any future disputes. I have invited you, our respected relatives, to offer your opinions on this matter."

He then extracted from his sleeve three copies of an agreement on property division, saying, "The apportionment has been conducted as fairly and equitably as possible, and all that is needed is the signature of the parties concerned."

When Mistress Yen realized that the family would split up and that her family would be on its own, tears trickled from her eyes and she cried, "My brothers, I am a widow and my children are still very young. We are like crabs without legs! How could I maintain a household? Since our late father left instructions not to split up the family, you should remain in charge of it. And once my children have grown up, you may give them whatever it pleases you to do so. I assure you we shall not argue over who gets what or how much."

But Xu Zhao replied, "Third Sister-in-Law, sooner or later all banquets come to an end, and even if we stayed together a thousand years, we would eventually part. Our father is dead, and his words need no longer be heeded. Your elder brother-in-law yesterday wanted to give you the ox or the horse, but since your children are too young to care for them, I thought it best to let you have Ah Ji. He is advancing in years, yet is still strong, and works better than a younger person. His woman is able to soak hemp and weave flax, and can earn her own keep. Their son will be able to tend the fields in a year or two. So you have nothing to worry about."

Mistress Yen wept all the more bitterly as she realized from her brother-in-law's manner of speech that his mind was made up and there was nothing she could do to change it. The relatives and neighbors read the agreement, and although they knew the division was inequitable, none spoke out against it since no one wished to make enemies. One after the other they affixed their names to the agreement, advised Mistress Yen to accept it, and then sat down to the food and drink.

Ah Ji in the meantime had been sent out early in the morning to do some shopping and invite some guests, though he knew not for what purpose. By the time he had invited a relative from South Village and returned to the house, the proceedings there had concluded. His wife met him at the gate, but fearing that he would again make unwelcome comments when he learned what had taken place, she drew him aside and told him, "The brothers have divided up the family property today. Do not try to interfere, lest you incur their displeasure!" Shocked by the news, Ah Ji protested, "The old master said in his will and testament that this property should not be divided! And now that Third Brother has died, how can his brothers abandon his widow and children? How will they live? Who will speak up if I do not say anything?"

He turned to enter the house, but the woman pulled him back, saying: "Even the best of judges are hard pressed to rule fairly in family disputes, and none of the friends and relatives here today has raised any objections. You are but an underling, not an elder in the clan, so what call have you to state your opinion?"

Ah Ji replied, "What you say is right, and I would say nothing if the division were fair. But if it is not, I will speak up even if I forfeit my life!" He then asked, "To which family have I been apportioned?" His wife replied, "I know not."

Ah Ji entered the main hall and saw the assemblage eating and drinking and making merry. Since it was inappropriate for him to ask any questions at this time, he stood to one side. A neighbor of the household caught sight of him and remarked: "Ah Ji, since you now belong to the Third Mistress and she is a widow, you should do your best to help her."

Ah Ji replied, "I am getting old and can do little work now." But even as he said this he reflected, "So they have given me to the third family! They must think I am of no further use and are using this opportunity to get rid of me. I shall show them! I shall start a business and let them see I am not to be laughed at!"

Instead of inquiring further about the division of property, he turned his steps toward Mistress Yen's room. When he reached the door, however, he heard the sound of weeping inside. Stopping outside the door, he stood and listened. Mistress Yen was lamenting, "Merciful Heaven! I had hoped to live with you until both our heads turned white! How could you abandon me halfway with so many children and no means of support? I had also hoped your brothers would help to raise the children. Who could have foreseen that they would split up the family even before your flesh and bones have become cold? I have no one to turn to now. How shall I make a living?" She continued, "As for the land shared out to me, they understand about such things while I do not, and I can only accept whatever they give me, whether it is good or bad. One thing suffices to show how mean and heartless they are! The ox can drag a plow, while the horse can be hired out. They have taken these useful things, leaving to me two old people who can only deplete my food and clothing."

On hearing these words, Ah Ji abruptly swept aside the door curtain and remonstrated, "Third Mistress, are you saying that I will only deplete your food and clothing, and that I am less useful than an ox or horse?" Taken aback by this sudden intrusion, Mistress Yen dried her tears and inquired, "What do you wish to say?"

Ah Ji continued, "The ox and the horse can plow the land or be hired out, but they will only bring a few taels of silver in profits, and will require people to tend to their needs. This old servant may be getting on in years, but I am still strong and able to go about and endure hardships. I have never engaged in business, but I know how it is done. If the Mistress will raise some seed money for me to go into business, a few turnovers a year will earn several times the profits earned by the ox or horse! As for my old woman, she is an industrious spinner and weaver and can help to earn your keep. And pay no heed to whether the land is good or bad. Rent it out for a few piculs of grain and become a landlord. You and your daughters could also do some needlework to eke out a living. But do not touch the seed money. After engaging in business for a few years, we will surely be able to set ourselves up. About that you need have no fears."

Mistress Yen saw that he spoke with assurance, but she could not help remarking, "It would indeed be good if you could help us in this way, but I fear you will be unable to bear such hardships at your age." Ah Ji replied, "To tell you the truth, Third Mistress, I may be old, but I am still hale and hearty. I go to sleep later and rise earlier than men younger than myself. You may rest assured on this score."

Mistress Yen then asked, "What business do you intend to engage in?" Ah Ji replied, "Generally speaking, people engage in big or small businesses according to the amount of capital at their disposal. I shall go forth and see what opportunities present themselves, and choose only those that are profitable. The decisions cannot be taken here at home." Mistress Yen agreed, saying, "Your words make sense. Let me consider the matter."

Ah Ji asked her for the property agreement and proceeded to verify and assemble the furniture and utensils listed in it. He then returned to the front hall to wait on the guests who drank late into the night before dispersing.

The next day, the eldest brother Xu Yan called in a carpenter to partition the house and make a separate entrance for Mistress Yen. As she rearranged her living quarters, she took out some of her jewelry and clothes and surreptitiously instructed Ah Ji to sell them. In this way she managed to put together a total of twelve taels of silver. These she entrusted to Ah Ji, saying, "This paltry sum is all I possess in the world and my entire family's sole means of survival. I do not expect you to obtain large returns on this. A small profit will be sufficient. Act judiciously, and take care on the road! And do not attempt to do anything you cannot accomplish, for the brothers will mock us." Her tears began to flow as she said this.

Ah Ji said, "Please set your mind at ease, for I know what I am doing and shall not fail you." Mistress Yen then asked, "When are you leaving?" Ah Ji replied, "Tomorrow morning, since I now have the seed money." Mistress Yen inquired, "Should you not choose an auspicious day?" To which Ah Ji replied, "The day I start to do business will be our auspicious day. There is no need to choose another one."

So saying, he secreted the silver among his undergarments and returned to his quarters. To his wife he said, "I am leaving tomorrow morning to engage in some business. Pack some old clothes for me." She was quite surprised by this announcement, for Ah Ji had discussed his intentions only with Mistress Yen and had not informed his wife. She asked, "Where are you going? And what business will you be doing?" Ah Ji then told her everything that had transpired.

"Aiya!" exclaimed his wife. "What is all this? In all the years you have lived, you have never set foot in the world of business, but now you have bragged and boasted yourself into this affair. A widow's money is nothing but trouble, and anyone who touches it invites censure. You will be reproached until the day you die if you lose her only means of livelihood! Take my advice and quickly return it to the Third Mistress. We are safer working in the fields as before, even if we must rise early and retire late and endure more hardships."

Ah Ji retorted, "What do you know, woman? All you say is nonsense! How can you be sure that I am no good at business and will make a mess of things? I do not need your gloomy predictions!" He refused to listen to his wife and went himself to pack some clothes and bedding. Having no bag to put them in, he tied them in a bundle, and then placed some victuals in a net. He then went to the marketplace to purchase an umbrella and a pair of hempen shoes.

Before leaving the next morning, he went to see Xu Yan and Xu Zhao and announced, "This old slave is leaving today for distant places to engage in business and there will be no one left to take care of the family. Although the families now live separately, I beg the two of you to go in the mornings and evenings to see how they are faring." The brothers could not refrain from smirking, and they said, "You need not remind us to do this. But remember us when you return after having made a profit." Ah Ji replied, "That goes without saying."

He went home, broke his fast, and bade farewell to Mistress Yen. Then he put on the hempen shoes, slung the bundle and umbrella over his back, and cautioned his wife to be careful at night and in the early mornings. Before he walked out of the gates, Mistress Yen repeated her instructions. Ah Ji nodded and strode off into the distance.

No sooner had Ah Ji left than the brothers laughed uproariously and Xu Yan commented, "Third Mistress is ridiculously ignorant. She has silver to do business with, but does not consult us. Instead, she listens to the words of that old slave, Ah Ji. I am certain that he has never done any business in all his life. He has cajoled the widow into giving him her silver, and has now gone to enjoy himself. That seed money is as good as lost!"

Xu Zhao said, "She never did anything with that silver when we were still one family, and it is only after we split up that she has asked Ah Ji to do business with it. I am sure she did not bring much of a dowry with her, so Third Brother must have wangled this silver from our father before he died, and it has only just come to light. At any rate, Third Mistress is doing things behind our backs, but she will say we are jealous if we reproach her for it. Let us wait for the day Ah Ji returns after losing everything. Then it will be our turn to laugh!"

As Ah Ji walked along, he kept thinking, "What business shall I engage in?" Suddenly he exclaimed, "I've heard that there is much profit to be made in the lacquer business, and it is not far from here. Why not give it a try?" Having made up his mind, he made straight for the Qingyun Mountains.

All the lacquer producers there had agencies, and Ah Ji took lodgings at one of these establishments. There were a good many buyers of lacquer, and these were served in the order of their arrival. Ah Ji reflected, "It would be a waste of time and money if I waited for my turn."

An idea occurred to him. During an interval in the business, he took the proprietor of the agency to the village inn and treated him to three bowls of wine. He said, "I am a small merchant with very little capital and cannot afford to wait. Since you and I are from the same county, I hope you will do me the favor of arranging matters so that I am served first. The next time I come, I shall host you in grand fashion."

As luck would have it, the proprietor of the agency was very much partial to drink and could not bring himself to refuse Ah Ji's request after he had imbibed the "mouth-softening" liquor. That evening, he went to several households in the village and collected enough lacquer to fill Ah Ji's order. Then the goods were packed and stored in a neighbor's house so that the other buyers would not find out and complain. He sent Ah Ji on his way before dawn the next morning.

Ah Ji was much delighted that his scheme had succeeded. He hired porters to carry the goods to the docks on the Xin'an River. It occurred to him that Hangzhou was too close to this district and his goods would hardly command a good price there. So he hired a boat and sailed all the way to Suzhou. It so happened that there was a shortage of lacquer in that city, and his goods were in great demand. They were sold out in less than three days. All clients paid for them in silver, and no one sought any credit. After deducting his traveling expenses and the cost of the goods, Ah Ji found he had more than doubled the money he had brought with him.

Ah Ji silently thanked Heaven and Earth, and then busied himself for the return trip. Then a thought struck him: "I shall be returning by boat without any goods, and the silver will be troublesome to take along. Why not ship back some merchandise and attempt to gain a bit of profit?" He learned that there was an abundance of rice at Fengqiao and its price had just fallen. He said to himself, "I reckon I can make a few taels of silver in the rice business." He purchased more than sixty piculs of rice and sold it in Hangzhou.

The time of year was the middle of the seventh moon and no rain had fallen in Hangzhou for more than thirty days. Seedlings died in parched paddy fields, and the price of rice was rising by leaps and bounds. Ah Ji's rice arrived just at the right time; the price per picul had increased by two tenths of a tael of silver so that he gained another dozen or so taels. He reflected, "Third Mistress must be having a run of good luck, for the business is proceeding extraordinarily well!"

Another thought occurred to him. "Since I am here, why not inquire about the price of lacquer? If it differs little from the price in Suzhou, I could save on the cost of transportation." His investigations revealed that the price of lacquer in Hangzhou was even higher than in Suzhou! Why? Because all merchants, assuming that the price in nearby Hangzhou would be low, shipped their goods to more distant places, and this resulted in frequent shortages in Hangzhou. As the saying goes: "There is no big or small merchandise; any goods bring in a high price if they are in short supply."

Ah Ji was highly pleased by this information and went back posthaste to the Qingyun Mountains, where he presented gifts to the proprietor of the agency and, as before, treated him to three bowls of wine. Gratified by these small considerations, the proprietor did as he had done on the previous occasion and surreptitiously served Ah Ji before his other clients. These goods were all sold in Hangzhou in less than three days' time. Ah Ji counted his profits and found that he had gained another several taels of silver. There was, however, no profit to be made on the return journey, so he decided that his next excursion would again be to more distant places.

He settled his accounts and prepared to set forth anew. But then he thought, "Since I have been away for quite some time now, Third Mistress must be concerned. I had better return to advise her of the circumstances and set her heart at ease." He also had another idea. "It will take a few days to assemble my next consignment of lacquer. So why not go first to the mountains and leave the silver with the proprietor so that he can begin to collect the goods, and then go home? That will save me both time and effort." Having decided on this course of action, he went into the mountains to give the silver to the agent before turning his steps homeward.

Meanwhile, Mistress Yen had been on tenterhooks ever since Ah Ji had departed. She was haunted by fears that Ah Ji might have forfeited the capital she had given him. Her vexation was aggravated by the brothers' constant tongue-wagging behind her back. As she was sitting in her room one day in a melancholy mood, her sons rushed into the house, shouting, "Ah Ji has come back!"

She hurried out of her room to see Ah Ji standing there with his wife behind him. He stepped forward and bowed deeply. At the sight of him, Mistress Yen felt her heart leap into her throat and throb wildly. She was terrified lest he had brought her bad news. She asked, "What business have you done? Have you made any profit?"

With his arms respectfully crossed before him, Ah Ji replied unhurriedly, "Thanks to Heaven's indulgence and to Third Mistress's good fortune, I have engaged in the lacquer business and made a profit five or six times greater than the original capital." He proceeded to give her a detailed account of his activities, concluding with the words, "Fearing that Third Mistress might feel uneasy, I have returned to give you this report."

Mistress Yen was elated by this Heaven-sent news and asked, "Where is the silver now?" Ah Ji replied, "I have not brought it back, for I left it with the agent who collects the lacquer. I shall be on my way again tomorrow morning."

The whole family was overjoyed. Ah Ji stayed one night, then rose early the next morning, bade farewell to Mistress Yen, and headed again for the Qingyun Mountains.

Xu Yan and Xu Zhao had dined the previous night at a neighbor's house and had ended up drunk, so they had known nothing about Ah Ji's return. The next morning they came together and asked, "We hear that Ah Ji has come back. How much silver did he gain?" Mistress Yen replied, "I was just about to inform you that he has engaged in the lacquer business and made a five- or sixfold profit." Xu Yan exclaimed, "What excellent fortune! If you continue to make money like this, you will become a rich family within a few years!" Mistress Yen replied, "Do not joke like that, Elder Brother. I will be content if we are spared from cold and hunger."

Xu Zhao then asked, "Where is he now? When did he leave? Why did he not come to see me? Such lack of courtesy!" Mistress Yen told him, "He left early this morning." Xu Zhao continued, "Why was he in such a hurry to leave?" And Xu Yan asked, "Have you seen the silver and counted it?" Mistress Yen replied, "He did not bring it back. He has left it with the agent to purchase more goods."

Xu Yan guffawed, then said, "I had assumed the capital and profits were all in your hands now. But it seems that all you have are empty words which are nice to listen to but do not fill one's belly. Your ears tingle with pleasure, but you know not where the capital and profits have gone. Do you believe his words? The right hand of a man of business does not trust his left hand. Would any man come home himself and leave his silver in another man's hands? As I see it, he has lost the seed money and is telling lies to hoodwink you."

Xu Zhao, too, said, "Third Mistress, this is your family's own business and we should not comment upon it. But you are a woman and do not know the ways of the world. Since you had the silver, you should have consulted the two of us. The best and most farsighted thing to do would have been to purchase some land. What does that Ah Ji know about doing business? You gave him the silver without letting us know and let him fool around with it. I surmise it was your dowry or Third Brother's savings and not stolen from anyone, so why did you part with it so readily?"

Mistress Yen could think of no reply to this duet of theirs. Doubts rose in her mind and she knew not whom to believe. All her delight was once again overshadowed by anxiety. And so we leave her for the time being.

Meanwhile, old Ah Ji hastened back to the Qingyun Mountains. The agent had already collected his goods and now counted them out and handed them over. This time, Ah Ji did not go to Suzhou or Hangzhou, but set out instead for Xinghua where a larger profit could be made. After selling his goods, he learned that the price of rice there was one tael of silver for three piculs, and that the measuring scoops were large. He remembered that the last time he had gone to drought-stricken Hangzhou, he had sold rice bought from other merchants and still made a profit. His earnings would presumably be twice as great if he procured rice in the region where it was produced.

Thus he purchased a large shipment of rice, which he sold in Hangzhou for precisely one and two tenths of a tael of silver per picul; the extra rice from the large measuring scoops was just enough to pay for the shipping. And when Ah Ji returned again to the mountains to purchase lacquer, he had become a big merchant, flattered and fawned upon by the agency proprietor. Mistress Yen's luck had something to do with this, but there is no denying that Ah Ji had become an astute businessman. All the goods he sold brought in large profits. And after a few more deals, his silver increased to more than two thousand taels.

The end of the year was approaching, and he reckoned, "Carrying around so much silver is no jesting matter for a solitary old man like myself! Should anything go wrong, all that has been gained might be lost. Besides, the year will soon end and the people at home must certainly be expecting me to return. I had best go back and discuss the purchase of some farmland. Once this basic investment has been made, I can come out again to do business with the remainder."

By now he possessed all the bags and containers a traveler might need. He wrapped and sealed the silver in tight packages, which he stowed away in traveling bags. Then he set forth, renting boats and hiring horses, taking to the road late and retiring early, and exercising the utmost caution.

He reached home a few days later and had his luggage taken in. His wife had seen him approaching and went to report his arrival to Mistress Yen. The latter was both happy and apprehensive—happy that Ah Ji had come back, but apprehensive because she knew naught of how his business endeavors had fared. In fact, her anxieties were even greater on account of the scoffing remarks uttered by Xu Yan and his brother.

Trotting as fast as her feet would take her, she hurried to the outer chamber. Her fears were somewhat allayed when she saw the pile of baggage, for it did not look like that of a merchant who has lost all his money. Unable to restrain herself, however, she asked, "How was the business this time? And have you brought back the silver?"

Ah Ji stepped forward and made an obeisance, saying, "Do not be so impatient, Third Mistress. I shall tell you everything in good time." He carried the luggage into Mistress Yen's chamber and then handed her the silver, package by package. Mistress Yen was overwhelmed by the sight of so much silver and made haste to put it away in her chests and trunks. Then Ah Ji gave her an account of his travels and business dealings.

Mistress Yen told him nothing about the remarks made by Xu Yan and his brother for fear of provoking an unpleasant confrontation. Instead, she said again and again, "All this is due to your efforts, Respected Elder. You must take a good rest!" But she enjoined him, "If the brothers ask you about this, do not tell them the truth." Ah Ji replied, "This old slave understands."

As they conversed, there was a knock at the front door. The Xu brothers had learned of Ah Ji's return and had come to make enquiries. Ah Ji stepped forward with obeisances to both.

Xu Yan said, "The last time we were apprised that your business was most successful. How much profit have you made this time?" Ah Ji replied, "Thanks to your good karma, this old slave made a net profit of fifty taels of silver after deducting expenses." Xu Zhao exclaimed, "Aiya! Last time you said you made a sixfold profit! Why has it shrunk again after all this time?" Xu Yan interrupted, "Never mind how much or how little you made. Did you bring the silver back this time?" Ah Ji replied, "I have given it all to Third Mistress." Saying no more, the brothers turned and departed.

During the next few days, Ah Ji consulted with Mistress Yen about the purchase of farmland and instituted discreet inquiries.

Rich families quite often produce wastrels. In Jinsha Village, there was a rich family named Yan that possessed enormous wealth and large tracts of farmland. The family had only one son, who was named Shibao, which means "born in this world to preserve property." But Yan Shibao did little else but whore and gamble, which so angered his father that the old man died in a fit of fury. All the villagers, knowing him to be a wastrel, called him Xian Shibao, or "giver-away of all property."

Xian Shibao consorted with a band of good-for-nothings who spent all their time carousing and pursuing pleasure. After squandering the family's entire store of money and valuables he began to sell off its property, and since disposing of it piecemeal did not bring in enough money for his needs, he put up for sale a thousand *mu* of land for some three thousand taels of silver, to be paid in one lump sum. Although there were other rich families in the village, none had that much silver on hand and thus no offers had been made.

As the end of the year approached, however, Xian Shibao became increasingly desperate for money, so he halved his asking price and added a homestead to the offer. Ah Ji learned of this and immediately sent a go-between to secure a pre-engagement on the land, for fear that someone else would take it. Conclusion of the deal was set for the very next day. Xian Shibao was extremely pleased that someone was purchasing the land. As a rule, he never stayed at home, but on this day he waited patiently for the go-between to come for him.

Ah Ji, on his part, surmised that Xian Shibao was partial to good food, and so went out early the morning to purchase viands and delicacies and hire a chef to prepare a banquet. He then said to Mistress Yen, "Today's transaction is of unusual importance. Third Mistress is a woman, and the two young masters are still children. I myself am only a servant and may only talk to our guest from one side, and not as an equal. The proper thing to do would be to ask the two masters next door to serve as witnesses." Mistress Yen replied, "If that is the case, ask them to come."

Ah Ji went next door where he found the brothers conversing. He announced, "Third Mistress will be purchasing some farmland today and asks you to preside over the formalities." The brothers consented to come but were again highly displeased because Mistress Yen had not sought their assistance in this matter. Xu Yan complained, "Why does she not ask for our advice when she wishes to purchase property, but lets Ah Ji take charge? She tells us only when the deal is about to be concluded. But if the truth be said, I know of no small lots of land for sale in this village." Xu Zhao said, "Do not waste time guessing, for we shall find out very soon."

The two sat before their doorway to wait. It was nigh upon midday when they saw Xian Shibao and a few middlemen coming down the road, laughing and clapping their hands and followed by a pair of young lackeys holding boxes for documents. The group walked into the neighboring gateway.

The brothers were astounded by this spectacle, and one exclaimed, "How strange! I have heard that Xian Shibao wishes to sell a thousand *mu* of farmland for three thousand taels of silver, but I am certain she does not have that much silver! Is he perhaps also selling small lots of ten or twenty *mu*?"

Puzzled, they too entered the gateway, and after greetings had been exchanged, hosts and guests seated themselves. Ah Ji stepped forward and stated, "Master Xian, the price was agreed upon yesterday, and we shall pay in full as you have requested. We hope you will not raise any side issues or change your mind." At this, Xian Shibao bridled and shouted, "Once a gentleman has given out his word, four horses cannot drag it back. If I change my mind, I am not born of a human being!" Ah Ji said, "In that case, let us first write out the contract and then count the silver." Paper, ink, and a brush had already been prepared and were now brought out. Xian Shibao picked up the brush and, with a big show of bravado, wrote out a final sales contract. He then said, "In case you have any doubts, this one may be considered a draft contract. What do you say?" Ah Ji replied, "This one is good."

The Xu brothers read the deed, which indeed was for the sale of one thousand *mu* of land and a house for the actual price of one thousand five hundred taels of silver. They stared at each other, so flabbergasted that their tongues protruded for several moments before going back into their mouths. Both were thinking, "However profitable Ah Ji's business has been, he could not have made that much money! Did he obtain it by robbing people or digging up hidden treasure? This is indeed hard to tell."

After the middlemen had signed the deed, Ah Ji gave it to Mistress Yen for safekeeping. A set of borrowed scales was placed on the table, and Ah Ji proceeded to weigh the silver, all of which was of the highest quality. At the sight of it, the Xu brothers' eyes flamed with greed and they could hardly restrain themselves from shoving the others aside and seizing the gleaming ingots.

When the silver had been measured, wine and food were placed on the table, and the drinking went on late into the night.

The next day, Ah Ji spoke to Mistress Yen, saying, "That house is quite spacious and we would do well to move there. Besides, it will be easier to oversee the rice harvests in the fields." Mistress Yen was also desirous of moving away, for she knew how envious the Xu brothers were. So she agreed to Ah Ji's proposal and moved on the sixth day of the first lunar month. Ah Ji then engaged a teacher to give lessons to the two young masters, the elder of whom was now named Xu Kuan and the younger, Xu Hong. The house itself was most handsomely refurbished.

When the villagers learned that Mistress Yen had purchased one thousand *mu* of farmland, they spread the tale that she had unearthed a vast trove of silver. It was even rumored that her outhouses were built of silver. All came to ingratiate themselves with the family.

In the meantime, Ah Ji out went as usual to do business after the family had settled in the new house. This time, however, he no longer limited his goods to lacquer, but traded in anything that would bring in a profit, including the grain harvested by the family. Within ten years' time, the family accumulated enormous wealth. By then, all of Xian Shibao's farmland and houses belonged to the third Xu family. The household bustled with activity, horses and cattle filled the pastures, and servants and hired hands numbered in the hundreds. Truly, a scene of prosperity!

All three daughters of Mistress Yen were married off to rich households in the vicinity, and the sons, now formally named Xu Kuan and Xu Hong, also took wives. Ah Ji took charge of all the wedding ceremonies and gifts, so that no exertions were required from Mistress Yen over these matters. And because the family had to pay heavy taxes on its extensive properties, Ah Ji secured titles as government scholars for Xu Kuan and Xu Hong, which exempted the family from some of the taxes.

Mistress Yen, on her part, arranged the nuptials for Ah Ji's son. Observing that the old man was getting on in years, she would not hear of him going out to do business anymore, but kept him at home as overseer and assigned a horse for him to ride. Even after he had begun making money for the family, Ah Ji had never indulged excessively in food or drink. Nor did he splurge on good clothing, but obtained Mistress Yen's approval before using any silk or cotton cloth. Abiding by the rules of etiquette, he would rise to his feet whenever members of the clan, young or old, entered the room, and dismount from his horse when he was on the road to let them pass first before going on his way. Hence, relatives and neighbors far and near held him in great esteem, and even Mistress Yen and her sons regarded him as a respected elder.

As for the brothers Xu Yan and Xu Zhao, they too acquired some more land and property, but nowhere near as much as Mistress Yen, and their eyes were often green with envy and their necks red with mortification. Knowing full well what was on their minds, the old man advised Mistress Yen to present each of them with a hundred taels of silver. He also had a new family tomb constructed, and Xu Zhe and his parents were laid to rest therein.

The old man lived until he was eighty years of age. Mistress Yen wished to send for a physician when he fell ill, but Ah Ji said, "Now that I have lived to eighty, it is my lot to die. Do not waste any money on me." And he flatly refused to take any medications. Mistress Yen and her sons came frequently to his bedside. They also prepared a coffin and burial garments for him.

After a few days of illness, Ah Ji, knowing he would not live much longer, asked Mistress Yen and her sons to come to his room. When they had seated themselves, he said, "This old slave has rendered faithful service and will die without regrets. But I before I do so, I would presume to offer a few suggestions. Please do not take offense!"

Tears streamed from Mistress Yen's eyes as she replied, "It is to you that my sons and I owe the life we now enjoy. We will obey whatever instructions you propose to give us."

The old man took two sheets of paper from beside his pillow and handed them to Mistress Yen. He then said, "The two young masters are grown men now and will some day request a share of the family property. Any argument over who should get what and how much is bound to hurt the ties of affection within the family. I have therefore made out a division of all the land, houses and valuables. These lists I now entrust to the safekeeping of the two young masters." As he did so, he cautioned them, "There are not many good people among the servants, so keep a careful eye on all matters and do not place too much trust in others."

Mistress Yen and her sons listened to his instructions with tears in their eyes. Ah Ji then addressed words of advice to his wife and son, who were also sobbing at his bedside.

Suddenly, Ah Ji said, "I have not yet bade farewell in person to the First Master and Second Master, and that is, after all, an omission. Please ask them to come." Mistress Yen dispatched a servant with an invitation.

The brothers, however, responded with the words, "Balderdash! He would not help us when he was in good health, and only thinks of us on his deathbed. We will not go!" The servant could do naught but return alone, whereupon Mistress Yen sent her youngest son, Xu Hong, to invite his uncles. Xu Yan and Xu Zhao could hardly reject a personal invitation from their own nephew, so they grudgingly came with him. By the time they arrived, however, Ah Ji was no longer able to speak. He looked at them, nodded, and quietly passed away.

His wife, son, and daughter-in-law wept, and even Mistress Yen and her sons wailed in deep sorrow. In fact, everyone in the household, whether old or young or man or woman, shed tears in memory of the kindnesses Ah Ji had performed for them—all except Xu Yan and Xu Zhao, who instead wore expressions of malicious glee. And thus died Ah Ji.

> *Like the diligent silkworm that spins the cocoon,*
> *And expires when the silk is unwound for the loom.*
> *Like the bee that takes honey from flowers in bloom,*
> *But whose sweetness is gathered for other men's boon.*

After a while, Mistress Yen and her sons left to make preparations for the funeral.

When Xu Yan and Xu Zhao saw the sturdy coffin and the elegant bedclothes and garments for the deceased, they drew their nephews aside and objected, saying, "He is but a servant of the family, and a passable funeral will do. Why go to such expense? Even your grandfather and father did not have such fine things when they died!" Xu Kuan replied, "Our family owes its prosperity to Ah Ji. Our consciences will not allow us to treat him shabbily!"

Xu Zhao laughed, "You are a grown man now, yet such a dolt! It is your mother's good luck that brought you this fortune, not his adroitness! And another thing. He has done business for many years and must have skimmed off a sizable sum for himself as insurance for his old age. So why should you carve money from your own flesh to pay for his burial?" Xu Hong protested, "Do not make such unfounded accusations! I have always seen him account to my mother for every bit of money passing through his hands, and never has he had a private hoard."

Xu Zhao sneered, "Would he let you see his private hoard if he had one hidden away? Since you do not believe me, go to his room and search it! I wager you will find at least a thousand taels of silver." Xu Kuan demurred, saying, "Even if he had that much, he earned it. Are you suggesting that we should take it away?" Xu Yan replied, "Not necessarily, but it will do no harm to clarify the matter."

Befuddled by their uncles' insinuations, the nephews agreed, and, without informing Mistress Yen, the four went together to Ah Ji's chamber. And having found an excuse to make the family depart, they shut the door and ransacked all the chests and boxes. All they found were some old clothes; there was no silver at all in the room. Xu Zhao then said, "It must be hidden in his son's room. Let us look there, too." There they found a bag containing less than two taels of silver as well as an account book. Upon examining the book, Xu Kuan learned that the silver was what remained of the three taels Mistress Yen had presented to Ah Ji's son on his wedding day.

Xu Hong said, "I told you he had no private savings, but you would insist on carrying out this search! We had best put the rooms back in order quickly, for we would look petty-minded indeed if someone were to happen upon us now!" Feeling very much put out, the uncles departed without even taking leave of Mistress Yen.

Mistress Yen was greatly distressed when the young brothers recounted this incident to her. She issued orders forthwith that the entire household put on mourning attire and held a public funeral ceremony to which all the villagers were invited and at which lavish tribute was paid to Ah Ji's faithful services. After the conclusion of the seven-times-seven days of mourning, Ah Ji was laid to rest beside the new Xu family tomb. All the burial rites and ceremonies were conducted with greater extravagance than would normally have been required.

The young brothers, mindful of Ah Ji's loyalty and diligence, and knowing now that he had amassed no savings of his own, could no longer bring themselves to regard his wife and son as household servants. After the funeral ceremonies they presented Ah Ji's family with property and wealth worth approximately one thousand taels of silver so that they could set up their own household.

Meanwhile, the local gentry jointly signed a petition in which they requested that Ah Ji be officially commended. The county authorities rewrote the petition as a report to the higher authorities, who in turn submitted it to the imperial court. The court thereupon decreed that a ceremonial arch be constructed and dedicated to Ah Ji's loyalty.

Thereafter, the Xu family had many sons and grandsons and became the richest clan in the country. Ah Ji's descendants, too, multiplied and prospered.

Judge Qiao Mismatches the
Mandarin Ducks

A marriage is predestined during the previous lives of the man and the woman and, in general, may not be changed by human intervention. The following story is about two matches, unforeseen by fate, that took place in Hangzhou Prefecture during the Jingyou reign of the Song Dynasty.

There lived in Hangzhou at the time a physician whose name was Liu Bingyi and who was known to all as Liu the Elder. His wife's maiden name was Dan, and they had two children. One of them, Liu Pu, a remarkably handsome boy in his teens, had been betrothed to Zhuyi, daughter of Widow Sun. Liu Pu had assiduously studied the classics since he was a child and was already quite an accomplished scholar. When he turned sixteen, his father Liu Bingyi wanted him to lay aside his books and learn the physician's trade. Liu Pu, however, was set on becoming a great scholar and refused to switch to a practitioner's calling. Liu the Elder's other child, a daughter whose childhood name was Huiniang, had just turned fifteen and had been engaged to the son of Pei the Ninth, the owner of an apothecary nearby. Exquisite of complexion and carriage, Huiniang was considered to be a girl of extraordinary beauty.

Now Liu the Elder, deeming his son to have grown up, talked with his wife, and the two thought it time to complete preparations for the boy's marriage. As they were waiting for the matchmaker to discuss the details of the marriage with the Sun family, the apothecary Pei the Ninth sent his matchmaker to arrange for Huiniang's wedding with his own son. Liu the Elder said to this matchmaker, "Please explain to our Pei in-laws that our daughter is still young and we have yet to assemble her trousseau, so more time will be needed. We will be able to attend to the girl's affairs only after our son's marriage has been consummated. There is definitely no way we can fulfill his request at the present moment." The matchmaker conveyed Liu's words to the Pei family.

It so happened that Pei the Ninth, the apothecary, had acquired his one and only son quite late in life, and he cherished the boy as he would prize a precious jewel. His greatest hope was to see the youngster grow up as quickly as a tree caressed by warm winds—to see him marry and have children without delay. He was therefore highly displeased with Liu the Elder for putting off the marriage. Consequently, he asked the matchmaker to go again to the Liu family with the message, "Your daughter, already fifteen years old, cannot be considered too young. Once she marries into my family, we will treat her like our own daughter, and I vow she will not feel ill-used. As for the size of her trousseau, we leave that to your discretion and will not haggle over it. We only hope you will accede to our request." But Liu the Elder refused to do so, since he had made up his mind that his son should marry before his daughter. So Pei the Ninth had no other choice but to wait. Had Liu the Elder agreed to the marriage, much fuss and pother would have been averted. Indeed, it was Liu's obstinacy that was the cause of the story that has been told and retold to this day.

Having refused the Pei family's request, Liu the Elder asked his matchmaker, Sixth Sister Zhang, to go to the Sun family to complete the arrangements for his son's marriage. Madame Sun, whose maiden name was Hu, had married Sun Heng, the scion of an old and venerable household, when she was sixteen. They first had a daughter, whom they named Zhuyi, and a year later a son to whom they gave the name Sun Ruen and the pet name Yulang. The father died while both children were still in swaddling clothes, and since the young widow was a chaste woman, she refused to marry again and brought up her children with the assistance of a nanny. She was thus known to all as Widow Sun.

As time passed and Widow Sun's two children grew up, the daughter Zhuyi was betrothed to the Liu family, whereas Yulang had since childhood been promised the hand of Wenge, daughter of the painter Xu Ya. Both Zhuyi and Yulang were of extremely pleasing appearance, as though cut from jade and fashioned from the finest of white rice flour. The two were also quite intelligent, the boy being a good student of books and the girl excelling at needlework and embroidery. And, as though talent and appearance were not yet enough, both were also most dutiful to their mother and devoted one to the other.

But let us get on with our story.

Sixth Sister Zhang proceeded to the Sun family home and transmitted Liu the Elder's message with regard to choosing an auspicious day for the wedding. Widow Sun and her daughter were deeply attached one to the other and would have preferred to stay together a bit longer. But the widow knew how important it was to see her children properly married, so she agreed and said to Sixth Sister Zhang, "Reply to my prospective in-laws that I am a widow with two orphans. There will be no large trousseau for my girl's marriage; merely a few simple, everyday cotton garments. I hope they will not find fault with us." Sixth Sister Zhang took this reply back to Liu the Elder, whereupon the Lius prepared a gift of eight boxes filled with confections and fruit, selected an auspicious date, and had these conveyed to the Sun family. Widow Sun agreed to the date and hastened to make ready her daughter's trousseau. Now that the wedding date was drawing near, the mother and the daughter, both loath to be parted one from the other, all day went about their business with tears in their eyes.

Quite unexpectedly, however, Liu Pu, the bridegroom, exposed himself to a chill wind while in a sweat and was struck down with an ague, as a consequence of which he lost consciousness and lay on the verge of death. All the medications administered to him might well have been poured on stones for all the good they did. Witch doctors and fortune-tellers were consulted, but all averred there was no hope for the boy. His parents were frightened out of their wits and wept softly as they sat by their son's bed. Liu the Elder said to his wife, "Our son's illness is too grave for the nuptials to take place. I think it would be best to ask the Suns to defer the ceremony and set another date after he recovers."

Mother Liu replied, "Old man, you have lived long enough to know what should be done in such circumstances. Many seriously ill persons can be brought back to health by a happy wedding. Why, even those who are not yet affianced look for someone to marry! I see no call to defer our son's wedding since the matter has already been decided." Liu the Elder said doubtfully, "From the looks of our son's illness, the signs are not good. It would, of course, be a great joy to us if his marriage gives him back his health. But should he fail to recover, we shall have harmed the girl, since she could only remarry as a widow." Mother Liu remonstrated, "Old man, why do you not think for us instead of for other people? You and I have expended too much time and money on finding a wife for our son, and it is indeed a stroke of bad luck that he should fall ill just before the nuptials. Now, if we defer the wedding and our son eventually recovers his health, all will be well and nothing more will need to be said. But if,

Heaven forbid, the worst should happen, we would be at the Suns' mercy and could count them as honest people if they gave us back even half of the betrothal gifts. We would lose both the girl and our money." Liu the Elder asked, "So what should we do?"

Mother Liu replied, "In my opinion, we should instruct Sixth Sister Zhang not to mention our son's illness and have her bring the girl to our house. We shall then treat the girl as a prospective daughter-in-law adopted into the family and choose a date to consummate the marriage after our son recovers his health. In the case that he fails to recover and the girl remarries, we can let her go after charging the other party the full price of the original betrothal fee we paid for her, plus all our other expenses. That, I believe, will best serve our interests." Liu the Elder had ears of cotton, so he agreed to his wife's proposal and hastily enjoined Sixth Sister Zhang not to tell anyone about their son's condition.

As the old saying goes, "If you do not wish other people to know what you do, do not do it!" Even as Liu the Elder tried to keep the truth from the Suns, however, he failed to reckon with his next-door neighbor, a man named Li Rong who had once managed considerable stores of money for various parties and was nicknamed "Mind-All Li." A wily and disreputable character, Mind-All Li found pleasure in prying into and gossiping about other people's private business. Moreover, having made some money through dubious practices as a money manager, and residing as he did next to Liu the Elder, he had more than once attempted to purchase Liu's house. Liu the Elder had rejected his offers, and the two families had never gotten along well. Indeed, Mind-All Li hoped the Liu family would encounter bad luck so that he could gloat over their misfortunes. On learning that Liu Pu had fallen critically ill, he was elated and hastened to inform the Suns. The news greatly alarmed Widow Sun. Concerned lest her future son-in-law's condition affect her daughter's future, she asked the nanny to summon Sixth Sister Zhang and questioned her about the matter.

Sixth Sister Zhang did not know what to say. She was afraid that Widow Sun would not forgive her if Liu Pu died, but she also feared that the Lius would hold it against her if she disclosed the truth. Caught in this dilemma, she started to speak, but stopped in mid-sentence. Widow Sun saw her hesitation and pressed her all the harder. Knowing she could not hide the truth any longer, Sixth Sister Zhang temporized, "He has caught a cold, but it is not serious. I am sure he will have recovered by the day of the wedding." Not satisfied, Widow Zhang said, "But I have heard his illness is most grievous. Why would you make light of it? This is no joking matter. I have borne much hardship to bring up my children and they are more precious to me than jewels. I will fight you to the death if I find you have trifled with my daughter's future. And when that happens, do not say that I failed to warn you!"

Widow Sun continued, "Go to the Liu's and, should the boy indeed be seriously ill, ask them if it would not be better to wait till he recovers before setting a date for the wedding. After all, both the boy and the girl are still young and there is no hurry. As soon as you have their answer, come back and report to me!"

Sixth Sister Zhang was about to leave with these instructions, when Widow Sun called her back again, saying, "I know you will not tell me the truth. I am ordering the nanny to go with you to find out what is transpiring." Reluctant to have the nanny accompany her, Sixth Sister Zhang quickly replied, "That will not be necessary. I shall not fail you." But Widow Sun would have none of it. She gave the nanny some instructions, then sent her off with Sixth Sister Zhang.

On the way, Sixth Sister Zhang attempted again but failed to shake off the nanny, so she had no choice but to take her along to the Liu's house. As they arrived, Liu the Elder happened to walk out of the gate. Sixth Sister Zhang knew the nanny had never met Liu the Elder, so she said to her, "Wait for me here. I must make some inquiries." Quickly accosting Liu the Elder, she drew him aside and recounted to him what Widow Sun wished to know, adding, "She does not trust me, so she sent the nanny with me to verify my report. How should we reply to her questions?" Disconcerted by the nanny's presence, Liu the Elder complained, "Why did you not prevent her from coming with you?" Sixth Sister Zhang replied, "I tried to dissuade her, but she would not listen. What else could I do? You had best ask her in and have her wait while you decide with your wife what to tell her. Do not leave me to take the blame!"

Before she had finished speaking, however, the nanny walked up to them. Sixth Sister Zhang hurriedly explained, "This is Liu the Elder." The nanny bowed her respects. Liu the Elder returned her greetings, saying,

"Please come inside." When the three had entered the parlor, Liu the Elder told Sixth Sister Zhang, "Keep this young woman company while I go and ask my wife to come out." Sixth Sister Zhang replied, "We await your pleasure, sir."

Liu the Elder hastened to the inner chambers and told his wife everything that had happened. He said, "The nanny is right out there. What shall we say to her? What if she demands to come in and see the boy? How can we disguise his condition? Would it not be best to change the date and be done with it?" Mother Liu snapped, "Do not be such a dolt! They have accepted the bride price, so the girl belongs to our family now. What is there to fear! Do not panic, there is always a solution." She then told their daughter, Huiniang, "Go straighten up the bridal chamber. I shall ask the Suns' nanny to partake of some refreshments there." Huiniang did as she was told.

Then Mother Liu went to greet the nanny, saying, "It is good of you to come to our humble abode. Is there something our in-law wishes to tell us?" The nanny replied, "Our mistress has heard that your young master is unwell. She is concerned and has sent this person to inquire about his health. Also, she wishes me to say to Master and Mistress that, should the young master be recovering from an illness, his health might not be able to support the exertions of a wedding. In that case it would be better to defer the occasion and choose a date after the young master has fully recovered."

Mother Liu replied, "We are grateful for our in-law's concern. The young master has indeed been somewhat indisposed, but it is merely a cold and nothing more serious. As for choosing another date, that is absolutely out of the question, since ours is a small family business and it has cost us much effort to achieve our present circumstances. Putting off the wedding would mean a great deal more trouble and expense for us. Furthermore, for those who are unwell, a wedding is just the thing to dispel the humors that sicken them. In fact, many are those who choose to get married when they are feeling unwell. Besides, we have long since announced the happy event and invited all our relatives to the wedding banquet. Should we suddenly put it off, they will not believe it is your family's idea but will think we cannot afford to pay for the wedding. The word will get around, we shall become a laughingstock, and our good name will be ruined. So please go back to your mistress and tell her not to trouble herself about this matter. We take all responsibility upon ourselves!"

Reluctantly, the nanny said, "There is reason in what you have said. However, please tell me where the young master is resting. I wish to give him my regards. That way, I can report back to my mistress and set her mind at ease." Mother Liu replied, "He has just taken a perspiration-inducing potion and is sleeping at the moment. I shall convey your regards to him. The situation is exactly as I have described it to you and there is nothing more to be said."

Sixth Sister Zhang interjected, "I said it was nothing more serious than a cold, but your mistress would not believe me and made you come. Now you can see I was not lying." The nanny said, "Since that is the case, I shall bid you farewell." As she stood up to leave, however, Mother Liu cried, "Nothing doing! We have been so busy talking that you have not even had a cup of tea. I cannot let you leave like this!" She invited the nanny to the inner chambers, saying, "This room is quite untidy, so let us sit in the wedding chamber."

She led the way to the wedding chamber. The nanny observed that it was most tastefully appointed. Mother Liu continued, "You see? We have made everything ready. How could we agree to change the wedding date? However, the young master will remain in my room for the time being and share the bride's bed only after he is fully recovered."

The sight of the well-prepared bridal chamber finally convinced the nanny. Mother Liu instructed a maidservant to bring tea and refreshments and asked Huiniang to come and meet the nanny. When she saw the girl, the nanny could not help thinking, "I never thought I would see another girl just as exceptional as our Zhuyi, who is herself a most beautiful girl!" Emptying her cup of tea, she bade farewell and departed with Sixth Sister Zhang. As they were leaving, Mother Liu repeatedly enjoined the matchmaker, "Make sure to report back to me."

When the nanny, together with Sixth Sister Zhang, returned to the Suns' house, she related to her mistress all of the above. Widow Sun was nonplussed by what she heard. She thought, "If I agree to hold the wedding and my son-in-law is indeed seriously ill, or if worse happens, I fear I will be harming my daughter. But if I do not agree and my son-in-law eventually recovers his health, we may not find another auspicious wedding date." Unable to make up her mind, she said to Sixth Sister Zhang, "Allow me some time to think about the matter. You may come for my answer tomorrow morning." Sixth Sister Zhang replied, "Take your time, Mistress Sun. I will be here tomorrow morning." So saying, the matchmaker departed.

Widow Sun then conferred with her son, Yulang. She asked, "What, in your opinion, should we do?" Yulang replied, "It appears that he is gravely ill. That is why the nanny was not permitted to see him. Should we insist on changing the date of the wedding, they would have nothing to say and could only agree to do so. However, all their preparations would have been for naught and our family would appear to be lacking in good will. And should the fellow get well some day, any further encounters between our two families would be quite embarrassing. Yet if we let them have their way, I fear his health may further decline. And in that case, we would find ourselves in a dilemma since it would be too late to change our minds. However, I do have a plan that will meet both contingencies. Is Mother willing to hear it?" Widow Sun replied, "Tell me about this plan that will meet both contingencies."

Yulang said, "We shall ask Sixth Sister Zhang to tell them tomorrow morning that we agree to the date, but that my sister will not take along her trousseau. Three days after the ceremony, we shall bring my sister home, and then, when the fellow regains his health, we will send her back together with her trousseau. That way, we will not be subject to their dictates. Such is my plan." Widow Sun snorted, "Such childish reasoning! They may pretend to agree to this arrangement, but what shall we do if they refuse to let your sister go on the third day?" Baffled, Yulang replied, "Indeed, what shall we do?"

Widow Sun thought for a moment, and then said, "We could tell Sixth Sister Zhang to reply to them as you have proposed. When the time comes, however, your sister should conceal herself while you dress up as the bride and go in her stead. You would take along a set of men's garments in your clothes chest. Should they allow you to leave on the third day, all will be well. In the case that they do not let you leave, you could stay there and wait to see what happens. And if things turn out badly, you would put on the man's garments and come home. No one could stop you."

Yulang protested, "I can do anything else, but not this! What if other people found out eventually? How could I live this matter down?" Vexed by her son's refusal, Mother Liu replied, "Even if people did find out, it will be seen as a joking matter and no great harm will have been done!" Yulang was after all a filial son and, seeing his mother's anger, he hastened to say, "I shall go. However, I do not know how to arrange my hair." Mollified, Widow Sun said, "I shall have the nanny go with you as your servant." And thus the plan was set.

When Sixth Sister Zhang came the following morning for the reply, Mother Liu put forth her terms and concluded with the words, "If they agree, they may come for the bride. If not, we shall select another date." Sixth Sister Zhang took this message to the Lius who forthwith agreed to all the terms. And why did they agree? Liu Pu's condition was not improving and they feared the worst. However, if they managed to bring the bride to their house, the deal would be as good as done. This would, of course, merely be the best of a bad bargain, but they were in no mood now to argue the advantages and disadvantages. Little did they know that Widow Sun had seen through their scheme and would be sending them false merchandise.

Mother Liu, on her part, would fall victim to her own wiles.

When the wedding day came, Widow Sun dressed Yulang up as a girl. Indeed, the boy looked so much like her daughter that even the mother could hardly tell them apart. She had also taught him all the rules of etiquette a woman should know. Everything, in fact, was quite perfect but for two objects that were difficult to conceal and might betray him. For one, there were his feet, which did not resemble those of a woman. Women's lily feet are pointed and arched, like the heads of phoenixes, and they look as pretty as flowers when they peek out from under the woman's silken skirts. Yulang's feet were about three or four times larger than those of a woman. Even if they were to be covered by skirts that swept the ground and Yulang walked with short, mincing steps, as he had been instructed, something would still look odd. Fortunately, his feet were down below and would remain hidden unless someone lifted his skirts.

The other objects that would cause difficulty were earrings, which are worn by all women. Some prefer them small and dainty and may insert a pair of clove-shaped devices in their ears. But even women from the poorest families—those who cannot afford earrings of gold or silver—purchase a pair made of copper or tin. On that day, Yulang, disguised as a bride, would have his entire head bedecked with pearls and precious stones. Would it look right if he did not sport a pair of earrings? His left ear had been pierced during childhood as a token to avert misfortune, but his right earlobe had no hole in it. What to do? Cudgeling her brains, Widow Sun came up with an idea. Can you guess what it was? She told the nanny to bring a small poultice and apply it to Yulang's right ear. To the curious they would say that the ear hole was infected and could not support an earring. Thus, only his left ear would be adorned.

When the son had been dressed up, Widow Sun hid her daughter in a back room and waited for the bridal escort to arrive. As dusk approached, the sound of drums and music broke forth and the bridal sedan chair was borne to the front door. Sixth Sister Zhang was the first to enter the house and was greatly pleased when she saw the bride so gorgeously garbed. However, she did not see Yulang and asked, "Where is the young master?" Widow Sun replied, "He has suddenly become indisposed and is sleeping. He will not be up today." The matchmaker did not suspect anything, so she asked no more questions. Widow Sun regaled all members of the bridal escort with food and wine, the master of ceremonies read out a poem, and the bride was invited to mount the sedan chair. Yulang covered his face with a red bridal kerchief and bade his mother farewell. Pretending to shed tears, Widow Sun saw him out of the door and onto the sedan chair. Sixth Sister Zhang followed them, bearing a leather garment case but no trousseau. As the procession left, Widow Sun once again enjoined the matchmaker, "I have said that the bride must be sent back after three days. They must not break faith with me." Sixth Sister Zhang assured her, "Of course not, of course not!"

Now let us leave Widow Sun for the time being.

The bridal escort, heralded by the shrill music of flutes and pipes and a blaze of light from lanterns and torches, proceeded to the door of the Liu residence, and the master of ceremonies entered the house. Displeased, he announced, "The bride has arrived, yet the bridegroom has not come out to meet her. Must she perform the ritual bows all by herself?" Liu the Elder anxiously whispered to his wife, "What do we do now? Shall we cancel the bowing?" Mother Liu replied, "I have an idea. Let our daughter bow together with her."

Huiniang was thereupon told to go to the door and welcome the bride. The master of ceremonies pronounced the ceremonial salutations, and then invited the bride to dismount from the sedan chair. The bride emerged, supported one on each side by the nanny and the matchmaker. Huiniang stepped forward to meet the bride, and together they walked into the main hall. Here, they bowed, first to Heaven and Earth, and then to the groom's parents and relatives. Seeing that both of them were girls, the spectators covered their mouths and snickered. When all had been duly greeted, the sisters-in-law bowed to each other.

Mother Liu then commanded, "Let us now go inside and take the good news to our son to hasten his recovery." The musicians blew their pipes and banged their drums as they led the assemblage into the son's chamber and right up to his bed. Mother Liu lifted the canopy and called out, "My son, your bride has come to bring you joy and hasten your recovery. You should make an effort to buck up your spirits!" She repeated the words three or four times, without, however, hearing any response. Liu the Elder held up a lantern, only to see his son's head slumped to one side. The boy had fainted. Debilitated as he was by his long illness, the racket of drums and gongs had been too much for him.

The father and mother were thrown into confusion. Pinching the *renzhong* acupoint on his upper lip, they ordered that hot soup be brought. After a few spoonfuls of this had been administered to the boy, he broke into a sweat and regained consciousness. Mother Liu instructed her husband to keep an eye on their son while she took the bride to the wedding chamber. There, the bride's kerchief was removed, uncovering a visage as lovely as a painting. All the relatives uttered exclamations of admiration at the sight of such beauty. Mother Liu, however, was secretly unhappy. "This daughter-in-law is indeed good-looking and a perfect match for our son," she reflected. "Should we have the two of them to serve us in our old age, our labors will not have been wasted. But alas! Who would have known the boy would become so ill just before his wedding? The chances are that he may never recover, and in case he dies, this daughter-in-law will eventually belong to someone else! So what good does it do to rejoice now?"

Let us leave Mother Liu to her thoughts for the time being.

When Yulang looked up at the relatives gathered in the room, he was captivated by the uncommon beauty of the bridegroom's sister. "What a girl!" he thought. "It is a pity I, Sun Ruen, am already betrothed. Had I known this girl to be so comely, I would certainly have wanted her to be my wife." And while Yulang was admiring Huiniang, she too was thinking, "I did not believe Sixth Sister Zhang when she said the girl is very pretty, but now I see she was speaking the truth. It is unfortunate for my brother that he cannot enjoy her tonight and that she will have to sleep alone. I would be lucky to have a husband as handsome as she is comely, but that may not be possible!"

After Mother Liu had treated the guests to a wedding banquet, all repaired to their own homes. The master of ceremonies and the orchestra were paid off, and Sixth Sister Zhang also returned to her own home, as there were no extra accommodations for her. Yulang sat in the bridal chamber while the nanny helped him remove the decorations from his hair, then remained seated by the lighted candle, not daring to go to bed. To Liu the Elder, Mother Liu said, "Now that our daughter-in-law has arrived, it would not be right for her to sleep alone. I think our daughter should keep her company." Liu the Elder demurred, "That may not be convenient or appropriate. Let her sleep alone." However, Mother Liu would not listen. She told Huiniang, "Go to the bridal chamber and sleep with your sister-in-law tonight, so that she will not feel lonely." This accorded with Huiniang's own wishes, as she had conceived a liking for her sister-in-law, and she readily agreed.

Thereupon Mother Liu took Huiniang to the wedding chamber and said, "My girl, your husband is unwell and cannot share a bed with you, so I have asked my daughter to keep you company." Fearful that his true identity would be betrayed, Yulang protested, "I am shy with strangers, and I do not need any company." But Mother Liu would not be deterred. "Aiya! You and your sister-in-law are of the same age and will be like sisters. This is a good opportunity for you to become acquainted. What are you afraid of? If you think it inconvenient, the two of you can sleep under separate coverlets." She then said to Huiniang, "Go get your own coverlet!" Huiniang left the room to do so.

Yulang felt both apprehensive and delighted—delighted because he felt very much attracted to the beautiful girl, and Mother Liu's injunction that they should share a bed gave him a heaven-sent opportunity to dally with her. But he also was afraid that she might resist his advances and cry out, and thereby place him in jeopardy. Then he reflected, "I shall have little chance of seeing her again if I miss this opportunity. The girl appears to have come of age, and I'll wager she feels the first stirrings of sensuality. If I stoke those flames judiciously, I have no doubt she will let me have my way." As he was thinking these thoughts, Huiniang returned with a maidservant carrying a coverlet. And when this had been spread on the bed, Mother Liu and the maidservant together left the room.

Huiniang shut the door and, all smiles, approached Yulang, saying, "Sister-in-law, I have not seen you eating anything. Are you not hungry?" Yulang replied, "No, I feel no hunger as yet." Huiniang continued, "Sister-in-law, if you should ever need anything, just let me know and I shall fetch it for you. Do not be shy." Secretly delighted by her graciousness, Yulang replied, "Thank you for your kind intentions!" Then Huiniang noticed the flame of the candlewick flaring in the form of a large flower and smiled, exclaiming, "Do you see that flower? It is blooming for you, and that means today is your good day!" Yulang laughed and said, "Do not make fun of me. If this is a good day, it is yours!" Huiniang rejoined, "What a teaser you are!"

After the two had exchanged some more small talk, Huiniang proposed, "Sister-in-law, it is getting late. Let us retire." Yulang said, "You be the first." Huiniang protested, "I cannot get into bed before you do, as I am the hostess and you are the guest." Yulang declared, "In this room, you are the guest!" Laughing, Huiniang gave in and said, "All right, I shall be the first!" Taking off her clothes, she climbed onto the bed.

The nanny, who had heard the two bantering with each other, felt that Yulang was harboring improper intentions. "Young Master," she whispered. "You must be more circumspect. This is no joking matter. If Mother Liu finds out, I too shall suffer the consequences!" Yulang replied, "You need not remind me. I am aware of that. Now go to bed!" The nanny repaired to a corner of the room where she made her own pallet and lay down.

Yulang took a lamp to the bedside, drew aside the canopy and looked in. He saw Huiniang curled up under her coverlet on the far side of the bed. Huiniang smiled and said: "Sister–in–law, come to bed. What are you looking at with that lamp?" Yulang smiled in return, saying, "I wanted to see on which side you are sleeping, so that I may know where to lie down." Placing the lamp on the bedside table, Yulang unfastened his clothing and ducked under the canopy. He asked Huiniang, "May I sleep with my pillow beside yours, so that we may converse and have some fun?" Huiniang agreed, saying, "I would like that."

Yulang went under his coverlet and removed his upper garments, but kept on his nether underwear. That done, he asked Huiniang, "How old are you, Sister?" Huiniang replied, "I am fifteen." Yulang pursued, "To which family are you betrothed?" When Huiniang shyly refused to answer, Yulang moved his head onto her pillow and whispered, "We are both girls, there is no need to be shy about it." Huiniang replied, "It is to the Pei family, the one that has the herb store." Yulang then asked: "For which auspicious date has the wedding been set?" Huiniang whispered, "Lately they have sent the matchmaker several times to discuss this matter, but my father declares I am still young and has told them to wait a little longer." Yulang laughed, "Does that not fill you with frustration?" Huiniang thrust a hand out of her coverlet and pushed Yulang's head off her pillow, saying, "You are a bad person! You wormed that out of me only to tease me about it! If you think *I* feel frustrated, I wonder how frustrated *you* must be feeling tonight!" Moving his head back onto her pillow, Yulang asked, "Tell me, why should I feel frustrated tonight?" Huiniang replied, "Because you do not have a mate on your wedding night, so of course you feel frustrated." Yulang countered, "Having you here as my mate, why should I feel frustrated?" Huiniang laughed, "In that case, you are my wife!" Yulang declared, "I am the elder, so I should be the husband!" Huiniang demurred, "I participated in the wedding ceremony on behalf of my brother. I am my brother, so I am the husband!" Yulang said, "All right, all right, let us not argue. We are a female couple. How is that?" As they twitted and teased each other, they became more and more intimate.

Sensing that the right moment had come, Yulang suggested, "Since we are husband and wife, we might as well sleep under one coverlet." So saying, he lifted the edge of Huiniang's coverlet and slipped in with her. He began to stroke her body, which as smooth and soft as silk—although her lower parts were still clad in underclothes. By this time, Huiniang was so aroused by Yulang's attentions that she forgot herself and submitted to his caresses without a word of protest. Yulang's hand groped toward her chest, and there found two small breasts arching up resiliently like wads of cotton and tipped with lovable little nipples that felt like the heads of newly hatched chicks. Huiniang, too, stretched out a hand to touch Yulang's body. "What a sleek and supple body you have, sister-in-law!" she said. Feeling his chest, she found only two tiny nipples and thought to herself, "She is as old as I, so why are her breasts so small?"

Having fondled Huiniang for a while, Yulang put both arms around her, placed his mouth against hers, and inserted the tip of his tongue between her lips. Huiniang, believing this to be a sort of game, also wound her arms around Yulang and began to suck his tongue. Then she thrust her own tongue into his mouth, whereupon Yulang drew it in and sucked so hard on it that Huiniang's whole body tingled. "Sister-in-law," Huiniang gasped, "we are behaving more like a true husband and wife than a make-believe husband and wife." Observing that she was fully aroused now, Yulang said, "Let us go all the way. What say we remove our underclothes as well and lie together in complete intimacy?" Huiniang said doubtfully, "No, I think that would be too embarrassing." But Yulang would not be deterred. "What is there to be embarrassed about, since this is but a game?" He undid her undergarment, drew it down, and reached for her private parts. Huiniang fended him off with both hands, protesting, "Sister-in-law, please desist!" Whereupon Yulang took her face between his hands, kissed her on the lips, and said: "What wrong have I done? You may also touch me!"

Huiniang actually did remove his undergarment and reached out a hand. What it encountered was a jade shaft, erect and as stiff as an iron rod! Shocked, she hastily withdrew her hand and asked, "Who are you? And why are you here, feigning to be my sister-in-law?" Yulang replied, "I am your husband now, so do not ask so many questions!" With these words, he mounted her and attempted to spread her legs apart. Huiniang pushed him away, saying, "Tell me the truth, or I shall cry out and land you in great trouble!"

Disconcerted by this threat, Yulang quickly said, "Please remain calm and allow me to explain. I am your sister-in-law's brother, Yulang. We learned that your elder brother is gravely ill, and that the outcome is still in doubt. Under these circumstances, my mother was unwilling to let my sister be married, but neither did she wish to let your family's auspicious date slip by, so she sent me in my sister's stead. She will allow my sister to come only after your brother has recovered from his illness. Who could have imagined that Heaven would form another happy match and make you and me husband and wife?! However, only you and I must know. Do not reveal this matter to anyone!" With that, he rolled onto Huiniang again.

Huiniang had taken a fancy to him even when she believed him to be a girl. Now that he had turned out to be a man, she was exceedingly delighted. Besides, she had already been carried away by Yulang's amorous advances, and with feelings mixed of consternation and joy, neither repelling nor abetting Yulang, she said: "What a seducer you are!" Yulang was in no mood to talk any further. Clasping Huiniang in his arms, he gave vent to his passions.

One was a boy, having his first taste of love; the other a virgin, enjoying a sweet initiation. Some say this candlelight encounter cemented their union, that a night's tryst gave rise to the love 'twixt a man and a woman. Others aver that marriages are destined during one's previous life and that matchmakers serve no great purpose. Still others insist that a solemn pledge, once given, must never be forgotten. Be that as it may, the two gave rein to their desires, with no thought for either sisters or brothers. They were like a brace of butterflies dancing among flowers, like a pair of mandarin ducks disporting themselves in water.

After their passions were spent, they fell asleep in each other's arms.

Meanwhile the nanny, fearful that Yulang would be up to some mischief, lay on her pallet without shutting her eyes. At first she heard the two whispering and laughing, then there was only the creaking of the bed and the sound of labored breathing. She knew then that they had done that thing, and she inwardly groaned.

When everyone rose the next morning, Huiniang repaired to her mother's chamber to perform her morning ablutions. As the nanny helped Yulang comb his hair and apply makeup, she said in a low voice, "Young Master, you made me a promise last night, but failed to keep your word and did that thing! What will you do if you are found out?" Yulang protested, "I did not ask her to come. She offered herself to me, so how could I decline?" The nanny only said, "You had best think of something." Yulang muttered defensively, "Believe me! No man can stand it when a girl as beautiful as a flower shares the same bed with him, even were he made of stone! How could I resist the temptation?! In any case, if you keep quiet about this matter, no one will find out."

His makeup completed, Yulang went to pay his respects to Mother Liu. Staring at him, Mother Liu remarked, "You have forgotten to put on an earring." The nanny hastened to explain, "She has not forgotten. She cannot wear it and must apply a poultice because there is an infection on her right ear." Mother Liu said, "So that is the reason."

Yulang returned to the wedding chamber and sat there to receive female relatives of the family. Sixth Sister Zhang was also present. When Huiniang came in the room after completing her morning toilette, she and Yulang looked at each other and smiled. That day, Liu the Elder gave a celebratory banquet for both his own and his wife's relatives, with music and wine-drinking that lasted until evening. When the last guests had gone home, Huiniang once more joined Yulang in the bridal chamber. The two frolicked like a pair of amorous phoenixes and exchanged pledges of eternal devotion, their love having redoubled since the previous night. During the next three days, the two became so inseparable that the nanny could no longer contain her anxiety. She urged Yulang, "Tell Auntie Liu that three days have passed and you wish to go home!" However, Yulang, who was now passionately enamored of Huiniang, had no intention of going home. He prevaricated, "How can I myself say such a thing? It would be best that my mother asked Sixth Sister Zhang to notify them." The nanny replied, "I suppose you are right," and forthwith went back to the Sun's house.

We now go to Widow Sun. Beset with feelings of unease and guilt after sending her son in place of the bride, she waited on tenterhooks for Sixth Sister Zhang to report what was happening. So when the nanny returned, she quickly questioned the latter. The nanny related to her in detail how ill her son-in-law had become, how his sister had come out in his stead to greet the bride, and how the two had slept together and fallen for each other. Widow Sun stamped her feet and cried in consternation,

"They must have done it! Go quickly and look for Sixth Sister Zhang!" Before long, the nanny came back with Sixth Sister Zhang. Widow Sun said to her, "Sixth Sister, the other day you promised they would send the bride back in three days. That time has passed, so I will trouble you to ask the Lius to send my daughter back without delay." Sixth Sister Zhang agreed to do so and returned to the Lius' house with the nanny.

It so happened that Mother Liu was holding forth in Yulang's room when Sixth Sister Zhang came to say that Widow Sun wanted the bride returned. Unwilling to be separated, Yulang and Huiniang whispered to each other, "Let us hope she does not agree." And indeed, Mother Liu said, "Sixth Sister, you are an old matchmaker. Have you no common sense? Does a bride ever go home on the third day? At first, her mother would not let her come and I could do nothing at the time. But now that she is in my house, she belongs to my family and her mother has no more say in the matter. I went through thick and thin to find this bride for my son, and it is not right to take her back on the third day. If her mother is so chary about letting her daughter go, she should not have pledged out her troth in the first place. She, too, has a son who will be getting married. Would she let his bride go on the third day? I hear our in-law is not ignorant of the rules of etiquette, so how could she make such a request?"

Sixth Sister Zhang had nothing to say to this. Nor did she dare go back with such a reply. The nanny, on the other hand, was afraid someone would barge into the bridal chamber unannounced and discover what was transpiring between the two young people, so she stayed at the house to guard the door and did not go home either.

Meanwhile, Liu Pu, after having broken into a sweat on the evening the bride had arrived, was gradually recovering. Happy in the knowledge that his bride was now in the house and that she was so good looking, he felt better and better. After a few days, he managed to raise himself to a half-reclining, half-seated position on his bed and was able to comb and wash himself. He then demanded to go to the bridal chamber to see his wife. Fearing he might overtax his newly found strength, Mother Liu told the maidservant to support him while she herself followed behind. Thus the three slowly wended their way to the bridal chamber. To the nanny seated at the threshold the maidservant announced, "Let the Young Master in." The nanny at once sprang to her feet and cried in a loud voice, "The Young Master is coming in!"

Yulang, who at this moment was hugging and engaged in amorous play with Huiniang, quickly distanced himself. Liu Pu drew aside the door curtain and stepped into the room. Huiniang hurriedly said, "Brother, I am so glad you have been able to perform your ablutions, but you should not tire yourself so!" Liu Pu replied, "Do not worry, I shall be up for only a little while and shall soon return to bed." He made a deep obeisance to Yulang, who at once turned his back on Liu Pu and merely uttered a formal greeting. Mother Liu cried, "My son, leave the bowing till later!" Then, observing that Yulang was keeping his back turned, she remonstrated, "Young lady, this is your husband. He has regained his health and has come expressly to see you. Why do you keep your back turned?" She stepped forward and pulled Yulang around to face her son and said, "My son, you two make a handsome pair." Liu Pu became quite animated at the sight of his lovely wife. Truly, happy events invigorate both the spirit and the body! However, Mother Liu admonished him, "Go back to your bed, my son. Do not abuse your constitution." Thus Liu Pu, supported by the maidservant, left the room. Huiniang went with them.

Yulang had seen that Liu Pu, although ill, was a man of fine appearance, and said to himself, "He would make a good match for my sister." But then he reflected, "Now that my brother-in-law is recovering his health, he will wish to share a bed with me and the truth will be exposed. I must leave at once!" That night, he said to Huiniang, "Since your brother is getting better, I cannot stay any longer. Try to persuade your mother to let me go home. Then my sister can take my place and this matter can be kept secret. My true colors will certainly be exposed if I do not depart at once." Huiniang protested, "It is easy for you to go home, but what about my future?" Yulang replied, "I have turned the matter over and over in my mind. However, you are engaged to another person, and so am I. I see no way out. There is nothing we can do." Huiniang declared, "If you find no way of marrying me, I swear my ghost will forever follow you, for I have no face now to marry anyone else!" She started to sob aloud. Yulang brushed the tears from her cheeks, saying, "Do not worry about this matter now. Let me think some more." Thus, carried away by mutual endearments, the two put aside the subject of Yulang's going home. One day, when the nanny went to another part of the house after lunch, they closed and locked the door and discussed the matter again. But try as they might, they could find no solution, and in their despair and frustration they held each other and wept.

In the meantime, it had come to Mother Liu's attention that her daughter never left her daughter-in-law's side, since the latter's arrival. They would shut the door and go to bed early in the evening and rise only when the sun stood three bamboo sticks above the horizon. Mother Liu was quite displeased. At first she did not give the matter much thought since she assumed her daughter and daughter-in-law had formed a deep bond of affection. However, when the same thing happened day after day, suspicions grew in her mind. Still, she would tell herself that these young people were merely a pair of lazy sleepyheads. Several times she was about to voice her displeasure but desisted when she reflected that the daughter-in-law, having only recently come to the house and not yet shared a bed with her son, might still be regarded as a guest. So she kept her counsel.

Yet it is only to be expected that there would be trouble. One day, as Mother Liu was walking past the bridal chamber, she was surprised to hear the sound of sobbing inside. She peeped through an interstice in the wall partition and saw her daughter and daughter-in-law holding each other and crying softly. Mother Liu sensed at once that something odd was going on. She was on the verge of flying into a rage, but restrained herself when she reflected that her son had barely recovered his health and would be greatly disturbed if he heard the commotion. She drew aside the door curtain, only to find the door tightly shut. So she called, "Open the door at once!" Hearing her voice outside, Yulang and Huiniang quickly dried their tears and unlocked the door.

Mother Liu burst in, asking, "Why are you hugging each other and crying behind locked doors in broad daylight?" The two young people grew red in the face and had nothing to say. Observing that they remained silent, Mother Liu knew now that something was greatly amiss. Her hands and feet grew numb with apprehension. Seizing Huiniang by the arm she cried, "What have you been up to? Come, I must have a word with you!" She dragged Huiniang toward an unoccupied room at the back of the house. The maidservant saw them coming and, fearing the worst, quickly ducked around a corner. Mother Liu pulled Huiniang into the room and bolted the door.

The maidservant, peering through a crack in the door, saw Mother Liu pick up a stick and yell, "You little sneak! Tell me the truth and I shall not beat or scold you. But try to hide anything, and I shall thrash your bottom to a pulp!" Huiniang at first denied that anything had happened, but Mother Liu shouted, "You cheap little slut! Let me ask you. Why is it that, so soon after she arrived, you and that girl became so inseparable? And why were you hugging and crying with the door locked?" When Huiniang could not reply, Mother Liu raised the stick to hit her yet had not the heart to do so.

Huiniang knew now that she could not hide the truth any longer. She thought to herself, "Since things have gotten this far, I might as well make a clean breast of the matter. I shall beg my father and mother to dismiss my betrothal to the Pei family and marry me to Yulang. If they refuse, I shall simply end my own life." So she said aloud, "When the Sun family learned that my brother was ill, they feared their daughter's future would be compromised and wished to see how things would turn out, consequently they asked father and you to choose another date. However, you refused their request, so they sent their son Yulang in his sister's stead. Then you had me keep him company, and we coupled as a man and a woman. We now love each other deeply and have pledged to remain together for the rest of our lives. Now that brother has recovered from his illness, Yulang fears he will be discovered and wants to go home and have his sister replace him. As I see it, one woman should not be with two men, and I have asked Yulang to find some way to take me as his wife. But he is unable to devise a plan, and we cannot bear to be parted from each other, which is why you found the two of us crying. That is the whole truth of the matter."

When Mother Liu heard this, she was filled with fury. Flinging aside the stick, she stamped her feet and ranted, "So that deceitful old beggar woman has cheated me by sending a man instead of a woman! No wonder she wanted the bride back on the third day! And now that fellow has ruined my daughter! I will not let him off so easily! I will get even with that carrion even if it costs me my old life!" She threw open the door to leave the room. Frantic with fear that her mother would beat up her beloved, Huiniang cast aside all decorum and attempted to seize her mother by the arm. Mother Liu shoved her aside, and she fell to the ground. By the time she had picked herself up, Mother Liu had rushed out of the room. Huiniang followed on her mother's heels with the maid-servant in close pursuit.

Meanwhile, when Mother Liu dragged Huiniang out of the bridal chamber, Yulang knew that his subterfuge was blown. As he waited in the room, distraught with anxiety, the nanny hurried in, crying, "Bad news, Young Master! Something has gone wrong! As I was coming from the back of the house I heard a loud commotion in one of the rooms. I peeped in and saw Mother Liu belaboring the Young Mistress with a big stick and questioning her about you." On learning that Huiniang was being beaten, Yulang felt as though a knife were being twisted in his heart and tears sprang from his eyes. As he stood there wondering what to do, the nanny said, "Disaster will befall us if we do not leave at once!" Yulang forthwith snatched the jeweled ornaments from his head and wound up his hair like a man's. He then opened his leather chest, drew out articles of male attire, dressed himself in these, and walked out of the bridal cham-ber, closing the door behind himself. He and the nanny left the Lius' house and, running and stumbling, made their way back home.

Widow Sun was happy to see her son coming home, but his evident haste and trepidation perturbed her. She asked, "Why are you in such a state?" And after the nanny recounted all that had happened, she cried angrily, "I sent you there merely as a temporary expedient. Why did you have to do such an outrageous thing? Had you returned on the third day, the matter would not have turned out so badly and might have passed unnoticed. Sixth Sister Zhang, that despicable old baggage, never came back to report to me after that day! And you, Nanny, you did not come back either and left me to stew day and night! Now the worst has hap-pened, and their daughter has been ruined. How shall I face them? What use do I have for such a no-good son!" As Yulang hung his head, fright-ened and shamed by his mother's wrathful recriminations, the nanny explained, "The Young Master did say he wanted to come home, but Mother Liu would not hear of it. I feared the young people would get into trouble, so I kept watch at their door and did not dare leave the Lius' house. It was only when I went to the back of the house today that

Mother Liu barged in on them. Fortunately we were able to escape before anything worse could take place. Perhaps the Young Master should go into hiding for a few days. With good fortune, we might not hear anything more from the Lius." For lack of a better idea, Widow Sun instructed her son to lie low, and then braced herself for further news from the Liu family.

Meanwhile, back at the Liu's house, Mother Liu saw that the door was shut when she came to the bridal chamber. Thinking that Yulang was still inside, she shouted: "Open up, you confounded little wretch! Who do you think I am, that you dare dupe me and ruin my daughter? I am here to pit my life against yours, and you shall see what I am capable of doing! Come out at once, else I shall force my way in!" As she was cursing and yelling, Huiniang arrived and tried to hold her mother back. Mother Liu scolded, "You cheap little hussy, have you no shame, that you dare dissuade me?" She wrenched herself away from Huiniang but exerted so much strength that both of them fell against the door. The door flew open, and both mother and daughter staggered in and collapsed in a heap on the floor. Mother Liu yelled, "You fit-to-be-killed scoundrel, now you have made this old mother take a fall!" Scrambling to her feet, she looked around for Yulang but saw no sign of him. When a further search proved fruitless, she remarked, "That scoundrel knows what is best for him. He is gone! However, I will run him down even if he flies up into the skies!" To Huiniang, she said, "Now that you have done this disgraceful thing, how will you face up to the Peis if they find out?" Huiniang replied tearfully, "I was wrong and have committed an error. However, I beg you to take pity on me. Persuade my father to think of some way of dismissing my betrothal to the Peis and marry me to Yulang, so that I might redeem my good name. Should you refuse to do so, all I can do is die!" Sobbing, she crouched on the floor.

Mother Liu said, "That is more easily said than done! The Peis have paid money for your betrothal and believe they have a daughter-in-law. Do you think they will cancel the arrangement so easily? If they ask about the reason for doing so, what will your father say? Can he tell them his daughter went and found a man by herself?" Shamed by her mother's words, Huiniang covered her face with her sleeves and wailed grievously.

Mother Liu, after all, cared for her daughter with the instinctive love of a female for her young, and she feared her daughter's health might suffer if she kept on weeping in such a manner. She said, "My child, you are not to blame. It is the fault of that old widow and her evil machinations. It is she who sent her fit-to-be-killed pup disguised as the bride. I, unknowingly, had you keep him company, and you fell for his wiles. Fortunately, no one else knows about this. We shall set the matter aside to save your reputation. That is best in the long run. However, there is absolutely no way your betrothal to the Peis can be dismissed or that you will marry that scoundrel." Seeing that her mother would not relent, Huiniang cried all the harder. Mother Liu felt sorry for the girl but angry at the same time, and was at loss what to do.

As this was going on, Liu the Elder came home after seeing some patients. As he passed by the bridal chamber, he heard the sound of weeping and his wife berating someone, and wondered what was happening. Curious, he drew aside the door curtain, asking, "What is the matter with you?" When Mother Liu told him everything that had happened, Liu the Elder was speechless with anger. After a moment's reflection, he began to reproach Mother Liu, saying, "You old crone, you are to blame for our daughter's misfortune! I wanted to change the marriage date when our son became ill, but you raised all sorts of objections and stubbornly refused to do so. Then Widow Sun sent the nanny to parley with us, and I would have consented, yet you again clacked that scurrilous tongue of yours and insisted on having your own way. When the bride arrived at our house, I told you to let her sleep alone, but you had to have our daughter keep her company. And such good company that was!"

Already in a vile mood because Yulang had escaped and because she felt sorry for her daughter, Mother Liu needed to let off steam. Now that her husband was shifting all the blame on her, she flew into a towering rage and cursed, "You old turtle, are you trying to say our daughter deserved to be cheated by that scoundrel?" She lowered her head and butted his chest. Seizing her, Liu the Elder furiously began to punch her. And when Huiniang tried to intercede, the three became embroiled in a tangle of arms and legs.

Frightened, the maidservant ran to Liu Pu's room and reported, "Young Master, come quickly! The Master and Mistress have come to blows in the bridal chamber!" Liu Pu clambered out of bed and went to settle the altercation. Seeing that their son was trying to pull them apart and concerned lest his health be impaired, the elderly couple finally stopped flailing at each other. However, they continued to hurl invective, insulting each other with names such as "old turtle" and "old crone." Liu Pu persuaded his father to leave the room, then asked his sister, "Why is everyone fighting here, and where is my wife?" Overcome with feelings of guilt, Huiniang covered her face and sobbed but dared not reply. Liu Pu impatiently inquired, "Who can tell me what is happening?" Only then did Mother Liu relate to him the whole course of events.

Liu Pu grew livid with anger. After a long while, he said, "This family shame must not be made public. If it becomes known, we shall be everybody's laughingstock. What has happened, has happened. We shall see what can be done about it." Mother Liu held her tongue and walked out of the room. Huiniang wished to remain there, but Mother Liu pulled her away and affixed a huge lock on the door. So the girl returned to her own room and, feeling disgraced, sat in a corner and sobbed.

Mind-All Li had heard much shouting in the Liu residence and pressed an ear against the wall to eavesdrop. He could tell that something was up, but the details escaped him. The next morning, when the maidservant came out of the gate, he called her to his house and questioned her. At first the maidservant was unwilling to say anything, but Mind-All Li counted out forty or fifty coins and wheedled, "If you tell me, you can have these to buy some goodies." Unable to resist the temptation, the maidservant took the coins, secreted them in her clothing, and recounted to Mind-All Li all that had transpired. Greatly elated, Mind-All Li thought, "If I report this scandal to the Pei family and egg them on, they will surely come to raise a ruckus, and the Lius will feel too ashamed to live here any longer. That house will be mine!"

He hurried over to the Peis and related to them all he had learned, adding details of his own invention to stoke their anger. Pei and his wife were already displeased by the Lius' refusal to set an early date for their son's wedding, and now they truly lost their temper when they heard about their daughter-in-law's scandalous behavior. Making straight for the Liu's house, Pei the Ninth called out Liu the Elder and shouted, "When I asked the matchmaker to see you about the wedding, you raised all sorts of objections. You said your daughter was still too young and would not agree to consummate the marriage. Yet all this time you have kept her at home and allowed her to conduct an affair with another man. This would never have happened if you had agreed to my request! Ours is a respectable household and I do not want that trash to sully our good name. Give me back the betrothal gifts at once, find her another man, and do not stand in the way of my son's happy event!"

As Pei the Ninth yelled, Liu the Elder's face paled and reddened by turns. He thought, "Those things happened at my house only just yesterday, so how did he find out about it already? This is strange!" He could not very well admit the truth, however, so he prevaricated, saying, "Dear in-law, what are you talking about? Why do you use such language to vilify my family? If other people hear you saying such things and believe you, where shall I hide my face?"

Pei the Ninth shouted, "You cheap scoundrel! You old turtle! Everyone knows about your daughter's scandalous behavior, yet you have the gall to tell me this bare-faced lie!" He stepped forward and poked Liu the Elder in the face, saying, "Have you no shame, you old turtle? Let me put a ghost's mask on you, the better for you to delude people."

Outraged by this insult, Liu the Elder swore, "You old fit-to-be-killed! Why do you come today to bully me like this?" He lowered his head and butted Pei so hard the latter tumbled to the ground. The two then began to brawl. Mother Liu and Liu Pu heard the commotion and came out to find out what was happening. Seeing Liu the Elder and Pei the Ninth engaged in fisticuffs, they hurried forward to pull them apart. Pei the Ninth pointed a finger at Liu the Elder and shouted, "You hit me, you old turtle! Fine! I shall see you at the yamen!" He then left, swearing loudly.

Liu Pu asked his father, "Why did Pei the Ninth come so early in the morning to pick a quarrel?" Liu the Elder told them what Pei the Ninth had said, whereupon Liu Pu mused, "How did he learn about those things? This is most strange." He continued, "What shall we do, now that this matter has become public knowledge?"

Still smarting from Pei the Ninth's insults, Liu the Elder turned his wrath on the Suns, averring, "This is all that old beggar woman Sun's fault! She has damaged our family's name and brought this evil down on our heads. I must sue her, otherwise I shall never live down this affront!" Liu Pu attempted to dissuade his father, but to no avail.

Liu the Elder asked someone to write out a complaint on his behalf, and then proceeded to the prefectural yamen where Judge Qiao was presiding over the morning's hearings. This judge came from another region, but he was a just and fair-minded person of considerable intelligence. He also had a fondness for talent and sympathized with the common people, and his judgments were god-like in their perspicacity. Everyone in the prefecture called him "Clear Sky Qiao."

Just as Liu the Elder arrived at the gate of the yamen, he came face to face with Pei the Ninth who had come to lodge his own complaint. On seeing Liu the Elder also with a complaint in his hands, Pei the Ninth assumed that Liu was suing him, and he shouted, "You old turtle! Your daughter does bad things, yet you come to sue me? We shall go in together to see the judge!" He seized Liu by the arm, and the two started to fight again. Both their written complaints were lost during the scuffle. They entered the courtroom, still grappling with each other. Judge Qiao ordered them to kneel down separately, one on each side of the room, and then asked, "What are your names? And why are you fighting like that?" When both started yelling at the same time, Judge Qiao snapped, "One at a time! Let the older one speak first!"

Pei the Ninth advanced on his knees and said, "This humble person's name is Pei the Ninth. I have one son, whose name is Pei Zheng, and who was engaged to Liu the Elder's daughter Huiniang when the two were quite young. Both are now fifteen years of age. My son was born when I was already quite advanced in years, and I wished to see his marriage consummated as soon as possible. Several times I asked the matchmaker to talk to the Liu the Elder about the wedding, but Liu the Elder arrogantly refused my request, insisting that his daughter was still too young. Yet he indulged the sexual escapades of his daughter who fell in love with Sun Ruen, and even brought the boy in secret to their house. Now he wants to repudiate the marriage agreement. I went this morning to talk to him about the matter, but he manhandled and insulted me instead. Driven beyond forbearance, I came before Your Honor's tribunal to seek redress, but he followed me and beat me up again. I beg Your Honor to uphold my rights and protect me."

After hearing him out, Judge Qiao ordered Pei the Ninth to stand down, called Liu the Elder forward, and asked, "What do you have to say?"

Liu the Elder presented his case, saying, "This humble person has one son and one daughter. My son Liu Pu has been betrothed to Widow Sun's daughter, and my daughter, to Pei the Ninth's son. Not long ago, Pei the Ninth wanted to take my daughter to his house, but I refused his request, because, for one, my daughter is still young and her trousseau is not yet ready, and secondly, I was busy with preparations for my son's wedding. Just at this time, however, my son unexpectedly fell ill, and we dared not let him share a bed with the bride. So we had our daughter keep our daughter-in-law company. Who would have imagined that Widow Sun was cheating us! She had hidden away her daughter and sent her son, Sun Ruen, in her stead, and Sun Ruen raped our daughter. I was about to sue Widow Sun, when Pei the Ninth found out what had happened and came to my house. He beat me up and cursed me, and in my anger I yelled at him. I had no intention of repudiating the marriage agreement."

Judge Qiao was highly intrigued when he heard of a man disguising himself as a woman. He said, "A man may clothe himself as a woman, but there still is a difference. Did you not identify him as a man?" Liu the Elder replied, "Of all the many marriages I have seen or heard about, I have never come across one where a man pretends to be the bride. Nor have I heard of any marriage where it has been necessary to verify whether the bride is indeed a woman. Besides, Sun Ruen is as well favored as any woman. My wife and I were both so delighted we never suspected anything."

Judge Qiao continued, "Since the Suns had promised to give you their daughter as a bride, why did they send their son instead? There must be a reason. Is Sun Ruen still at your house?" Liu the Elder replied, "No, he ran away and went home." Judge Qiao thereupon ordered bailiffs to arraign the entire Sun Family of three. He also sent people to summon Liu Pu and Huiniang to the hearing. In a short time all of them arrived at the yamen.

Judge Qiao looked at Yulang and his sister and found both to be virtually identical in their good looks. Liu Pu was also quite handsome, and Huiniang, exceptionally beautiful. Judge thought to himself admiringly, "What fine pairs of young people!" and already was of a mind to accommodate them in their marital affairs. He asked Widow Sun, "Why did your son pretend to be a girl, thereby to deceive the Lius and abuse their daughter?" Widow Sun explained how she found out that her son-in-law was critically ill, how she feared for her daughter's future, how she instructed her son take her daughter's place at the wedding, and how she told him to return in three days. She explained that this had only been meant as a temporary expedient. She had never expected that the Lius would have their daughter sleep in the wedding chamber and that the young people would do such a thing.

Judge Qiao observed, "So that is how it was!" He then addressed Liu the Elder, "Since your son was so ill at the time, you should, by rights, have agreed to change the wedding date. Why did you not do so? Had you agreed to the Sun family's request, your daughter would not be implicated in such a scandal. You got your daughter in trouble by your own acts." Liu the Elder replied, "I should not have listened to my wife. I now regret this no end." Judge Qiao reproved him, saying, "That is nonsense! You are the head of the family, yet you let yourself be swayed by your woman."

The judge then instructed Yulang and Huiniang to come forward. To Sun Ruen, he said: "Sun Ruen, you, a man, were already in error when you passed yourself off as a woman. Yet you deceived a virgin and had illicit sexual relations with her. Do you know this is a crime?" Yulang kowtowed and replied, "This humble person committed a crime, but I did not do so by premeditation. Mother Liu herself sent her daughter to keep me company." Judge Qiao said, "She had her daughter keep you company because she did not know you are a man. Her intentions were honorable. Why did you not decline her offer?" Yulang replied, "This humble person tried hard to decline, but she insisted." Judge Qiao said, "If I were to go by the law, I should have you caned. However, in consideration of your youth and the fact that the parents in both families brought on this situation, I shall let you off this time." Yulang kowtowed and tearfully thanked the judge.

Judge Qiao then spoke to Huiniang, saying, "What you did was wrong, but we shall not dwell upon that matter. Tell me, with whom do you wish to be? The Peis? Sun Ruen? Tell me the truth." Sobbing, Huinang replied, "This lowly woman has compromised her virtue by communing with a man without the services of a matchmaker. I am no longer fit to serve another man. Besides, I have conceived a deep affection for Sun Ruen and have sworn not to marry any other. Should Your Honor order us to part, I shall have no choice but to end my life, for I have forfeited my reputation and cannot face other people's derision." Having said this, Huiniang wept aloud. Judge Qiao could see that Huiniang had spoken with truth and sincerity, and he felt a deep sympathy for the girl. He ordered her to stand aside.

Calling up Pei the Ninth again, Judge Qiao announced, "I should, by rights, have adjudged that Huiniang go back to your household. However, she has lost her chastity to Sun Ruen and compromised her virtue. Should you wed her to your son, your family's name will be damaged and you will become a laughingstock. The girl will also be known as having two husbands, and that will be a source of discord for all concerned. It is therefore my decision that Huiniang shall become Sun Ruen's wife so that her reputation may be redeemed. I also order that Liu the Elder return to you the betrothal gifts you have given to his family and that you look for another wife for your son."

Pei the Ninth demurred, saying, "Now that the girl is a figure of scandal, I of course do not want her. However, Sun Ruen has ruined my family's nuptial dispositions, and giving the girl to him would be tantamount to allowing an adulterous man and woman to attain their nefarious goal. I cannot accept that! I would rather relinquish the betrothal gifts and request that My Lord order that this woman marry someone else. Only that would help to assuage some of my anger and vexation." Judge Qiao asked, "You have already said you do not want the girl, have you not? Why go to the trouble of making enemies of her and her family?"

At this point, Liu the Elder approached the Judge and said, "You Honor, Sun Ruen is already betrothed to another. Surely, you would not have my daughter become his concubine!" Judge Qiao had not known that Sun Ruen was betrothed when he pronounced his arbitration. Learning now that Sun Ruen already had a prospective wife, he exclaimed in dismay, "Now what am I to do!" He first scolded Sun Ruen, saying, "Since you already had a wife, it was absolutely wrong of you to molest another family's virgin daughter. What are we to do now with the girl?" Sun Ruen was too frightened to reply. Judge Qiao continued, "To which family does your wife belong? Has the marriage been consummated?" Sun Ruen mumbled, "This humble person's wife is the daughter of Xu Ya. The marriage has not been consummated."

Relieved, the judge declared, "Then it is easy." Raising his voice, he said, "Pei the Ninth! Sun Ruen has not consummated his marriage. Since he will now be getting your intended daughter-in-law, I shall rule that his intended wife be given to your son as compensation. That should allay your vexation." Pei the Ninth acquiesced, saying, "I can only obey Your Honor's wise ruling. However, I fear that Xu Ya might not be willing." Judge Qiao declared, "Once I make a decision, no one may disobey it. Go home and get your son. I shall have Xu Ya bring his daughter and arrange the match right here before my tribunal."

Pei the Ninth hurried home to get his son. Xu Ya and his daughter were also summoned. When all had arrived, Judge Qiao inspected the young people of all three families. He found that all six were of handsome appearance and would make good matches, so he informed Xu Ya, "Sun Ruen has seduced Liu the Elder's daughter, and I have ordered that the two become man and wife. It is now my ruling that your daughter shall be joined in marriage with Pei the Ninth's son Pei Zheng. The marriage arrangements of all three families are to be concluded and reported to me this very day. Anyone who fails to comply shall be subject to heavy sanctions." Xu Ya could only accede to Judge Qiao's ruling. All other parties expressed satisfaction.

Judge Qiao then picked up his brush and wrote the following:

The brother appeared at the wedding in his sister's stead, and the sister-in-law shared the bride's bed. These dispositions were not, in themselves, reprehensible, as they sprang from the parents' love for their children. However, the unexpected happened when the bride turned out to be a man. Dry wood, placed next to a blazing fire, will burst into flames. Bring together a handsome man and an attractive woman, and they will soon become a couple. The Suns' son found a wife through his sister; he needed not to scale any walls to embrace the virgin. The Lius' daughter thought the man to be her sister-in-law; she did not seduce him with flirtatious advances. Happy with each other, they became a couple. True sentiments led to new commitments, and previous betrothals were forsaken. However, compromises have now been devised. Xu Ya has been enjoined to renounce his son-in-law Sun Ruen. Pei the Ninth's son, Pei Zheng, will instead marry Sun Ruen's betrothed, and Sun

Ruen, who purloined a man's wife shall forfeit his own wife to another. Thus the resentments kindled among the three families will be laid to rest, further distur- bances will be averted, and three couples will savor the bliss of fish in water. Partners have been interchanged, but all else will remain the same. The spouses will be from families other than originally ordained, yet time will prove the matching to be fully satisfactory. Because of love for their children, the parents have unwittingly become matchmakers. Although not a parent, this court has perforce served as the Old Man of the Moon. The court has now made its ruling. May all go forth to celebrate the happy events.

When Judge Qiao had finished writing his verdict, he asked the clerk to read it aloud. All persons present agreed with the judge's reasoning and kowtowed in appreciation. Judge Qiao drew six lengths of red silk from the yamen's warehouse and had these draped across the shoulders of the three new couples. He also engaged three wedding orchestras and hired three sedan chairs for the brides, after which the bridegrooms and the parents walked behind the sedan chairs out of the yamen. The ruling cre- ated a stir in Hangzhou prefecture. Everyone extolled Judge Qiao's resourcefulness, and one and all called him a benevolent and wise man. The marriages were consummated in all three families, and everyone was content.

Mind-All Li had fully expected to benefit from pitting Widow Sun and Pei the Ninth against Liu the Elder. Never had he imagined that Judge Qiao would not only fail to punish the families but would even contrive a happy union for Sun Yulang. Moreover, much to Mind-All Li's chagrin, the entire affair was told and retold in the city as a felicitous fable and not at all regarded as a scandal.

Less than a year later, Judge Qiao accepted both Liu Pu and Sun Ruen as candidates for *xiu cai* and sent them to take the imperial examinations. Mind-All Li, haunted by his shameful deeds and feeling insecure in Hangzhou, moved to a house in the countryside. In later years, Liu Pu and Sun Ruen successfully passed examinations of higher levels, were appointed to positions in the capital, and enjoyed considerable fame. They also helped Pei Zheng acquire an official position. The three families, all of them related by marriage, became quite wealthy and powerful, and Liu Pu even ascended to the post of Scholar of the Long Tu Pavilion. By that time, Mind-All Li's house had come into the Liu family's possession, which only goes to show that naught is to be gained by being a wily little villain! Judge Qiao, on the other hand, was lauded by later generations for his wise and benevolent matchmaking, and all agreed that he deserved to be called "Qiao Clear Sky."

The Woman in White Under Thunder Peak Pagoda

白娘子永鎮雷峯塔

The scenery around West Lake is famed for its unique hills and waterways. During the Xianhe era of the Jin Dynasty (265–420 A.D.), a great flood surged down from the mountains and swept up to the western gate of the city of Hangzhou. A gold-colored ox appeared amid the waters, and when the floodwaters receded, the ox was observed going toward the hills to the north, but it was soon lost to sight. This event caused a sensation among the city's residents, who believed it to be some sort of divine manifestation. Consequently they built a temple and named it the Golden Ox Temple. A monastery named the Monastery of General Jinhua was also established by the western gate, which is today called the Flood-of-Gold Gate.

At about that time, the Indian monk Huili came here to visit nearby Wulin County, and as he admired mountain scenery he remarked, "A small peak that used to stand before Mount Nimble Vulture suddenly vanished and would seem to have flown to this place." People did not believe the monk's words, so he said, "If my memory serves me well, the small peak—which was called Nimble Vulture Peak and that stood before Mount Nimble Vulture—has a cave inhabited by a white ape. I shall call out the white ape to prove my contention." And when he called, a white ape indeed came out of the cave. The peak was consequently called Feilai Feng, which means the Peak That Flew from Afar. A pavilion called Cool Spring Pavilion stands before this peak.

In the middle of West Lake rises Solitary Hill Islet where the scholar Lin Hejing led a hermit-like existence. He hired laborers to transport earth and rocks and build a walkway that linked Duan Qiao, or Broken Bridge, with the Evening Clouds Mountain Range to the west, and that walkway was called the Solitary Hill Road.

During the Tang Dynasty, Governor Bai Letian, who was the famous poet Bai Juyi, constructed a road linking Cuiping Hill in the south with Evening Clouds Mountain Range. Called the Lord Bai Causeway, it was more than once washed away by floodwaters from the mountains and repaired by means of official funds.

In the Southern Song Dynasty the poet Su Dongpo, who served as the local prefect, noted the damage done to these two roads by floodwaters. So he purchased timber and stone, hired laborers, and built a solid causeway, the balustrades on both sides of which were painted vermilion and the levees planted with willow and peach trees. The scenery here was so charming in springtime that it became the subject of many paintings. The road has since acquired the name Lord Su Causeway.

Two stone bridges, built along the Solitary Hill Road, enable people to cross the waters of the lake. The bridge on the east has been named Broken Bridge, and the one on the west, Xining Qiao, or Bridge of Western Serenity.

This storyteller has dwelt at length on the scenery at West Lake and on its legends and ancient relics. Now let me tell you about a handsome young man who met two women while visiting West Lake, and about the bizarre events that stirred up such a commotion in the streets and lanes of the surrounding cities and towns. Indeed, these events have inspired writers to compose not a few stories that enjoy much popularity.

So what was the name of this handsome young man? Who were the women he met? And what were the bizarre things that transpired?

The events in this tale took place in the Shaoxing era of the Song Dynasty (960–1279) when Emperor Gaozong fled to the south from the northern Jin invaders. An official called Li Ren lived in Black Pearl Lane by Guojun Bridge in the Lin'an Prefecture of Hangzhou. He held the position of Procurator of South Court Pavilion and oversaw the monies and grain stores of Defender-in-Chief Shao. His wife had a younger brother called Xu Xuan who also answered to the name Xiaoyi. Xu Xuan's father had once operated a store that sold dried medicinal herbs, but both his parents had passed away when he was a young boy, and now, at twenty-two years of age, he was in charge of the apothecary belonging to an uncle, Storekeeper Li. The apothecary was situated at the mouth of Guan Lane.

One day as Xu Xuan stood at the counter conducting his business, a monk came to the door, greeted him, and said, "This lowly monk is from the monastery at Baoshu Pagoda. A few days ago I delivered some rolls and steamed buns to your house. The Qingming Festival is approaching and it will soon be time to remember our ancestors. I hope Brother Xiaoyi will come to light incense at our monastery. Please do not forget." And Xu Xuan replied, "I shall certainly come." The monk bade him farewell and departed.

That evening Xu Xuan returned to his brother-in-law's house. He was still living in his sister's home since he had not yet married. He told his sister, "A monk from Baoshu Pagoda monastery came and invited me to burn offerings to our ancestors tomorrow. I intend to go."

The next morning, he purchased paper horses, wax candles, sutra streamers, paper money, and other items. He then broke his fast, put on new shoes and socks and fresh garments, wrapped his purchases in a bundle, and set out for his uncle's store at Guan Lane. His uncle asked him where he was going, and he replied, "I must go to the Baoshu Pagoda to burn offerings to our ancestors. Pray, allow me to take a day off." Storekeeper Li said, "You may go, but come back without delay."

Xu Xuan left the store and walked through Shou'an Lane and Flower Market Street. He crossed the Well Pavilion Bridge, strode along Clear River Street to the Qiantang Gate, and then passed over a stone bridge to reach the monastery at Baoshu Pagoda. There, he sought the monk who had previously sent him the steamed buns, performed rites of penance, burned sacrificial offerings, and then proceeded to the hall of worship to observe the assembled monks recite the sutras. After sharing a vegetarian meal with the monks and bidding them farewell, he left the monastery and took a roundabout route back home. He wandered by the Bridge of Western Serenity, and then turned his steps to walk along the Solitary Hill Road to the Temple of the Four Immortals, where he paid his respects at the grave of the scholar Lin Heqian and strolled by the Liu Yi Spring.

Without forewarning, dark clouds rolled in from the northwest, a dense fog shrouded the southeast, and a light drizzle gave way to a steady downpour. One might have surmised the gods were marking the Qingming Festival by sending rain to hasten the growth of flowers. The ground being wet, Xu Xuan removed his new shoes and socks and then hurried out of the Temple of the Four Immortals in the hope of finding a boat. None could be seen. As he stood undecided, however, he caught sight of a small boat rowed by an old man. Xu Xuan was delighted since he knew the old man, and he cried, "Grandfather Zhang, please give me a ride." The old man, hearing his name called, peered through the rain and recognized Xu Xuan. He rowed his boat over to Xu Xuan and asked, "Young Master Xiaoyi, you are soaked with rain! Where do you wish to go ashore?" Xu Xuan replied, "At the Flood-of-Gold Gate."

The old man helped Xu Xuan step into the boat, then pushed off and rowed in the direction of Pavilion of Abundant Joy. They had traveled but a distance of a hundred or more paces when they heard someone calling, "Grandfather, give us a ride!" Xu Xuan looked around and saw a woman on the riverbank. She had her hair coiled up in mourning and secured with white combs, and she was clad in a white silk upper garment and a skirt of fine linen. By her side stood a maidservant dressed in black and wearing her hair done up in a double topknot—of the sort affected by young maidens—interwoven with two crimson bands and adorned with a piece or two of jewelry. She held a bundle in her hands.

The old man said to Xu Xuan, "As they say, 'Little is needed to keep fires burning when tender breezes blow.' Let us give them a ride too!" Xu Xuan assented, so the old man brought the boat next to the riverbank.

As the young woman stepped in the boat with her maidservant, she parted her rosy lips in a smile, revealing two rows of jade-white teeth, and greeted Xu Xuan with a deep curtsey. Xu Xuan rose in haste to return the greeting, and waited for the woman and her maidservant to be seated.

The woman then cast bewitching glances at Xu Xuan. On his part, Xu Xuan, having received a sheltered upbringing, could not help but feel stirred by the sight of this beautiful woman and her pretty maidservant. The woman asked, "May I ask this young master his family and given name?" Xu Xuan replied, "This humble person is from the Xu family. My personal name is Xuan, and I am the first male in the generational line." The woman then asked, "Where is your home?" and Xu Xuan replied, "My humble abode is in Black Pearl Lane near Guojun Bridge. I tend to sales at an apothecary."

Having answered all these questions, he reflected, "I too should ask her some questions." So he rose to his feet and asked, "May I inquire your name and place of abode?" The woman replied, "This humble woman is the younger sister of Eunuch Bai, a member of the Three Ranks of Court Attendants. I was wedded to a certain Master Zhang, who has unfortunately passed away and is now buried at Thunder Peak. Since the Qingming Festival is nearing, I have come with my maidservant to make offerings and sweep his grave. Today's rain is quite unexpected, and we would have ended up a sorry sight indeed had you not given us this ride."

As they passed the time with such small talk, the boat arrived at their destination, whereupon the woman declared, "I left home in such haste that I neglected to bring along any cash. Will you lend me some money with which to pay the boatman? I will most certainly pay you back." To which Xu Xuan declared, "Do what suits you. It does not matter. That paltry boat fee is of no importance." He paid the boatman and helped the women disembark. It was raining harder now, and the woman said, "We live at the entrance of Twin Teahouse Lane by Arrow Bridge. If you can spare the time, come to my humble abode for a cup of tea, and I shall reimburse you for the boat fee." But Xu Xuan declined, saying, "A trifling matter, not worth your concern! Besides, it is getting late. I shall visit you another day."

The woman and her maidservant took their leave. Xu Xuan entered Flood-of-Gold Gate and hurried forward, seeking shelter from the rain under the eaves of the residences along the way. He soon reached Three Bridges Street and approached an apothecary that belonged to Storekeeper Li's brother. As Xu Xuan walked up to the store, Li the Younger, who was standing in the doorway, asked, "Brother Xiaoyi, where are you going at this late hour?" Xu Xuan replied, "I went to burn offerings at the Baoshu Temple and was caught in the rain. Could you lend me an umbrella?" Li the Younger turned and called out, "Old Chen! Fetch an umbrella for Master Xiaoyi." An elderly servant soon came out bearing an umbrella. Opening it, he said to Xu Xuan, "Master Xiaoyi, this is an umbrella made by Honest Shu of Eight Signs Bridge at Clear Lake. It is of the best quality and has eighty-four ribs and a handle of purple bamboo. It has never been damaged or mended, so take good care of it." And Xu Xuan replied, "That goes without saying."

Having thanked Li the Younger, Xu Xuan took the umbrella and set forth. He walked out of Sheep's Dyke and had come to Back Market Street when he heard someone calling, "Young Master Xiaoyi!" He turned around to see a woman standing under the eaves of a residence on Small Teahouse Lane. On closer inspection he saw that it was Mistress Bai. "What are you doing here?" he asked, and she replied, "The rain kept falling and my shoes became wet, so I sent Qingqing home to fetch umbrellas and shoes. But it is getting late. Could you accompany me for a few steps?"

Sharing one umbrella, the two walked to the end of the dyke, where-upon Xu Xuan asked, "Which way are you going?" And she replied, "Across the bridge to Arrow Bridge." Xu Xuan said, "I am going to Guojun Bridge, which is much closer. Better that you take the umbrella with you, and I shall go to retrieve it tomorrow." Mistress Bai hesitated before declaring, "That is hardly appropriate. But I thank you for your generosity."

Xu Xuan made his way home in the rain, seeking what shelter he could under the eaves of residences. Went he got home, Wang An, his brother-in-law's servant who had been sent out with an umbrella and boots and who had failed to find him, also returned to the house.

At his sister's house, Xu Xuan had a meal and went to bed. He tossed and turned all night, thinking about the woman in white. Visions rose in his mind's eye of the time they spent together that day, and of intimacies shared. But when he awoke to the crowing of a rooster, he realized it was all a dream.

He rose at dawn, performed his ablutions, broke his fast, and went to the apothecary. His thoughts, however, were in turmoil, and he could not keep his mind on his work. After the noon hour a thought occurred to him. "If I do not make up an excuse, I will not be able to get the umbrella and restore it to its owner." To Storekeeper Li who was sitting at the counter, Xu Xuan announced, "My brother-in-law has asked me to take half a day off and go home early to do someone a favor." Storekeeper Li granted him leave, but added, "Come in earlier tomorrow!"

Bidding his uncle a good day, Xu Xuan made straight for Twin Teahouse Lane by Arrow Bridge to seek Mistress Bai's house. He made many inquiries, but no one appeared to have heard of her. As he stood nonplussed, he saw Mistress Bai's maidservant Qingqing approaching from the east, and he asked her, "Sister, where do you live? I have come to retrieve the umbrella." Qingqing replied, "Come with me, sir." He fol-lowed her, and when they had walked a short distance she told him, "This is the place."

Xu Xuan looked around and saw a two-story house facing the rear wall of a mansion owned by Prince Xiu. The house had a gate of two doors, four of the panels of which were pierced with peepholes for look-ing out into the street. Inside, an exquisitely woven red curtain was suspended across the entrance to a hall of reception. On the four sides of the hall were ranged twelve black lacquered armchairs, and on each of the four walls hung an ancient landscape painting by some well-known artist.

The maidservant held open the curtain and said to Xu Xuan, "Sir, please enter and have a seat." And when Xu Xuan had done so, she called out softly, "Mistress! Master Xu is here." From an inner chamber Mistress Bai called back, "Ask him to come in for a cup of tea."

Xu Xuan stood undecided at first, and only entered after Qingqing had urged him several times to do so. Walking past a row of trellised windows, he lifted a black curtain and saw a small boudoir with a potted calamus on a table and four paintings of beautiful women adorning the walls on both sides. At the center hung the portrait of a god, and under it, on a small table, stood an antique vase-shaped incense burner.

Stepping forward, Mistress Bai made a deep curtsey and said, "I cannot thank you enough for rendering me such assistance yesterday evening despite our brief acquaintance." Xu Xuan replied, "A trifling matter, not worthy of mention."

"Stay a moment for a cup of tea," said Mistress Bai, and when the tea was served she proposed, "I would like you to stay a while longer and have three cups of wine whereby to express my gratitude." Before Xu Xuan could decline, Qingqing was already laying out dishes of fruit and vegetables, and Xu Xuan could only say, "I thank you for the wine, but truly do not deserve such generosity on your part."

Xu Xuan partook of a few cups of wine, and then rose to his feet, declaring, "The hour is late and I have a long way to go. Permit me to take my leave." Mistress Bai told him, "A relative of mine has borrowed the umbrella. Stay for some more wine while I send for it." Xu Xuan protested, "It is too late now. I must go." Mistress Bai attempted once more to detain him, saying, "Do have just one more cup of wine." But Xu Xuan refused, saying, "I have had my fill of food and drink, for which I thank you very much." Seeing that she could not persuade him to stay, Mistress Bai finally stated, "Since you must go, come and get the umbrella tomorrow." Only then was Xu Xuan able to take his leave and depart.

On the next day, Xu Xuan went to work as usual at the apothecary. He once more concocted an excuse to ask for leave, and forthwith went to Mistress Bai's house for the umbrella. When Mistress Bai again asked him to stay for some wine and food, he said, "Simply return the umbrella to me and do not put yourself to so much inconvenience." But Mistress Bai would not be deterred. "Since everything has been prepared," she said, "stay for just one cup of wine." Xu Xuan had no choice but to seat himself at the table. Mistress Bai poured a cup of wine and handed it to Xu Xuan. As she did so, she parted her cherry-like lips and revealed teeth as delicate as pomegranate seeds. Then, in dulcet tones and assuming a most appealing look, she spoke the following words: "I shall not attempt to deceive you, sir. As you know I am a widow, yet I am convinced you and I are destined by fate to be married, and I have been deeply attracted to you from the instant we met. If you share with me such feelings, I beg you to engage a matchmaker to join us together in eternal matrimony. Would that not be the best course, since we are evidently born to be husband and wife?"

Her words set Xu Xuan to thinking, "This would indeed be a good match, and I would do well to marry this woman, which I am most willing to do. Yet there is one obstacle. I tend to Storekeeper Li's store by day and sleep at my brother-in-law's house at night, and the little money I make barely suffices to buy the clothes on my back. Where would I find the money to get married and raise a family?"

As he remained silent, Mistress Bai pressed him to speak, asking, "Why do not say something?" Reluctantly, Xu Xuan replied, "I am much moved by your sentiments. I must confess, however, that my financial circumstances do not permit me to do what you propose." With a wave of her hand, Mistress Bai declared, "That is easily resolved. I have money to spare." She turned to Qingqing and said, "Go upstairs and get an ingot of silver."

The maidservant mounted a flight of steps, holding onto the banisters, and returned in a few moments with a package. This she handed to Mistress Bai, who in turn tendered it to Xu Xuan with the words, "Take this, sir. And come to me for more if it does not suffice you for your needs." Xu Xuan opened the package and found an ingot of the purest silver. Secreting this in his sleeve, he rose to take his leave. Qingqing had by now retrieved the umbrella and she gave it to Xu Xuan, who forthwith went home, hid the silver, and turned in for the night.

After rising the next morning, Xu Xuan went to Three Bridges Street and returned the umbrella to Li the Younger. He then spent a few odd pieces of silver purchasing a fat roast goose, fresh fish, lean pork, a tender chicken, and some vegetables, and took all of this back home with a jar of wine. He then ordered the nanny and maidservants to make preparations for a dinner. His brother-in-law, Procurator Li, was at home that day, and when all was ready Xu Xuan invited his sister and her husband to the feast. Much astonished by this lavish meal, Procurator Li thought, "Why does he splurge in this manner today? Wine is rarely served in this house, so what is going on?" Thus when all three had seated themselves in proper order and emptied a few cups of wine, he asked, "Brother-in-law, why do you waste your silver for no good reason?" Xu Xuan replied, "Do not mock me for what I am about to say. This meal is merely my inadequate way of thanking you for all the care you have shown me over the years. Yet I have grown up now, and should not impose on your hospitability any longer. I do, however, have concerns about finding someone who will look to my needs hereafter. Thus I am bringing up the matter of making a match for myself, which I hope you—my brother-in-law and my sister—will arrange for me, as that will settle an important event in my life and be a good thing."

While his brother-in-law and sister listened to his words, they thought, "Xu Xuan is usually too pinchfisted to pull a single hair from his head for anyone else. Did he spend all this money today so that we will pay for his wedding?" The couple looked at each other askance and made no reply. After dinner, Xu Xuan went off to work at the store.

When two or three days had gone by, Xu Xuan wondered, "Why does my sister not say anything?" And so he asked her, "Have you conferred with my brother-in-law about my request?" When she replied, "No," he inquired, "Why not?" The sister hemmed and hawed a moment, then said, "This is no simple matter and cannot be decided in haste. Besides, your brother-in-law has been in a vile mood these days and I have not dared ask him for fear of adding to his vexations." With a frown of impatience, Xu Xuan said, "Sister, why do you not make an effort? What is so difficult about my request? Are you ignoring it because you fear I will ask my brother-in-law to put up his own money for the wedding?"

Xu Xuan went to his bedroom, took the silver ingot out of his coffer, and went back with it to his sister, saying, "Do not make any more excuses. Just tell my brother-in-law to get on with it." His sister exclaimed, "So you have managed to put aside all this silver while you worked at your uncle's store! And all for the purpose of getting married! Go now, and leave this matter to me!"

When Procurator Li came home that evening, his wife said to him, "Husband, you know that my brother wishes to get married. It seems that he has saved no small amount of silver. He says we may use whatever we need of it to arrange the wedding for him." Surprised, Procurator Li said, "Is that indeed so? Well, he has done well to salt away all that silver. Let me see it!" His wife hastily brought the silver ingot to her husband, who examined it, turning it this way and that. All at once, he noticed some characters etched on the ingot and cried out aloud, "Horror! This thing will be the perdition of our whole family!" Bewildered, his wife asked, "My husband, what terrible thing has happened?"

Collecting himself, Procurator Li explained, "A few days ago, fifty ingots of silver somehow vanished from the treasury managed by Defender-in-Chief Shao. The locks and seals of the treasury were intact, and no tunnels have been brought to light. The Lin'an Prefecture was ordered posthaste to apprehend the thief, but there were no clues, and not a few innocent people have been implicated. A notice of arrest has been posted. It describes the markings on the ingots and the number of ingots stolen, and says: 'Whosoever apprehends the thief and recovers the silver shall be rewarded with fifty taels of silver. Whosoever knows about the theft but does not report to the authorities, or conspires to conceal the thief, shall be exiled to the frontier regions together with his entire family.' This ingot bears markings like those described in the notice of arrest, so it must be from Defender-in-Chief Shao's treasury. As they say, 'When fire burns close, one can only look out for oneself and not one's relatives.' Should this matter come to light, we will not be able to explain ourselves. I care not whether Xu Xuan stole the silver or borrowed it. I would rather he suffer than see myself implicated. The only way to save our whole family from disaster is to report this silver to the authorities!"

His wife heard this recital with mouth agape and eyes wide with fright, and she made no protest when Procurator Li took the silver and sent it straightaway to the Lin'an Prefecture. The prefectural magistrate was so consternated by the procurator's revelation that he did not sleep a wink all night. The next morning, he hastily summoned the Officer of Detentions Ho Li, who, together with a number of his colleagues and a band of handpicked agents, proceeded to the Li family's apothecary at the entrance to Guan Lane to arrest Xu Xuan. Swarming up to the apothecary's counter with vociferous yells, they seized Xu Xuan, bound him with ropes, and, beating a drum and a gong, hauled him to the Lin'an Prefecture.

Magistrate Han forthwith ascended to the bench. He ordered that Xu Xuan be brought into the courtroom, forced to his knees, and administered a beating. Xu Xuan cried, "I beg My Lord not to apply the tortures, for I know not of what crime I am guilty!" Irritated, the magistrate snapped, "Since both the thief and the loot are in evidence, what have you to say? Do you claim to be innocent? Fifty ingots of first-grade silver, which were secured under locks and seals, have vanished from Defender-in-Chief Shao's mansion, and, by Procurator Li's information, you must still be in possession of forty-nine of them. Moreover, the silver disappeared without the seals being tampered with, which would indicate that you are a demon!" Addressing his minions, he commanded, "Do not put ordinary shackles on him, and sprinkle him with unclean blood to counter his evil powers!"

Aware now of what the affair was about, Xu Xuan cried, "I am not a demon! Allow me to explain!" The magistrate ordered his minions, "Desist!" then said to Xu Xuan, "Tell me how you obtained this silver." Thereupon Xu Xuan recounted in detail how he had lent Mistress Bai the umbrella, and all that transpired on the occasions he went to retrieve it. When he had concluded, the magistrate asked, "What manner of person is this Mistress Bai? And where does she live?" Xu Xuan replied, "She told me she is a blood sister to Eunuch Bai, member of the Three Ranks of Court Attendants. She resides at the entrance of Twin Teahouse Lane by Arrow Bridge, in a black two-story house facing the rear wall of Prince Xiu's mansion."

The magistrate ordered Officer of Detentions Ho Li to go with Xu Xuan to Twin Teahouse Lane and arrest the woman. Ho Li thereupon proceeded with a band of minions to the black two-story building on Twin Teahouse Lane. There they saw the entryway with the double doors and four panels, but the steps leading up to it were littered with refuse and a thick bamboo pole barred the entrance. Ho Li and his men stared with surprise. After a while, they rounded up the neighbors who lived on both sides of the house—one called Qiu the Elder made paper flowers, and the other, Old Man Sun, was a cobbler. So alarmed was Old Man Sun at being hustled out of his house that his hernia burst and he fell fainting to the ground. Other neighbors then came forward and reported, "There has never been a Mistress Bai in this house. Some five or six years ago, a certain Inspector Mao resided here, but he and his whole family perished of the plague. Since then, ghosts have been seen coming out in broad daylight to make purchases, but no one has dared live in this house. A madman has come here during the last few days and stood before the gate, uttering nonsensical words."

Ho Li ordered his men to remove the bamboo pole that blocked the entrance and went in. No one was to be seen inside, but a gust of wind suddenly arose, sweeping with it a fetid odor of corruption. Fearfully, everyone recoiled several steps while Xu Xuan stood speechless with dread.

It so happened that among the agents there was a daredevil of a man named Wang who ranked second in his family and loved to drink, and was thus called Tippler Wang the Second. He now called, "Follow me!" With loud shouts, all the agents charged into the house, running along the paneled walls and past the tables and chairs that stood in the reception hall. Tippler Wang the Second led the way up the flight of stairs. Everything was thickly covered with inches of dust. Coming to a room, they pushed open the door and looked in. Within the room stood a canopied bed together with an assortment of hampers and boxes, and seated on the bed was a woman of delicate beauty, clad entirely in white. The agents stopped in their tracks, and no one dared approach her. One of them ventured, "Are you a ghost or a demon? We are here by order of the magistrate of Lin'an Prefecture to arraign you as witness in the trial of Xu Xuan." The woman did not stir. Tippler Wang the Second blustered, "How, now! So no one dares to step forward? Someone bring me a pot of wine! I shall drink it to ward off evil, and then take this woman to the magistrate!"

Several agents hurried down the stairs and soon returned with a pot of wine.

Tearing off the seal, Tippler Wang the Second emptied the pot in one draught. "Now you cannot harm me!" he whooped, and thereupon hurled the empty pot toward the canopy.

There had been no disturbance before he threw the pot, but once he did so, a loud report ensued, like a peal of thunder in a clear sky. All the agents toppled to the ground in panic, and when they scrambled to their feet again the woman was no longer on the bed. They saw instead a pile of gleaming silver ingots. Someone said with relief, "That is more like it!" and they set themselves to counting the ingots. There were forty-nine in all. One agent proposed, "Let us take the silver to the magistrate and be done with this matter!"

And so, each carrying some of the silver on his shoulders, the agents returned to the Lin'an Prefecture. Ho Li made a full report to the magistrate, who remarked, "Then she must have been a demon! So be it. The neighbors are innocent and may be sent home in peace." He then had the fifty ingots of silver returned to Defender-in-Chief Shao's house with a detailed account of what had transpired. Xu Xuan was administered a caning for "committing such acts as should not have been committed," but spared a branding as a criminal. He was then sentenced to a term of labor at a prison city under the jurisdiction of Suzhou Prefecture, to be released after he had completed his sentence.

In the meantime, Procurator Li, who now felt pangs of guilt about his role in reporting Xu Xuan to the authorities, gave all the fifty taels of reward money he had received to his brother-in-law to serve the latter on his journey. Storekeeper Li wrote two letters, one to Director Fan of the Bureau of Detentions, and the other to Master Wang, proprietor of an inn at the foot of Jili Bridge.

Xu Xuan wept heartbrokenly as he bade farewell to his sister and brother-in-law. A lightweight cangue for the journey was then fitted around his neck, after which he left Hangzhou escorted by two guards and boarded a boat at Dongxin Bridge. Less than a day later, Xu Xuan arrived in Suzhou. The first thing he did there was to have the letters delivered to Director Fan of the Bureau of Detentions and to Master Wang. Master Wang forthwith had some gratuities distributed at the local government offices, and then sent the two guards to the Suzhou Prefecture to complete the documentation required for delivery and receipt of their charge. That done, the two guards returned to Hangzhou.

Director Fan and Master Wang then posted bond for Xu Xuan, which allowed the latter to remain out of prison and to stay in a room over Master Wang's inn.

Overcome with depression and frustration, Xu Xuan inscribed the following poem on the walls of his room:

> *Alone in this chamber I gaze toward my hometown,*
> *Watching the sunshine slant over the window.*
> *E'er have I striven to be a good, honest fellow.*
> *What brought me nigh to that treacherous widow?*
> *To where has that temptress betaken herself?*
> *And where is Qingqing, her conniving companion?*
> *Kith and kin have I forsaken to come to Suzhou.*
> *Longing rends my heart as I yearn for my dear ones.*

Thus stood matters as time flew like an arrow and the sun and moon shuttled across the heavens. Xu Xuan had by now spent more than half a year at Master Wang's house.

One day, in the last ten days of the ninth moon, Master Wang happened to be sitting at the door of his inn and watching people walk by, when he saw a sedan chair approach from the distance, followed by a maidservant. The sedan chair stopped at the inn, and the maidservant said, "May I inquire whether this is the house of Master Wang?" Master Wang quickly rose to his feet and replied, "It is indeed. Whom do you seek?" The maidservant declared, "Young Master Xu Xiaoyi who has come from Lin'an Prefecture." Master Wang said, "Wait here while I ask him to come out!"

The sedan chair was set down before the door, and Master Wang went in and shouted, "Brother Xiaoyi, you have a visitor!" Xu Xuan hurried out with Master Wang, only to see Qingqing and then the sedan chair with Mistress Bai in it. At the sight of her, he railed, "You spiteful woman! Do you know how much suffering you have caused me with that silver you stole from the official treasury? Do you know I had no way of pleading my innocence, or what plight you have plunged me in? Why have you come here? Have you no shame?!" Mistress Bai replied, "Master Xiaoyi, do not reproach me for what transpired. I have come expressly to clarify the matter. Let me go into the inn and talk to you there." She instructed Qingqing to take some bundles from the sedan, but Xu Xuan cried, "You are a ghost and a demon! I will not permit you to enter!" and he barred entrance to the inn.

Mistress Bai turned and dropped a deep curtsey to Master Wang, saying, "Esteemed owner of this inn, I am not deceiving anyone. First of all, how could I be a ghost? Do you not see the seams in my clothing, and the shadow my body casts under the sun's rays? Alas! I rue the day my husband died, leaving me a widow to be maligned and mistreated by others! If any wrongs were committed, these were committed by my husband and have naught to do with me." To Xu Xuan she said, "I feared you would hold a grudge against me, and so I came to explain myself. After doing so, I will willingly depart again."

Thereupon the innkeeper intervened and said, "Why does the mistress not come in and talk inside?" And Mistress Bai agreed, saying, "I shall go in and speak in the presence of your wife." And when the onlookers gathered at the door heard her say this, they all dispersed and went their own ways.

Xu Xuan also went in and declared to Master Wang and his wife, "I was put on trial and went through all that suffering because she stole silver from the official treasury. And now she comes here! What does she have to say for herself?"

Mistress Bai responded, "That silver was left to me by my late husband, and I gave it to you out of good intentions. I do not know how he came in possession of that silver." Xu Xuan retorted, "Then why is it that when the agents came to arrest you, your doorway was filled with garbage? And why did you suddenly vanish from inside the canopy?" Mistress Bai explained, "When I learned you had been arrested on account of the silver, I feared you would tell the officials about me, which would only result in my being arrested and submitted to much loss of face. In desperation I sought refuge at my aunt's residence in front of Huazang Temple. I had someone pile garbage in front of the gate, placed the remaining silver on the bed, and asked the neighbors not to say anything about me."

Xu Xuan cried, "So you absconded, leaving me to face the authorities?" Mistress Bai defended herself, saying, "I assumed that leaving the silver on the bed would make things easier for you. How was I to know that such dire consequences would ensue? I put together some money and came here as soon as I learned that you had been exiled to this place. And now that all has been clarified, I shall go away. I daresay you and I were never destined to be man and wife."

Master Wang interjected, "Why leave so soon after you traveled so far to come here? Stay a few days and see how matters turn out." And Qingqing chimed in, saying, "Why not stay here for a day or two, since Master Wang has time and again invited you to do so? Besides, you once offered to marry Master Xiaoyi, did you not?" Mistress Bai responded dismissively, "Do not embarrass me so! It is not as though no one would want me as a wife! Anyhow, I only came to clear my name." Master Wang demurred, "Why leave now, since you and Brother Xiaoyi had agreed to get married? I insist that you stay here!" And he forthwith paid off and sent away the sedan-chair bearers.

In the next few days, Mistress Bai had inserted herself into the good graces of Master Wang's wife, who thereupon prevailed upon her husband to patch matters up between Xu Xuan and Mistress Bai. And when that had been done, the eleventh day of the eleventh moon was chosen as the day for tying the marriage knot.

Time passed swiftly, and when the auspicious day approached, Mistress Bai produced some silver and asked Master Wang to arrange for the wedding feast. Mistress Bai and Xu Xuan performed the formal rites of marriage, and after the banquet the two retired behind the gauze curtains of the nuptial bed. Mistress Bai exercised all manner of seductions and charms as they consummated their union as man and wife. Xu Xuan, in his transports of joy, felt as though he was communing with a fairy from the land of immortals, and he regretted that this encounter had been delayed so long. So engrossed were the two in their delights that they failed to notice it when the golden rooster crowed thrice and the sky grew pale in the east.

Thereafter, the two were as inseparable as fish and water and spent their days in trance-like indulgence in their chambers at Master Wang's inn.

As the sun and the moon came and went, half a year passed by. Spring drew near, bringing balmy weather and blooming flowers. One day, horses and carts crowded the streets and the town was filled with activity. Xu

Xuan asked his host, "Why so many people and so much excitement?" Master Wang replied, "Today is the fifteenth day of the second moon, when all men and women go to see the Sleeping Buddha. It would do you good to take a walk around the Temple That Holds Up the Heavens." Thereupon Xu Xuan said, "Yes, I shall let my wife know and go look at the temple." He went up the stairs and said to Mistress Bai, "Today is the fifteenth day of the second moon when men and women go to see the Sleeping Buddha. I will go take a look and then return. Should anyone ask for me, say I am not at home. And do not go out to meet them." Mistress Bai responded disapprovingly, "What is there to see? You would do better to stay at home." But Xu Xuan insisted, "I shall amuse myself for a while and then come back. I see no harm in that."

Xu Xuan left the inn and went together with a few acquaintances to the temple to see the Sleeping Buddha. They strolled through the corridors and halls, and as they emerged from the temple they saw a Daoist priest seated before the gate. He was clad in a Daoist robe belted with a yellow cord, wore a casual head cloth and a pair of hempen sandals, and was selling potions and dispensing talismans. Xu Xuan stopped to look at him, and the Daoist priest chanted, "This humble priest is from Mount Zhongnan. I wander far and wide, dispensing incantations and talismans which deliver people from sickness and disaster. Anyone with such troubles, please step forward!"

As he said these words, he espied Xu Xuan among the bystanders and saw a black miasma wafting over his head. Deducing that Xu Xuan was being importuned by a demon, he called him over and said, "A demon has imposed itself on you of late and may cause you grievous harm. I shall give you two talismans which will save your life. One of these you shall burn during the third watch of the night, and the other you must wear in your hair." Xu Xuan accepted the talismans and kowtowed to the priest, thinking to himself, "I had always suspected that the woman was a demon. So it is indeed true!" He thanked the priest and returned to the inn.

That night, after Mistress Bai and Qingqing had fallen asleep, Xu Xuan rose from the bed. "It must be about the third watch now," he told himself. Having placed one of the talismans in his hair, he was just about to set fire to the other when Mistress Bai heaved a sighed and said, "Brother Xiaoyi, you and I have been husband and wife for a goodly while now, yet you still do not feel any affection for me. You let yourself be persuaded by other people's words and burn a talisman in the third watch of the night to put a curse on me. Go ahead and burn it!" As Xu Xuan hesitated, she rose, snatched the talisman from him and set fire to it. Nothing happened. Mistress Bai scolded, "What now? Say again that I am a demon!" Xu Xuan said defensively, "I am not to blame! A wandering priest I saw before the temple of the Sleeping Buddha claimed he knew you to be a demon." Mistress Bai declared, "I will go with you tomorrow to see what kind of a priest he is."

The next morning, Mistress Bai rose early, performed her ablutions, put on her adornments and a set of plain garments, and told Qingqing to look after their upstairs chambers. Husband and wife then proceeded to the temple of the Sleeping Buddha. There they saw a crowd of people assembled around the priest who was dispensing amulets and talismans. Mistress Bai strode up to him and, glaring fiercely, cried, "What impudence! You, who have taken the vows, have the gall to tell my husband I am a demon and then give him a talisman purportedly to unmask me!" The priest countered, "I practice the orthodox doctrine of the Five Thunders and Heavenly Center. Any demon that swallows one of my talismans will at once be revealed in its true form." Mistress Bai snapped, "Write out a talisman in everyone's presence. I shall swallow it and we shall see what transpires." The priest accordingly wrote out a talisman and handed it to Mistress Bai, who forthwith swallowed it under the eyes of the onlookers. After a while, when nothing happened, some people jeered at the priest and cried, "Why do you accuse this respectable woman of being a demon?" Then everyone began to curse the priest who stood speechless, mouth open and eyes wide with alarm. Mistress Bai announced, "As all of you will bear witness, he has failed to unmask me. I, however, learned a few magic tricks as a child, so let me try one on him before your eyes!"

So saying, she uttered a few incomprehensible words, and the priest huddled in upon himself as though seized by some gigantic hand and rose into the air. All the onlookers were greatly astonished, and Xu Xuan stood dumbstruck. Mistress Bai said to the onlookers, "I could keep him suspended up there for a full year, but I shall not offend your sensibilities." She blew a breath of air. The priest at once tumbled to the ground and fled forthwith as though regretting his parents had not provided him with a pair of wings!

The onlookers dispersed, and husband and wife went back to the inn. Life returned to normal, and other than the fact that it was Mistress Bai who paid their daily expenses, Xu Xuan resumed his husbandly authority, and the two disported themselves both day and night.

Time sped by like an arrow, and soon it was the eighth day of the fourth moon, the birthday of Buddha Sakyamuni. Cedar-wood pavilions that symbolized the bathing of Buddha were borne through the streets by monks, and every household presented them with alms. To Master Wang, Xu Xuan commented nostalgically, "This is just like in Hangzhou!"

Just then, a boy named Ironhead, who lived in a neighboring house, said, "Master Xiaoyi, a Buddhist festival is being held today at the Temple That Holds Up the Heavens.

You should go and take a look!" Intrigued, Xu Xuan went at once to tell Mistress Bai, who responded unhappily, "What is there to see? Do not go!" But Xu Xuan insisted, saying, "I wish to go, if only to dispel my boredom." Mistress Bai relented, "All right, then go. But your garments are worn and unsightly. Let me dress you up."

Upon her instructions, Qingqing brought out a new set of garments, which fitted Xu Xuan as though they had been tailored for him, being neither too short nor too long. He wore a lacquered cap with a brace of white jade circlets affixed at the back, and a long black gown. His boots were also black, but he held in his hands a fine silken fan of a hundred folds, which had beautiful women traced on it in gold and from which hung a coral pendant. When he was all dressed up, Mistress Bai cooed to him sweetly, "Come back quickly, my husband. Do not make me worry about you!"

Xu Xuan left with Ironhead for the Temple That Holds Up the Heavens to join in the Buddhist festivities. Everyone there admired him for his elegance. As he walked about he overheard someone saying, "Last night, pearls and other valuables worth around four or five thousand strings of cash vanished from the storeroom at Shopkeeper Zhou's pawnshop. He has made a list of the stolen objects and submitted it to the authorities, but investigations have yet to turn up the thief." Xu Xuan heard these words but knew not what they portended, and he continued to seek entertainment with Ironhead. There was much to see at the temple that day, with many rich patrons, both male and female, burning incense and sauntering here and there. After a while he reflected, "My wife asked me to go back quickly, so I had better return." He had, however, lost sight of Ironhead among the crowds, so he walked out the temple gate alone. As he did so, he saw five or six men attired like police agents and with tablets of authority attached to their waists. One of these remarked to his companions, "Do the objects worn and held by this fellow not look like those goods?" And another agent who knew Xu Xuan said, "Master Xiaoyi, let me have your fan so that I may admire it." Not suspecting that this was a ruse, Xu Xuan handed over the fan. The agent exclaimed, "See the fan and the pendant? They are none other than those described on the list!" The rest of the agents cried, "Arrest him!" and trussed Xu Xuan up with ropes. It was no different from:

> *A flock of black eagles pouncing on a swallow,*
> *A pack of ravening tigers rending a young lamb.*

Xu Xuan cried, "Do not make a mistake! I have committed no crime!" But the head agent responded, "Go with us to the prefecture and let Shopkeeper Zhou determine whether or not you have committed a crime! Stolen from his pawnshop were gold, pearls, and other valuables worth five thousand strings of cash, and among them were rings of white jade and a fine silken fan of a hundred folds with a coral pendant. And you claim you have committed no crime? We now have both the thief and the loot, so what have you to say for yourself? You have some gall, to come out in public bedecked from head to toe with objects stolen from his house!"

Stunned, Xu Xuan remained silent for a long moment. Then he said, "So that's how it is! No matter! No matter! I know who the thief is." To which the agents replied, "Then go tell that to the Suzhou Prefecture!"

The next day, the magistrate of the Suzhou Prefecture ascended to his bench, and Xu Xuan was brought into his presence. The magistrate asked, "Where have you put the objects you stole from the Shopkeeper Zhou's storeroom? Confess, and you shall be spared the torture." Xu Xuan replied, "May it please My Lord, all the garments and accoutrements on this small person pertain to my wife, Mistress Bai. I do not know their provenance." The Magistrate inquired, "Where is your wife?" And Xu Xuan told him, "Look for her at the house of Master Wang below Jili Bridge."

The magistrate ordered Yuan Ziming, the Officer of Detentions, to arrest Mistress Bai at once and to take Xu Xuan along. When they arrived at the inn, Master Wang was greatly surprised and asked, "What is going on?" Xu Xuan inquired, "Is Mistress Bai upstairs?" And Master Wang replied, "Soon after you left with Ironhead yesterday morning for the Temple That Holds Up the Heavens, she said to me, 'My husband went to amuse himself at the temple and asked Qingqing and myself to take care of our chambers upstairs, but he has not returned yet, so Qingqing and I will go to the temple to look for him. Please keep an eye on our chambers.' Then she went out, but did not return last night. I assumed they had gone with you to visit relatives. In any case she has not come back today."

The agents then told Master Wang they had come to arrest Mistress Bai, and they ransacked the inn front and back but found nothing. So Yuan Ziming took Master Wang to the magistrate for interrogation.

The magistrate asked, "Where is Mistress Bai at this time?" Master Wang recounted all that had transpired, and concluded with the words, "Mistress Bai is a demon." The magistrate questioned the agents, and then commanded, "Throw Xu Xuan in prison." Master Wang, however, produced some money and bailed Xu Xuan out so that he could await further proceedings in freedom.

In the meantime, the owner of the pawnshop, Shopkeeper Zhou, was whiling the time away in a teahouse across the street when a servant reported, "All the gold and jewels have reappeared, and are now in an empty chest in the attic of the storehouse." Upon hearing this news, Shopkeeper Zhou hastened back to his home. The purloined objects had indeed reappeared! The only items missing were a headdress, some jade circlets, and a fan with a pendant. Shopkeeper Zhou exclaimed, "I have manifestly wronged Xu Xuan. It is not right to harm a man for no good reason!" And he forthwith went to the authorities and asked that Xu Xuan be convicted of a lesser crime.

It so happened that Xu Xuan's brother-in-law Procurator Li had just been dispatched to Suzhou on some matter. He found lodgings at the inn operated by Master Wang, who recounted to him in detail how Xu Xuan had come here, and how he had once more fallen afoul of the law. Procurator Li thought to himself, "He is, after all, my relative and I cannot see him suffer!" And he distributed some money in high and low places so that Xu Xuan would not be maltreated.

A few days later, the magistrate summoned Xu Xuan and reviewed the accusations against him. The magistrate then assigned all culpability for the theft to Mistress Bai and merely charged Xu Xuan with "failing to inform the authorities of a demon," for which offense he sentenced Xu Xuan to a hundred strokes of the cane and to exile in the prison city at Zhenjiang prefecture, three hundred sixty *li* away.

Procurator Li remarked, "Going to Zhenjiang is not so bad! I have there an uncle who is father of a sworn brother of mine and whose name is Li Keyong. He has an apothecary at Needle Bridge. I shall write to him and he will take care of you." Xu Xuan borrowed some money for the road from his brother-in-law, and kowtowed to him and to Master Wang. He then purchased some wine and food for the bailiffs who would escort him, packed a few belongings, and left Suzhou. Master Wang and his brother-in-law saw him off for a short distance before returning each to their own homes.

Xu Xuan spent a few days on the road, eating when hungry and drinking when thirsty, and before long arrived in Zhenjiang. He and his escorts first sought Esquire Li Keyong's residence. When they arrived at the apothecary at Needle Bridge, a manager was selling herbal remedies at the door, and the esquire, who was owner of the apothecary, happened to walk out. The two bailiffs and Xu Xuan hastened to greet him, and Xu Xuan said, "I am from the family of Procurator Li of Hangzhou. I have a letter for you." The manager took the letter and handed it to Esquire Li, who opened it and read it right away. Li Keyong remarked, "So you are Xu Xuan!" To which Xu Xuan replied, "This small person is he." The esquire had a meal prepared for Xu Xuan and his escorts, and then instructed a clerk to go with them to the prefecture, whence the escorts submitted their documents of delivery. The esquire also produced some money to post bail for Xu Xuan. Then the escorts, having obtained a receipt for their charge, went back to Suzhou.

Xu Xuan returned to the apothecary with the clerk, kowtowed his thanks to Li Keyong, and met the elderly mistress of the house. Having learned from Procurator Li's letter that Xu Xuan had once managed an apothecary, Li Keyong kept him to work at his store. He also arranged for Xu Xuan to sleep at night in the house of Old Man Wang, a bean-curd maker who lived on Fifth Lane. Li Keyong was gratified to see that Xu Xuan carried out his duties at the apothecary carefully and consci-entiously.

Now, before Xu Xuan's arrival, there were two managers at the apothecary—Manager Zhang and Manager Zhao. Manager Zhao had always been an honest and dutiful man, whereas Manager Zhang was mean and crafty and took advantage of his seniority to bully his younger colleagues. The addition of Xu Xuan to the apothecary's staff displeased him, for he feared he might be dismissed. So he began to devise strategies to discredit Xu Xuan.

One day, Li Keyong came to the apothecary to look around, and he asked Manager Zhang, "How is the new man performing his tasks?"

These words at once set Manager Zhang to thinking, "Aha! Here is my chance to dig a pitfall!" Aloud, he said, "He will do, only . . ." Li Keyong inquired, "Only what?" Manager Zhang continued, "He is only interested in dealing with big clients and sends smaller clients away, which is why some people disapprove of him. I have spoken to him several times already, but he will not listen." Whereupon Esquire Li declared, "That is easily resolved. I shall speak to him and he will listen to my words."

Manager Zhao overheard this exchange and, seeking an occasion, said to Manager Zhang in private, "We should strive to maintain harmony among ourselves. Xu Xuan is a newcomer, and you and I should take him under our wing. Should he do anything wrong, would it not be better to say so to his face instead of behind his back? He would only think we bear him ill will if he learns about such comments." But Manager Zhang riposted, "What do you younger people know about such matters!"

As the hour was getting late, everyone at the apothecary went home. Manager Zhao accompanied Xu Xuan to his lodgings, and told him, "Manager Zhang has spoken ill of you before the esquire. Henceforth be more cautious, and treat all clients, big and small, in the same manner." Xu Xuan said gratefully, "I thank you for your advice. Now let us go out for a cup of wine!"

The two found a tavern and seated themselves across from each other. Each drank a few cups of wine as a waiter served dishes of food and fruit. Manager Zhao told Xu Xuan, "The old master is a man of blunt temperament who brooks no impertinence. You would do well to humor him and exercise patience when at work." Whereupon Xu Xuan once more expressed his gratitude, saying, "Elder brother, I cannot thank you enough for your kind concern." Both drank two more cups of wine. Then, as night was falling, Manager Zhao said, "The streets are dark and difficult at night. Let us meet some other time." Xu Xuan paid for the wine and food, and they parted company.

Xu Xuan knew he had imbibed too much wine and, lest he bump into people, he made his way homeward along the walls of the houses lining the streets. As he weaved along, a window in an upstairs room opened and ashes from a flatiron flew out and landed squarely on his head. He halted his steps and yelled, "What sort of man or woman are you? Have you no eyes? Such impudence!" A moment later, a woman hurriedly came down and cried, "Please sir, do not shout! It was my fault, a careless mistake! Do not hold it against me!"

Xu Xuan, still half drunk, looked up and steadied his gaze. It was Mistress Bai! Rage suffused his breast and the flames of fury flared high, high up! Filled with righteous anger, Xu Xuan swore, "You cheap, despicable demon! Do you know how I have suffered? Twice have I fallen afoul of the law because of you! And why are you here again? Do you deny you are a demon?" Pursuing her into the house, he seized her and shouted, "How do you wish to settle this matter? In court or in private?"

Smiling, Mistress Bai replied, "My dear husband. As they say, 'One night of connubial bliss begets a hundred nights of affection.' I have much to tell you, so please hear me out! Those garments were left to me by my late husband, and I presented them to you because of the deep love we share. You, however, repay kindness with ingratitude, and treat me like a bitter enemy." Xu Xuan interrupted, "Why were you gone that day, when I came back to seek you? Master Wang told me you and Qingqing went to the temple to look for me. And what are you doing here now?" Mistress Bai replied, "When I arrived at the temple, I heard you had been arrested. Qingqing also made enquiries about you, but to no avail, so I assumed you had escaped. Fearing they would come for me too, I quickly had Qingqing hire a boat, which took us to my maternal uncle's home in Jiankang Prefecture. Only yesterday did we return. I hesitated to go to you, for I know you have had two brushes with the authorities on my account! But of what use are recriminations? Seeing as how congenial we used to be, and how well we communed as man and wife, how can we think of parting company now? My love for you is as high as Mount Tai and as deep as the Eastern Sea. Did we not swear to share life and death? Thus for the sake of the good times we once spent as man and wife, I beg you to take me back, so that we may live together to a ripe old age! Is that not the best for both of us?"

Mollified by Mistress Bai's blandishments, Xu Xuan fell silent. And then, as lust and desire once again befuddled his brains, he decided not to return to his lodgings but to spend the night with Mistress Bai in her chambers.

The next day, Xu Xuan returned to Old Man Wang's house on Fifth Lane and said to his landlord, "My wife has returned from Suzhou with her handmaid." Spinning an account of what had transpired, he concluded with the request, "May I bring them here to live together with me?" Old Man Wang readily agreed, saying, "That is a good thing. You need not even have asked." That very day, Mistress Bai and Qingqing moved into a set of upstairs chambers at the house.

The following day, the Xu family invited the neighbors to have tea with them, and on the third day the latter gave a dinner to welcome the new arrivals. These amenities disposed of, Xu Xuan rose early on the fourth day, and after completing his ablutions, told his wife, "Today I shall thank the neighbors living on both sides and then return to work at the apothecary. Stay upstairs with Qingqing to look after things, and on no account go out of the house!" Having given her these instructions, he went back to the apothecary, and thenceforth worked assiduously, leaving home early in the morning and returning late at night.

Another month slipped by almost unnoticed as the sun and moon alternated in the skies. Then one day, Xu Xuan conferred with Mistress Bai about her going to visit Esquire Li, his wife, and other members of his household. Mistress Bai concurred, saying, "Now that you are a manager at the apothecary, paying our respects to the family will enable us to engage in regular relations with them." So the next day, Xu Xuan hired a sedan chair and invited Mistress Bai to mount into it. He asked Old Man Wang to help carry boxes of gifts and, with Qingqing following behind, they soon arrived at Li Keyong's residence. Alighting from the sedan chair, Mistress Bai went in and asked to see Esquire Li, who came out at once. Mistress Bai curtseyed deeply and made two obeisances. These last were returned by the mistress of the house, who then introduced Mistress Bai to all the womenfolk in the family.

Now, Esquire Li, though advancing in years, was a man obsessed with lecherous fantasies, and when he observed Mistress Bai's beauty—the sort of beauty that can bring down kingdoms—his soul well nigh flew from his body and his eyes kept staring at Mistress Bai. At this time, wine and food were being prepared to entertain the visitors. His wife remarked, "She is indeed a lovely woman. Her features are most attractive, she has a gentle, amiable manner, and her behavior would seem to be decent and demure." He replied, "Ah, yes! Women from Hangzhou are known for their charm!"

After the dinner had concluded and Mistress Bai had thanked her hosts and returned to her home, Li Keyong kept thinking, "How can I get her to sleep one night with me?" Furrowing his brow he pondered mightily, and then struck upon an idea. "My birthday comes on the thirteenth day of the sixth moon," he thought. "No fear! That woman will fall for my wiles!"

Time again flew by, and after the fifth day of the fifth moon—marked by all people as the Dragon Boat Festival—came the sixth moon, and Li Keyong said to his wife, "Mother, as you know, the thirteenth day of this moon is my birthday, and I wish to give a banquet and invite all my relatives to enjoy themselves, for that is the happiest day in a man's lifetime." Thereupon invitations were sent to all relatives, friends and neighbors as well as to the managers at the apothecary. The next day, all the male heads of households sent such gifts as candles, pastries, kerchiefs, and the like, and on the thirteenth they came to the banquet and were wined and dined for a full day. On the following day the womenfolk came to wish Li Keyong a happy birthday. There were more than a score of them, among them Mistress Bai, who was most attractively attired in a black manteau embroidered with gold thread and a crimson chiffon skirt, and wore an array of pearl, jade, gold and silver ornaments in her hair. Bringing along

Qingqing, she entered the house and congratulated Li Keyong on his birthday and paid her respects to the mistress of the house. She then joined the rest of the female guests at the banquet tables ranged in the eastern pavilion.

Li Keyong was a stingy man, of the sort that insists on saving a hind leg even when dining on no more than a louse. In his eagerness to lay hands on the comely Mistress Bai, however, he laid out a princely banquet. After many drinks and dishes had been consumed, Mistress Bai rose from the table to change her garments and wash her hands.

Li Keyong had foreseen such an event, and had instructed a nanny—who was also his confidante—as follows: "Should Mistress Bai wish to use a lavatory, take her to the secluded one at the back of the house." Having made this disposition, he concealed himself, also in the back of the house.

All was ready for him to:

> *Indulge in the stolen favors of a beauteous woman,*
> *With no crawling through holes or climbing over walls.*

And so, when Mistress Bai asked to be directed to a lavatory, the nanny led her to the secluded one at the back of the house, and then departed. Burning with lust, Li Keyong could scarcely restrain himself, yet he dared not enter immediately but peered through a crack in the door. What he saw threw him into such terror that he reeled back and fell to the ground.

What Esquire Li had seen in the room was not the jade-like figure of a delicate woman, but the coarse coils of a great white snake as thick around as a well bucket and with eyes that glittered like golden globes! Frightened half to death, he picked himself up and stumbled away, only to swoon after a few steps. The maidservants who raised him up observed that his countenance was blue and his lips had turned deathly pale, so the family's caretaker administered a nerve-soothing potion, which helped him recover his senses. His wife and other people gathered around to inquire about his health, asking, "What alarmed you so? What happened?" But Li Keyong would not tell them, and merely replied, "I rose too early this morning. That, added to the fatigue of the past two days, made my head dizzy—an old ailment of mine." He was then helped to his bed to take a rest.

The guests then returned to the seats and drank a few more cups of wine before they wound up their merrymaking, thanked their hostess, and went home.

At home, Mistress Bai turned the incident over in her mind. Fearing that Li Keyong would divulge the truth of the matter to her husband when they met at the apothecary on the morrow, she devised a stratagem. That night, as she disrobed before retiring, she sighed loudly. Xu Xuan asked, "Why the sigh? Did you not enjoy yourself at the banquet today?" Mistress Bai replied, "My dear husband, this is a difficult thing to say. Esquire Li's celebrating his birthday was merely a pretense. He had evil intentions. When I had to visit the lavatory during the banquet, he was hidden there and attempted to assault me. He plucked at my skirt and my drawers and made advances. I wanted to cry out, but too many people were present and I did not wish to stir up a scandal so I pushed him, and he fell to the ground. He was too ashamed to admit the truth and pretended he had swooned. However, I shall seek redress for the alarm I suffered!"

Xu Xuan hesitated before venturing, "He did not violate you, and he is my employer. I see no way out but to swallow the insult and stay away from his house in future." Mistress Bai retorted, "Do you refuse to stand up for me? How will you be able to live with yourself?!" Pained, Xu Xuan replied, "I came to his house for assistance on the strength of a letter written by my brother-in-law. He willingly took me in and has made me a manager at his apothecary. What would you have me do?" Mistress Bai cried, "And you call yourself a man! He insults me in such a manner, and you still wish to work as his manager?" Xu Xuan protested, "Where would you have me go? What would I do for my subsistence?" Mistress Bai replied, "To work for another man, even as a manager, is a lowly calling. You would do better to set up your own apothecary." Xu Xuan snorted, "More easily said than done! Where would I find the capital?" Mistress Bai stated, "That poses no difficulty. I will give you some silver tomorrow. Go rent a place, and we shall speak further about this matter."

These days, as in olden times, one will always find warmhearted people willing to help a person out. There was a next-door neighbor by the name of Jiang Ho who all his life had been one ready and generous in helping those in need. Having obtained some silver from his wife the next day, Xu Xuan went with Jiang Ho to Zhenjiang Harbor. With Jiang Ho's help, Xu Xuan rented a room, purchased some apothecary shelves, and began to procure various medicinal herbs. By the tenth moon all was ready, so Xu Xuan left his employment as manager and chose a date to open up his own apothecary. Esquire Li, haunted by his own fears, made no attempt to detain Xu Xuan.

Business at the new store was brisk, and Xu Xuan prospered. One day, as he was selling herbs at the front of his store, a monk clasping a donation registry approached him and said, "This humble monk is from the Gold Mountain Monastery. The seventh day of the seventh moon is the birthday of the valiant Dragon King, and I respectfully request that the master come to our monastery to burn incense and contribute some incense money." Xu Xuan said, "You need not put my name in the registry. However, I have a piece of the best incense which you may take." He opened a chest, took out the incense, and presented it to the monk. As he accepted the incense, the monk nevertheless said before departing, "Sir, I do so hope you will come to our monastery."

Mistress Bai had espied this exchange, and she berated Xu Xuan, saying, "You good-for-nothing! Why did you give him that good incense? That bald-headed thief will only trade it for meat and wine!" Xu Xuan responded, "I gave it to him in all sincerity. How he disposes of it is his own affair!"

The seventh day of the seventh moon soon came around. As Xu Xuan was conducting his business in the store, he noticed that there was more activity than usual in the street, with many people coming and going. Jiang Ho, now his assistant, said, "Master Xiaoyi donated a piece of incense the other day, so why do you not go to the monastery and look around?" Xu Xuan at once replied, "Wait a moment while I put things in order, then we shall go together." And Jiang Ho declared, "I will accompany you with pleasure."

Xu Xuan hurriedly tidied up the apothecary, and then went in to tell his wife, "I shall go to burn incense at the Gold Mountain Monastery. Stay here to take care of the house." Said Mistress Bai disapprovingly, "As they say, 'Never go to a monastery unless you must.' Why do you go there?" Xu Xuan remonstrated defiantly, "For one thing, I have never visited Gold Mountain Monastery and I wish to see it. And for another, I contributed alms to the monastery the other day, and I should burn some incense today!"

With obvious reluctance, Mistress Bai said, "If you must go, I cannot hold you back. But you must promise me three things." Xu Xuan asked, "What three things?" And Mistress Bai stated, "One, do not enter the abbot's room. Two, do not speak with any monk. And, three, go and come back quickly. I shall go after you if you tarry." Xu Xuan said, "I see no difficulty. You have my promise!"

Xu Xuan put on fresh garments, shoes and socks, secreted a box of incense in his sleeve, and went with Jiang Ho to the riverbank, where they boarded a boat that took them to Gold Mountain Monastery. There, they first burned incense at the Hall of the Dragon King, and then strolled around the monastery. As they followed other visitors who were walking around, they came to the entrance of the hall in which the abbot was seated. Xu Xuan suddenly exclaimed, "My wife told me not to enter into the abbot's presence!" He halted in his steps and refused to enter the hall, but Jiang Ho wished to go in, and said, "What does it matter? She is at home, and you need not tell her you went in!" So the two stepped in, peered around for a while, and then came out again.

Now, the abbot who was seated in the center of the hall was a man of the most distinguished appearance. He wore a round bonnet and a wide, flowing robe, and looked every inch a pious, venerable monk. When he saw Xu Xuan walking past, he called his attendants and ordered, "Quick! Bring that young man to me!" The attendants sought the "young man," but not knowing whom to look for among the thousands of people milling about, they reported, "We do not know where he has gone."

The monk snatched up his staff, hastened out of the hall, and searched through the grounds of the monastery, without, however, finding Xu Xuan. He then sallied from the monastery and saw many people by the river, waiting for the wind and waves to subside so they could take a ferry. But the wind and waves only grew stronger, and a bystander remarked, "No boat can sail at this time!"

At this very moment, a small boat sped toward them from the middle of the river. Astonished, Xu Xuan said to Jiang Ho, "Even a ferry cannot cross the river in such a wind. How can that little boat survive?"

As people watched, the little boat drew near the riverbank. On it

stood two women, one clad in white and the other in black. Taking a
closer look, Xu Xuan was greatly shocked to see that they were Mistress
Bai and Qingqing. The boat touched land, and Mistress Bai cried, "Why
did you not come back? Come on the boat at once!" Xu Xuan was on
the verge of complying when a voice behind him thundered, "What are
those creatures doing here?" Xu Xuan looked back, and someone said,
"Master Fahai is here!" Master Fahai said in a loud voice, "You evil
creatures! Have you come to stir trouble and hurt people again? It is on
your account that I am here!" At the sight of the monk, Mistress Bai
punted the boat away from the riverbank. That done, she and Qingqing
overturned the boat and they plunged themselves into the waves and
disappeared in the depths of the river.

Xu Xuan turned around. Looking piteously at the monk, he kowtowed and said, "I beg the master to save my unworthy life!" The Master
asked, "How did you meet that woman?" And Xu Xuan launched into an
account of all that had transpired. After hearing him out, the Master
declared, "That woman is indeed a demon. You should return to
Hangzhou at once, and should she bother you again, come to me at the
Monastery of Pure Benevolence on the south side of the lake. You must
keep this in mind:

> *"She is a demon disguised as a woman,*
> *Crooning her song on the banks of these lakes.*
> *Blind to her mischief you fell for her wiles,*
> *Meet me at South Lake if trouble she makes."*

Xu Xuan once more kowtowed his gratitude to Master Fahai, and
then together with Jiang Ho took a ferry, crossed the river, and went
home. Both Mistress Bai and Qingqing were nowhere to be found,
which finally convinced Xu Xuan they were demons. He asked Jiang Ho
to keep him company that night, but being disturbed and depressed he
did not sleep a wink. Rising early the next morning, he told Jiang Ho to
take care of the store and went to pay a call on Esquire Li. Xu Xuan
recounted all that had happened to him, whereupon Li Keyong told him,
"On the day of my birthday, I entered a lavatory without warning and
saw this demon. I fainted from fright and dared not tell you about this

matter. But now that we both know, you had best come live at my house and see how things turn out." Xu Xuan thanked Li Keyong and soon moved into his house.

Two more months passed by. One day, as Xu Xuan stood at the door, he saw the head of the local precinct directing all homes and businesses to make ready such objects as incense, flowers, and candles for the gracious pardons to be granted by the emperor. It so happened that Emperor Gaozong of the Song Dynasty was to pass the throne to his successor, Xiaozong and, in order to mark the event, he had announced an empire-wide amnesty for all criminals except murderers. Persons convicted of lesser crimes would be pardoned and permitted to go home. In his elation that he, too, would be pardoned, Xu Xuan recited a poem, which goes:

> My thanks to the Emperor for granting this pardon,
> Which opens the cage and confers me new life.
> Thus die shall I not as a ghost in strange lands,
> But live to go back to the place of my birth.
> Alas! Caught am I now in the coils of a demon!
> Oh, when may I sever the roots of my sins?
> Once home I will fill up my censers with incense,
> And pray that the gods, too, will pity my lot.

Having recited this poem, Xu Xuan asked Li Keyong to distribute gratuities to officials high and low at the yamen. The magistrate then granted him an audience and gave him a formal notice permitting him to go home. Xu Xuan thanked and bade farewell to all the neighbors, to Esquire Li and his wife and all other members of the household, and to the two managers at the apothecary. Finally, he asked the ever-helpful Jiang Ho to purchase some local produce, which he took back to Hangzhou.

When he arrived at his home in Hangzhou, he kowtowed four times in greeting to his sister and her husband. Procurator Li, however, said to him angrily, "A fine one you are! I wrote two letters asking other people to render you assistance, but you did not deign even to write a single letter letting us know you took a wife during your stay with Esquire Li. You are an ingrate!" Xu Xuan attempted to prevaricate, saying, "I have never taken a wife!" But his brother-in-law told him, "Two months earlier, a woman with a maidservant came and told us she is your wife. She said you had gone to Gold Mountain Monastery to burn incense but had not returned. She looked for you, but without success. Just recently she learned that you would be returning to Hangzhou. She and her maidservant have been waiting here for you for two months."

Procurator Li then instructed that the woman and the maid be brought out to meet Xu Xuan. They were indeed Mistress Bai and Qingqing! So shaken was Xu Xuan that his eyes bulged and his mouth fell open. Yet he could not divulge the truth of the matter to his sister and her husband, and could only suffer his brother-in-law's berating in silence. Procurator Li then had Xu Xuan and Mistress Bai shown to chambers where they could take up residence for the time being.

As evening drew near, Xu Xuan grew ever more fearful of Mistress Bai. He dared not approach her and, succumbing to panic, fell to his knees before her and cried, "I know not what manner of ghost or demon you are, but I beg you to spare me my life!" Mistress Bai said soothingly, "Brother Xiaoyi, why do you say that? Never, in the all the time we have lived as husband and wife, have I ever mistreated you. Why such untoward remarks?" Xu Xuan mumbled, "I have already fallen out twice with the law since becoming acquainted with you. After the first time, you pursued me to Zhenjiang Prefecture. And the other day, when I went to burn incense at Gold Mountain Monastery and was tardy coming home, you and Qingqing again came after me. You leapt into the river when you saw the Buddhist master, and I thought you had died. I know not how or by what means, but you contrived to come here before I did. Have pity on me and spare me this misery!"

Mistress Bai, her eyes glaring balefully, replied, "Xiaoyi, all I have done was for our good, yet you reproach me! You and I have rested our heads on the same pillow, slept under the same coverlet, and shared much love and affection. But now you let yourself be persuaded by false rumors and bring disharmony between us. Let me tell you frankly, if you listen to my words and live happily with me, all will be well. But should you attempt to leave me, I shall see to it that this city is washed in blood, that all people in it are swallowed by waves and flounder in mud and die fearful deaths!"

Quaking and mute with terror, Xu Xuan shrank away from Mistress Bai. Qingqing then exhorted Xu Xuan, saying, "Master, my mistress has always been attracted to you handsome men from Hangzhou and admires you for your kindly and affectionate nature. Why do you not restore harmony with my mistress and lay your doubts to rest?" Unable to withstand the onslaught mounted by both mistress and servant, Xu Xuan cried, "Woe is me!"

His sister, who happened to be in the courtyard enjoying the evening's cool air, overheard Xu Xuan's plaintive cry and, assuming the couple to be bickering, hurried into their room and drew her brother out. Mistress Bai shut the door behind them and lay down to sleep.

Xu Xuan recounted to his sister all that had transpired. As they spoke, the brother-in-law returned from a stroll outside the house and his wife told him, "The two have had a fight. I know not whether she is sleeping now, but go and take a look!" Procurator Li went to their room. The lights had been extinguished, but a dim glow illuminated the window. Procurator licked a hole in the window paper with his tongue and peered in.

Had he not done so, this tale might have ended differently, but he did, and he saw curled on the bed a python as big around as a well bucket. It was stretching its head toward the skylight to catch the cool breeze, and its scales gave off a luminescence that lit up the entire room. Astounded, Procurator Li turned back and returned to his chambers. He held his tongue and merely said, "She appears to be sleeping. I saw nothing."

That night, Xu Xuan remained in his sister's chambers and dared not show his face outside. Nor did his brother-in-law ask him any questions.

The next day, Procurator Li called Xu Xuan out and, leading him to a secluded spot, asked, "Where did you get your wife? Tell me the truth, and do not attempt to hide anything! Last night I saw with my own eyes that she is a big white snake, but I said nothing, for I did not wish to alarm your sister."

Xu Xuan recounted to Procurator Li, from beginning to end, all that had happened. After a moment's reflection, Procurator Li said, "In that case, there is, in front of White Horse Temple, a snake charmer called Master Dai who is skilled at catching snakes. Let us bring him here."

The two went to White Horse Temple and found Snake-charmer Dai before the gate. "Greetings, Master," they said, and Master Dai asked,

"How can I help you?" Xu Xuan said, "There is a big snake in our house, and we would be obliged if you capture it." "Where do you live?" inquired Master Dai, and Xu Xuan told him, "At the house of Procurator Li in Black Pearl Lane, just past Guojun Bridge." Extracting a tael of silver from his sleeve, he said, "Take this as a retainer. We will recompense you with more after you have snared the snake." Master Dai took the silver and promised, "You two gentlemen go back first! I will come in short order!"

So Procurator Li and Xu Xuan went home, while Master Dai filled a bottle with a potion made of the poison realgar. That done, he set out for Black Pearl Lane. Once there, he inquired where Procurator Li lived, and he was told, "In that two-story building just ahead."

Master Dai walked up to the door, rapped on it, and coughed, but no one came out. After he had knocked several more times, a young woman appeared and asked, "Whose house are you seeking?" Master Dai inquired, "Is this Procurator Li's residence?" The woman replied, "It is."

Master Dai then explained, "Two gentlemen told me there is a big snake in this house and asked me to capture it." Feigning surprise, the woman said, "A big snake in this house? Surely, you are mistaken!" Master Dai was not to be deterred. He said, "The gentlemen gave me a tael of silver as a retainer and promised much more once I capture the snake." The young woman, who was in fact Mistress Bai, insisted, "There are no snakes here. Do not let them bamboozle you!" But Master Dai countered, "Why should they do that?"

Observing that her efforts to dismiss the snake charmer bore no fruit, Mistress Bai lost her temper and queried mockingly, "Are you truly able to capture the snake? What if you fail in the attempt?" Master Dai assured her, "Snake charming has been my family's vocation for seven or eight generations. I see no difficulty in catching just one snake." Mistress Bai sneered, "So you say. But I fear you will run away once you see it!" Master Dai expostulated, "Nothing of the sort! I shall not run away! If I do, you may have that one tael of silver!" Whereupon Mistress Bai commanded, "Follow me!"

In the courtyard, Mistress Bai abruptly turned a corner and entered her chambers, leaving Master Dai outside with the bottle of realgar in his hands. In an instant, a chill wind arose, and a huge snake slid out of the chambers and darted straight at the snake charmer. Terrified, Master Dai fell backward, dropping and shattering the bottle. The snake yawned its blood-red maw to reveal gleaming white fangs and prepared to strike. Staggering to his feet—and regretting that his parents had not furnished him with an extra pair of legs—Master Dai fled all the way to the bridge and right into the arms of Procurator Li and Xu Xuan.

Xu Xuan asked, "How did it go?" And Master Dai cried, "There is something you must know!" And he forthwith launched into a detailed account of what had transpired. He then took out the one tael of silver and, handing it to Procurator Li, declared, "Were it not for this pair of feet, I would have lost my life. Feel free to engage someone else!" So saying, he quickly walked away.

Xu Xuan said, "Brother-in-law, what do we do now?" After a moment's thought Procurator Li replied, "At least we know it is a demon! Now, there is a certain Zhang Cheng who owes me one thousand strings of cash. He lives by Red Hill Pier, a tranquil place. Go to him and ask for a room to live in. After you leave, the demon will naturally go away." Having no better ideas of his own, Xu Xuan reluctantly agreed.

When they arrived at the brother-in-law's house, all was quiet as though nothing had transpired. Procurator Li wrote out a letter and enclosed the original loan compact for Xu Xuan to take to Red Hill Pier.

All at once, Mistress Bai summoned Xu Xuan to her chambers and scolded, "So you had the gall to call in a snake catcher! Let me tell you, if you are nice to me, I shall be merciful toward you. If not, you shall suffer together with all people in this city, and every one of you will die unspeakable deaths!" Terrified and quaking in his shoes, Xu Xuan dared not utter a word in reply.

Some time later, he placed the loan compact in his sleeve and went with a heavy heart to Red Hill Pier. He found Zhang Cheng, but when he felt in his sleeve for the loan compact, it was not there! With a cry of dismay, he turned back and retraced his steps to search for the compact but found nothing.

As he walked along, plunged in despondence, he passed by the gates of the Monastery of Pure Benevolence and suddenly recalled the admonition of Buddhist Master Fahai at the Gold Mountain Monastery: "Return to Hangzhou at once, and if the demon bothers you again, come to me at the Monastery of Pure Benevolence!" And he reflected, "When should I go to him, if not now?" So he hastened to enter the monastery, and he asked the superintending monk, "I wish to inquire whether Master Fahai has come to this monastery." But the monk replied, "No, he has not." These words only deepened Xu Xuan's despair. He turned back, and when he came to the ramp of Long Bridge, he muttered to himself, "As they say 'Nothing goes right when one's luck runs out.' Of what use is this life to me?"

He stared at the clear waters of the lake and was about to throw himself in when he heard someone behind him call out, "Why do you, a man, make so light of your own life? Does life mean so little to you? Why do you not come to me if you are in trouble?" Xu Xuan turned around and saw Master Fahai approaching, staff in hand. Clearly, he had only just arrived, as he was bearing a large bundle on his back.

Xu Xuan was apparently not destined to die yet, for if Fahai had tarried for the time needed to consume but one bowl of rice, Xu Xuan would have been dead!

Xu Xuan at once kowtowed to the master and cried, "Please save me!" The abbot asked, "Where is that creature?" Xu Xuan told the master all that had happened, saying, "She has found me once more! Master, I beg you to save my life!"

The master took a large earthen alms bowl from his sleeve and handed it to Xu Xuan with the words, "When you go home, find a moment when the woman is distracted and push this bowl over her head. Do not hesitate and do not panic. Hold the bowl down with all your strength. Go now!"

Xu Xuan thanked the master and went home. He found Mistress Bai seated in a room, fretting and fuming. "Someone is sowing discord between my husband and myself! I do not know who it is, but when I find out, see how I make him pay for it!"

That was precisely the moment of distraction Xu Xuan was seeking! Watchfully, he stole up behind her and with one fell swoop clapped the bowl over her head, driving it down with every ounce of his strength. The woman form gradually dissolved as the bowl bore down, but Xu Xuan did not dare relent and only pressed the harder.

After a while, he heard a voice coming from under the bowl. "We have been a couple for many a year. How can you be so unfeeling? Let up a bit, I beg you!"

Just as Xu Xuan was at loss what to do, a servant reported, "A monk is outside. He claims he has come to exorcise a demon." Xu Xuan quickly asked Procurator Li to bring the monk in at once, and when that was done, he pleaded, "Master, rescue me!"

The monk muttered a few words, and then carefully lifted up the bowl. They saw Mistress Bai curled on the floor with her eyes shut, reduced to the size of a clay puppet two handspans long. Master Fahai thundered, "What manner of evil creature are you, that you dare inflict yourself on human beings? Out with it!"

Mistress Bai replied, "Founding Father, I am a python. I came and settled down in West Lake, together with Qingqing, after a great thunderstorm. When I encountered Xu Xuan I was carried away by lustful desires and thus violated the rules of heaven. But I have never slain or harmed any person. Have mercy on me!" The master asked, "What sort of demon is Qingqing?" And Mistress Bai said, "She is a black fish from the pool under the Third Bridge at West Lake and had lain there for a thousand years. After we met, I persuaded her to join me, but she has never had even a single night's carnal enjoyment. I beg you to have pity on her!"

After some reflection, the Master Fahai declared, "In consideration of your thousand years of cultivating the essence of life, I will not put you to death. But you must revert to your original form!" Mistress Bai refused to do so. Greatly angered, the abbot again muttered an incantation and cried, "Oh, Gyate, Protector of the Dharma, where art thou? Seize the Black Fish, and reveal the White Snake in its true form! I shall decide their fate!"

An instant later a fierce wind rose, followed by a loud crash. A huge black fish, bigger in size than a man, fell from the sky, flopped about a few times, and then shrank until it was less than a handspan long. In the meantime, Mistress Bai changed into a white snake three feet in length, and it kept lifting its head to look at Xu Xuan.

Master Fahai placed the two creatures in the alms bowl, tore a length of cloth from his cassock, and tied this over the mouth of the bowl to seal it. He then took the bowl to Thunder Peak Monastery, buried it in the ground, and had bricks and stones brought to build a pagoda over the spot.

Having suppressed the two demons, Master Fahai proceeded to compose an admonitory verse of eight lines, which reads as follows:

All men would do well to abjure sensual lust,
Since lust is a bane that bewitches the mind.
Corruption retreats when a heart is well strung,
Can evil invade when the flesh holds up strong?
Hence lust was the reason for Xu Xuan's ill luck,
For all his mishaps and disputes with the law.
To Buddha he owes that this monk did him save,
From being devoured by the fearful White Snake.

After Master Fahai had recited this verse, his listeners went their own respective ways—all but Xu Xuan, who asked Fahai to be his mentor, and who then became a monk. He donned a cassock and shaved his head under the Thunder Peak Pagoda, and thereafter devoted his remaining years to practicing the Buddhist religion. When eventually he died, seated in meditation, his fellow monks cremated his remains and built a stupa as an eternal resting place for his ashes.

In his later years, Xu Xuan assembled a sufficient sum of money in alms and donations to replace the first pagoda with a bigger and more magnificent one seven tiers high—one that would prevent the White Snake and Black Fish from ever appearing in the world again.

Weaver Shi Meets a Friend at the Strand

施潤澤灘闕遇友

Allow me to begin with a story from ancient times—a story about unsung virtue. It has to do with Pei Du, Lord of Jin during the Tang Dynasty. Before Pei Du achieved renown, he was utterly destitute as well as unsuccessful in all his endeavors. So he sought a soothsayer—of the kind that tells a man's fortune by reading his physiognomy—to see what he should do. And the soothsayer said, "There is naught, I fear, to be said about either fame or fortune. But I can tell you something else if you promise not to reproach me for speaking too bluntly." And Pei Du replied, "This young person seeks your advice because I know not where my destiny is bound. I will, of course, not reproach you." Whereupon the soothsayer said, "Those lines that run from your nose to your mouth tell me that in a few years hence, you shall starve to death in some roadside ditch." The soothsayer then departed, refusing to accept any fee. And Pei Du, a sensible man, did not take the matter to heart.

One day, as he strolled around the hall of a temple at Fragrant Hills, his attention was drawn to a glittering object on the altar. He went closer and saw that it was a bejeweled girdle. Picking up the girdle, he examined it and thought, "What brings a precious girdle to this out-of-the-way temple?" As he turned it about in his hands, he surmised, "An important person must have been praying to Buddha here and then gone to relieve himself, whereupon his attendants left the girdle here on the altar in a moment of carelessness. They are bound to come back for it." So he seated himself on a balustrade and proceeded to wait.

Soon, a young woman hurried into the temple and made straight for the hall. She looked at the altar and uttered a wail of despair, and then fell weeping to the ground. Pei Du approached her and inquired, "Young Mistress, why do you weep?" And the woman said, "This humble woman's father was imprisoned on false accusations, with no place to plead his innocence, so I have come daily to pray to Buddha for his deliverance. Just recently, his sentence was reduced, and he may be set free upon payment of a sum of money. But we are poor and have no money or means to secure his release. Yesterday, a noble person took pity on us and presented me with a valuable girdle. Believing this to be a manifestation of Buddha's power, I came here, placed the girdle before Buddha and kowtowed my thanks. But in my eagerness to bail my father out, I departed in great haste and left the girdle here, and only realized the oversight when I had walked halfway home. I returned at once, but someone has already taken it. Now that I have lost the girdle, my father will never come out of prison!" And with that, she began to weep again.

Pei Du said, "Young Mistress, do not grieve. It was I who took the girdle, and for that reason have been waiting here." Having said that, he gave her the girdle. The young woman dried her tears, kowtowed her thanks, and then asked, "Please tell me your name, so that when my father is released he may kowtow his thanks to you in person." But Pei Du said, "I see your distress, and it shames me to say that I myself am too penurious to offer you any assistance, however little. However, returning other people's lost property is the rightful thing to do and does not deserve any thanks." And without telling her his name, Pei Du took his leave.

A few days later, Pei Du happened to come across the aforementioned soothsayer, and the latter exclaimed in astonishment, "What good deeds have you done of late?" And Pei Du replied, "None." The soothsayer told him, "Your facial features have undergone remarkable changes since the last time we met. They now bear clear lines of the performance of praiseworthy deeds and indicate that you will become a high official, live to a venerable old age, and acquire wealth beyond measure."

Pei Du dismissed these words as a pleasantry, but they were eventually borne out in full when he attained high military and civil positions, held power under four different dynastic rules, gained the title Lord of the State of Jin, and enjoyed exceptional longevity.

★ ★ ★

Seventy *li* from Suzhou Prefecture, in the county of Wujiang, lies a township called Shengze. The inhabitants of this populous township are by nature modest and industrious, and most are engaged in the silkworm and mulberry-leaf industries. As all men and women here are hardworking people, the clacking of looms can be heard all night long. The banks of the river that flows through the township are lined with more than a thousand brokerages, and the owners of village workshops far and near come here to market the silks and satins they weave. So many merchants from all over the country flock to this township to purchase its products that one can hardly squeeze through the market streets or, indeed, even set foot in them. And although the regions south of the Yangtze River abound in silkworm breeding areas, none is as prosperous as Shengze.

Now during the Jiajing reign (1522-1567), there lived in Shengze a man by the name of Shi Fu. He and his wife, Mistress Yu, had neither sons nor daughters. They possessed one silk-weaving loom, raised a few trays of silkworms every year, and with the woman spinning silk and the man weaving fabrics, they made a tolerably good living. Most of the households in this township were fairly well off and would put together ten bolts of fabrics, or at least five or six bolts, before taking these to the market. The bigger households stored up larger quantities of fabrics and did not go to the market, since the brokers would bring visiting merchants straight to their doors. Shi Fu, however, was a small producer with little capital, so he would sell his silks on the market when he had assembled three or four bolts.

One day, having accumulated four bolts of silk, Shi Fu folded them into neat squares, wrapped them in a length of cloth, and took them to the township. The marketplace was a scene of animated activity, with people jostling one another and talking loudly. Shi Fu went to a broker with whom he was well acquainted. Many sellers of silk stood by the door while several visiting merchants sat inside. The owner of the store stood before the counter, examining lengths of fabric and chanting out his estimation of their worth. Shi Fu made his way to the counter and handed his bundle of silks to the owner. Taking the bundle, the owner unwrapped it, unfolded and inspected each bolt of silk, had them weighed, and set a price on them. He then passed the silk to a merchant, saying, "Master Shi is an honest man and has never given me any trouble. Pay him with good silver."

The merchant accordingly brought out some high-grade silver and gave it to Shi Fu, who forthwith took out a set of scales and weighed the silver. When he found it to be somewhat wanting in weight, the merchant agreed to add a *fen* or two, and thus the deal was done. Shi Fu asked for a sheet of paper, wrapped up the silver, and tucked it in his money belt. Then, folding his hands in an obeisance, he thanked the owner and left the brokerage.

He had walked but half an arrow's flight when he noticed a small black pouch lying beside the doorstep of another brokerage. He hastened to retrieve it, and then sought a secluded spot. There he opened the pouch and saw that it contained two ingots and several smaller pieces of silver, plus some loose cash. Hefting the silver in his hand, he surmised that it weighed about six taels. He was overjoyed and exclaimed, "What a stroke of luck! This silver will be a most welcome addition to my capital!" Quickly returning the silver to the pouch, he secreted the latter in his money belt and turned his steps homeward.

As he walked along, he thought to himself, "The loom I have now merely suffices me for my everyday needs. With this silver, I can purchase another loom, which will produce such-and-such an amount of silk every month and so much silver in profits. I shall pretend that the silver is not there and refrain from using it, and in a year I shall have accumulated such-and-such an amount of profits and buy another loom. In this manner, I will, in ten years, have accumulated a thousand taels of gold, with which I can build this-and-that number of houses and purchase such-and-such an amount of land."

As he approached his home, engrossed in such calculations, a sudden thought struck him. "If this silver was dropped there by a rich man, it would be of as much consequence to him as a hair from the hide of an ox but will serve me well. If, however, the silver belongs to a visiting merchant who leaves his wife and children at home, suffers all the hardships of the road, and works hard for his money, this loss must be most vexing. Should he have sufficient capital, he will be able to even out the loss and not be overly inconvenienced. But if he is a small operator and has only so much capital, or, like me, struggles to make a living by selling silk or reeling silk thread, these two ingots of silver would be his very lifeblood, and losing it will choke the very air from his throat. With nothing to live on, he and his wife will bicker with each other and might even have to sell themselves or their children. And who knows, if he is a self-willed man he might even wastefully take his own life. Although I have not committed any great transgression by picking up this silver, the thought of what might have happened to this man will give me no peace of mind in the days to come. Moreover, having this bit of silver will not necessarily cause my business to prosper, and had I not found it I could still continue to live as I have until now. I had best go back and wait for the owner to come looking for the silver and then return it to him. In that way I shall be at peace with myself."

Shi Fu turned about, retraced his steps to the place where he had found the silver, and stood next to the broker's counter. He waited a long time, but no one came to seek the silver. Shi Fu had left home that morning without breaking his fast, and now he felt increasingly hungry. He thought of going home to eat something, yet feared that the man would come looking for the silver while he was away and they would miss each other. So he endured his discomfort and continued to wait.

Some time later, a young man of rustic appearance rushed into the brokerage, his face bathed in perspiration, and he cried, "Proprietor, I left my silver on your counter. Have you picked it up?" The proprietor shot back, "What impudence! I gave you the silver this morning, and now you ask me for it? Not to mention one packet of silver, had you left ten packets of silver on my counter, all would have been taken away by now!"

Stamping his feet in despair, the young man lamented, "I was counting on that silver to plant my crops. Now that it is gone, what shall I do?" Shi Fu approached him and asked, "About how much silver did you lose?" The young man replied, "Six taels and two *qian*, the amount for which I sold my silk." Shi Fu asked again, "How was it wrapped, and how many pieces were there?" The young man declared, "There were two whole ingots and three or four smaller pieces, all contained in a pouch of black cloth." Shi Fu said, "Then you need not worry. I have found the silver and have been waiting here for you to come." As he spoke, he drew the pouch out of his money belt and handed it to the young man.

Having thanked Shi Fu most profusely, the young man took the pouch and opened it, and found that none of its contents were missing. Passersby noticed that something unusual had occurred and crowded around, asking, "Where did you find it?" Pointing, Shi Fu replied, "Right by that doorstep." The young man then said to Shi Fu, "Elder Brother, few are the kindhearted persons who would wait here to return the silver. This would not have happened had it fallen in someone else's hands. Now that I have recovered the silver, I am willing to give you half of it." But Shi Fu demurred, "Had I wanted the silver, I would have taken all instead of only half of it." Whereupon the young man said, "Since that is the case, then let me show my gratitude by giving you one tael, so that you may purchase some sweetmeats." Shi Fu laughed and replied, "What a dolt you are! Why would I want one tael when I have already declined six?" The young man asked, "Then how can I thank you, since you refuse to take any silver?"

At this time, some onlookers declared, "This is obviously an honest and virtuous gentleman who will not accept any recompense. You had best take him to a wine shop and treat him to three cups of wine to show your appreciation." The young man said, "You are right," and forthwith invited Shi Fu to go with him to a wine shop, but Shi Fu refused. "That will not be necessary. I have matters to attend to at home, so please do not take up my time." So saying, he turned on his heel and left, and the young man was unable to detain him. The onlookers remarked, "You are indeed fortunate! You lose your silver and then get it back at no cost at all." And even the proprietor added, "That is true. I would never have thought that such a good man exists in this world."

The young man put away his silver, apologized to the proprietor for any inconvenience caused, and strode out of the store. The onlookers then dispersed, commenting among themselves. Some said, "Shi Fu is a fool. He finds silver, but instead of using it for himself, stands there and waits to return it." But others opined, "He has accumulated merits for himself in the nether world and will certainly benefit from them."

When Shi Fu arrived at his home, his wife asked, "What kept you away for so long?" Shi Fu replied, "Let us not talk about that. I had just about reached home when I had to go back for some matter and was thus delayed." But his wife insisted, "What is it that delayed you?" Whereupon Shi Fu apprised her about the silver he had picked up and returned. His wife declared, "You did well. The ancients have told us, 'A windfall does not make rich those fated to be poor.' For all we know, if we are not destined to find such wealth, doing so may only visit disaster upon us." Shi Fu agreed, saying, "And for that reason I returned the money to him."

Neither Shi Fu nor his wife took pleasure in picking up other people's silver, but instead found contentment in returning the silver to its owner. The high-mindedness of such unlettered commoners as Shi Fu and his wife is most gratifying when one reflects that many richly bedecked gentlefolk throw all morality to the winds when they see the possibility of profits for themselves.

Thereafter, Shi Fu gained great profits from raising silkworms, and his fortunes began gradually to improve.

Now, many skills are needed for raising silkworms, but the most essential of these is the choice of good strains. A good strain of worms spins small, translucent, and compact cocoons from which good strands of silk may be reeled. If, on the other hand, the strain is poor, then the cocoons are flaccid and cottony and produce inferior silk, so that one's profits are many times smaller. One must also be blessed with good fortune. Those who are so blessed may also obtain good cocoons from an inferior strain. However, less fortunate persons succeed only in obtaining cotton-like cocoons from good strains.

Northern silkworms molt thrice before they weave their cocoons, whereas southern silkworms molt four times. When they wake up after each molting, they must be promptly fed with mulberry leaves. Silkworms are also averse to both cold and heat and they grow best in moderate temperatures. For them, a day may be compared to the four seasons, with morning and evening being like spring and autumn, and midday and nighttime, like summer and winter. Thus taking good care of silkworms presents many difficulties.

Shi Fu was careful to select the best strains, and he had consistent good luck. Hence none of his silkworms produced poor cocoons, and the strands reeled from the latter were clear and glossy and none came in uneven thicknesses. Moreover, he harvested much more silk from each tray of silkworms than other families. His fabrics, woven in the same manner as other people's, were more shiny and lustrous than any on the market, so that brokers vied for them, paying him a good deal more silver for his products than for other people's silks and satins.

With this run of good fortune, Shi Fu was able to purchase three or four new looms within a few years' time, and his family became quite prosperous. Indeed, villagers in neighborhood applauded his accomplishments by nicknaming him "Shi the Lustrous." He sired a son whom he dedicated to Guanyin, the Goddess of Mercy, and named him Guanbao, which means "Protected by Guanyin." And when two years old, Guanbao was already a sturdy child of the most pleasing appearance.

But enough of these details for now!

One year, just after the third molting during the silkworm-raising sea-son, there was a grave shortage of mulberry leaves throughout Shengze Township. And when Shi Fu's household was down to their last two days' supply of leaves, they were greatly consternated, as they did not know where to find any more.

Had there been rainy or cloudy weather during the raising season, there would have been a surplus of mulberry leaves, for as much as half a crop of silkworms may curl up and die when exposed to cold and damp air, or when fed leaves moist with cold dew. However, in this year, the days had been warm and sunny and no family had suffered losses, so that mul-berry leaves were in short supply.

Just as Shi Fu was close to desperation, a neighbor informed him that there was an abundance of leaves at Mount Dongting and that ten or more families were sending people across Lake Tai to purchase some sup-plies. No sooner did Shi Fu hear this news than he tied his bedding in a bundle and hurried to the boat, taking along a few taels of silver. Shortly after the noon hour, the boatman lowered the stern sweep and rowed out of the township.

After passing Pingwang, the boat came to a village called the Strand, situated on the bank of Lake Tai at some forty *li*'s distance from Shengze. Since evening was approaching and time did not suffice to cross the lake before nightfall, the boat was steered into a small cove and securely moored. But when the company prepared to cook supper, they found that no one had brought flint and tinder. They asked one another, "Who will go ashore to borrow a firebrand?" As though prompted by some unknown spirit or god, Shi Fu stated, "I shall go!" And he forthwith picked up a bunch of slow-burning flax roots and jumped ashore.

In the village, he observed that every door was shut. So why is it that all the doors were shut before nightfall? That is because silkworm breed-ers most scrupulously avoid intrusions by strangers at a certain season. During some forty days from the time the worms are hatched to when they weave their cocoons, every household keeps its doors tightly shut and no one goes visiting, not even on matters of the greatest urgency.

As Shi Fu walked past several houses, he felt somewhat mystified at first, and he thought, "Do these people fear being dragged away by demons, that they shut their doors when the sky is not yet dark?" Then with sudden realization, he exclaimed, "Hah! How could I, a seasoned silkworm breeder, have forgotten that I would be violating taboos by knocking on people's doors! I have taken on an impossible task. Nowhere will I get a firebrand!" He started to turn back but another thought struck him. "All would be well and good had I not volunteered. But if I return empty-handed now and someone else comes ashore and succeeds, I shall be the butt of much ridicule. There are, perhaps, families that do not raise silkworms."

As he proceeded further, he saw the door of one house slightly ajar. Brashly, he hastened toward the house, but his courage failed him when he came under its eaves. Standing outside the door, he craned his neck to look in and called, "Is anyone at home?"

A woman stepped out, asking, "Who are you?" Shi Fu, wreathing his face in a smile, said, "Big Sister, I am here to borrow a firebrand." The woman remarked, "Other families would refuse to oblige you during this season. However, we have no such taboo and I will be glad to help you."

Shi Fu forthwith handed his bunch of flax roots to the woman, who entered the house and soon came out with the roots already smoldering. Taking the roots, Shi Fu said, "Many thanks." Then he turned his steps toward the cove. He had walked past two houses when he heard the woman calling, "Borrower of fire, you have lost something!" Shi Fu turned around, thinking, "What can I have lost?" The woman then said, "You dropped your money belt here." Thereupon she handed the money belt to Shi Fu, who thanked her effusively, saying, "Kindhearted people like you are indeed rare." But the woman demurred, "Not at all! A few years ago, my husband went to Shengze to sell silk and lost more than six taels of silver. But a good person found it and waited for the person who had lost it to return, and when my husband arrived, he found that none of the silver was missing. The man would not even accept a cup of wine as recompense. That was truly a kindhearted person!"

Shi Fu was astonished to hear the woman's account, for it concurred with his own actions years earlier. He asked, "When did this thing happen?" Counting on her fingers, the woman replied, "Six years ago." Shi Fu ventured, "To be honest with you, Big Sister, I am from Shengze, and six years ago I picked up more than six taels of silver that had been lost by a seller of silk. I waited for the man to come back and returned the silver to him. He wished to treat me to wine, but I declined. Could that man have been your husband?"

"How amazing!" exclaimed the woman. "Let me call my husband out and see if you recognize each other!" Shi Fu wished to stop her, for he feared his companions on the boat might become impatient. But the flax roots in his hand were burning out, so he said, "Big Sister, I would be much obliged if you should get me a paper spill to sustain the spark of fire." Without saying a word, the woman entered the house, and a moment later a young man hurried out. He looked at Shi Fu, and though six years had passed since their last encounter, he recognized the man who had returned him his silver.

The young man folded his hands in a deep obeisance and said, "I have always kept you in mind, brother, but could not find you to pay you my respects. It is Heaven's will that has sent you to my poor abode." Shi Fu returned the obeisance, and the man's wife also bowed to Shi Fu.

The young man then said, "I was in such haste on the day I benefited from your kindness that I neglected to ask your name and place of residence. Since then I have sold silk several times to the same brokerage in your township, but the owner could not tell me your name. I also made other enquiries, but to no avail. Now Heaven has unexpectedly brought you right to our humble village. Please come in and sit down."

However, Shi Fu replied, "I thank you for your kindly remembrances, but friends of mine are in a boat, waiting for some fire to cook their supper. I ought not to go in." Whereupon the young man said, "Why do we not invite all of them here?" But Shi Fu demurred, saying, "No, that would not be proper." The young man then said, "If so, then come back and sit a while after sending them a firebrand."

He then told his wife to bring a paper spill. While she was doing this, the young man asked, "What is my elder brother's name? And where are you going?" Shi Fu replied, "My name is Shi Fu. People call me Shi the Lustrous. There is a dearth of mulberry leaves in our township, and we are crossing the lake to purchase some leaves at Mount Dongting." The young man declared, "If you should need mulberry leaves, I have plenty to spare. Why do you not spend the night here and let your companions go on their way? I will take you back home on my boat. What say you to that?"

Much pleased to hear that the young man could provide him with mulberry leaves, Shi Fu exclaimed, "If you have leaves, I would be saved the trouble of crossing the lake! Allow me to tell my companions I shall not be going with them."

At this time the woman came out of the house. The young man took the lighted paper spill from her, saying, "I shall be going with my elder brother." He then instructed his wife to prepare supper.

When the two men came to the boat, they handed the paper spill to those on board. These had been chafing over their long wait, and they complained, "What was so difficult about getting a firebrand, that you tarried at such length?" Shi Fu replied, "Need I explain? No one would give me a firebrand as all are tending to their silkworms. Moreover, I happened to meet a friend and spoke a few words with him, which is the reason I am late. I offer my apologies." He continued, "This friend has some spare leaves at home and I have purchased them. Thus I shall not be sailing with you across the lake. My bundle is in the cabin, so I must ask someone the favor of bringing it to me." When one of Shi Fu's companions had retrieved the bundle, the young man took it, saying, "Let me carry it!" Whereupon Shi Fu called out, "Fellow villagers, we part for the time being and shall meet again back home."

Having taken his leave, Shi Fu departed with the young man. As they walked along, he inquired, "What is your honorable name, my brother? I was too preoccupied to ask earlier." The young man replied, "This humble one's name is Zhu En, and my style name is Ziyi." Shi Fu then asked, "How old are you?" And the young man replied, "Twenty-eight years old." "Then you are eight years my junior," said Shi Fu.

He then continued, "Does your respected father live with you?" And Zhu En informed him, "He passed away long ago, and only my mother is with us. She is sixty-eight years old and has lived abstemiously for many years."

As they spoke, they came to Zhu En's house. Pushing open the door, Zhu En asked Shi Fu to come and sit inside. A candle was already lit on the table. Setting down the bundle, Zhu En called out, "Wife, bring us some tea!" No sooner had he spoken that his wife came from behind a curtained door with two cups of tea. These she handed to Zhu En, who then offered one to Shi Fu and retained the other to keep his guest company. He inquired, "Wife, has the chicken been killed?" The wife replied, "I was waiting for you to help me do that." At this, Zhu En laid down his cup and sprang up to take a chicken from a coop to the left side of the room. However, Shi Fu detained him, saying, "I appreciate your hospitality, but must you kill that chicken? Any dishes to go with the rice will be sufficient to show your hospitality. Besides, the chicken has already retired for the night, and it would pain me to see it dispatched for my benefit." Zhu En saw that his guest was a man of his own mind, so he relented and, seating himself again, said, "Since you say so. Let us then have it for dinner tomorrow." Calling to his wife, he said, "Never mind the chicken. Serve us anything that is available. And hurry, for our guest must be starving. Bring the wine well warmed up!"

Shi Fu commented, "I have come to bother you during the busiest time of the year. Happily, your house does not observe the taboo." Zhu En replied, "To tell you the truth, ours used to be the house with the most taboos in this village. Now we are the only one that does not have any at all." "Why is that?" asked Shi Fu, and Zhu En explained, "After you returned the silver to me, we came to the realization that all things are predestined and not decided by man. We therefore eschewed all the taboos. Yet we have since made profits as good as any in previous years. So we know now that people create their own ghosts and demons, and that taboos are of no consequence. Evil is caused by men who believe in evil." Shi Fu remarked, "My brother's words are reasonable and make good sense."

Shi En continued, "There is another strange thing. In past years we have raised ten trays of silkworms but never gathered a sufficient amount of leaves from our own mulberry trees and had to purchase more elsewhere. This year we started up fifteen trays, but without adding a single new tree we not only plucked enough leaves for ourselves but even have a large surplus to supply your needs. It would seem that these leaves were predetermined to be yours, my elder brother." Shi Fu observed, "That also makes sense, as our meeting itself would also seem to have been preordained. You met me that year because you lost your silver, and now we meet again because your wife returned to me silver that I lost and we started talking about that past event." Zhu En marveled, "It would seem that we were predestined during some past life to meet again. It would please me if we could become sworn brothers. What say you to that?" And Shi replied, "I would be greatly honored, for I have no brothers of my own."

Without further ado, the two kowtowed eight times to each other right there in the room, and formally swore brotherhood. Shi Fu asked that Zhu En's mother be invited out of her chambers so that he might kowtow to her, while Zhu En called to his wife to come and meet her sworn brother-in-law, and there was much good cheer. Wine and food were served, though the plates held merely the usual fare of fish and pork.

As the two sat and drank, Zhu En asked, "How many sons do you have, Elder Brother?" "Only one," said Shi Fu, "and he is but two years old. How many do you have?" Zhu En replied, "I only have one child, a daughter. She too is two years old." He forthwith asked his wife to bring the girl out to show to Shi Fu. All at once, Zhu En had another idea. "Elder Brother, what say you if, in addition to being brothers, we also became in-laws?" Shi Fu smiled, saying, "That would be excellent, but I fear my family is too poor to aspire to such a distinction." Zhu En protested, "How can you say such a thing, Elder Brother?" And the two then and there agreed to the match, which only brought them closer together.

The two then went back to their drinking, toasting each other back and forth. After more than a watch had passed in this manner, Zhu En got up and brought over a door plank. Propping up both ends of the plank with stools, he improvised a bed at the right side of the room and laid a mat on it. Shi Fu undid his bundle and took out a quilt, which he spread on top of the mat. Then, Zhu En bade Shi Fu a good night and retired to the inner rooms, closing the intervening door.

Shi Fu blew out the candle and lay down but could not fall asleep. As he tossed and turned, he heard a chicken clucking restlessly in the coop and wondered, "What is the matter with that chicken?" An hour or two passed, when suddenly all the chickens began to squawk loudly as though something were chasing them. Thinking that a yellow weasel had come to steal a chicken, Shi Fu sprang out of bed and threw on some clothes, intending to go over to the chicken coop. He had taken barely three or four steps from his bed, when there was a tremendous cracking sound, as though the ground had split open, and something crashed onto the bed. Fear rooted Shi Fu to the spot.

In the meantime, Zhu En and his wife and mother had been feeding their silkworms when they heard the chickens squawking. They too assumed that a weasel had entered the chicken coop, and they sallied forth with torches in their hands. They had just reached the door, when they heard the loud crash. Zhu En stamped his foot in anguish, and cried, "What has happened? Have I caused my brother to lose his life?" He rushed out, closely followed by his wife and his mother, both of whom were exclaiming "Alas! Alas!"

As Zhu En stepped through the door, he saw Shi Fu standing in the middle of the room, and he cried with relief, "Elder Brother, I almost died of fright! How fortunate that you happened to get up, and thus escaped with your life!" Gathering his wits, Shi Fu said, "I rose to see why the chickens were creating such a row. Had I not done so, I would have been smashed into little pieces. What is it that fell down?" Zhu En replied contritely, "It is a wagon axle that I placed up there for safekeeping. I cannot imagine how it could have dropped down."

They examined the bed by the light of the torches and saw that the door plank had been smashed to bits and the stools flung aside. The axle itself, a full hand span in thickness, had rolled next to the wall. Shi Fu was so aghast his tongue stuck out and remained hanging outside his mouth.

After a while, Zhu En's mother and wife, having ascertained that Shi Fu was safe and sound, returned to their chambers. The chickens, too, had quieted down. Zhu En remarked, "Elder Brother, you asked me not to kill that chicken, and now it has saved your life." The two men then and there swore a solemn oath that they would never again kill livestock and chickens. Zhu En then lit candles, rolled up Shi Fu's bedding, brought some hay, and made a bed for Shi Fu to sleep on.

It started to rain the next morning. After breakfast, Shi Fu prepared to depart but Zhu En protested, "It was a rare chance that brought you here. Why not stay here one more day? I shall take you back tomorrow." Shi Fu demurred, "This is a busy time for both you and me, and neither of us would feel tranquil if I stayed another day. I had best go back now. When I am less busy, we could visit together for a few days with our minds at ease." Zhu En cried, "Not so! Not so! In any case you would have gone to Mount Dongting today, so stay and talk with me for one more day."

Zhu En's mother also came out of her room and exhorted him to stay longer, so Shi Fu could only accede to their requests.

At around nine in the morning, a powerful windstorm blew up, driving before it clouds of dust and uprooting trees, and it was followed by torrential rain. Zhu En exclaimed, "Elder Brother, it is Heaven's will that you should stay with me instead of going further on your trip. All who are crossing the lake must now be in peril." Shi Fu agreed, "That is true. This windstorm is truly unexpected, and quite fearsome!"

By nightfall, the wind had gradually stilled, and so had the rain. Shi stayed one more night. When he rose the next morning, Zhu En had already plucked a quantity of mulberry leaves and loaded them in his own boat, and after breakfast they were ready to leave. Shi Fu had considered giving Zhu En some money for the leaves, but surmised the latter would not accept any, so he said, "Dear Younger Brother, I suppose you will not let me pay you for the leaves, so I will not go through the motions. However, you are needed at home and would lose two days by taking me back. Would it not be convenient for both of us if I hired a man to row the boat?" But Zhu En disagreed, "I would like to see where you live, so that I may know how to find you next time. Do you not want me to go? Besides, I am not indispensable at home."

Since Zhu En was so insistent, Shi Fu no longer endeavored to dissuade him. Bidding farewell to Zhu En's wife and mother, he mounted the boat, and with Zhu En rowing, they arrived in Shengze just after midday. They moored the boat and proceeded to unload the mulberry leaves. Other people in the neighborhood, worried because of the windstorm of the previous day, were standing at their doorways, waiting for news. When they saw Shi Fu, they exclaimed in relief, "It is well. They have returned." Then they came to ask, "Why don't we see your companions? And how many leaves did you buy?" Shi Fu replied, "These leaves were given me by a relative whom I met at the Strand and who had some to spare. I did not sail across the lake with the others." A neighbor remarked enviously, "You are quite fortunate. I wonder how those who crossed the lake are faring." Shi Fu replied, "I surmise they are safe and sound." And the neighbor said doubtfully, "I would indeed hope so."

Shi Fu then asked some of his fellow villagers to help him take the leaves to his home. When this was done, he thanked them and they departed. His wife told him, "I had been worrying about you. The wind was so strong yesterday, I was wondering how you were, crossing the lake." Shi Fu said, "First come and meet your brother-in-law Zhu En, then I shall tell you what happened." Zhu En stepped forward and, with his hands folded, made a deep obeisance. Mistress Yu returned the greetings, after which Shi Fu continued, "Please be seated, my good brother." To his wife, he said, "Please serve us some tea, and bring our son out to meet his father-in-law."

Never having met Zhu En, Mistress Yu was mystified to hear this stranger being called her brother-in-law and her son's father-in-law, and wondered who he was. She hastened to bring two cups of tea, and then led out the little boy. Shi Fu handed a cup of tea to Zhu En, but instead of drinking tea himself, he took the boy in his arms and showed him to Zhu En. The boy's fine and delicate features greatly pleased Zhu En, who set down his bowl of tea and took the boy in his arms, the better to look at him. Not a bit shy, the little boy smiled and chuckled as though he were acquainted with Zhu En.

Shi Fu then told his wife, "Brother Zhu is the man who lost his silver a few years ago. His home is at The Strand." Mistress Yu exclaimed, "So that's who he is! How did you meet him this time?"

Shi Fu recounted in full detail how he had gone ashore to seek a firebrand and lost his money belt, how his conversation with Zhu En's wife had led to their reunion, how he had stayed at The Strand that night, how he and Zhu En had kowtowed to each other to become sworn brothers, and how they had decided to betroth their children. He also related how he asked that the chicken's life be spared, and how the chicken's warning had saved him from being crushed by the cart axle, and why he had not sailed across the lake but had brought back the mulberry leaves on this day.

Mistress Yu marveled at this account, then set about preparing wine and food to treat their visitor.

As they were eating and drinking, the sound of weeping and wailing suddenly arose in some neighboring houses. Shi Fu wondered what had happened, and when he went out to inquire, he learned that the boat on which his ten or more companions were crossing the lake to purchase mulberry leaves had capsized, drowning all of its passengers except for one man, who had kept himself afloat by hanging onto a wooden plank. Rescued by a fishing vessel, the man had only just returned to bring back the evil tidings.

Shi Fu was appalled. He came back to tell Zhu En and his wife what he had learned, then clasped his hands together and offered his thanks to Heaven. He said to Zhu En, "If you had not persuaded me to stay at your house, my good brother, I would have suffered the same fate!" But Zhu En would hear none of it, and said, "Your life has been spared because of the goodness and kindness you show to others. It has nothing to do with me."

Shi Fu kept Zhu En for the night, and after breakfast the next morning said to him, "I should by rights have you stay a few more days to show you around, but I know you are busy at home and dare not detain you any longer. I shall invite you to come again after the silkworm season is over." Zhu En replied, "There will be no need for any express invitation, as I am a frequent visitor to these parts."

Shi Fu bought two boxes of sweetmeats and presented these to Zhu En who accepted them without argument. Zhu En then bid farewell to Mistress Yu, untied his boat, and cast off. Shi Fu saw him to the very edge of the township, for,

> The gratitude for silver lost and returned,
> Had blossomed into brotherly esteem.

Shi Fu's profits from his silk manufacturing increased several-fold that year, and he wished to install another loom. But his house was too small for such an addition.

When a man has a run of good luck, everything would seem to fall in place of its own accord. As Shi Fu fretted about the lack of space for his new loom, his next-door neighbor announced that he was putting up his two rooms for sale. The neighbor had been losing money on his silkworms and mulberry leaves and blamed it on the site's poor *feng shui*. This suited Shi Fu's intentions.

The neighbor had offered to sell for a low price, since there were no takers. But once Shi Fu agreed to the deal, the perfidious neighbor raised the price, intentionally put up obstacles, and moved away only after all his demands had been satisfied. Moreover he stripped the rooms so bare they looked more like horse stables.

Shi Fu engaged a number of laborers to refurbish the rooms and chose an auspicious date for putting in the loom. He himself took up a hoe to prepare the foundation for the loom, and had dug down a foot or more when his hoe struck a large, square pavement block. Lifting the pavement block, he uncovered the round mouth of a big jar, which was apparently filled with mildewed rice. Shi Fu thought to himself, "What a waste of good rice! Why should a jar of rice be buried in the ground?" Then he thought, "The top layer of rice may be mildewed, but further down it may still be good." He set down his hoe and began to scoop out the rice with both hands. A layer less than an inch thick was removed when something white and silvery came to light. Upon further inspection, these turned out to be two ingots of the best silver, tilted up at both ends and slightly concave in the middle. Shi Fu's first thought was to take them out at once, but fearing that a laborer might come upon him and spread the news, he quickly covered the jar again with earth and told his wife about his discovery. Only after nightfall, after the laborers had left, did he and his wife take the silver home. It amounted to about one thousand taels! The couple was truly overjoyed.

Having now escaped two major disasters and acquired this treasure, Shi Fu became even more charitable and performed every good deed that lay within his means, yet he was careful not to overreach himself. Nor did he and his wife abandon their frugal ways, and they continued to work from dawn till dusk. Hence he became a respected elder in his locality.

In no more than ten years, they augmented their assets to several thousand taels of silver. They also purchased a bigger house in the vicinity, operated thirty or forty looms, hired a number of helpers and servants, and put their household affairs in a most admirable state of felicity. For his son, Guanbao, he even engaged a private tutor to teach the boy how to read and write. He changed the boy's name to Deyin, which means "virtuous offspring" and formally betrothed Zhu En's daughter to become his future daughter-in-law. As the saying goes, "All six kin share one man's good fortune." Zhu En's affairs, too, prospered splendidly, and the two men consorted with each other frequently and as affectionately as though they were blood brothers.

But, to come back to my story. Everything about Shi Fu's newly purchased house was in good condition—all except the main hall, which tilted perceptibly to one side and appeared to be in danger of falling down. Shi Fu had no choice but to rebuild it. He himself was accustomed to hard work, as he had been born in a poor family and had toiled for a living all his life. So rather than put on the airs of a rich man, he spent all his time with the laborers, carrying bricks and stones and fetching water and mortar. The laborers, however, did not comprehend his habit of working hard and suspected he was using this as a pretext to keep an eye on them, and so none dared to dawdle or loaf on the job.

After two weeks of work, an auspicious day and hour were chosen for raising the pillars and hoisting the beams. Before dawn, all the laborers were wined and dined to ensure good luck for that event. Shi Fu stayed alone at the work site to inspect the pillar foundations on both sides, and added bricks and stones to level the rough spots. He found that the foundation for the central pillar to the left of the room was slightly higher on one side than on the other, and he attempted to correct this flaw. Strangely enough, the foundation remained uneven no matter how he rearranged the bricks, so he finally took apart the entire base. When he had done so, he found the reason: a triangular chunk of sandstone lay underneath the bricks with one corner jutting upward. "What a slipshod piece of work!" he grumbled. "How could they leave that rock there!" As he lifted out the piece of sandstone, to his astonishment he uncovered a pit filled with shining silver ingots of various sizes. Gleaming brightly at the top of the pile were several large ingots, all of the same size and with bright red ribbons knotted around their midsections.

Shi Fu was both delighted and mystified—delighted that he had found another cache of treasure, and mystified that the ingots with the red ribbons still glistened with such a fresh glow although they must have lain buried for a long time. However, he did not waste any time on conjecture. He bundled as many ingots as possible in the folds of his garments, covered the pit with the rock, hurried back to his house, and emptied out the ingots on his bed. Mistress Yu observed him doing this and inquired, "Where did you get all that silver?" Shi Fu did not stop to explain, but called to his son who was also in the room, "Guanbao, come with me at once!" As he spoke, he was already running helter-skelter from the room, and Mistress Yu surmised that something unusual had taken place.

Father and son returned to the main hall, and while Guanbao maintained a lookout, Shi Fu made several trips to move all the silver into his own chambers. By the time he had finished, the laborers had not yet returned from their drinking.

Shi Fu then recounted to his wife how he had found the silver, and all three in the family were immensely pleased. Locking the doors, they secreted away the silver, which amounted to some two thousand taels. Eight of the ingots had red ribbons tied around them and weighed exactly three taels apiece. When all the ingots had been hidden away, Shi Fu knelt and kowtowed his gratitude to Heaven and Earth. Then, having changed his garments, he came out to watch the laborers going about busily with preparations to erect the pillars. When the latter saw that the base for one of the pillars had been torn up, they asked, "Who has made this mess? This will require a good deal more work!" But Shi Fu announced, "It was poorly laid and must be remade." Hearing this, the laborers knew that it was the master's doing and dared not say anything else. They quickly repaired the foundation without ever learning the true reason it had been taken apart.

At this time, Shi Fu looked up at the sky and declared, "Daybreak has come. Erect the pillars!" The laborers all pitched in and soon pulled up the pillars and positioned the beams on top of them. When this was done, a large platter of steamed buns to celebrate the successful raising of the beams was brought out and distributed among the laborers, and all the neighbors came with sweetmeats and wine to congratulate Shi Fu. His happiness enhanced by his recent discovery, Shi Fu drank until he was quite tipsy.

When he had seen his visitors off, Shi Fu removed his ceremonial cap and robe and, once more attired in his customary short tunic, went to assist the laborers. Just before the noon hour, he happened to take a stroll outside the house and saw a man in his sixties with shaggy eyebrows and gray hair approaching the door. The elderly man eyed him for a moment, and then asked, "Is this the Shi residence?" Shi Fu replied, "It is indeed. And whom do you seek?" The elderly man stated, "I wish to see the head of the house to ask him a question." Shi Fu said, "I am he. What do you wish to know? Please come in and be seated." Upon learning that Shi Fu was the head of the household, the elderly man looked him up and down and again asked, "Are you truly the master here?" Shi Fu smiled, "I am but an ordinary person. Who would wish to impersonate me?"

The elderly man waved his hand and said, "This old person will not stand on ceremony. I merely ask for a few moments of your time." He drew Shi Fu aside and asked, "Did you erect pillars and beams at your house today?" Shi Fu replied, "Indeed we did." The elderly man continued, "Did you find any silver under the left central pillar?"

Shi Fu was greatly astonished by the elderly man's question and thought to himself, "Is this a man or an immortal?" But as such a thing had indeed happened, he could not deny it, and he replied, "Yes, there was some." The elderly man went on, "Were there eight ingots with red ribbons tied around them?" Shi Fu was even more astounded, and he acknowledged, "Yes, there were. But how do you know these details?" The elderly man stated, "I know, because these ingots belonged to me!" Shi Fu protested, "If they were yours, why were they under my pillars?"

The elderly man explained, "There is a story behind all of this. I live at the eastern side of South Township, and my name is Bo Youshou. My old wife and I are alone, as we have no children. In front of our house we run a confectionery where we sell pastry, rice noodles, tea, and refreshments. It provides us with more than our everyday needs, and every time we save up two or three taels of silver, we have it smelted into an ingot. My old wife, being of a playful nature, ties a red silk ribbon around each of the ingots, though merely as a token of respect. Because the wall around our house is low and the rooms are poorly hidden from view, and because we fear inquisitive eyes, we have sewn the ingots into a large cushion so as to be on the safe side. In the past few years we have laid aside eight such ingots, which we believed would be more than sufficient to provide us with a decent funeral.

"Early this morning, however, at about the time of the fifth watch, I dreamed I saw eight young men in white robes standing beside the cushion, and all had red sashes tied around their waists. They were engaged in a discussion before my bed, and one said, 'At daybreak, pillars will be erected at the Shi family residence in Shengze, and all our relatives who should be there have already gone there. It is time that we joined them.'

One of them asked, 'Where will we find them at the house?' And another replied, 'Under the central pillar on the left side.' As they turned to leave, one said, 'We have lived here a long time, and it would be uncivil of us to go without first bidding the master farewell.' So they turned to me and said, 'We thank you for caring for us all these years, but we must leave now. Please do not take offense.'

"In this dream, I did not recognize these eight young men and knew not where they were from, so I inquired, 'Where do you eight young masters come from? Why is it that I do not know you?' And one of them replied, 'You have seen us only once since we came to your house, and you have doubtless forgotten us. We know you, but you do not know us.' Pointing to the red sash around his waist, he said, 'You gave me this when we first met. Now do you remember me?'

"I still did not recall when I had presented them with the red sashes. But I was reminded that I had no sons of my own, and seeing that they were all so handsome, I wished to keep them as my foster sons, so I pleaded, 'Since you are here already, why do you not make this your home? I shall treat you as though you were my own sons.' But the young men laughed, and one replied, 'You want us to be your sons only because you need us for the time you die. But we must go to a more prosperous establishment—a place, sir, that yours cannot equal.' And with that they walked out of the door.

"I was still in bed, yet somehow I found myself outside the house, begging them again and again to stay, but they did not even look back. I heard one of them say, 'It is getting late, and we must hurry!' And they took to their heels. I ran after them but tripped on some grass roots—and woke up. I recounted to my wife what I had dreamed. She suspected that it had something to do with the eight ingots of silver, so we unstitched the cushion that morning and found that the ingots were gone. I have come because I wish to verify my dream. So it is true!"

Dumbfounded by this story, Shi Fu exclaimed, "What a strange thing! But please do not worry, and come inside my house and sit awhile." Old Man Bo declined, saying, "The dream has been verified, so there is no need for me to go in." But Shi Fu would not hear of it. He insisted, "For a man of your age you have come a long distance and must be hungry. Allow me to offer you some breakfast before you leave."

When he heard he was being offered breakfast, Old Man Bo relented and followed Shi Fu into the house. There he saw a tall and spacious three-room main hall newly constructed of thick and sturdy timbers. All the laborers were banging away vigorously with axes and chisels, making more of a racket than usual. Why were they working so industriously? The reason was that custom called for a banquet of reward and a propitiatory bonus on the day a new building was completed. The laborers were looking forward to a generous supply of wine and money, and put on a special performance to please the master when they saw him coming.

Old Man Bo was quite impressed, and he thought with regret, "No wonder those ingots thought I was unequal to their ambitions and sought a more prosperous establishment. This house is thriving, and is just the place to satisfy their hoity-toity aspirations!"

Shi Fu invited Old Man Bo to a small parlor and asked him to be seated while he himself hurried to tell his wife what had transpired. Mistress Yu, too, was astounded by Old Man Bo's story, and she told her husband, "Since those ingots are meant to defray his funeral expenses, why do we not return them to him as a gesture of good will?" Shi Fu agreed, and said, "That is precisely what I was thinking, and why I came in to inform you." Mistress Yu wrapped the ingots in a piece of cloth, and Shi Fu placed the bundle in his sleeve, and then ordered that food and drink be taken to his guest. Returning to the parlor, he placed the bundle before Old Man Bo and said, "Please see if these are the eight ingots you mentioned." Old Man Bo opened the bundle and at once recognized the ingots. "Yes," he replied, "these are the eight rascals." He examined them, turning them this way and that and muttering all the while, "I had you sewn in a cushion, so how did you leave our stretch of the river and walk all the ten *li* to this place? That is no mean distance even for a human being, and you also would have to take a ferry. With no feet to walk with, how did you come here in such a short while?" Tears sprang to his eyes as he thought of how much hardship he had undergone to earn and save this silver, and how easily he had lost it.

Shi Fu attempted to comfort him with the words, "Do not grieve, old man! This humble person will return the ingots to you so that they may serve you in your old age." However, Old Man Bo demurred, saying, "I am grateful to you for your kind intentions, but they left me because it is not my good fortune to have them. Should I take them back, they will only leave again, so why should I put myself to more misery?" Shi Fu argued, "But there should be no more trouble this time as I am giving them to you." Old Man Bo waved his hand. "No! I do not want them! I know my destiny. No good comes of putting fate to a test."

Seeing that Old Man Bo would not be persuaded, Shi Fu went again to consult with his wife. She stated, "Although he refuses to take the ingots, we would not feel comfortable with keeping them ourselves. If he will not agree to taking all of them, perhaps he can accept one or two?" Shi Fu told her, "He refuses to take even a single ingot." After a moment's thought, Mistress Yu replied, "I have an idea. I will insert two of the ingots in some steamed buns for him to take along. Once he is at home and finds them, he will let the matter pass. He would hardly bring them back again, would he?" Shi Fu agreed, and Mistress Yu forthwith went to set out wine and food for their visitor.

Shi Fu placed Old Man Bo in the guests' seat of honor and sat down to keep him company. Old Man Bo said apologetically, "It is not right that I importune you in this manner." And Shi Fu assured him, "That is not so. Nothing here has been prepared especially for you." They ate and drank for a while. Old Man Bo, who was not a big drinker, soon became tipsy, and so Shi Fu ordered rice to complete the meal. Just as Old Man Bo was ready to take his leave, a servant brought two buns on a tray. Shi Fu announced, "These two buns are for you to eat on your way home." Old Man Bo protested, "I have had so much food and drink I will even forgo my evening meal. Why should I take anything for the road?" Shi Fu hastily replied, "If so, then take them to your wife." But Old Man Bo declined. "That will not be necessary. We make and sell such buns for a living and eat them all the time. You had best keep them for someone else." At a loss what else to say, Shi Fu picked up the buns and thrust them in Old Man Bo's sleeve, declaring, "The filling in my buns is different from that in the ones you sell. That you will find out when you try them at home."

Unable to refuse his host's hospitality any longer, Old Man Bo could only say, "I came on some paltry matter but end up eating your food and even taking some away. I feel quite guilty!" Then, folding his hands in an obeisance, he thanked Shi Fu and turned to leave.

As Shi Fu saw his visitor out of the gate, he heard Old Man Bo mutter to himself, "Coming here was easy, but I wonder where I can find a boat to take me back." Aware that Old Man Bo was somewhat inebriated, and concerned about the ingots in the buns, Shi Fu declared, "Not to worry, old man. I have my own boat and will have a servant take you home." Old Man Bo nodded and said gratefully, "You are truly a warmhearted man. I do not wonder now that you have such good fortune!" Shi Fu summoned a servant and enjoined him, "Take this old uncle back home in the boat. Accompany him to his doorstep and remember where he lives, so that I will know where to find him again."

Old Man Bo took his leave and stepped into the boat, which took him out of the township toward the Huangjiang stretch of the river where he lived. Animated by the wine he had imbibed, Old Man Bo was quite talkative and asked the servant about this and that. Before long, they arrived at Huangjiang, The servant helped Old Man Bo go ashore, and then saw him all the way home.

Old Man Bo's wife came out to meet them and asked, "Old man, is it true?" And he replied, "Absolutely true." Old Man Bo then retrieved the two buns from his sleeve and handed them to Shi Fu's servant with the words, "I will not invite you in for a cup of tea as I know you are quite busy at the house. But allow me to give you these buns." The servant attempted to decline, saying, "These were given you by my master. I cannot take them." But Old Man Bo insisted, "I have already thanked your master for the buns, and now I am giving them to you to thank you for your services. So do not refuse me." Realizing that nothing he said would change the old man's mind, the servant accepted the buns, returned to the boat, and rowed himself back to Shengze.

He moored the boat and had just gone ashore with the buns when he came face to face with Shi Fu who was coming out of the house. Shi Fu espied the buns and inquired, "Why did you bring the buns back? I gave them to Old Man Bo." The servant explained, "He gave them to me instead of a cup of tea and would not listen when I tried to refuse. I had to take them." Smiling to himself, Shi Fu thought, "I return two ingots to the old man but he gives them away again. Truly, he is not destined to have them. Perhaps this man is more fortunate." Aloud, he enjoined the servant, "These buns have a special flavor. Do not give them to anyone else." The servant replied, "I hear you, master." He went in the house, found his wife, and handed the buns to her. But before he could explain who had given them to him, he was called away by his colleagues to join in the banquet of celebration.

The servant had two children, and it so happened that both of them were indisposed with the colic. As their mother took the buns, she thought, "If the children see these buns and eat them on the sly, their illness may grow worse. I had best go to the mistress and see if she will exchange them for some other pastries." So she took the buns to the Mistress Yu and said, "I do not know how my husband obtained these two buns, but my children have the colic and I fear they may become sicker if they eat them. If the mistress is willing, I would like to exchange these buns for something that will better agree with their digestions." So saying, she placed the buns on the table. Unaware of what had taken place earlier, Mistress Yu chose some other pastries for the servant's wife and put the buns away.

Some time later, Shi Fu came in the house and related to his wife how Old Man Bo had given the buns to the servant, and then remarked, "Who would have imagined he would be the lucky one!" Mistress Yu knew now where the buns had come from. She exclaimed, "How strange!" Bringing the buns to her husband, she urged him, "Break these open and look inside!"

Not knowing why he was asked to do this, Shi Fu broke open a bun. An object fell out and clinked on the table, and when he looked down, he saw a silver ingot tied around the middle with a red ribbon! Astonished, he asked, "Where did you get these buns?" And Mistress told him how the servant's wife had brought them to her.

Shi Fu and his wife marveled over this matter, and they came to the conclusion that wealth resides in a person's destiny; it cannot be ordered to depart, nor will it come even if one entreats it to do so.

Shi Fu felt much compassion for Old Man Bo. He frequently sent him money and rice and treated him like a kinsman, and when the old couple died he purchased a piece of land for their burial.

His son, Shi Deyin, grew up to marry Zhu En's daughter, and the young people were most dutiful to their parents. Shi Fu became the richest man in his township. Both he and his wife lived to a ripe old age and died in peace. Their family tree flourished and intermarried with the Zhu household of the Strand for many subsequent generations.

And, as the verses tell us:

> *Just six taels of silver are not a large sum,*
> *Yet Heaven was moved by the virtuous deed.*
> *As shown by the fateful events at the Strand,*
> *A good man will reap the rewards he deserves.*

Lord Kuang Solves the Case of the Dead Infant

況太守斷死孩兒

During the Xuande reign (1426-1436), there lived in Yizhen County of Yangzhou Prefecture in the southern part of Zhili a man of moderate wealth named Qiu Yuanji. His wife, Mistress Shao, was a woman of outstanding appearance and carriage as well as of much moral strength and virtue. The two were deeply devoted to each other, yet in six years of married life they failed to beget any offspring.

Qiu Yuanji died of a sudden illness when Mistress Shao was only twenty-three years old. In her sorrow and pain she declared her intention to remain a widow for as long as she lived and never to marry again. After the requisite three years' of mourning had been observed, however, her parents, mindful that she was still young and had a long life ahead of her, advised her to remarry. Even Qiu Dasheng, an uncle-in-law on her deceased husband's side, sent his wife several times to try to talk to Mistress Shao and bring her around. But her mind was set in iron and stone and she would not be persuaded. She uttered a vow, saying, "To my late husband by the Nine Fountains in the nether world, I, his wife, swear I will die by the blade or the rope rather than take another surname or a second husband." And when people saw how determined she was, no one dared to broach the subject with her again.

As the time-honored saying goes: "She who resolves to embrace the solitude of widowhood must have the stomach to swallow three casks of vinegar." It is in truth not easy for a woman to remain a widow. In her long-term interests, Mistress Shao would have done better to marry another man. True, in doing so she would not be entitled to a place among women of the highest caliber, but she could at least be regarded as a woman of middling virtue and would have been spared the scandal that eventually ensued. One must indeed be practical in all matters and not seek vain renown!

Because of her uncompromising attitude, Mistress Shao was called everything from "virtuous" to "foolish." While some people were lavish with praise, others viewed her with skepticism. Yet Mistress Shao herself was firm in her resolve to remain chaste and saw strictly to the sanctity of her bedchamber. She had for company only one maidservant, a girl named Xiugu with whom she eked a living by sewing and embroidering.

A boy called Degui, who was not yet ten years old, guarded the interior gate to her private quarters and passed in all purchases of firewood and water. All male servants were dismissed by the time they approached manhood. There were no extraneous hangers-on in her house, and the atmosphere in the inner and outer courtyards was at all times hushed and solemn. After several years of this, people were finally convinced, and all acknowledged that Mistress Shao, though still young, displayed steadfastness beyond her years and managed a well-ordered household.

Time flew like an arrow, and as the tenth anniversary of Qiu Yuanji's death drew near, Mistress Shao conceived the idea of holding a religious ceremony in memory of her beloved husband. She had Degui invite her uncle-in-law Qiu Dasheng to her house to discuss the details, and it was decided to engage seven Buddhist monks for three days and nights of pious prayers and rites. Mistress Shao then declared, "I am but a widow, and I depend on you to preside over these proceedings." And Qui Dasheng agreed to do so.

It so happened that a man named Zhi Zhu had recently moved into the neighborhood. A ne'er-do-well born in an impoverished family, Zhi Zhu had no proper occupation and spent most of his time sniffing out scandals and prying in other people's affairs. Having heard that Mistress Shao was that seldom-encountered combination of a chaste widow who is also quite young and very becoming, he had his doubts, and he loitered around the Shao residence from dawn till dusk. Sure enough, no outsiders frequented the house and the only person to pass through its doors was the houseboy, Degui.

So Zhi Zhu struck up an acquaintance with Degui and gradually wormed his way into the boy's confidence. As they were chatting one day, he asked, "I have heard that your mistress is quite a comely woman. Is that true?" Degui, who had been born and bred in a family with high principles and always told the truth, replied, "It is true." Zhi Zhu asked again, "Does your mistress ever come out for a stroll in the marketplace?" Waving a hand dismissively, Degui declared, "She never comes out of her courtyard, much less strolls around in the marketplace."

One day, Zhi Zhu came upon Degui as the latter was purchasing vegetarian provisions, and he inquired, "Why are you buying so much monkish food?" Degui told him, "It will soon be the tenth anniversary of my master's passing away. This will be used for a religious ceremony." Zhi Zhu asked, "When will that be?" And Degui replied, "Starting tomorrow, for three days and nights. I will be quite busy."

Zhi Zhu reflected privately, "Since the memorial ceremony will be for her late husband, she must come out to light the incense. This will be my chance to see for myself whether she really fulfills the description of a chaste widow!"

On the next day, Uncle-in-Law Qiu Dasheng hosted a vegetarian meal for the seven monks, all of whom had taken the vows of abstinence. Portraits of Buddha were then enshrined in the main hall of the house, drums and cymbals were beaten, and sutras were chanted, all contributing to an atmosphere of pious devotion. Qiu Dasheng dutifully kowtowed before Buddha. Mistress Shao then came out to light incense in the mornings and evenings, after which she returned forthwith to her chambers. On several occasions, Zhi Zhu took advantage of the hustle and bustle of the religious rites to insinuate himself into the house, but did not catch sight of Mistress Shao. He asked Degui why this was so, and was told she only emerged once in the daytime, and then only to light incense before the morning meal.

On the third day, Zhi Zhu came before breakfast, slipped into the house, and hid behind a partition. He saw the monks, clad in their cassocks, either blowing or striking their musical instruments or chanting sutras, while a tender of censers hurried about replacing the previous day's incense sticks and candles with new ones. The only domestic servant present to attend to various exigencies was Degui, and he was too busy to keep an eye on the premises. Qiu Dasheng and some other relatives were also there, but they were absorbed with watching the proceedings and none paid any attention to Zhi Zhu. Soon, Mistress Shao came out to light sticks of incense, and Zhi Zhu carefully observed her. As the saying goes, "to look charming, put on mourning." The plain and unadorned garments she wore only accentuated her natural purity and elegance.

Zhi Zhu felt his whole body tingle at the sight of Mistress Shao, and even after he went home he could not put her out of his mind. Meanwhile, the religious rites concluded that night and the monks left at daybreak. Nor did Mistress Shao come out of her chambers any more. Zhi

Zhu was disappointed, but he thought to himself, "Degui is a simple-minded fellow. I shall use him to bait my hook."

It was then the fifth day of the fifth moon, when people celebrate the Dragon Boat Festival. That day, Zhi Zhu waylaid Degui and asked him to his house for a cup of yellow rice wine. Degui attempted to decline the invitation, saying, "I am not a drinker of wine, and if I go home with my face flushed from drinking, the Mistress will surely scold me." To which Zhi Zhu replied, "Then we shall not drink wine, but simply have some glutinous rice dumplings." So saying, he dragged Degui to his house and instructed his wife to prepare a plateful of rice dumplings. This she did, and placed them on the table with a dish of sugar, a bowl of meat, a bowl of fish, two pairs of chopsticks, and two wine cups. As Zhi Zhu began to warm a pot of wine, Degui protested, "I said I would not drink any wine. Do not warm any!" But Zhi Zhu insisted, saying, "Have just one cup with me to celebrate the festival. This wine is not strong and will not hurt you."

By dint of such wheedling, Zhi Zhu prevailed on Degui to drink a cup of the wine. He did not stop there, however, but continued, "Young men do not take single cups of wine. They should drink them in pairs." Unable to refuse, Degui emptied another cup of wine. Zhi Zhu himself had one round of wine, holding forth all the while with sundry bits of neighborhood gossip. He then filled Degui's cup again and urged him to drink up. Degui remonstrated, "My face is all red from drinking. Truly I cannot take any more." But Zhi Zhu placated him, saying, "Since your face is already red, you might as well sit here a while longer before going home. Just drink this one cup, and I will not urge you any further."

By this time Degui had downed three cups of wine. Having lived since childhood under Mistress Shao's strict supervision, he had never tasted wine in his lifetime, and now, with so much of it in his belly, he felt his head spinning. Taking advantage of Degui's befuddlement, Zhi Zhu lowered his voice and said, "Brother Degui, I would like to ask you about an inconsequential matter." Degui mumbled, "Ask whatever you wish." Zhi Zhu drew closer and inquired confidentially, "Your mistress has been widowed for many a year now, and I am convinced she knows stirrings of desire. Would it please her if a man were to sleep with her? Widows have always yearned for men, but few have any chance of meeting one. What say you spirit me into her house and let me have a go at her? If anything comes of it, I would be heavily in your debt."

Degui retorted sharply, "What are you saying? Have you no fear of blaspheming? My mistress is most correct in her behavior, and her comportment is irreproachable. No man may enter her chambers by day, and in the evenings she and her maidservant light lanterns and examine every corner of the house before locking up and going to bed. Where would I hide you even if I did spirit you in? Besides, her maidservant is constantly at her side and it is not possible for me to broach such a matter to the mistress. What you propose is complete nonsense!"

Zhi Zhu pondered a moment, and then asked, "In that case, does she examine your door as well?" Degui replied, "Of course she does." Zhi Zhu then inquired, "Brother Degui, how old are you?" Degui told him, "I am seventeen." Zhi Zhu continued, "The male essence is stimulated when boys turn sixteen. You are seventeen now. Have you never thought of a woman?" Degui grinned, "What good would it do me even if I did?" Zhi Zhu snorted, "With such a beautiful woman near you day in and day out, do you not feel any desire for her?" Degui retorted, "How can you say such a thing? She is the mistress of the household. She can scold and beat me at her pleasure, and I am afraid of her. Shame on you for making light of my feelings!" Zhi Zhu sniggered, "Well, since you will not take me to her, what say you if I taught you how to get her for yourself?" Degui shook his head and cried, "No, no! I cannot do such a thing. Nor would I dare to do so!" Ignoring the boy's protestations, Zhi Zhu continued, "Never mind what you should or should not do. I will teach you a stratagem, and you can try your luck with it. If it succeeds, do not forget that you owe me a favor."

Degui, who had indeed come of age, felt an itch rising in his heart, and made reckless by the wine he had imbibed, inquired, "What is this stratagem you would have me try out?" Zhi Zhu explained, "Leave your door open when you retire to your bed tonight. This is the fifth moon and the nights are warm, so lie naked on your back and make your dingus hard and stiff. Pretend to be asleep when she looks in your door. She will be aroused when she sees you, and after a night or two she will succumb to the temptation and come to you of her own accord." Degui asked, "And what if she doesn't come?" Zhi Zhu assured him, "Even if this stratagem fails, she cannot very well reproach you for anything. So you have nothing to lose." Degui reflected a moment, and then said, "I shall follow your advice, and if it is good I will not forget to recompense you." After a while, the effects of the wine dissipated somewhat and Degui took his leave, resolved to carry out the stratagem that very same night.

By rights, Mistress Shao, who maintained strict household rules, should have avoided any suspicions of impropriety by dismissing Degui when he turned seventeen and by engaging a younger boy. That would have been best all around. However, Degui had been a docile servitor ever since he was a child, and he impressed her as being well behaved albeit not very bright. Mistress Shao herself was fully determined to keep to the straight and narrow and did not contemplate any other eventualities, so she had let the matter slide.

That night, Mistress Shao and her maidservant came out as usual with lanterns to inspect the premises. When she saw Degui lying naked on his bed, she exclaimed, "That young knave! What does he think he is doing, sleeping unclothed like that with the door open!" She instructed Xiugu to shut the door.

Had Mistress Shao been firm of mind, she would have summoned Degui the next morning, told him he was negligent and impertinent, given him a tongue-lashing or a few slaps, and Degui would have not dared to repeat his performance. She, however, had not lain with a man for many a year and was oddly disturbed by the unfamiliar spectacle of Degui's nakedness. Thus she made no mention of the incident.

This merely encouraged Degui to do the same thing the next night. When Mistress Shao and the maidservant did their rounds and saw him, she scolded, "That insolent cur! Why doesn't he have the decency to cover himself?" She told Xiugu to draw the bed sheet over him without, however, awakening him. Excitement stirred within her but was kept in check by the presence of the maidservant.

The next day, Degui went out of the house on an errand and bumped into Zhi Zhu, who asked him whether he had used the stratagem. The boy guilelessly related the happenings of the two previous nights, and Zhi Zhu chortled, "So she asked to maid to cover you but not wake you up! That means she is attracted to you. Something good will surely take place tonight!"

When darkness fell, Degui again left the door ajar and pretended to be asleep. Meanwhile, Mistress Shao purposely instructed the maidservant not to accompany her on her inspection. She took a lantern and made straight for Degui's bedside, only to see him lying naked on his back with his member pointing straight up like a spear. All she knew now was a surge of lust, a burning desire. She hurriedly removed her undergarments and climbed into the bed. Not wishing to wake the boy up, she carefully positioned herself astride his hips and bore down on him. Suddenly, Degui threw his arms about her and, rolling his mistress underneath, began to make rain and clouds with her.

The one had long missed such pleasurable encounters; the other enjoyed his first taste of a woman. The one was loath to forgo a remembered delight; the other reveled in the new sweetness. The one so hungered for him she minded not his callowness; the other, knowing he was desired, forgot his fears of his stern mistress.

Once a beautiful flower, its trellis was now entwined by an evil vine; the pristine snow, melted and gone for all time. Ten years of purity, sullied and thrown to the winds in one night of unmentionable debauchery.

When they were done, Mistress Shao said, "I have tried so hard to preserve my virtue, only to forfeit it to you in one night. I have no doubt sinned in my previous life. However, you must remain silent about this night and not tell any person, and I will of course see to your interests." Degui hastily replied, "I dare not disobey my mistress's orders!"

Thereafter, Mistress Shao came to Degui each and every night on the pretext of checking the doors and disported herself with him before retiring. For fear that Xiugu would discover and spread word about her trysts, Mistress Shao had Degui seduce the girl. Then she made a pretense of berating Xiugu, yet instructed the maidservant to bring the boy to her bed, and thus sealed the girl's lips. With all sharing the same secret now, none needed to conceal anything from the other. Meanwhile, Degui, out of gratitude to Zhi Zhu for his advice, often asked Mistress Shao for various objects which he then presented to Zhi Zhu. The latter demanded time and again that Degui take him to Mistress Shao, but Degui feared his mistress would rebuke him and dared not mention the subject to her. And when Zhi Zhu repeatedly insisted on being told what was transpiring, he could only keep procrastinating.

For the next few months, Mistress Shao and Degui communed like husband and wife. And in the end it was inevitable that their secret should betray itself. Mistress Shao had never been with child in all her six years of married life, but now her bosom rose and her belly swelled and she was manifestly pregnant. Fearing the disgrace of being discovered, she gave some silver to Degui and told him to secretly purchase a potion with which to expel the fetus and thus avoid eventual scandal. However, Degui was a simple soul. For one, he knew not what potions to use for abortions, and for another, he saw Zhi Zhu as his benefactor ever since the day he had accepted the latter's advice, and he confided in him on all matters. And so, on this day, he also told Zhi Zhu about the circumstances of his private affair with his mistress.

Zhi Zhu, a scoundrel by any measure, had been incensed by Degui's unwillingness to take him into the house, and he now saw an opportunity to exact revenge and secure some benefits for himself. A scheme suddenly occurred to him, and he said to Degui, "An acquaintance of mine makes the most efficacious potion. Let me purchase some for you." He then went to an apothecary's and bought four doses of a fetus-securing medication and gave it to Degui to take back home.

Mistress Shao made four preparations of the medicine and took them, but nothing happened in her belly. She told Degui to go elsewhere and purchase something more effective. So Degui went once more to Zhi Zhu and asked, "Why did the potion fail to take effect?" Zhi Zhu prevaricated and finally stated, "One may attempt to expel the fetus only once. Should one fail the first time, no further attempt must be made. That fetus must be very firmly ensconced since it refused to be banished this time, and the mother's life may be imperiled if one resorts to potions of greater violence." Degui repeated these words to Mistress Shao, and she believed him.

The tenth month came around, and Zhi Zhu, surmising that Mistress Shao should be giving birth any day now, sought Degui and said, "I intend to brew a health-preserving tonic and need a new-born infant. Your mistress is about give birth, and I am sure she does not intend to keep the baby. Whether it is a boy or a girl, bring it to me. By doing so, you can repay me for everything you owe me. It will not cost you anything, but do not tell your mistress about this matter." And Degui agreed.

A few days later, Mistress Shao gave birth to a male infant. She then drowned the infant, wrapped it in a rush bag, and instructed Degui to take it out and bury it. Degui promised to do so, but instead of burying the infant, he took it surreptitiously to Zhi Zhu. After the latter had hidden the infant away, however, he seized Degui by the arm and said in a loud voice, "Your Mistress is the wife of Qiu Yuanji who has been dead many years now. Being a widow, how would she have a child? I shall report the matter to the authorities." Panic-stricken, Degui covered Zhi Zhu's mouth with his hand and cried, "I have regarded you as my benefactor and consulted with you in all matters. Why do you suddenly turn against me?" Zhi Zhu's face darkened, and he said harshly, "Do you know what you have done? You have defiled your mistress, a crime punishable by the death of a thousand cuts. Do you imagine you can put me off simply by calling me your benefactor? Moreover, since you knew you had benefited from my services you should have repaid me in kind, but what have you ever done for me? If you would have me keep my mouth shut, go ask your mistress for one hundred taels of silver and bring it to me, and I shall overlook your misdeeds. But I shall not let the matter drop if I see no silver. I have the newborn infant as evidence, and you shall go before the tribunal to explain yourself, and even your mistress will have her name dragged through the mud. I shall wait here for your answer. And be quick about it!"

With tears of fear and frustration in his eyes, Degui went home. He knew he could not conceal this matter from Mistress Shao, so he told her everything that had transpired. Mistress Shao reproached him bitterly, saying, "How could you make him a gift of such a thing! Do you know what trouble you have landed me in?" And with that, she started to weep. Degui attempted to defend himself, declaring, "I would not have given it to him if he were someone else. But he was my benefactor, and I could not refuse him." Mistress Shao asked, "Your benefactor? What has he done for you?" Degui replied, "Back then, it was he who advised me to lie unclothed on my bed so as to arouse your desires. If it were not for him, would you and I be sharing such love today? When he told me he wished to have the newborn infant for brewing a health-preserving tonic, what could I do but give it to him? How could I know he was up to no good?" Ruefully, Mistress Shao stated, "What an utterly reprehensible thing you did! Yet it was because I myself had a moment of weakness that I fell victim to this blackguard's wiles. However, it is too late now for regrets. If I do not buy back the infant, he will assuredly take it to the authorities, and nothing will save us then."

Seeing no other recourse, Mistress Shao took out forty taels of silver and told Degui to redeem the dead infant from Zhi Zhu, bury it in secret and thus eliminate this source of trouble. Degui returned to Zhi Zhu, and then guilelessly handed him the silver, saying, "This is all she has. Give me back the infant." But the silver only served to whet the scoundrel's greed, and he thought, "That woman is good-looking and quite well-heeled. If I use this opportunity to press myself upon her and seize control over her affairs, I shall be rolling in clover!" So he said to Degui, "I was only joking when I said I wanted silver. Since you have brought it, however, I must accept it. I have already buried the dead infant. I want you to take me to your mistress and tell her I wish to consort with her. Should she agree, I shall take care of the household in Mistress Shao's stead, and henceforth no one will dare bully her. That would be an ideal arrangement for both parties, would it not? If she does not agree, I will dig up the dead infant and report her to the authorities. You have five days to bring back her reply." Degui had no alternative but to go home and tell his mistress what Zhi Zhu had proposed. Mistress Shao flew into a fury and cried: "Who does that blackguard think he is! Ignore him!" And Degui did not dare say anything more.

Meanwhile, Zhi Zhu embalmed the dead infant in lime, placed it back in the rush bag, and hid the sack in a secret location. Five days passed, but Degui did not return. He decided to wait for another five days. When the ten days were up, surmising that Mistress Shao had by then fully recovered her health after childbirth, he went to the Qiu household's gate and accosted Degui as the latter came out. "Is she amenable?" he inquired. Degui shook his head and replied, "No, no! She does not agree!" Without further ado, Zhi Zhu turned and barged through the gate. Degui dared not bar his way, but fled into the street and waited in the distance to see what would happen.

When Mistress Shao saw a man entering the second courtyard, she scolded, "Outsiders are not to enter a household's inner sanctums. Who are you, that you dare break into my chambers like this?" Zhi Zhu replied, "This humble person's name is Zhi Zhu, and I am Degui's benefactor." Knowing now with whom she was dealing, Mistress Shao temporized, "If you wish to see Degui, go outside. You have no call to come in here." Undaunted, Zhi Zhu continued, "I have long yearned for you, like a thirsty man for water. Although I have no great abilities, I believe I am in no way inferior to Degui, so why do you reject me so abruptly?" Having no intention of pursuing such a conversation, Mistress Shao turned to leave. But Zhi Zhu stepped forward and threw his arms around her, hissing, "I have your misbegotten infant, and I shall show it to the authorities if you do not bend to my will." Mistress Shao's anger knew no bounds, but she saw no other way of extricating herself, so she attempted to cajole Zhi Zhu with the words, "Other people will notice us in the daytime. I will have Degui bring you here when night falls." Zhi Zhu insisted, "That is a promise. Keep it!" He released Mistress Shao and started to walk away. Then he spun around and declared, "I know you will not dare go back on your word!" After which he walked out of the door.

Mistress Shao stood speechless with fury, tears streaming down her face. After a while, she shut the door and sat by herself on a stool, turning the matter over in her mind. As she did so, she could find no one to blame but herself. She had refused to remarry after her husband's death, hoping thereby to find a place among the most superior of women. Now that she was about to make a laughingstock of herself, how would she face all the relatives? She reflected, "I vowed then to die by the blade or the rope rather than take a second surname or a second husband. But now, how can I meet my deceased husband by the Nine Fountains, unclean as I am?"

Xiugu saw her Mistress sobbing and weeping, but she dared not attempt to console her. Standing by the gate of the second courtyard, she waited for Degui to return.

Degui loitered in the street and came back to the house only after he saw Zhi Zhu leave. At the gate of the second courtyard, he asked Xiugu, "Where is the Mistress?" Pointing with a finger, Xiugu replied, "In there." Degui pushed open the door and stepped in.

In the meantime, Mistress Shao had taken a dagger, kept for emergencies at the head of her bed, with the intention of cutting her own throat. But her hand would not obey her will. With a sob, she set the dagger down on a table and proceeded to unwind an eight-foot-long sash from her waist. With this, she fashioned a noose, suspended it from a beam, and prepared to place it around her own neck. Then, overcome with misery and despair, she uttered whimpers of anguish.

Just at this juncture, Degui opened the door and came in. At the sight of him, it suddenly crossed Mistress Shao mind: "This is the cur who set the trap, made a fool of me, and ruined my name and virtue!" Seized with a sudden hatred and resentment, she snatched up the dagger and hacked at Degui's head. The blade, swift as the wind and driven by the redoubled force of rage, clove Degui's skull in twain. Blood flowed across the ground as Degui gave up the ghost. Aghast at the realization of what she had done, Mistress Shao drew the noose over her head, kicked the stool from under her feet, and swung from the beam in the ceiling.

As they say: "Gambling breeds theft, adultery begets death." On this day, adultery alone took two lives.

Meanwhile, Xiugu was accustomed to seeing Degui enter Mistress Shao's chambers, but sensed that something out of the ordinary was taking place this time and made herself scarce. But when no more sounds issued from the room, doubts arose in her mind. She peered in through the door and was frightened out of her wits to see a body hanging from the ceiling and another lying on the floor. After she had collected herself somewhat, she shut the door, and then hastened to Uncle Qiu Dasheng's house to report what had transpired. Qiu Dasheng was thunderstruck. He notified Mistress Shao's parents and went together with them to the Qius' house, where they shut the gate behind them and proceeded to interrogate Xiugu about the cause of the deaths. Xiugu did not know Zhi Zhu, nor had she been told about the forty taels of silver the latter had demanded as blackmail for the dead infant. She recounted that Mistress Shao and Degui had been carrying on an affair, but under repeated questioning insisted, "I have no idea why the two died today." Shame and embarrassment suffused the faces of the elder Shaos when they learned of their daughter's affair, and washing their hands of the matter, they forthwith went home. All Qiu Dasheng could do was to take Xiugu to the county yamen and report the deaths.

The county prefect ordered the bodies examined. It was established that the man, named Degui, had been killed by a blow to the head from a sharp instrument, and that the women, known as Mistress Shao, had died of hanging by the neck. Xiugu was then interrogated, after which the county prefect stated, "It is a fact that Mistress Shao and Degui had a liaison, during which the distinction between mistress and servant was dismissed. It would appear that Degui said something offensive that angered Mistress Shao; that she, in her anger, committed an act of violence that accidentally deprived Degui of his life; and that she, overcome with fright, then committed suicide by hanging herself by the neck. No other circumstances are in evidence." The prefect ordered Qiu Dasheng to have the deceased put in coffins and interred. Xiugu, as a maidservant who had connived with the pair's misdeeds, was administered a caning and sold into bondage by the authorities.

In the meantime, Zhi Zhu had returned to his home after Mistress Shao had repulsed his advances, but he continued to fantasize about an assignation that night. Thus he was greatly shocked and affrighted when he learned that both Mistress Shao and Degui were dead, doubtless as a result of his machinations. For several days he dared not show his face outside his door.

Then early one morning, on a sudden impulse he retrieved the infant he had preserved in lime, took it to the riverbank, and flung it in the water. As he did so, an acquaintance of his named Bao the Ninth came up and inquired, "Brother Zhi, what did you throw in the river?" Flustered, Zhi Zhu quickly replied, "It is only some beef that I salted and wrapped up. I had intended to eat it at some later date, but unfortunately it has rotted. Ninth Brother, are you busy these days? Come to my home some time for a few cups of wine." But Bao the Ninth declined, saying, "I shall be occupied today, for the government post boat that is transporting Lord Kuang Zhong of the Suzhou Magistracy is putting in here, and I must oversee the dock hands." "If that is the case," said Zhi Zhu, "let us meet some other day." And he hurried away.

Now, Kuang Zhong, formerly a minor administrative clerk, had been elevated to the post of magistrate of Suzhou upon the recommendation of Minister of Rites Hu Rong, and though he had served as such for only a year, the populace had acclaimed him as "Kuang Clear Skies." He had returned to his hometown as required by ritual after his father passed away, but had been reinstated by imperial edict and was now traveling by government post boat as sign of imperial favor.

Lord Kuang was seated in the ship's cabin, reading a book, when the post boat arrived at the Yizhen Locks. All at once he heard the cry of an infant on the river. Surmising that a child might have fallen in the water, he dispatched an attendant to investigate. The attendant soon came back and reported, "I saw nothing." Precisely the same thing happened a second time, and, when this took place a third time, Lord Kuang asked his entourage if they had heard an infant crying. All denied hearing anything, whereupon Lord Kuang commented that this was indeed strange.

Lord Kuang then opened the window of the cabin, and he caught sight of a small rush bag floating in the river. He instructed a boatman to fish the parcel out of the water. When this had been retrieved and opened, the boatman reported, "It contains an infant." Lord Kuang inquired, "Is it alive or dead?" And the boatman said, "It has been preserved in lime and appears to have been dead for quite some time." Puzzled, Lord Kuang cogitated, "How is it that a dead infant can cry? And why should it be preserved in lime? One would normally just bury it and be done with it. There must be a reason for this."

He instructed the boat's crew to place the infant and the rush bag in the bow of the ship, and said, "Should anyone say something about the provenance of this infant, inform me in confidence, and there shall be a generous reward." Whereupon the boat's crew placed the infant in the bow of the ship.

It so happened that Bao the Ninth caught sight of the bag and at once recognized it as the one Zhi Zhu had thrown in the river. He exclaimed, "He said the bag contained rotted beef. How did a dead infant get in it?" He was taken into the boat's cabin, where he reported to Lord Kuang, "This small person does not know where the dead infant comes from, but the bag is the one Zhi Zhu threw into the river." Lord Kuang observed, "Good! Now that we have a name, we can get to the bottom of this affair."

He ordered that Zhi Zhu be arrested in secret, and then issued an invitation to the prefect of Yizhen to appear at the court of inquiry for an investigation. Lord Kuang himself proceeded to the court of inquiry with the body of the infant, and sat down to wait. Before long the prefect arrived, and bailiffs brought in Zhi Zhu. Lord Kuang then took the seat of honor while the prefect seated himself on his left. Lord Kuang, quite aware that Yizhen County was not within his area of jurisdiction, had no desire to appear overbearing by presiding over the case, and thus had asked the prefect to open the inquiry. The latter, however, knew that Lord Kuang had recently received an imperial decree and was reputed to be man of unusual ability, so he did not wish to appear brash or presumptuous. Since the prefect time and again declined to take charge of the inquiry, Lord Kuang had no alternative but start the proceedings.

Raising his voice, he asked, "Zhi Zhu! From where did you get this lime-preserved infant?" Zhi Zhu was on the verge of denying all knowledge of the rush bag and its contents, when he saw Bao the Ninth kneeling to one side, evidently ready to bear witness about the matter. So he corrected himself at the last moment and said, "This small person saw this filthy thing lying by the roadside. Finding it objectionable, I threw it into the river. I do not know where it came from." Lord Kuang then asked Bao the Ninth, "Did you see him pick it up by the roadside?" And Bao the Ninth replied, "I saw this thing only as he was throwing it in the river. I asked him what it was, and he told me it was some beef that he had tried to salt but that had rotted."

Lord Kuang grew angry and snapped, "Since he already lied once by stating it was rotted beef, he must be attempting to hide something!" He ordered a bailiff to select a thick wooden stave and administer twenty blows before continuing with the interrogation. Those were fearsome blows. Twenty blows were like forty or more, and left Zhi Zhu's flesh broken and bleeding, yet he would not confess. So Lord Kuang shouted that finger vises be applied. The vise rods were no less fearsome. Zhi Zhu contrived to bear the first round of torture but broke down under the second and cried, "The dead infant was Widow Shao's. She had an illicit affair with her houseboy Degui and begot this illegitimate baby. Degui begged me to bury the infant for him, but dogs scratched it out of the ground, so I threw it in the river."

Lord Kuang felt that something did not make sense in Zhi Zhu's account, so he asked again: "Since you were willing to bury her infant, you must have been on close terms with the family, were you not?" Zhi Zhu replied, "No, I was not. I was merely acquainted with Degui."

Lord Kuang then tried another tack and inquired, "Why was the infant preserved in lime? If they wanted it buried, it would seem that they would also wish to see it decompose." Zhi Zhu hemmed and hawed, but could not come up with an explanation. Finally he kowtowed and declared, "Lord Clear Skies, it was actually this small person who embalmed the infant with lime. I knew the widow was quite well off, and I preserved the body in the hope of getting a few taels of silver from her. But my hopes fell through when both of them died unexpectedly, so I dropped the infant into the river." Lord Kuang asked in surprise, "Then are both the woman and the young fellow dead?"

The prefect rose to his feet, and with a bow, replied, "They are indeed both dead. It is this prefect who personally examined the matter." Lord Kuang asked, "How did they die?" And the prefect reported, "The servant was hacked to death with a dagger, and the woman hanged herself. This prefect inquired closely into the matter and found that they had for some time been engaged in an adulterous relationship, in which the distinction between mistress and servant was long flouted. The young fellow must have said something to offend the woman, who then lost her temper and attacked him with the dagger, accidentally killing him. She then hanged herself in a fit of fear and remorse. That is the only possible explanation."

Lord Kuang hesitated, reflecting, "Since the two were carnally on such intimate terms, a minor verbal spat would hardly lead to an act of manslaughter! There must be some reason I heard the infant crying this morning." So he inquired, "Was there any other person in the Shao household?" And the prefect replied, "There was also a servant girl named Xiugu. She has since been sold into bondage by official quarters." Lord Kuang observed, "If official quarters sold her into bondage, she must certainly be in this locality. I would trouble your staff to find her and bring her here. She may shed some light on the circumstances."

The prefect promptly sent out runners, and before long Xiugu was brought in. Asked to relate the events of that day, she gave the same account as the prefect's.

Lord Kuang pondered the matter for a while, then descended from his dais and pointed at Zhi Zhu. "Do you know this person?" he asked. Xiugu took a close look, and stated, "This humble woman does not know his name or surname, but I do recognize that disagreeable countenance of his." Lord Kuang grunted, "I thought as much. He and Degui were well acquainted, so he must have come to the house with Degui. Tell me truthfully what you know, for if I detect the least bit of ambiguity, I shall apply the finger press." Alarmed, Xiugu cried, "I never saw him come to the house earlier, and that is the truth! It was only on the last day that he suddenly forced his way into the middle hall and attempted to molest the mistress, who then chased him out. Degui arrived after he had departed and as the mistress was sobbing and weeping in the room. Degui went in, and soon after that both were dead."

Lord Kuang thundered at Zhi Zhu, "You scoundrel! You would not have dared to break into the middle hall were you not in league with Degui! You were the cause of both those deaths!" He ordered the bailiffs, "Apply the vises!"

Swooning with pain, and no longer master of his own tongue, Zhi Zhu recounted from beginning to end how he had incited Degui to seduce his mistress, how he tricked Degui into bringing him the dead infant and extorted silver from Mistress Shao, how he had coerced Degui into admitting him to the house for a carnal encounter, how he had intruded into the middle hall, thrown his arms around Mistress Shao and attempted to ravish her, and how she had coaxed him into leaving the house. He ended his detailed account with the words, "I, in all truth, do not know what transpired afterward and what brought on their deaths." Lord Kuang remarked, "This, I believe, is the truth." He forthwith ordered that the vises be removed and that a scribe take down the confession. And all this while the prefect listened to the proceedings, sorely embarrassed by the knowledge that Lord Kuang's talents far outshone his own.

Lord Kuang now raised his brush and wrote his verdict:

> The hearing has shown Zhi Zhu to be a lecherous scoundrel who conceived evil intentions after observing the beauty of a widow. He attempted to fulfill his scheme by taking advantage of the foolishness of a weak-willed servant whom he persuaded to seduce his mistress by lying in bed unclothed with the door open. And when she became pregnant he further plotted to secure the fetus and seize it. Failing in his attempt to take possession of the widow adulterously, he turned to taking possession of her property. Yet taking her property failed to satisfy his desires and he wished to have her carnally as well.

After Mistress Shao had erred in a moment of weakness, she attempted to cover up her indiscretion. However, Zhi Zhu continued to harass her, preying upon her both financially and sexually, and her hatred for him translated into hatred for Degui, with intimacy eroding into animosity. She then slew Degui, and subsequently herself, though her death does naught to mitigate her shame and guilt.

Now that the mistress and servant are both deceased, nothing more need be said on their account; and the maidservant who connived in the affair has received the caning she deserves. Solely the chief culprit remains outside the meshes of the law. It would appear that Heaven willed Bao the Ninth's chance encounter and the wailing of the embalmed infant, for Zhi Zhu's crimes can in no way be countenanced! It is fitting that Zhi Zhu be put to death, and that all his ill-gotten gains be sought and recovered.

Lord Kuang read out his verdict, and even Zhi Zhu could raise no objections.

Lord Kuang then submitted his report on the case to his superiors, and all people lauded his perspicacity. Indeed, the common people all sang his praises, asserting that the legendary Judge Bao had returned to this world! As the ditty bears witness:

Fair Mistress Shao succumbs to temptations that addle her wits.
And foolish Degui seduces his mistress then loses his life.
All on account of the wretched Zhi Zhu and his rascally wiles.
But naught can escape the miraculous ken of Kuang Clear Sky!

The Man Who Lost His Yin-Yang Cord and His Life in a Nunnery

郝
大
卿
遺
恨
鴛
鴦
絛

During the Xuande era (1426–1436) of our current dynasty, there was, in Xingan County of Jiangxi's Linjiang Prefecture, a *jian sheng* named Daqing who was of the household of Ho. Handsome and romantic, he had scant regard for social convention and was so enamored of the sensual pleasures that he could hardly tear himself away from the streets and lanes that were famed for singsong houses and brothels. Indeed, he felt so much at home in such places, and frequented them so often, that he slowly but surely squandered away much of his not inconsiderable inheritance.

His wife, Mistress Lu, enjoined him time and again not to be so profligate. But he accused her of lacking in wifely humility and often raised his voice in anger. So Mistress Lu swore to wash her hands of him, and thereafter let him pursue his dissolute ways. She herself, with their three-year-old son, withdrew in abstinence to her chambers where she led a life of vegetarian frugality and spent her days praying to the gods.

One day during the Qingming Festival, Daqing dressed himself in his finest and went out alone to enjoy the scenery in the countryside. He sought only those places where many women were to be found, and he followed them around, preening and parading himself in the hope that some beauty would be drawn to him. To his disappointment and disgust, however, none showed any interest in having an encounter, so he entered a tavern to drink away his boredom. He mounted to the second floor where a waiter served him with wine and a few choice dishes; there he drank by himself, leaning against the railing to watch the jostling crowds in the streets below. After he had downed numerous cups, he began to feel somewhat inebriated. So he went downstairs, paid his bill, and left the tavern to stroll aimlessly here and there.

By now it was mid-afternoon, and when he had walked for a while, the wine he imbibed had the effect of parching his mouth and tongue and he craved a cup of tea to quench his thirst. As he cast about in vain for a teahouse, he caught sight of a number of scripture banners fluttering over the woods before him and heard the mellifluous chiming of a bronze bell. Surmising that some sort of monastery stood there, he was intrigued and quickened his steps in that direction.

At the other side of the woods he came upon a cluster of grand temple buildings surrounded with a white-painted wall. Ten or more weeping willows graced the approach to the south-facing main gate, over the double doors of which hung a sign inscribed with gilt characters that read "Non-Void Nunnery." With a nod, Ho Daqing told himself, "I have often heard that there are some good-looking nuns at the Non-Void Nunnery, yet I have never had the occasion to visit this place. This is a fine opportunity to do so."

Straightening his attire, he strode through the gate and turned right onto a quietly elegant pebble path lined with elm trees. A few more steps brought him to another gate that opened on a small three-room courtyard in which an effigy of the warrior saint Skanda was enshrined. Tall pines and cypresses in the courtyard reached to the sky and provided perches for trilling and chirping birds. Beyond the courtyard lay a cross path. Ho Daqing took the eastern branch toward an elaborately carved gate tower. The door in the gate tower was shut, but after Daqing rapped lightly on it a few times it creaked open to reveal a young novice, neatly attired in a black robe caught up at the waist with a silken cord. She greeted Ho Daqing, who replied with an obeisance and stepped through the door into a courtyard. There he saw three halls which were not very big, but sufficiently spacious to accommodate three large buddhas with austere, gold-tinted visages. Daqing bowed to the buddhas, then said to the novice, "Please inform your abbess that she has a visitor."

The girl asked him to be seated and then went to report his arrival. Before long, a young nun appeared and bowed to Daqing. He sprang to his feet and returned the bow, all the while closely examining her with the half-squinting, flirtatious expression that he usually reserved for amatory advances. The nun, who might have been about twenty years old, had an exquisite jade-white face and bore herself with exceptional poise. Daqing made a deep obeisance. He was so smitten by her beauty he sagged like a glutinous rice patty fresh out of the steamer and could hardly straighten himself up again.

When the initial greetings had been disposed of, host and guest seated themselves and Daqing reflected, "I chase around all day without finding a woman to my taste, only to find one hidden in a nunnery! If I use my powers of persuasion and succeed in arousing her, I wager she will readily take the hook!" As Daqing secretly drew up a strategy, however, little did he suspect that the nun was doing exactly the same thing!

It has always been the rule at nunneries that the abbess comes out to meet any visitors and answer inquiries. The younger ones are held in strict seclusion, much like the young ladies of wealthy households, and only make an appearance when the visitors are relatives or are well known to the nunnery. Should the abbess happen to be away from the nunnery or indisposed, all visits are declined. Even when a highly prominent personage insists on meeting a younger nun, he must make repeated requests before she is allowed to come out, and then he will, more often than not, be constrained to wait until his patience is well nigh exhausted.

So why had that young nun come out so boldly? There was, of course, a reason. She was the sort of nun who chants the sutras yet does not follow the tenets piously, who yearns for romance, who detests solitude, and who therefore hates being a nun. She had happened to look through a crack in the door when Daqing entered the courtyard and had been attracted by his handsome carriage, and so she simply sallied forth on her own.

And now, with her eyes fixed upon Daqing like pins drawn by a magnet, she smiled and inquired, "May I ask, sir, what is your name? Where do you come from? And what counsel do you have for our humble nunnery?" And Daqing replied, "This small person's name is Ho Daqing and I live in the city. I happened to pass by during a spring outing in the countryside today, and as I have long admired the virtues of the pious women here, I decided to drop in." The nun thanked him and declared modestly, "Residing as I do in these remote wilds, this humble nun has no virtues or abilities to speak of. I am greatly honored by your gracious presence. However, many people come and go in this courtyard, so I would have you come to an inner chamber for some tea." Daqing was elated. This invitation to take tea further within the nunnery augured well for his intentions.

Daqing rose from his seat and followed the nun through a series of rooms and a winding corridor. Soon they came to a small courtyard with three elegantly appointed rooms fronted by balustrades. In the courtyard were two parasol trees, a few sprigs of bamboo, and a profusion of flowers that gave off a heady fragrance. Right at the center of the main room, in the place of honor, hung a plain black-and-white portrait of the goddess Guanyin. Before the portrait stood an ancient bronze censer with the smoke of incense curling in the air above it, and on the floor below rested a cattail hassock. The room on the left contained four vermilion cabinets, all of which were locked and presumably served as repositories for sutras. The room on the right was hidden from view by a screen, and when Daqing stepped in he saw a rectangular pinewood writing table, to the left of which stood a small wicker chair. On its right, against the wall, was placed a couch made of speckled bamboo. A seven-stringed zither hung on the wall.

On the spotlessly clean writing table lay an exquisite set of writing implements, and stacked beside these were a number of calligraphic texts. Daqing picked up a text at random. It was a sutra rendered in small characters in imitation of the brushwork of the famous calligrapher Zhao Songxue. Recorded below it were the year and the date when the copying had been completed as well as the name of the copyist, given as "Disciple Kongzhao, after perfumed ablutions." Daqing inquired, "Who is this Kongzhao?" To which the nun replied, "That is the humble name of this insignificant nun." Daqing examined the writing with admiration and voiced lavish praises.

The two then seated themselves face to face across the writing table while the novice served tea. Kongzhao took a cup of tea and tendered it to Daqing with both hands. Daqing observed that she had lovely white hands tipped with long, tapering fingers. Taking a sip of the tea, Daqing found it to be excellent.

Setting down the cup, Daqing inquired, "How many of you are in this sacrosanct nunnery?" Kongzhao replied, "There are four of us. This humble nun is currently in charge, as my mentor, the abbess, is old and ailing and has of late been confined to her bed." Pointing to the novice who was sitting nearby, she added, "This is one of my apprentices. A younger one is in her room, chanting sutras." Daqing then asked, "How long is it since you left home to enter this nunnery?" Kongzhao told him, "I was seven when my father passed away and I was brought here to enter this order. That was twelve years ago." After some mental calculations, Daqing remarked, "So you must be nineteen now and in the best years of your life. How can you endure such solitude?" Kongzhao countered, "Do not mock me, sir. But being a nun is many times better than being a lay woman." Curious, Daqing inquired, "How so?"

Kangzhao stated, "We nuns are not tied down with trivial worldly matters, nor are we trammeled with children. We spend our days chanting the sutras, indulge now and then in a censer of excellent incense or a pot of tea, lie down to sleep within our painted paper canopies when we feel tired, and play on the lute when we have the time and inclination to do so. We lead a truly peaceful and leisurely life." Daqing commented, "Playing on musical instruments is a fine thing, but when you do so would it not be best to have someone with you who appreciates and applauds your music? Yet, I feel that is of less consequence than sleeping alone in that painted canopy. Are you not afraid that a demon may appear in your dreams—with no one there to wake you up?"

Kongzhao knew now that Daqing was baiting his hook. With a smile, she replied, "You, sir, are not required to pay for it if a dream demon takes someone's life." Daqing laughed, "I am not concerned if a dream demon takes even ten thousand lives, but it would be a pity if a person of your qualities were to lose hers!"

As their badinage increasingly overstepped the limits of propriety, Daqing suddenly said, "I would much appreciate another pot of this excellent tea." Kongzhao understood what he meant, and she instructed the novice to go to the porch to boil water for another pot of tea. After the girl had left, Daqing asked, "Would you show me where you sleep and what a painted paper canopy looks like? I would like very much to know."

By now, Kongzhao could no longer suppress the flames of desire. Even as she asked "Why would you want to know?" she rose to her feet. Daqing quickly stepped forward, embraced Kongzhao, and pressed his lips to hers. Disengaging herself, Kongzhao turned around and walked to the back of the room with Daqing at her heels. She drew aside a partition to reveal another room. It was her bedchamber and it was even more tastefully furnished than the room they stood in. Daqing, however, was in no mood just then to examine it. Arms around each other, the two entered the bedchamber and surrendered themselves to the pleasures of making clouds and rain.

Just as they were most deliciously engaged, the novice came through the door with a pot of tea, compelling Daqing and Kongzhao to hastily interrupt their lovemaking. The girl put her hand over her mouth to hide a smile, then placed the pot of tea on the table and left the room.

Since it was growing dark, Kongzhao lit lamps and candles. Then she brought wine, fruit, and vegetables for a meal and sat down at the table with Daqing. Fearing, however, that the novices might disclose to others the affair she was having, she told both of them to stay and share their dinner. Kongzhao said to Daqing regretfully, "This being a nunnery, we subsist on a vegetarian diet. We had no idea that you were coming, so please excuse us for neglecting to prepare any meat dishes." Daqing replied, "I am already overwhelmed by your graciousness, and such apologies only disquiet me."

The four imbibed cup after cup of wine, and when all were half inebriated, Daqing edged closer to Kongzhao and threw an arm around her neck. He then drank half of the wine in his cup and lifted the cup to her lips. Reaching forward with her mouth, Kongzhao drained the rest of the wine. The two novices were embarrassed by such intemperate conduct and rose to their feet to leave the room, but Kongzhao detained them, declaring, "Since you are here already, do not imagine I will let you off so easily."

Not being permitted to depart, the novices modestly covered their eyes with their sleeves. But Daqing rose from his seat and put his arms around both of them. Brushing aside the sleeves that hid their faces he kissed them by turns. It so happened that both the girls were mature enough to know the stirrings of lust, and since their teacher was not averse to their presence they gladly joined in the merry-making. With arms and bodies intertwined, the four continued to drink until they were fully intoxicated. Then they lay down on the same bed and clung to one another as though painted or glued together. Daqing strove to satisfy all of them. And, this being the first time these nuns knew such sweetness, they coupled with vim and vigor.

The next morning, Kongzhao gave the tender of censers three *qian* of silver to ensure his discretion as well as some cash to purchase meat, fish, wine and fruit. This old tender of censers, whose daily fare consisted of nothing more succulent or nutritious than boiled vegetables and plain rice, was bleary of vision, hard of hearing, flaccid of body, and slow of movement. But now that he possessed three *qian* of silver and had been told to purchase wine and meat, his vision cleared, his movements grew sprightly, his body became as vigorous as a tiger's, and he virtually flew on his feet. Before two hours passed, he returned with all his purchases and set about preparing a repast for Daqing.

Now, the Non-Void Nunnery was presided over by two senior nuns. East Pavilion was in the charge of Kongzhao, whereas the administration of West Pavilion had been entrusted to Jingzhen, a nun of equally loose morals. Jingzhen had her own tender of censers and a single novice.

For several days on end, the tender of censers at West Pavilion noticed his East Pavilion colleague going out to purchase wine and meat. He reported what he had seen to Jingzhen, and she at once deduced that Kongzhao was engaged in some dubious pursuit. Instructing her novice to look after the pavilion, she went to see what was going on.

As Jingzhen approached the gate of East Pavilion, its tender of censers happened to come out with a large wine pot in one hand and a basket in the other. The tender of censers asked, "Where are you going, Senior Nun?" Jingzhen replied, "I have come to converse with my younger colleague." The tender of censers hastily declared, "In that case, I shall announce your arrival." But Jingzhen stopped him, saying, "I know what is going on, so there is no need for you to announce me." His subterfuge exposed, the tender of censers grew red in the face and he said no more. He followed Jingzhen back into the pavilion and shut its doors, and when they arrived at the main room, he called in a loud voice, "The senior nun of West Pavilion has come on a visit!"

When she heard this, Kongzhao flew into a panic. Making no reply, she instructed Daqing to conceal himself behind a screen, and then went to greet her visitor. Jingzhen seized her by the sleeve, crying, "So this is the way a person who has taken the vows comports herself! You have defiled our nunnery! You shall go with me to the administrator of the community and explain yourself!" So saying, she pulled Kongzhao toward the door. Kongzhao was so frightened her face assumed various hues of red and green, her heart thumped as though belabored by a thousand hammers, and she stood as though paralyzed, unable either to speak or to move. Seeing her in such a state of craven fear, Jingzhen laughed and said, "Do not worry, sister. I was merely teasing you. But why do you hide your wonderful guest instead of sharing him with me? Ask him to come out so that I may meet him!"

Greatly relieved by these words, Kongzhao called Daqing out of his hiding place. As Daqing greeted Jingzhen, he saw a beautiful and seductive nun in her mid-twenties. Although she was older than Kongzhao, he deemed her even more alluring than her younger colleague. He asked, "Where do you reside?" And Jingzhen replied, "This humble nun lives in West Pavilion of this nunnery, only a few steps from here." Daqing declared, "Had I known that, I would have gone to pay my respects."

As the two exchanged more small talk, Jingzhen found Daqing's manners quite pleasing and his conversation most engaging. She gazed at him longingly and sighed, "That there should be such a ravishing man under Heaven! My younger sister is most fortunate to have him all to herself." Kongzhao hastened to assure her, "Sister, you need not be envious. If you do not mind doing so, we could very well share the pleasures he can provide." Brightening, Jingzhen exclaimed, "If that could be done, I would be most appreciative. Pray, accept my invitation to come to my chambers this evening." And with that, she took her leave and returned to West Pavilion to prepare a dinner for her guests.

Before long, Kongzhao and Daqing came to West Pavilion and were welcomed at the gate by the novice. Daqing found the buildings, porches, and flower gardens as subtly charming as those at East Pavilion, and the nun's chambers even more elegant. Elated at the sight of Daqing, Jingzhen dispensed with the formal courtesies and at once seated her guests. Tea was served, after which fruit, wine, and a variety of dishes was laid out. Kongzhao had Jingzhen sit next to Daqing while she seated herself across the table. The novice was also placed next to Daqing. Then the four proceeded to drink and dine. After some time, Daqing lifted Jingzhen onto his lap and asked Kongzhao to sit beside him. Placing his arms around them, he caressed and fondled them this way and that, so that even Jingzhen's novice sitting next to them became flushed in the face with excitement.

When darkness fell, Kongzhao rose from the table and said to Daqing, "Do your part as bridegroom, and I shall come again tomorrow to congratulate both of you." She asked for a lantern, then was seen to the gate and returned alone to East Pavilion.

After she left, the novice instructed the tender of censers to close the pavilion up for the night, while she herself cleared the table and made hot water for Jingzhen and her guest to wash their hands and feet. That done, Daqing lifted up Jingzhen in his arms and placed her on her bed, and when they had disrobed each other they slipped under the covers, pressing their bosoms together and intertwining their arms and legs. Stimulated by the wine he had imbibed, Daqing put all his skill and prowess into his performance, up to such time as Jingzhen's soul finally took flight, her body fell back drained and spent, and her limbs lay limp on the bed. Then both slept until late the next morning before getting up. Thereafter, the tenders of censers at both pavilions were bribed to secrecy, and the carousing took place in each pavilion by turns. Ho Daqing's lust knew no bounds, and the pleasures he enjoyed drove all thought of home from his mind.

Yet after two months of this he commenced to feel fatigued. He could no longer deliver as before and he wished to go home. But the nuns, both at an age when they most craved the carnal delights, would not hear of it. Daqing pleaded again and again, "I appreciate your wondrous love and am loath to leave you. But I have been here for a full two moons without my family being aware of my whereabouts, and they must be worried. Let me go home to relieve my wife and child of their anxieties and I shall then come back to keep you company. As that should require no more than four or five days, why should you be so reluctant?" At long length, Kongzhao said, "All right, if you insist on going, we will prepare a farewell dinner and let you leave tomorrow morning. But you must keep your word and not renege on it." And Daqing declared, "I swear of this day never to forget your kindness to me."

Kongzhao went to West Pavilion and informed Jingzhen of this agreement. But after the older nun had given the matter some thought, she declared, "His pledge may be sincere, but he might not come back after he leaves." Kongzhao inquired, "And why is that?" Jingzhen explained, "He is a handsome and romantic man loved by many women. Moreover, he has always been most partial to pleasures of the flesh and knows many places where he can obtain such enjoyment. Once he goes back to those women they will wish to keep him, and he may not be able to come back to us even if he desires to do so." Kongzhao asked, "Then what do you think we should do?" Jingzhen replied, "I have an excellent solution, one that will hold him here without resort to ropes or chains, and will resign him to staying with us for good." Kongzhao quickly asked what she intended to do. Jingzhen raised two fingers and ticked them off as she said, "At the farewell dinner this evening, we will make him drunk and then shave off his hair. That, for one, will prevent him from going home. And since his looks resemble a woman's, once he is attired like us, even Bodhidharma, our founding teacher, would not recognize him as a man, and we could go on forever with our merrymaking. Secondly, no one could accuse us of keeping a man in the nunnery. So we would achieve two purposes at one stroke." Kongzhao cried admiringly, "An excellent plan. I would never have thought of that!"

That evening, Jingzhen asked her novice to take care of the pavilion and went alone to East Pavilion. When she saw Daqing, she said reproachfully, "We are having so much pleasure together, why do you suddenly wish to leave us? Why are you so uncaring?" Daqing protested, "It is not that I am uncaring, but because I have stayed away from home for so long that my wife and son are no doubt worried about me. I shall be gone for only a few days and will soon come back to you. Never would I abandon you or forget our affections." With a show of reluctance, Jingzhen replied, "Since my younger colleague has agreed to your going home, I cannot compel you to stay. But I hope you do not disappoint us and will remain true to your word." Daqing assured her, "Of that you need not remind me any further."

The banquet was promptly laid out, and all five—four nuns and Daqing—sat down together at the table. Jingzhen declared, "Since this is a farewell banquet, everyone should drink their fill." And Kongzhao chimed in, "That goes without saying!" Then they began to ply Daqing with wine, and by the time of the third drum, Daqing was sodden drunk and bereft of his senses. Jingzhen rose from her seat to remove Daqing's head cloth, after which Kongzhao brought out a razor and shaved every strand of hair from Daqing's head. Then they carried him to the bedchamber and all repaired to their respective beds.

Daqing did not wake up until the next morning. He found himself lying beside Kongzhao, and as he rolled around to look at her he sensed the skin of his scalp touching the pillow. Hastily he raised his hand to see why that was so. His pate was as naked as a gourd! Shocked, he quickly sat up and exclaimed, "What is this? What has happened?" Kongzhao was awakened by his cries, and seeing him so alarmed, she too sat up. "My dear man," she said, "Do not be angry. You insisted on going home, but we could not bear to let you go. Having no other recourse, we came up with this distressful scheme, and from now on we shall disguise you as a nun so that we may forever enjoy ourselves." She fell into his arms with so many whispers of cajolery and whimpers of lust that Daqing was completely befuddled. All he could say was, "I know your intentions were good, but your means are extreme. How shall I meet people from now on?" Kongzhao consoled him, "Your hair will grow back, and it will not be too long before you can meet people again."

Having no alternative, Daqing agreed to being disguised as a nun and live at the nunnery, there to spend his days and nights in lubricious revelry. Kongzhao and Jingzhen of course did not spare him, and to their ardors were added those of Kongzhao's two novices.

Sometimes all communed on the same bed; at other times the encounters were joined at random. Those who demanded would not yield their turn; he who serviced dared not stint his energies. A stick of dry firewood soon splinters under the attacks of two sharp axes; one weary soldier cannot withstand the assaults of four strong generals. Thus the flickering lamp, lit again and again, gave off but a waning flame, and the depleted hourglass, never replenished, dribbled its last grains of sand. Even a man of iron would have melted and perished in such circumstances.

Daqing was already ill but received scant sympathy from the nuns. When, at first, he performed three times well and twice badly, they assumed he was shirking his duties. But later, when he was confined for longer and longer periods to his bed, they began to feel concerned. They contemplated sending him home, but he had no hair, and if he were to be questioned by his family and the matter taken to court, the nunnery's reputation would be ruined and their livelihood jeopardized. But if they kept him at the nunnery and he died, it would be difficult to dispose of the body. And if the local authorities found out and the matter came to light, their own lives would be forfeit. Nor did they dare call in physicians. So they had the tenders of censers go to apothecaries and solicit medications by describing the symptoms. However such medicines had little more effect than water poured on a stone.

For lack of anything better, Kongzhao and Jingzhen brewed the medications and tended to Daqing day and night, hoping against hope that he might recover some day. But his condition only worsened, and soon he was at death's door. Kangzhao asked Jingzhen, "What shall we do now? I see no hope for him." Jingzhen reflected a moment, and then said, "Have no fear! Just tell the tenders of censers to purchase a few loads of lime. When he passes away, we will not ask any outsiders to prepare the corpse, but shall ourselves dress him up as a nun. Nor will we need to purchase a coffin, for we shall lay him in the one prepared for our old abbess. Then, with the assistance of the tenders of censers and the novices, you and I will carry him to the vacant lot in the rear courtyard, dig a deep pit, pour in the lime, and bury him there. Neither gods nor ghosts will be any the wiser!"

In the meantime, Daqing languished in Kongzhao's bedchamber. Tears rained from his eyes as he thought of his family and saw none of his dear ones at his bedside. Kongzhao wiped away his tears and attempted to comfort him by saying, "Do not worry, you will get better some day." But Daqing lamented, "I met the two of you by chance and had hoped to share intimacies with you forever. It grieves me profoundly that my lot is so shallow and that we must part so soon. Since all this began with my acquaintance with you, there is something important you must promise me, and I beg you not to go back on your word." Kongzhao declared, "Tell me what you want of me, and I shall not go back on my word." Daqing reached under his pillow and took out a yin-yang cord.

Now what is a yin-yang cord? It is a cord braided half with parrot-green and half with goose-brown silk. Because it combines these two colors, it is also known as a mandarin duck cord.

Daqing handed the cord to Kongzhao and said with tears in his eyes, "My family has heard nothing from me since I came here. Now that I am to part with them forever, I wish to send them this cord, so that my wife may be informed and come to see me one last time. I will then be able to close my eyes when I die."

Kongzhao took the cord, and then instructed a novice to bring Jingzhen to a side room of East Pavilion. She showed Jingzhen the cord and told her about Daqing's request. Appalled, Jingzhen expostulated, "You and I, who have taken the vows, have already breached unequivocal rules by concealing a man here. And that is to say nothing of the fact that we have done him almost to death. If his wife comes here, she will not forgive us and will certainly stir up a fearful scandal. How will we deal with that?"

Being more softhearted, Kongzhao could not bear to see Daqing suffer so much. As she hesitated, however, Jingzhen snatched the yin-yang cord out of her hands and tossed it into the rafters where much time would presumably elapse before it was ever found again. Kongzhao protested, "What shall I say to Daqing, now that you have thrown the cord away?" Jingzhen replied, "Just tell him you have instructed the tender of censers to deliver the cord. If his wife does not choose to come, he cannot accuse us of going back on our word, can he?" Kongzhao did as she was told. For several days after that, Daqing inquired whether there had been any response, and when there was none he assumed that his wife, in her bitterness, refused to see him. So great was his misery that he uttered loud wails. Soon his time came, and he expired.

The two nuns dared not weep aloud over his death. They could only sob softly as they boiled hot water, cleansed his corpse, and dressed it in a set of new clothes. That done, they summoned both tenders of censers, gave them an abundant meal of wine and meat, lit candles for them, and had them dig a deep pit under a tall cypress in the nunnery's rear courtyard. Into the pit the tenders of censers poured lime and lowered the old abbess's coffin. When everything was ready, all returned to the chamber in which Daqing lay. Then, with no regard for whether the day or hour was propitious for an interment, the corpse was rolled onto a door plank and the tenders of censers, helped by the novices, bore it to the rear courtyard. Daqing was properly laid out in the coffin, the lid was nailed fast, and more lime was poured in. Then earth was shoveled on top and patted smooth to leave no trace of the burial.

Poor Ho Daqing! Not four months after he became embroiled with the nuns during the Qingming Festival, he lost his life, left behind no small amount of property, and was buried in a backyard without ever seeing his wife and child again. A sad affair indeed!

Now back to Ho Daqing's wife, Mistress Lu. When Daqing failed to return four or five days after his outing during the Qingming Festival, Mistress Lu had not been particularly concerned, since she assumed he had once again been detained at some house of prostitution. But when more than ten days had passed and he still did not reappear, she instructed servants to make inquiries at his usual haunts. They were told he had not been seen since the Qingming Festival. Mistress Lu began to worry, especially after a month and more elapsed without any news about Daqing. At home she wept all day, wrote handbills offering rewards, and had these posted throughout the city, but still there was no sign of her husband. Anxiety pervaded the entire household.

In autumn that year, heavy rains fell for many days and damaged several of the Ho family's houses. However, distracted by the disappearance of the master of the household, no one was inclined to attend to such matters, and only in the eleventh moon were a number of craftsmen engaged to make repairs. One day, Mistress Lu came out to see for herself how the work was progressing. As she walked around, she noticed a craftsman wearing around his waist a yin-yang cord exactly like the one her husband sported. Startled, she hastily summoned a maidservant and had her ask the craftsman to show her the cord.

Craftsman Kuai the Third was known for his skills at masonry and carpentry. The Hos were one of his main clients, and everyone in the household knew him. Advised that the mistress of the household wished to see his yin-yang cord, he untied it and handed it to the maidservant, who passed it to her mistress. Mistress Lu carefully examined the cord. There was no doubt that it was her husband's! She and her husband had once purchased two identical yin-yang cords and each had worn one of them.

Tears sprang to her eyes at the sight of the cord. Calling to Kuai the Third to come over, she proceeded to question him. "Where did you get this cord?" she asked, and Kuai the Third replied, "I found it in a nunnery outside the city." Mistress Lu continued, "What is the nunnery called, and what are the names of the nuns there?" She was told, "It is the well-known Non-Void Nunnery, the one with two pavilions. One of these, East Pavilion, is managed by a nun called Kongzhao, and the other, West Pavilion, by Jingzhen. There are also a number of novices there who have yet to shave their heads." Mistress Lu quickly asked, "How old are those two nuns?" And Kuai the Third replied, "I would say they are in their twenties, and both are quite pleasing to the eye."

This information set Mistress Lu to thinking, "My husband must have taken a fancy to these two nuns and hidden himself in the nunnery. A full search will surely turn him up. I shall send several men there with this cord and have Kuai the Third go along as witness." As the craftsman turned to leave, however, it suddenly occurred to her, "What if this cord was not left there by my husband? I cannot wrongly accuse nuns who have taken the vows. I must ask him for more details." Calling the craftsman back, she queried, "When did you find this cord?" And he replied, "Less than half a moon ago." Mistress Lu reflected, "Could my husband still have been in that nunnery half a moon ago? I must make sure of that." So she asked again, "Where exactly did you find this cord?" And Kuai the Third stated, "In a room at East Pavilion, among the rafters. Their roofs, too, were leaking after the rains, and I was hired to retile them. That is how I found the cord. But may I inquire why the mistress is asking me so many questions about this cord?"

Mistress Lu decided to confide in him. She said, "This cord belongs to the master. He left home in the spring, and nothing has been heard about him since. His yin-yang cord has come to light now, and he must be where it was discovered. I want you to go with us when we demand that the nuns return my husband."

Kuai the Third was flabbergasted. "What?" he thought, "Does she want me to ask for her husband?" Aloud, he protested, "I did find that cord, but I know nothing about the master." But Mistress Lu would not listen to any excuse. She asked, "For how many days did you work at the nunnery?" Kuai the Third replied, "More than ten days at both pavilions. They still owe me my payment." Mistress Lu pursued, "Did you see the master there?" Resentfully, the craftsman replied, "I would never lie about this. All those days we worked there, we were allowed to enter every single room. I never saw so much as Master Ho's shadow!"

Mistress Lu reflected, "If my husband is not in the nunnery, I cannot confront them, even though I have the cord." After some thought she came to a decision. "There must be some reason his cord was in the nunnery," she told herself. "Who knows, he may have been hidden somewhere else. Since Kuai the Third claims they still owe him payment, I shall give him a tael of silver and have him look around there every now and then, on the excuse of asking for his money. He may find some clue or other. Then I can tie my husband's disappearance to those nuns and find out where they are keeping him." Telling Kuai the Third to come closer, she instructed him to do this, that, and the other, then stated, "I shall first give you one tael of silver. A bigger reward will be yours if you bring me reliable information."

When Kuai the Third heard that he would receive a tael of silver, with more to follow, his objections evaporated, and he promised to fulfill all her instructions. Mistress Lu went to her chambers and came back with a tael of silver. Kuai the Third accepted it with thanks, after which he went home.

The next morning, Kuai the Third tarried until after his noon meal, and then, taking his time, sauntered to the gate of the nunnery. There he saw West Pavilion's tender of censers seated on the threshold in the warm sunshine. The old man had removed his outer garments and was searching them for lice. Kuai the Third called out to him. The old man raised his rheumy eyes and, recognizing the craftsman, said, "It has been quite a few days since I last saw you. How is it that you have the time to stroll around? The senior nun has been asking about you. She has some small jobs for you, so you've come at the right time." Kuai the Third felt this suited his purpose just fine, and he inquired, "Do you know what the senior nun wants me to do?" The old man replied, "No, I do not. She did not specify. Come in with me and ask her."

Putting on his garments, the tender of censers led Kuai the Third through winding corridors and paths to the nun's chambers. Jingzhen was seated at a table, copying a sutra. The old man reported, "Senior Nun, the craftsman Kuai the Third is here." Jingzhen laid down her brush and said, "I am glad you have come. I had just asked the tender of censers to bring you here for some work." Kuai the Third inquired, "What does the senior nun wish me to do?" And Jingzhen explained, "The sacrificial table before Buddha is an inheritance from the founders of the nunnery, and the lacquer on it is cracked and peeling with age. I have always wished to replace it but found no donors until a few days ago when Madame Meng kindly bestowed a few cords of lumber. Also, I want you to make a sutra cabinet like the one at East Pavilion. You may start tomorrow, as I have ascertained that it is an auspicious day. But you must complete the work with your own hands. I do not trust any assistant to do it properly. As for payment, I might as well give it to you together with what I already owe you."

Kuai the Third promised to return the next day. As he spoke, his gaze swept around the chamber, but it was sparsely furnished and afforded no hiding place for a man. He then turned and retraced his steps toward the gate of West Pavilion, all the while looking this way and that. An idea occurred to him. "Since I found the cord in East Pavilion, I should look there for clues."

Bidding farewell to the tender of censers, he walked out of the gate and bent his steps toward East Pavilion. Its gate was only half shut, and Kuai the Third looked in. Seeing no sign of human activity, he pushed the gate open and stole into the courtyard. The doors to the chambers were locked, so he peered through the cracks but saw nothing of interest. He then proceeded to the kitchen. All at once he heard laughter inside and he stopped in his tracks. Finding a pinhole in the window paper, he peeped in, only to see the two novices tussling playfully with each other. A moment later, the younger one tumbled to the ground, whereupon the older one hoisted her legs onto her own shoulders. Kissing the younger girl, she mounted her like a man in the act of copulation, and when the younger one cried out as though in pain, the older one jested, "He made your hole bigger, so why such a fuss?"

Kuai the Third was watching them with much amusement, when he suddenly sneezed. The novices jumped up in alarm and called out, "Who is there?" Kuai the Third approached the door and said, "It is I. May I see the senior nun?" While he spoke, he was unable to repress a chuckle as he recalled the novices' behavior, and both girls, sensing that he had observed them, grew red in the face. One of them asked, "What do you want, Craftsman Kuai?" And he replied, "Nothing of importance. I merely wish to borrow something from the payment owed to me." The novice snapped, "Senior Nun Kongzhao is not in. Come some other day."

Thus rebuffed, Kuai the Third could not very well go in, so he retraced his steps and left the pavilion. As the two novices shut the gate behind him, one of them scolded, "That boor came in like a burglar and sneaked right up to the kitchen. What a horrible man!" Kuai the Third overheard her but could hardly shout back at her since he had seen nothing that was truly reprehensible. As he walked home, he mused, "'He made your hole bigger.' I do not know what that means, but it sounds questionable. When I go back tomorrow I will look further into the matter."

The next morning, he went to West Pavilion with his tools, and while he measured and marked the lumber and cut it with axe and saw, he kept his eyes and ears open for any sign or indication of Ho Daqing.

At around the noon hour, Jingzhen came to look at his work and exchanged a few pleasantries with him. She suddenly noticed that the incense lamp had gone out and instructed her novice to fetch a light. The novice soon returned with a taper and, having set it down on a table, proceeded to undo the rope by which the incense lamp was suspended. She then began to lower the lamp, but gave out too much rope so that the lamp slithered down. By coincidence, Jingzhen was standing below the lamp, and it fell straight on her head. With a thud, it split in two parts, drenching Jingzhen from head to foot with oil.

Jingzhen flew into a rage. Disregarding the oil that covered her, she sprang forward to seize the girl by the hair and commenced to kick and punch her, shrieking, "You lecherous little slattern! Has some man diddled you out of your wits? You have besmirched all my clothing!" Kuai the Third laid down his axe and chisel and hastened to pull them apart. Still cursing furiously, Jingzhen returned to her chambers to change her clothing. The novice, bruised and with her hair straggling all over her back, sobbed piteously. Glaring at Jingzhen's retreating figure, she muttered, "You beat and curse me when all I did was spill some oil. How should you be punished for doing a man to death?!" When Kuai the Third heard her say this, he quickly asked what she meant.

It so happened that this novice had also attained pubescence, and when she saw Daqing and Jingzhen engage in all sorts of dalliances, she too wished to have a taste of such pleasures. Jingzhen, however, was quite different from Kongzhao, in that she was mean and inordinately jealous. She had countenanced Kongzhao because it was the latter who had set the whole affair going. But she was the sort of woman who, once she had a man in her bed, would not be content even with swallowing him whole, and would never be willing to let anyone else have a taste of him! The novice had long held down feelings of resentment, but on this day, in her anger, she blurted out the truth, which was precisely what interested Kuai the Third, and he inquired. "Who did she do to death?" The novice replied, "A *jian sheng*. Day and night she and those sluts at East Pavilion took turns carousing with him, right until he died." Kuai the Third asked again, "Where is he now?" And the novice told him, "Buried under the big cypress behind East Pavilion." Kuai the Third wished to ask more, but the tender of censers came out into the courtyard. Both fell silent, and the novice, still sobbing, went back to her room.

Kuai the Third turned the novice's words over in his mind. They fitted in with what the novices at East Pavilion had said the day before. He felt he now had nine tenths of the information he needed, so before the day was out, he put away his tools and left the nunnery on the pretext that he had some matter to attend to. Without pausing to catch his breath, he ran all the way to the Ho's residence, asked to see Mistress Lu, and reported to her all he had learned.

Mistress Lu broke into loud laments when she heard that her husband was dead. The same evening, she assembled members of the clan to discuss what should be done, and Kuai the Third was asked to stay the night. The next morning, more than twenty servants and retainers gathered, all bringing hoes, spades, or hatchets. Mistress Lu left her son in his nanny's care and stepped in a sedan chair, and then all set forth.

Very soon they arrived at the nunnery, as it stood no more than three *li* from the city. Stepping out of the sedan chair, Mistress Lu instructed half of the men to stand guard at the main gate. The remainder, armed with spades and hoes, went with her into the nunnery. Kuai the Third showed them the way to East Pavilion and knocked on the door.

Although the nunnery's main gate was open, the nuns and novices had only just risen from their beds, so it was the tender of censers who came to the door. Opening it and looking out, he saw a woman among the people there and assumed they had come to burn incense. He went to Kongzhao to report that visitors had come.

Meanwhile, the group broke down the door and entered the pavilion, guided by Kuai the Third who was familiar with all its ways and byways. They came face to face with Kongzhao, and she, seeing a woman among them, stepped forward to greet them, saying, "You must be Kuai the

Third's family members." Making no response, Kuai the Third and Mistress Lu shoved her aside and marched toward the rear courtyard with the rest of the group. Kongzhao was surprised at their temerity. Wondering what they were up to, she followed them. She saw them make straight for the big cypress and then commence to tear up the ground under it with hoes and spades. Kongzhao knew now that the secret was out, and she turned pale with fear. Hurrying back to the pavilion, she told the novices, "This is dreadful! Master Ho's death has been discovered! Come with me, we must flee for our lives!" She then dashed out of East Pavilion with the terrified novices hard on her heels. But when they came to the nunnery's main hall of worship, the tender of censers told them, "For some unknown reason many men are guarding the gate. They will not let me go out!" Kongzhao cried, "Quick! Let us go to West Pavilion and see what we can do!"

The foursome ran to West Pavilion and pounded on the gate, then instructed the tender of censers to shut it behind them. Kongzhao told him, "Do not open it for anyone!" Then she hurried into the senior nun's chambers. The door was shut and Jingzhen had not yet risen from her bed. Kongzhao rapped on door, calling frantically to be let in. Recognizing her voice, Jingzhen put on some clothes and went out, asking, "Sister, why all the commotion?" Kongzhao told her, "It's about Master Ho. Someone has divulged our secret. That scoundrel Craftsman Kuai came with a large number of people and went straight to the rear courtyard. They are digging there! I tried to escape, but the tender of censers said the front gate is being guarded and no one can get out. So I have come to confer with you."

Dazed by this news, Jingzhen queried, "But Craftsman Kuai was working here just yesterday, was he not? Why did he bring those people here today? And how does he know things in such detail? That cur could only have reported such information because someone here leaked it to him. How else would he know about this matter?" Hearing this, her novice was frightened and sorely regretted her indiscretions of the previous day, but before she could say anything, an East Pavilion novice stated, "Kuai the Third must have had something in mind for several days. We found him eavesdropping by our kitchen the other day and drove him away. But who could have told him such things?"

Kongzhao interrupted, "We will discuss that later. The important thing now is, what should we do?" Jingzhen declared, "There is only one thing we can do—abscond!" Kongzhen ventured, "But the front gate is being guarded!" Whereupon Jingzhen cried, "Then see if anyone is at the back gate!" A tender of censers was sent to reconnoiter, and he returned with the information that no one was there. Greatly relieved, Jingzhen instructed her tender of censers to lock all doors on their way out. She herself returned to her chambers where she retrieved some silver but abandoned everything else that belonged to her. Then all seven, counting the tenders of censers, went out of the back gate and locked it behind themselves. Kongzhao inquired. "Where should we go now?" Jingzhen replied, "We cannot travel along the main roads, as we will certainly be seen. The best thing is to take seldom-used side roads. We shall hide temporarily at the Nunnery of Ultimate Bliss. Few people know about this nunnery, as it is situated in a sparsely inhabited place. Moreover, its abbess, Liaoyuan, is on good terms with me, and I do not think she will refuse us sanctuary. We shall make further plans after things have calmed down somewhat." Kongzhao agreed. Then the group set out, walking along rough and narrow paths, in order to seek refuge at the Nunnery of Ultimate Bliss.

Now back to Mistress Lu, who was overseeing Kuai the Third and the other men as they toiled under the tall cypress tree. Having dug open the topsoil, they came upon a layer of lime, and all believed they had found what they were seeking. However, moisture had caused the lime to harden and it cost them much time and effort to break it apart. When at last the coffin lid was uncovered, Mistress Lu began to sob loudly.

Using their spades, the men chipped away the lime on both sides of the coffin, but were unable to pry up its lid. In the meantime, those waiting outside the gate became impatient, and all ran in to see what was happening. When they observed that little progress was being made, all pitched in to dig deeper, and they finally raised the coffin to the surface. Then with axes they loosened the lid. When they lifted it off, however, what they found inside the coffin was not the body of a man but that of a nun! Dumbfounded, they looked at each other, and then hurriedly replaced the lid without taking the time to examine the corpse.

One moment, storyteller, I have a question for you. Ho Daqing had been dead for less than a year, and although he had no more hair, his wife would surely have recognized him, would she not?

As we all know, esteemed listener, Ho Daqing was a handsome fellow with ruddy cheeks and a fair complexion when he left home, but by the time he died, his excesses at the nunnery and the many days he lay ill there had reduced him to a bag of bones. Even he would not have recognized himself had he looked at a mirror. Besides, it was only natural that all should assume the corpse to be that of a nun when they saw it had a bald pate.

Mistress Lu at once took Kuai the Third to task. "I had you come here to obtain reliable information," she cried. "Why did you not verify your findings, instead of bringing me a false report?" Kuai the Third remonstrated, "That was no false report! The novice told me quite definitely that he was buried here." One of the men commented, "Why do you argue? We all saw it was a nun." Hopefully, Kuai the Third said, "Perhaps we have looked in the wrong place? Let us try digging somewhere else." But an older clansman hastily objected, "No, no! According to law, beheading is the punishment for those who break open a coffin and expose the corpse. Digging up a grave is also punishable by decapitation. We are already guilty of one crime, and if we disinter another nun we shall face two death sentences. Is that what you wish? We should quickly report this matter to the authorities and ask them to interrogate the novice who spoke to you yesterday. That is the only way we can expect a fair hearing. Should the nuns send in a report before we do, we will be in grave trouble."

All the men agreed. They led Mistress Lu away and departed in such haste that they left their hoes and spades in the rear courtyard. On their way to the gate of the nunnery, they did not see a single nun or novice, and the elderly clansman cried, "This bodes no good! The nuns must have gone, either to fetch the local constable or to press charges. Let us hurry!" All were so frightened their only thought was to put the nunnery behind them as quickly as possible. They placed Mistress Lu in the sedan chair and ran pell-mell toward Xingan County to report to the authorities. By the time they reached the city, half of the relatives had vanished.

Now, among the men Mistress Lu had brought to the nunnery was a hired hand known as Mao the Mischief-Maker. He assumed that some objects must have been placed in the coffin with the corpse, so he slipped away and waited until everyone had departed. He then removed the coffin's lid again and searched the garments on the corpse, looking for something of value. He found nothing, but as luck would have it, as he tweaked and tugged at the garments the corpse's trousers slipped off, revealing a male's phallus! Mao the Mischief-Maker grinned, then said, "So it was a monk, not a nun!"

He replaced the lid and walked around the nunnery, looking here and there, and when he saw no one, he entered one of the chambers, which happened to be Kongzhao's bedchamber. Taking a few pieces of jewelry and thrusting them in his bosom, he left the nunnery and hurried to the county yamen. Mistress Lu and the others were still there, waiting for the magistrate who had gone out to pay his respects to some visiting dignitaries.

Mao the Mischief-Maker went up to them and said, "Have no worries. I had my doubts, so I returned to look again. That body was not the master's, but neither was it that of a nun. The deceased was a monk!" All were mightily relieved, and the elderly clansman declared, "That makes things better! But it still remains to be seen to which monastery the monk belonged and how he was slain by those nuns."

Talk about coincidences—just as they were conferring among themselves, an old monk approached them and inquired, "What monk was slain, and in which nunnery? What did he look like?" He was told, "It was at the East Pavilion of Non-Void Nunnery just outside the city. A tall, sallow young monk, who looked as though he had died not too long ago." Hearing this, the old monk declared, "If that is so, he must be my disciple." Someone asked, "How would he have died in a nunnery?" And the old monk replied, "I am Jueyuan, abbot of the Ten Thousand Dharmas Monastery. I have a disciple named Qufei who is twenty-six years of age and who has never learned to behave himself. Nor have I ever been able to keep him in line. He left the monastery in the eighth moon and has not been heard of since. His parents are so protective of him, they refuse to admit he is a wastrel and accuse this humble monk of murdering him. That is why I am here waiting to be tried. If the body you mentioned is truly his, I would be exculpated."

Mao the Mischief-Maker proposed, "Old Master, I will take you to see the corpse if you promise to treat me to some wine. What say you?"

And the old monk exclaimed, "That would be most felicitous!" Just as they were leaving, however, an elderly man with his wife in tow came over to the old monk and slapped him twice on the face and railed, "You bald thief! Where have you put our murdered son?" The old monk replied, "Do not shout! I have found a clue to your son's whereabouts." The elderly man inquired, "So where is he now?" And the old monk told him, "Your son had a liaison with a nun at the Non-Void Nunnery. He may have died there and been buried in the nunnery's rear courtyard." Pointing to Mao the Mischief-Maker, he continued, "This is the witness." So saying he seized Mao the Mischief-Maker by the arm and strode off, and the elderly man and his wife went with them to the Non-Void Nunnery.

By then, residents in the vicinity of the nunnery were aware that something had happened there, and all people, old and young, had come to satisfy their curiosity. Mao the Mischief-Maker took the old monk into the nunnery. They heard someone call out as they passed one of the chambers, and when Mao the Mischief-Maker opened the door and looked in, he saw an old nun lying on a bed, evidently close to death. She cried weakly, "I am hungry! Why do they not bring me some food?" Mao the Mischief-Maker paid no heed to her. Shutting the door, he proceeded with the old monk to the cypress in the rear courtyard and opened the coffin. The elderly couple rubbed their old eyes and peered in, and thinking that the body resembled their son, they began to wail at the top of their voices.

Onlookers clustered around to inquire what was going on, and Mao the Mischief-Maker told them with much gesticulating and embellishment. The old monk, on his part, was concerned only with extricating himself from his troubles. Seeing that the elderly couple acknowledged the body to be their son's, and not caring whether this was true or not, he tugged at the elderly man and urged, "Come, come! You have your son now. Let us go quickly to the authorities, request that the nuns be arrested, and have them interrogated until all has been clarified. You will have time to weep then."

The elderly man ceased his wailing and closed up the coffin. Then all four hurried back to the city. When they arrived at the county yamen, the magistrate had just returned, and the bailiffs in the old monk's case, having lost both the plaintiffs and the defendant, were searching everywhere, their faces lined with anxiety and dripping with perspiration.

When the Ho family saw Mao the Mischief-Maker and the old monk coming back, all asked the old monk, "Is it indeed your disciple?" And he replied, "Absolutely!" The Ho family members then proposed, "Let us combine the cases and go in to report to the magistrate what we have found." The bailiffs took them into the yamen and made all of them kneel down.

First, the Ho family went before the magistrate with a detailed account of when their master had disappeared, where Kuai the Third had found the yin-yang cord, what he had learned from the novices, and how they had opened up the coffin only to find the body of a monk. Then the old monk reported that the body was that of a disciple of his, that his disciple abruptly left the monastery three months ago and died in the nunnery, and that he himself was now being wrongly accused by the disciple's parents. He ended with the words, "Since it is clear now that I am innocent, I plead to be exonerated."

The magistrate asked the elderly man, "Is the body truly that of your son? There must be no mistake!" The elderly man replied, "There is no mistake. The body is indeed that of my son."

The magistrate then dispatched four bailiffs to the nunnery to bring in the nuns for examination. With this order, the bailiffs proceeded swiftly to the nunnery. There, they saw large numbers of onlookers milling in and out of the gate. They pushed their way in and came upon a dying old nun, lying on a bed in one of the chambers. Other than that, they found no trace of any nuns or novices. One of the bailiffs said, "They may be hiding in West Pavilion." So they hurried over to West Pavilion. The gate was shut, and when they had hammered on it for a while and no one answered, they became impatient and clambered over the back wall. Inside, they found the doors to all the chambers, both front and back, secured with locks. Breaking the locks as they went along, they searched the entire pavilion but saw no one there. The bailiffs all helped themselves to some articles of value, then detained the local constable and took him back to the yamen.

To the magistrate, who was waiting for them, they reported, "The nuns at Non-Void Nunnery have fled, and their whereabouts are unknown. We have brought the local constable back for questioning." The magistrate then asked the constable, "Do you know where the nuns are hiding?" The constable replied defiantly, "How could this insignificant person know where they went?" Angered, the magistrate snapped, "Nuns in your locality hid a monk in their nunnery and murdered him, yet you failed to report this. Now that the matter has come to light, you allow them to escape and pretend to know nothing. Of what use is a constable like you?!" He ordered that the man be taken out and beaten, and it was only after the latter begged for mercy that he retracted his order. However, he gave the constable three days to produce the fugitives. The magistrate then set all the detainees free on bail, pending trial after the nuns were apprehended, and issued two paper seal strips with which to seal the gates of the nunnery.

Now let us go back to Kongzhao, Jingzhen, the novices, and tenders of censers. When these arrived at the Nunnery of Ultimate Bliss, they found the gates of the nunnery tightly shut and had to knock for a long time before the nunnery's tender of censers emerged. All rushed headlong into the nunnery, telling the tender of censers to close the gate behind them.

Liaoyuan, the abbess, had come to the gate to meet the visitors. She recognized all of them as coming from the Non-Void Nunnery and, seeing them in such a state of panic, surmised that something had gone seriously amiss at that nunnery. She invited the nuns to be seated in the hall of worship and sent her tender of censers out to prepare tea. Then she asked her visitors why they had come. Jingzhen drew her aside, told her all that had happened, and requested temporary sanctuary. Liaoyuan was greatly shocked. After a long moment, she said, "You and Kongzhao are my sisters in religion, and were you to seek refuge here because of some other difficulty, I would normally take you in. But your affair is no small matter, and you must go far away if you hope to avoid disaster. The walls here are too thin to protect you from inquisitive eyes and ears. If your presence is detected, you could not escape, and even I would be stuck in this morass."

Why was Liaoyuan unwilling to help them? It so happened that she was a libertine open to all comers, and was just then carrying on a liaison with young monk Qufei from the Ten Thousand Dharmas Monastery, whom she had kept hidden in the nunnery for more than three months and lived with as a bald-headed couple. Although Qufei was also disguised as a nun, the two were constantly apprehensive of being found out, and therefore kept a tight check on the nunnery's gates. When she learned that Jingzhen and Kongzhao were seeking refuge because an affair such as her own had been exposed, she feared the two would be seized at her nunnery, in which case her own conduct might be laid bare. That was the true reason for her refusal.

Kongzhao and her novices were stunned by Liaoyuan's reply and looked helplessly at one another. But Jingzhen was, after all, more canny than her colleagues. She knew that Liaoyuan was a greedy person, so she extracted two or three taels of silver from her sleeve and handed these to Liaoyuan, saying, "What you have said makes sense, but all happened so suddenly we had no time to plan where to go in such an emergency. I hope you will, for old times' sake, allow us to stay for two or three days. We shall leave after the situation eases. This bit of silver is for our upkeep."

Just as she had anticipated, at the sight of this silver Liaoyuan forgot what was at stake, and she said, "If you stay only two or three days, there should be no problem. And I cannot accept this silver." But Jingzhen insisted, "We cannot let you go to any expense on our account, as the way we have imposed ourselves on you is inappropriate enough." After hypocritically refusing the silver a few more times, Liaoyuan took it, and then led her visitors to a place of concealment in the nunnery.

By this time, the monk Qufei had learned from the tender of censers that five nuns and novices had arrived from the Non-Void Nunnery and that all were quite agreeable to the eyes. As he hurried out to take a look, Qufei came squarely face to face with them. During the exchange of greetings, Kongzhao carefully scrutinized this young "nun," and not recognizing her, asked Jingzhen, "To which nunnery does this sister belong? Why is it that I have never seen her?" Liaoyuan prevaricated, "You do not know her because she has just recently taken the vows." Meanwhile, Qufei was elated when he saw that these nuns and novices were better favored than Liaoyuan. He told himself, "I am in luck! Since Heaven has seen fit to send these beauties here, I shall of course cozy up to them and make merry with each and every one of them by turn."

Liaoyuan treated her visitors to a vegetarian repast. However, Jingzhen and Kongzhao were preoccupied with their thoughts and ate little. Ears flushed and eyelids twitching, they fidgeted nervously. In the afternoon, they asked Liaoyuan, "We wonder what is going on at our nunnery. Could you ask your tender of censers to go there and see what has happened? We would like to know, so that we may plan what to do next." Liaoyuan agreed to do so.

That tender of censers was a simple old soul and knew not the import of his mission. He went to the Non-Void Nunnery and proceeded to look about. At the time, local constables had just received orders from the magistrate to close and seal the gates. With no regard for the fate of the old nun within the nunnery, they placed locks on the gates and then sealed these by pasting strips of paper crosswise on the two leaves of the gates. They were about to leave when they remarked an old man peering around furtively, and at once knew him to be a spy. They surrounded him and shouted, "You come right in time! The yamen wants you arrested!" And one of them threw a rope around the old man's neck.

The tender of censers was so terrified that his legs quivered and grew weak, and he cried, "They came to hide at our nunnery and asked me to find out what is going on here. Actually, I have nothing to do with them!" The constables declared, "We know you came here to spy out the situation. From which nunnery do you come?" And the tender of censers replied, "From the Nunnery of Ultimate Bliss." Having secured this information, the constables called for reinforcements and, taking the tender of censers with them, set out together for the Nunnery of Ultimate Bliss.

Once there, the constables posted guards both behind and in front of the nunnery before knocking at the gate. Liaoyuan, believing that the tender of censers had returned, came in person to open the gate, and the constables swarmed in. They first seized Liaoyuan, and then made her go with them as they ransacked the entire nunnery. Not one person escaped. The terrified young monk attempted to conceal himself under a bed, but he too was discovered and detained. In desperation, Liaoyuan pleaded with her captors, "They only sought temporary sanctuary, and I had nothing to do with whatever they did. I shall give all of you some wine money for doing me a convenience and sparing my nunnery!" But the constables declared, "This we cannot do! Our magistrate is an unforgiving man. What shall we tell him if he were to ask us where we apprehended those nuns? And how do we know you are not implicated in this matter? You must go before the magistrate to clarify these questions."

Liaoyuan then said, "That will be no problem for me. But my disciple has only recently taken the vows, so leave her out of this matter. I beg you to do me this favor!" Most of the constables hoped to receive some silver and would have agreed to this request, but one of them dissented, saying, "Nothing doing! If that nun were not implicated, why would she be so flustered and hide under a bed? There is something fishy about her, and we cannot bear responsibility for letting her go." The others reluctantly concurred.

They bound all ten captives, both men and women, with ropes, stringing them one behind the other like the rice dumplings wrapped in bamboo leaves that people consume during the Dragon Boat Festival. Then they left the nunnery, locked and sealed the gates behind them, and returned to Xingan County. All the way, Liaoyuan bitterly reproached Jingzhen, and the latter could find nothing to say.

The magistrate had already left the yamen when they arrived at Xingan County, so the constables had to take their captives home for the night. While no one was looking, Liaoyuan whispered to the young monk, "When we are in court tomorrow, admit only that you are my disciple and that you have only just taken the vows. Do not say anything else. Let me do the talking. All will be well."

The next morning, when the magistrate convened the morning hearing, a constable went in and reported, "The Non-Void Nunnery nuns had concealed themselves in the Nunnery of Ultimate Bliss. We have apprehended them and brought them here together with some occupants of the Nunnery of Ultimate Bliss." The magistrate ordered that all be brought in and made to kneel to the left of the dais. He then sent bailiffs to summon the old monk, Ho Daqing's family members, Kuai the Third, and the young monk's parents to the hearing. These soon arrived and were ordered to kneel to the right of the dais. The young monk stole a glance at them and was astonished. "How has my teacher become involved in this matter? And even my father and mother are here! How strange!" However, he dared not call out to them and, fearing that his teacher might recognize him, he averted his face and crouched to the ground.

At this time, his parents, disregarding the rules of the court, began to weep and to berate Jingzhen and Kongzhao, "You shameless she-dogs! Why did you murder our son? Give him back to us alive!" These words only puzzled the young monk all the more, and he thought, "I am here, alive and well. Why do my parents accuse those nuns of killing me?" As for Jingzhen and Kongzhao, they dared not utter a word, believing the elderly man and his wife to be Ho Daqing's parents.

The magistrate ordered the elderly couple to hold their tongues, then called Jingzhen and Kongzhao to come forward and said, "Both of you are nuns. Why did you break your vows of chastity, conceal a monk in your nunnery, and then conspire to do him to death? Confess, if you do not wish to be put to torture!"

Jingzhen and Kongzhao knew the gravity of their crimes, and their bowels constricted with fear. But now that the magistrate was questioning them about some monk or other instead of Ho Daqing, they were completely bewildered. Even the nimble-tongued Jingzhen was speechless, and her words lodged in her throat as though stuck there with fishglue. The magistrate repeated his questions four or five times before she managed to say, "This humble nun did not murder a monk!" Whereupon the magistrate roared, "You dare deny that you murdered the monk Qufei of the Ten Thousand Dharmas Monastery and buried him in your rear courtyard? Apply the vises to them!" With ferocious yells, the yamen beadles on both sides set their hands on the nuns.

Liaoyuan reeled with shock and amazement when she realized that the magistrate believed the corpse to be that of Qufei, and that he was proceeding accordingly. She thought to herself, "What is this all about? They find Ho Daqing's body at the Non-Void Nunnery, but instead of pursuing that affair, they confused it with mine. How strange!" She glanced surreptitiously at Qufei. He, too, was aware that his parents had misidentified the body, and he and Liaoyuan stared at each other in disbelief.

In the meantime, Jingzhen and Kongzhao, whose pampered bodies and delicate flesh had never known such mistreatment, almost swooned when the vise rods commenced to tighten, and they cried, "My Lord, do not torture us! We will tell you the whole truth!" The magistrate told the beadles to desist while he heard their confessions.

The two nuns cried in unison, "The body buried in our backyard is not that of a monk. It is that of Ho Daqing!" Hearing that it was their master's body, the members of the Ho family, together with Kuai the Third, crept closer to the bench. The magistrate asked, "If so, why was his head shaved?"

The nuns proceeded to recount how Ho Daqing came to visit their nunnery, how mutual seduction had led to adultery, how they schemed to shave his head and disguise him as a nun, how he fell ill and died, and how he was buried. The magistrate knew they were telling the truth, as their words fitted in with what the Ho family had said the day before. He announced, "The matter of *jian sheng* Ho has been resolved. But where have you hidden the monk? Confess!" The nuns wailed, "We truly do not know! We would not be able to tell you, even if you have us beaten to death!"

The magistrate then called forward the novices and tenders of censers and questioned them each in turn, and as all of them said the same thing, he concluded that the two nuns had naught to do with the young monk. Then he had Liaoyuan and the young monk come forward and declared, "Since you concealed Jingzhen and Kongzhao in your nunnery, you must be in league with them!" To the beadles, he said, "Give them a taste of the vise!"

But Liaoyuan had gained in confidence, since the confessions by Jingzhen and Kongzhao distanced her from the supposed death of the young monk. She said calmly, "My Lord, you need not apply torture to us. Allow this humble nun to tell you all that I know. When Jingzhen and her companions arrived at our nunnery, she told us they were being subjected to blackmail and requested that I allow them stay for a few days, to which I misguidedly agreed. As for their debaucheries, I truly had no knowledge of such things." Pointing to the young monk, she continued, "This disciple has recently entered the nunnery and has never met Jingzhen or any of her companions. It is quite manifest that their shameless conduct brings disgrace to the Buddhist faith. Although I was unaware of it when they came, I would certainly have condemned them to the authorities had I later gained the least inkling of what they had done, and would never have consented to hiding them. Now that My Lord knows the facts, I crave your indulgence."

The magistrate deemed her arguments reasonable, and he smiled, "You are quite eloquent, but I would hope your words come from your heart." That said, he told her to kneel to one side.

The magistrate then ordered the beadles to administer fifty strokes with their canes to both Kongzhao and Jingzhen, thirty strokes to the novices of East Pavilion, and twenty strokes to both of the tenders of censers. Each of the blows broke skin and drew blood. The magistrate then pronounced the following verdicts: For instigating illicit acts of fornication and doing a man to death, Jingzhen and Kongzhao were sentenced to death according to law. The novices at East Pavilion were given the lesser punishment of eighty strokes of the cane, after which they were to be sold into bondage by the authorities. For knowingly concealing unlawful acts, the two tenders of censers were sentenced to additional caning. The Non-Void Nunnery, having been turned into a den of iniquity, would be demolished and its site confiscated by the authorities. Although Liaoyuan and her disciple were ignorant of what had transpired at the other nunnery, they had nevertheless concealed fugitives from the law and were sentenced to caning, but were permitted to buy themselves off with fines. The novice at West Pavilion was ordered to return to secular life. To Ho Daqing, who had died in the course of his transgressions, no further punishment would be meted, and his family was ordered to retrieve his coffin and bury it. After the sentencings, all parties were made to affix their mark on the transcripts of their depositions.

Meanwhile the elderly man knew now that the body at the nunnery was not that of his son. He felt he had made a fool of himself by weeping and wailing the day before, and his anger grew. He again approached the magistrate on his knees and repeated his demands that the old monk give him back his son. The old monk, on his part, accused the young monk of having stolen things from the monastery and then hidden himself at home while his parents blamed the monastery for his disappearance. Even the magistrate was at loss how to resolve the dispute. He believed the old monk might have done the younger one to death, but no conviction was possible in the absence of any evidence of the crime. Yet if the young monk were hidden at home, why would the elderly man be demanding that the old monk return him his son? After mulling over the matter, the magistrate told the elderly man, "I cannot judge this case as there is no evidence as to whether your son is dead or alive. Go now, and come back when you have found reliable proof."

Then Kongzhao, Jingzhen and the two novices from East Pavilion were led away to prison. Liaoyuan, her "novice," and all the tenders of censers were released on bail, while the old monk and the elderly couple, accompanied by bailiffs, went forth to seek evidence about the young monk's whereabouts. All others who had been embroiled in the case were sent home.

It is the rule at all yamens that people enter from the eastern side and go out on the western side. And now, as people left the yamen by the vermilion-painted steps on the western side, both Liaoyuan and the young monk secretly exulted, as they had succeeded in duping the magistrate and avoiding exposure. The young monk, however, still feared he might be recognized and walked behind the others with his head lowered to his breast. Yet it was fated that his true colors should be revealed.

As people filed out of the western gate, the elderly man seized the old monk and fulminated, "You bald old thief! You kill my son and then try to use someone else's corpse to gull me? Eh?!" And with that, he proceeded to rain blows on the old monk's head and face. The old monk attempted to shield himself, crying that he was being wronged.

It so happened that more than a score of the old monk's disciples and disciple's disciples were at the gate, waiting to hear the outcome of the proceedings. When they saw their teacher being beaten, they rushed forward, pushed the elderly man to the ground, and pummeled him with their fists. Seeing his father treated in such fashion, the young monk became so agitated that he forgot he was feigning to be a nun. He stepped forward and cried, "Brothers, I beg you to desist!" The monks looked up and saw that it was Qufei. Casting aside the elderly man, they pounced on him and shouted, "Teacher, all is well! Qufei is here!" Bewildered, the bailiffs who were taking Qufei to post bail ordered the monks to fall back and declared, "This is a nun from the Nunnery of Ultimate Bliss whom we are taking to post bail. You have mistaken her for someone else!" But the monks would not be deterred, and they clamored, "Ha! So he disguises himself as a nun and gallivants in the Nunnery of Ultimate Bliss, leaving our teacher to face all this trouble!"

Only now did the crowd of onlookers realize that the nun was a monk in disguise, and all burst out laughing. The only person who failed to be amused was Liaoyuan. She bitterly bemoaned her ill luck, and her face turned blue with fear. The old monk pushed through the crowd, pulled Qufei forward, and dealt him several slaps across the face. "You Heaven-condemned slave dog!" he fumed. "You disport yourself and make me suffer! We shall see what the Magistrate has to say about this!" And he forthwith turned his steps toward the yamen, dragging Qufei along with him.

The elderly man knew now that his son was alive and had masqueraded as a nun. And he knew full well that the magistrate would punish Qufei. Falling on his knees, he kowtowed to the old monk, pleading, "Old Teacher! I have wrongly accused you and offended you! I am willing to make whatever amends you wish, but I beg you to spare my son. He is, after all, your disciple! Do not take him before the magistrate!" The much-tormented old monk, however, would not relent and, tightly clutching the young monk's arm, went back into the yamen. The bailiffs followed them in, with Liaoyuan in close custody.

Surprised to see them, the magistrate inquired, "Why is the old monk dragging in that nun again?" The old monk cried, "My Lord, this is no nun! This is my disciple Qufei in nun's attire!" Hearing this, the magistrate could not help but laugh, and he exclaimed, "How much more bizarre can this matter become?!" He then ordered the young monk to confess the whole truth. Knowing he could no longer maintain his deception, Qufei told the court everything that he had done. The magistrate had all his words recorded and ordered that forty strokes of the cane be administered to both the young monk and Liaoyuan. Then he decreed that Qufei be sent into exile, that Liaoyuan be sold into bondage by the authorities, and that the Nunnery of Ultimate Bliss be torn down. The old monk and the elderly man were set free without punishment.

Lastly, Qufei and Liaoyuan were locked in cangues for exhibiting miscreants. Then one side of their faces was painted black, and they were paraded throughout the city and put on public display. The elderly man and his wife had nothing to say, since their son had broken the law. With tears and snot trickling down their faces, they followed Qufei as he staggered out of the yamen, and they helped him hold up the heavy wooden collar. The affair created a great stir in the city, and all people, old and young alike, flocked to see what was going on. A wag composed a ditty that went like this:

Poor old bonze! Where is his missing boy bonze?
Hidden away by a young woman bonze!

What beyond doubt is a masculine bonze,
Was made up to look like a feminine bonze.

Troubles galore for some genuine bonzes,
All on account of a counterfeit bonze.

Judgment declared on a dead-and-gone bonze,
Shows up the pranks of a much-alive bonze.

Cries at the court call for caning the bonzes;
Crowds in the streets come to ogle the bonzes.

Letch for the crotches of poker-stiff bonzes,
Brings on the downfall of lustful girl bonzes.

In the meantime, members of the Ho household and Kuai the Third hurried back and reported all that had happened, and Mistress Lu well nigh wept herself to death when she learned that Daqing had indeed died. That same night she prepared a coffin and a suit of burial garments, and the next morning, after notifying the magistrate, went in person to the Non-Void Nunnery to prepare Ho Daqing's corpse for burial. That done, she had his coffin transported to the Ho family's ancestral graveyard and chose an appropriate day to bury it.

Needless to say, the old abbess at the Non-Void Nunnery had already starved to death, and the local constable reported this to the authorities and had her properly interred.

Mistress Lu was painfully aware that her husband's early death was due to his uncontrolled lust for women and his refusal to mend his philandering ways. So she gave her son a most correct and strict education. The boy did so well that he was chosen to be a *ming jing*, and was eventually appointed to a highly respectable official position.

GLOSSARY

Dates of Some Chinese Dynasties:

Tang Dynasty   (A.D. 618–907)
Song Dynasty   (A.D. 960–1279)
Yuan Dynasty   (A.D. 1271–1368)
Ming Dynasty   (A.D. 1368–1644)

Titles Conferred by China's Imperial Examinations:

tongsheng   Candidate for the lowest degree in the imperial examination system.

xiucai   One who passed the imperial service examinations at the county level in dynastic times.

juren   One who passed the imperial service examinations at the provincial level in dynastic times.

jinshi   One who passed the highest imperial service examinations.

zhuangyuan   Title conferred on one who came first in the highest imperial service examinations.

Other Titles:

jian sheng   A student of the national university.
ming jing   During the Ming Dynasty, one of several categories of nominees considered for official appointments.

Some Chinese Weights and Measurements

li   A unit of distance equivalent to approximately one third of a mile.

mu   A unit of land measure equivalent to approximately one fifth of an acre.

picul   A unit of weight equivalent to approximately 133 pounds.

tael (or *liang*)   A unit of weight roughly equivalent to $1\frac{1}{2}$ ounces, used, among other purposes, for measuring silver.

qian   One tenth of a *liang*.
fen   One tenth of a *qian*.

Miscellaneous

yamen	The headquarters or residence of an official or government department in imperial China.
"watch" or "drum"	In older times, the night was divided into five two-hour periods. These began at dusk and ended at dawn. The third watch, for example, corresponded to about midnight, and the fifth watch to the hours just before dawn. The beginning of each watch was usually marked, in cities, with the beating of a drum in the city's drum tower.
cangue	A large, portable square wooden collar affixed as punishment around a convicted prisoner's neck and sometimes also his hands.
Nine Fountains	In Chinese mythology, the place where the spirits of the dead reside.
Mid-Autumn Festival	The 15th day of the 8th lunar month, when families got together to thank the gods for the year's harvests. People still observe it today by partying and eating "moon cakes."
Qingming Festival	Or, Pure Brightness, one of the 24 solar periods, occurring on April 4, 5, or 6. On this day, people traditionally visit, or "sweep," the graves of their ancestors.

Literary Terms

Make clouds and rain	A poetic allusion to the act of love-making.

About the Authors

Feng Menglong (1574–1646), a Ming Dynasty scholar and writer, wrote down hundreds of stories in three volumes called *Instructive Tales to Enlighten the World, Popular Tales to Admonish the World*, and *Lasting Tales to Waken the World*—or "Three Tales"—in China's famous teahouse storytelling tradition.

Ted Wang majored in English and Russian at Yanjing and Beijing universities. An experienced translator both from English to Chinese and Chinese to English, his main works are translations of Chinese novels, plays, screenplays, and a vast number of social science papers in Chinese studies.

Chen Chen was musicologist in her youthful years in China. She became a translator and editor in the late 1970s, working both in China and the United States. She is the author of the critically acclaimed memoir *Come Watch the Sun Go Home* (1998).